The Storm of Endless Tears

The Storm of Endless Tears

Katie Booth

iUniverse, Inc.
New York Lincoln Shanghai

The Storm of Endless Tears

Copyright © 2005 by Katie Booth

iUniverse books may be ordered through booksellers or by contacting:

iUniverse
2021 Pine Lake Road, Suite 100
Lincoln, NE 68512
www.iuniverse.com
1-800-Authors (1-800-288-4677)

ISBN-13: 978-0-595-36428-2 (pbk)
ISBN-13: 978-0-595-80860-1 (ebk)
ISBN-10: 0-595-36428-4 (pbk)
ISBN-10: 0-595-80860-3 (ebk)

Printed in the United States of America

This book is dedicated to my parents who were always there for me and
to Ryan Lancaster who kept encouraging me.
And a very special thanks goes to Karen Booth,
who made it all possible with all her hard work and dedication.

Chapter 1

In the world of the animals where no humans ever set foot, a howl could be heard. The howl belonged to a wolf, one of the most respected creatures in the world of Verinaul. The wolf had given birth; now she was dying from it. The pack gathered to honor their stricken leader.

In a large cave, Serval lay, breathing heavily.

"Leader, your pup will grow into a healthy male," her mate told her, walking in sadly.

Quite large with heavy yellow eyes, he gazed down on Red Eyes; he couldn't bear to see her down, and all the other wolves idolized her too. If they saw her now, they would claim she couldn't be the legendary wolf. Her pup whimpered from deep within the cave. "Quiet!" the older wolf snarled. It was this little creature that had reduced Serval to this.

"Please don't hate our son," Serval breathed.

"Leader, I can't see you this way. It can't be," the wolf muttered hanging his head.

"Don't look at me like that, Fergath. It doesn't suit you. My son...watch over him. He is destined for great things. His name will be heard throughout the land—Hero." Serval smiled.

She closed her eyes and never opened them again. Fergath clenched his teeth together as the pup, Hero, crawled to his fallen mother.

Hero wasn't very old. However, since Serval had given birth to him, she had been weak. He nudged her cooling body with his nose. Fergath left the cave, and the wolves gathered and peered anxiously around him, trying to see Serval.

"Our great Leader, Serval Red Eyes, has left us. We shall watch over Hero as she wished, until he is old enough to become a Leader himself. Go in peace, Leader," Fergath said.

He began to howl a long, clear note, the funeral note that guided wolves to their final resting place. Soon, another howl floated into the air, followed by another until the whole pack joined in.

Inside the cave, Hero continued to whimper. He was not yet old enough to howl or even talk. But he let his whimpers join the long howls coming from the pack. His pack.

Hero woke early that day. He shook himself as he felt that same oppression weighing down on him. All of the wolves felt it, even more as the years passed. They didn't quite know what it could be, so for the most part, they ignored it completely. It felt rather like a thunderstorm that might rear its ugly head at any time.

Hero left his cave and heard his name. He looked over to his left and saw his best friend, Nakoomu, trotting over to him.

"Hello," he said rubbing his head on her shoulder.

"Hi," she replied following suit. "So, you wanted to show me something today?"

"Yes, something secret. No one else knows about it," Hero bragged.

He started to walk away from the network of caves.

"Are you sure about this? We aren't really suppose to leave the pack until we're older," Nakoomu warned.

"So what? I leave all the time and no one notices," Hero laughed. He began to sneak away again. Nakoomu licked her mouth, and then she followed.

The two young wolves walked through the dense forest surrounding their caves.

"Hero," Nakoomu began.

"Yes?" Hero replied.

"Where are you taking me?" she finished.

"You'll see. Why do females always have to be so impatient?" Hero grumbled, pushing past thick bushes.

Nakoomu growled indignantly. Hero looked down a snowy hill and saw his destination. He glanced over his shoulder at Nakoomu and smiled. She joined him at the top of the rise and drew in her breath.

Below them a large pond glistened. Wisps of steam rose lazily into the air and disappeared into the trees and bushes that surrounded the pond. Fireflies flitted about above the center of the green water.

"Hero, it's so beautiful," Nakoomu breathed.

She shook some cold snow off her white fur. Nakoomu was completely white like her mother. Hero was a mixture of white and gray, with black ears and strange eyes. His left eye was red like his mother's, but his right eye was yellow like his father's.

"Come on," Hero laughed, running toward the water.

"Wait, you aren't going to swim in there are you?" Nakoomu asked.

"What else would I do?" Hero called back.

He had reached the edge of the pond and felt that same strange sensation that he felt the first time he went into the water. What he felt was raw power and a release from the peculiar force that seemed to follow him everywhere. He smiled and ignored Nakoomu as she called for him to stop; instead, he jumped in.

"Hero!" Nakoomu shrieked.

She ran to the water's edge and scanned the surface. She felt none of the power emitting from the pond as Hero had. She started to feel quite scared until Hero broke through the surface and grasped her shoulder with his mouth. He dragged her into the water. Nakoomu yelped and quickly scrambled back to land.

"You should have seen your face," Hero jeered.

"Oh, you awful wolf," Nakoomu snarled.

"Come on, you have to admit, it was a good one," Hero smiled, showing pointed teeth.

"Shut your yap," Nakoomu barked.

She shook herself dry.

"Where are you going?" Hero asked.

"Home," she answered.

"Make sure you aren't seen," he warned as she stormed away in a temper.

Hero swam to the deepest part of the pond, wondering why females were so sensitive.

When Hero climbed out of the water, he shook himself dry and headed back home immediately.

"Nakoomu better not have said anything," he thought to himself.

He could just see Fergath's face if he found out that Hero had wandered off again. He stared at the puddle of melted snow and his own face stared back. He turned away, hating the face. He never wanted to be a Leader. He wanted to be normal, but with two different colored eyes, he knew he could never be that.

Gazing every which way, Hero dashed from the tree line. He ran behind all the caves until he arrived home. He looked around again and then raced inside. No one was home. His father must have been out hunting or something.

"Hello, Hero," a voice growled.

It was Fergath.

"Hello Leader," Hero said bowing his head.

"Where were you?" his father demanded.

"What do you mean? I've been here all day," Hero lied.

"No you haven't. Gerb saw both you and Nakoomu go off into the woods. I didn't want to believe him, but it was true," the older wolf sighed.

"What the heck is so dangerous about us going a little ways away?" Hero asked, his cover blown.

"Other animals would kill you for meat!" Fergath yelled.

"Hah, they wouldn't touch the son of Serval Red Eyes," Hero boasted.

"If you think that way, you will surely never see the day when you are a grown wolf," Fergath sighed.

"Well, then I guess I won't," Hero said carelessly.

Fergath barked and raked his paw against Hero's shoulder, leaving behind ragged cuts.

"For your insolence!" he snapped, leaving the cave.

The next day, Hero's cuts had hardened, and his shoulder was stiff. He wouldn't be going anywhere today. He looked around and saw Nakoomu stepping gingerly toward him. Judging by her step, he knew that her father must have had hit her too.

"Hi," she said miserably.

"Hello," Hero replied guiltily.

"Just so you know, I can't stay with you today. Father's orders," Nakoomu said.

"Oh, well. Just today?" Hero asked.

"Yeah," Nakoomu said.

"Hey lover wolves," a rude voice called.

It was Rasco, the only completely black wolf of the pack and the only jerk in the pack too.

"What do you want?" Hero barked sharply.

"Just wanted to talk with Nakoomu," Rasco answered.

Everyone knew Rasco's greatest dream was for Nakoomu to be his mate. Not for love, though. He only had two reasons. One, Nakoomu was pretty, and, two, he wanted to see if his pups would be black and white, an unusual combination.

"Well, I'm talking to Hero," Nakoomu said, snuggling up next to Hero's unwounded shoulder.

She always acted as if she loved Hero when Rasco was around. Hero did too, because it made Rasco burn with jealously.

"Well, you can talk to him later," Rasco snarled.

"No, I'm talking to him about the future. We're thinking of becoming mates," Nakoomu answered.

"What?" Rasco howled.

"Oh yes. She'll make a lovely mate. We were thinking of discussing it with Leader," Hero said, playing along.

"But...I...You...Damn!" Rasco growled.

He hung his head low, as though thinking furiously about something. Hero winced as another wave of oppression washed over him. He saw Nakoomu and Rasco shiver slightly as well.

"Hero, may I speak with you for a minute?" Rasco asked sweetly.

Hero and Nakoomu glanced at each other in surprise. Hero sighed and thought that Rasco planned some kind of a trap. He looked at the black wolf. Rasco was larger than he, but Hero was sure that he could match his strength. He stepped forward and faltered when his wounded shoulder throbbed painfully.

"Well, are you too good to talk to me or something?" Rasco asked, with that same sweet smile on his face.

"Fine," Hero replied. "I'll talk with you."

Hero saw Nakoomu give him an anxious look, but she didn't say anything to stop him. Rasco led Hero behind a cave and turned to face him.

"So what do you want to talk about?" Hero asked impatiently.

"Nakoomu," Rasco said silkily.

"Well I don't," Hero replied heatedly.

"Hold up now. You can't just leave like that. This is really important," Rasco snarled, jumping ahead of Hero.

"Hurry up then," Hero sighed.

"Listen, I want Nakoomu to be my mate. You can have another wolf. One more closely connected with your bloodline, you know? How about it?" the black wolf asked.

"You are not stealing my mate. Now get out of my sight," Hero ordered.

"Who're you kidding? I'm not about to take the orders from a wolf I can beat up," Rasco taunted.

"You better. I know you could beat me now, with my wounded shoulder, but you know Fergath would never let this go. He could easily defeat you and turn you from the pack. Just as he did with your father," Hero said.

It was true. Rasco's father had defied a direct order from Fergath. Now he wandered all alone in the wilds of Verinaul. Rasco did remember. He always got furious when somebody mentioned it to him. He arched his back and bared his teeth. Hero suddenly felt reckless, so he continued.

"Maybe if you get hurled out of here, you can find him and live together until you starve to death, if he hasn't already."

Rasco let out a small howl of rage and leapt upon Hero. Being a lot heavier, he quickly wrestled Hero to the ground and began biting any place he could find. Hero kicked at his face furiously, biting his snout whenever it got close enough.

The fight was brutal, and Hero was surprised that he wasn't killed. He had managed to free himself from Rasco and turned to bite the larger wolf in the back. Rasco snarled and shook Hero off, causing Hero to rip a large chunk of skin away. The black wolf charged at Hero and bit him on the scruff of the neck. He easily tossed Hero into a nearby rock. Hero gasped and quickly regained his footing. He rushed at Rasco and bit at his leg. Rasco dodged and snapped his jaws onto the back of Hero's neck. Hero twisted his head so that he could bite Rasco's chest. Both wolves backed away, bleeding heavily from their wounds.

"Not so tough now are you?" Rasco sneered as Hero strained to remain standing.

Hero groaned but rushed at the taunting wolf anyway. Rasco dodged Hero and dug his teeth into Hero's back. Hero yelped and shied away.

"I wonder what Nakoomu would think if she saw you now," Rasco said.

"You better stop this now," Hero snarled.

"Well, I'm not going to. You haven't learned your lesson yet. Unless you apologize of course. And let me have Nakoomu," Rasco sneered.

"I would never do that. Neither of them," Hero snarled.

Rasco shook his head. Ignoring his injuries, he charged at Hero and bit him on the neck, completely cutting off his breath. Hero struggled madly, but to no avail. Rasco's hold was too strong. Hero knew he couldn't remain conscious for long. With renewed energy, he backed as far away as he could and raised his paw, jamming it into Rasco's eye.

Howling in pain, he jumped into the air, and Hero took the opportunity to run into the nearest cave. He could hear Rasco barking and scrabbling outside, searching for him. But he passed by the cave where Hero hid, and Hero let out a sigh of relief. He would have to stay near the stronger adults for a few days, until his wounds healed, or else Rasco might actually kill him.

Chapter 2

In the days that followed, Hero's good friend Swift Paw visited him often. Hero smiled as he watched his friend quiver with happiness. Apparently, after much pleading from his mother, Swift Paw had been allowed to hunt with the pack. He had caught himself a plump rabbit. It was a record. None of the other young wolves that went out ever actually caught anything. Swift Paw had returned yesterday, but Hero had been cooped up inside his cave, waiting for his injuries to heal and avoiding Rasco.

"You should have seen me! I was all over that rabbit!" Swift Paw bragged.

"I'm really proud of you, Swift Paw. This will be remembered throughout history," Hero said truthfully.

"We're having a feast in my honor tonight. I heard you tore out Rasco's eye and have been hiding, but I really want you to be there," Swift Paw pleaded.

"Don't worry. I'll be there," Hero said.

"Thanks, Hero," Swift Paw grinned.

With that, Swift Paw raced from the cave. Hero knew that Rasco probably knew he was hiding out in his cave, but it was forbidden to enter the Leader's cave unless given permission. And Fergath rarely gave anyone permission; he'd rather discuss things in the wild.

As Hero leisurely stretched out, Fergath entered the cave. The Leader of the pack entered slowly, taking things at his own pace, as he always did.

"What is your problem, my son? Why have you not left this cave for days?" he asked.

"I have a problem with Rasco, Leader," Hero answered.

He had always hated having to call his father "Leader." It made him envious to see his friends walking with their fathers, laughing and talking pleasantly.

"Why haven't you dealt with it then? What is going on between you two?" Fergath asked stiffly.

"Rasco attacked me a few days ago. To defend myself, I hit him in the eye. I heard that I actually tore it out. Well, I'm afraid that he will try to kill me if I step foot outside, Leader," Hero explained.

"Why would Rasco attack the son of his Leader? Did you taunt him, Hero?" Fergath asked.

"Rasco tried to persuade me to release my bond with Nakoomu, Leader. He wanted me to let him take her as his own. I refused, and he got angry. I did make a rude comment about his father, and that was when he attacked," Hero replied.

"That little…How dare he try to defend his despicable father? That wolf had no right to even exist. I should have killed him. Well, have no worry, my son. I will sort this out so you can join us at your friend's feast without looking over your shoulder. Though, I would rather have seen you take care of him. With your wounds I know that you cannot, so don't think about it," Fergath said.

He gave Hero a rare smile and added slyly, "Never let anyone steal what you desire." Then, he left the cave.

Hero smiled. His father had never talked with him for so long. He half expected Fergath to yell at him and tell him that it was his own fault for not finishing Rasco off. Hero's smile grew as Nakoomu entered the cave.

"Leader told me to come visit you," she said.

"Good. I've been bored out of my mind," Hero answered.

"Thank you for fighting for me. I know you don't really like me as a mate, but you could have just let Rasco claim me. You were so brave, thanks," Nakoomu said, her voice shaking with emotion.

"Don't worry. I won't let you spend your life with a wolf you hate," Hero said.

They sat in silence for a while, until Fergath reappeared in the cave's entrance.

Nakoomu leapt up and left, bowing her head to Fergath as she passed.

"It is over. I have exiled Rasco," the Leader said.

"Exiled? Why go to that extreme, Leader?" Hero asked.

"Attacking a future leader is a crime. Worse so than just talking back," Fergath explained.

"I see. Thank you, Leader," Hero answered.

Fergath left. So Rasco had been exiled. Hero didn't think his father would do that. He walked out of his cave for the first time in days. The sky was gray again; it usually was in winter. He saw another one of his friends walking at the bottom of the hill.

"Keelok," he yelled.

The white-gray wolf looked up at him, his yellow eyes glinting. Keelok wasn't one of his best friends. He had been friends with Rasco more than Hero. However, he waited up for him. Hero smiled at him, but Keelok looked away angrily.

"What's wrong?" Hero asked.

"Rasco was kicked out because of you, did you know that?" Keelok growled.

"Yes. But I didn't mean for it to happen. I was just concerned that I would be killed if I left my cave. I'm sorry. I only wanted him to let me be," Hero explained.

"Well, he will certainly leave you alone now!" Keelok snapped, trotting away.

Hero sighed. It would take Keelok about a month to forgive him. He had the reputation of being the only wolf to hold a grudge for more than a week.

Hero walked off to find Swift Paw. He saw him re-telling his tale of the hunt to his sister Shira. Shira looked over at Hero and smiled.

"Hey, Hero, coming out of hiding?" she smirked playfully.

"Rasco has been exiled. Didn't you hear?" Hero asked.

"What? Really? Wow, that's pretty awful,' Shira said.

"At least you don't have to worry about him now," Swift Paw stated.

Hero agreed with a bowed head. He walked off, not wanting to discuss Rasco. He had hated him. But wolves were meant to live with their pack, unless they wanted to start their own. Hero couldn't shake off his guilt. It was his fault. If he had just talked to Rasco, had just faced him like an adult, he wouldn't have been banned. As he walked, he realized that he had walked straight to Rasco's cave. He heard mournful wails. Rasco's mother was now alone, and it was his fault.

Hero heard the bear before he saw it. He was making his way to the center of the caves when he heard a deep voice that he did not recognize. When Hero walked around a bush, he saw the bear. Bears never entered a wolf's area. By the looks on the other wolves' faces, they thought the same thing. Hero walked closer so that he could clearly hear the conversation.

"You're certain? The Wise Ones told you this?" Fergath demanded with urgency.

"Yes. Just another ten years until it happens. Then a hero will be sent to the human world of Nazberath to save both worlds—a hero who will be called Lone Wolf in Verinaul," the bear explained.

"I see. If we could prevent it before it happened?" Fergath began.

"Not possible. There is no way to stop it from actually happening. No one even knows who Lone Wolf is...or rather, will be," the bear sighed.

"The Wise Ones leave us nothing but fear," Fergath said.

"Not entirely," the bear said. "We now know the cause of this oppressive feeling that has plagued us our entire lives."

With that said, the bear bowed its huge head and tumbled out of the large clearing. Fergath looked around at all the wolves that had gathered around.

"Well, carry on. After the feast I will explain what happened," he said, walking off.

Nakoomu caught Hero's eye and jerked her head behind her. She wanted to go to their little hideaway under the bushes. Hero trotted over and saw her tail heading not to the bushes, but out of the clearing.

"Where are we going?" he asked.

"To that pond. It's the only place we'll have total privacy," Nakoomu said.

They disappeared behind the trees. Within minutes they arrived at the green pond. Hero felt a great desire to plunge in again, but Nakoomu seemed to be in no mood to play around. He waited patiently for her to start talking. She just stood there, however, gazing at the cloudy sky.

"Nakoomu?" Hero asked.

She shook herself and said, "I'm worried."

"About what?" Hero asked.

"About that bear. You might not have heard what he said that 'it' was. I did. He said that 'it' was the Storm of Endless Tears. You know, the storm that legend says will wipe out our entire planet unless..."

"A wolf from our world goes to Nazberath," Hero finished dully. "I can't understand why you actually believe that stuff."

"Humph! Well if the Wise Ones say that it will happen, then it will happen. We have ten more years until we get wiped out," Nakoomu snapped.

"Maybe the Wise Ones were kidding," Hero sighed.

"*Kidding!*" Nakoomu shrieked. "Since when were you so *stupid*? The Wise Ones never joke around!"

Hero backed away. He had forgotten how much Nakoomu looked up to the Wise Ones. He admitted that he himself thought the owls were incredible. He felt rather bad now that he made that crack about them. Nakoomu seethed. She started to storm back to the caves.

"Wait for me," he hissed.

They crept back toward the cave and prayed that they wouldn't get caught this time.

All was quiet in the clearing as they made their way back. Then it hit them. Swift Paw's feast had begun. They gave a sheepish gulp and then ran toward the meeting cave.

Long and high and easily the largest around, the meeting cave stood a good ten feet from the ground. Inside was warm and dry, as the bears had helped to pad it with mud a good five years ago. There was plenty of room for the two young wolves to squeeze in. The wolves on either side gave them a hard glance. But preoccupied by Swift Paw, Hero did not notice.

Fergath began by announcing Swift Paw's great skills. The wolves gathered before the two wolves smiled with pride.

"Swift Paw, son of Hura, turn and be recognized," Fergath finished.

Swift Paw turned to look to the rest of the pack. All started to yip and yap, howl and bark. They were all very happy for him. It had been Swift Paw's dream to catch something on his first hunt. He gave Hero, Shira and Nakoomu an extra grin. They grinned back.

"And now, without further ado—Swift Paw's feast," Fergath shouted above the din.

Several wolves dragged in the meat. Mostly deer and pig. But placed in the middle of the feast, sat Swift Paw's plump rabbit. The wolves dug into the meat, keen to let Swift Paw cut in front of them. Hero pushed his way over and finally got face-to-face with Swift Paw and Shira.

"Wow, Swift Paw, you really made us proud," he said.

Swift Paw blushed deeply.

"Come off it, Hero. If you keep going on like that, he'll actually get used to it," Shira smirked.

"No I won't," Swift Paw argued.

Hero and Shira laughed. Swift Paw had always enjoyed a little extra attention. They smiled wickedly at him, and he dropped his mock-angry frown and burst out laughing. Infused by his laugh, Hero and Shira soon laughed as hard as they could. The older wolves looked down on them proudly. To see them get along so well would mean good hunting partners.

When the feast ended, Hero retreated to his cave. He felt full of food and beyond content and flopped down onto the ground, drowsiness settling in. He hadn't bothered to listen to Fergath make his speech about the ridiculous Storm of Endless Tears. He didn't believe in that sort of nonsense, even if it did feel as though a storm had been brewing all his life. However, in about an hour he had reason to feel very sorry he had missed out on the speech.

Fergath came storming into the cave, eyes blazing in anger. He spotted Hero flat on his stomach and growled loudly.

"Y-yes Leader?" Hero stammered.

"Where did you run off to?" he snarled.

"I was tired," Hero admitted.

"Do you realize that I spent a whole hour explaining about this storm so *you* could hear?" he demanded.

"M-me? Why do you need me to hear it?" Hero asked.

"I believe that you might be that one who will be called Lone Wolf. The one that goes to Nazberath."

"That's crazy. I'll never go to the human world!" Hero yelled.

"Why not? Are you that much of a coward? Are you not Serval Red Eyes' son?" Fergath bellowed.

"I don't *want* to be her son! I never *wanted* to be a Leader in the first place. It is all too much! And no one cares what I say or do. They ignore me like I'm an outcast!" Hero shouted.

He had wanted to find an opportunity to say this for years.

"You are more foolish than I thought. You are Serval's son. Nothing can alter that. No matter what you may say, what you may try to do, you will always be the one to become our Leader," Fergath said calmly.

"Why does it have to be me? I don't want this. I just don't."

"Then you must learn to want it...as I did," Fergath replied.

Hero looked at him. He wanted to ask more, but Fergath had already disappeared. He had never thought of Fergath as one who would not like power. He knew he was a nice wolf, but he did like to be the one in control. Hero turned onto his side. He wasn't very tired anymore.

The next day, Hero ran into Swift Paw. They walked together toward the meeting cave. When they entered, they saw Jeru, an old wolf on the brink of death. He had been an excellent hunter and fighter in his youth. Swift Paw and Hero stared at him in awe. Jeru wasn't out of his cave often, and he was a hero to the younger wolves.

"Hello, young ones," he said in a deep voice.

"Hello, Jeru," they answered quickly.

"Tell me, is the sun shining my friends?" Jeru asked.

"Yes sir," Hero replied.

"Brighter than ever, sir," Swift Paw added.

"Then today is a good day to depart to the afterlife," Jeru replied.

He stepped slowly toward the young wolves. Without another word, he passed by them and went out into the rare sunshine. Hero followed him. The old warrior stumbled into the woods, toward the pond. Hero almost cried out to stop him. He didn't want anything to die near something so pure as the pond.

When Hero reached the pond, he saw Jeru walk into the heated waters. He never made it past his chest. With a groan, he fell down and closed his eyes slowly. Hero was horror-stricken. Now there was a dead wolf *in* the water. But something was happening to the now shriveled flesh. It shook, as if the dead wolf was laughing. Hero stepped back, frightened at what he saw next.

Jeru's body was slowly shrinking, and at the same time sinking deeper into the water. The fur disappeared around his body, leaving the skin exposed. His front legs grew smaller and smaller, while his back legs changed shape. They bent at the knees, and Jeru's feet grew longer and his toes multiplied to five. His front feet changed as well. The three-clawed toes became skinny and long. Five long toes appeared on each 'foot.' Jeru's snout shrunk so much that only a small portion protruded from his face. His forehead grew, and pink lips surrounded his now small mouth. His eyes closed, and the now very young thing opened a toothless mouth and gave a shrill wail. The tips of Jeru's ears had vanished, becoming round and smooth. The thing sunk deeper into the pond and soon disappeared out of sight.

Hero ran as fast as he could, heedless of making any noise. He knew what Jeru had changed into. The Wise Ones had explained human babies well enough for Jeru's description to fit. But how could Jeru turn into a human? Hero ran into Fergath as soon as he broke away from the trees.

"Hero, what?"

"I *need* to speak with a Wise One, immediately," Hero panted.

"What are you talking about? Why were you away from the clearing again?" Fergath demanded.

"There is no time for this! I need a Wise One right away. Where can I find one?" Hero shouted.

"North of our cave. Look for a red pine tree," Fergath answered, seeing the anxiety in Hero's mismatched eyes.

Hero raced to his cave. He ran behind it and plunged into the woods once again.

It didn't take long to find a Wise One. He heard her before he saw her. A pretty little hooting sound reached his sharp ears. He ran through a thorn bush and saw the female owl singing on a low pine branch.

She turned her head at the noise and noticed Hero, panting and with bits of twig tangled in his fur.

"Ah, Son of Serval Red Eyes, what is it you need to know?" she asked all too calmly.

"Wise One, I have seen what should not have been seen," Hero exclaimed.

"Slowly pup, calm yourself and clear your mind."

Hero took a deep breath and sat himself down in front of her branch.

"Very good. Now, what did you see?" the owl asked.

"Jeru, an old and respected wolf has died today," Hero began. "He was a hero to me."

"Well, you have my sympathy. I knew Jeru. He was most kind," the Wise One nodded.

"Yes, well, before he died, he went to this green pond where I've been before. When he got in, he died. But, the thing is, he changed," Hero trailed off.

"Continue Son of Serval," the Wise One commanded.

"He turned into a human, I think. He lost all his fur, and his shape changed a lot," Hero finished.

"You, like some before you, have discovered the Pond of Change. Any animal may enter this pond on the brink of death to become a human," the owl explained.

"Wise One, who would choose to be a human?" Hero said scornfully.

"Ahh young one, humans are not a bad choice. They have many qualities that most animals dream about," she explained.

"I guess," Hero muttered. "Well, I should really be getting back now. Thank you for your knowledge," he added.

"Good luck, Hero," the Wise One said.

Hero was not sure why she would say this, but he didn't inquire further. He had enough to think about. The Pond of Change...would he decide to become a human before he died? He shook his head and picked up his pace. Fergath would not be pleased if he were gone too long.

Chapter 3

A few years passed. Hero had grown into a fine young male. He was big, and his fur was full and smooth. Many females tried to catch his eye, eager to show they could be his perfect mate. He would not be unkind to them, but he had eyes for one wolf only—Nakoomu.

"Hello," he said as he passed her.

"Hello Hero, how are you?" she asked.

"Fine, you?" he replied.

"Wonderful," she answered.

They walked off together. Since they were older now, it wasn't against the rules for them to leave the clearing. They would often go on walks together, but never to the pond after learning its true nature.

Today was a very special day for Hero. It was going to be his first hunt with Fergath and the others. Nakoomu, Swift Paw and Shira were going too. Hero blew a loud sigh out of his mouth.

"What is it?" Nakoomu asked.

"I'm a little nervous about the hunt today. I am expected to catch something, being the Leader's son and all," he explained.

"Oh, don't think on it, Hero. We'll do fine," Nakoomu laughed.

Hero smiled. Nakoomu always made him feel better inside. She knew she did too. Hero wasn't sure, but he thought that Nakoomu might also be interested in being his mate. He wanted to find out before she chose another wolf instead.

"Nakoomu," he began, "do you like me?"

"Yes I do. I have been your friend since we were pups," Nakoomu giggled.

"No, I mean really like me. You know, like enough to be my mate," he said.

"Now why would you want to know that?" she asked rather stiffly.

"Oh, you know...wolves were just talking about it. I heard one say that he thought we'd make a great couple," Hero pressed on.

"Oh really? And what do you think?" she asked.

"Huh?" Hero replied. He wasn't expecting that.

"Do you think we make a perfect couple?"

"I think that we get along good, yeah," he answered.

"Are you trying to tell me that you want to be mates, but are just too scared to say it openly?" she asked slyly.

"Well," he stammered. "I guess so."

"I'll tell you what. I will consider your offer. But there is no guarantee, okay? I mean we *have* been friends for so long, I'm not sure I'd like that to change," she finished.

With that she walked away from him and back toward the clearing. Hero sighed. Nakoomu was known for not giving a straight answer right away. He hoped that she would just say yes. He shook his head and went back to the clearing as well. His hunt was nearly upon him.

Before the hunt, Fergath took Hero aside. He looked into his son's eyes. Red and yellow stared back at him.

"Listen, don't try to go after anything too big. Go after a fox or rabbit, okay?" he said.

"What about a deer?" Hero asked.

"Deer...I suppose you could try, though I doubt you'd be able to catch one on your first hunt," Fergath smiled.

Hero smiled back at him, and they walked over to the other wolves. Swift Paw gave him a goofy smile. Shira and Nakoomu were in deep conversation. By the way they kept shooting glances at Hero, he thought he knew the subject.

"The hunt begins now. All those who feel unready may stay behind," Fergath announced.

None of the younger wolves backed down an inch. Fergath led them into the forest. Hero felt excitement course through him. Being on a hunt led him farther from home then he had ever ventured. The wolves kept their noses to the wind, searching for the scent of prey.

Not long after, they came across their first target—a deer looking for grass in the snow-covered clearing. Hero hunched his shoulders. Now was his chance. He glanced at Fergath and was surprised to see the older wolf staring pointedly at him. He wanted him to do it. Hero crawled forward inch-by-inch. The deer started when Hero accidentally snapped a twig. He held his breath for a moment, and the unsuspecting deer continued its search for food.

When Hero thought he was close enough, he prepared to lunge. He shifted his shoulders and then leapt at his prey. The deer tried to leap away, but Hero landed on top of it. He bit at the deer's throat until it stopped kicking him. The blood poured into his mouth as he gave one hard chomp just to make sure. He turned around and saw the others looking at him.

"Hero," Nakoomu whispered.

"Well done, my son," Fergath said.

"Thank you, Leader," Hero answered.

One of the older wolves grabbed the dead deer by the mouth and dragged it back to the clearing. Hero felt very proud of himself as the others started to make their way back home. The whole pack was going to be very impressed with him. He caught a deer on his first hunt, without any help.

By the time they returned from the hunt, Hero felt rather tired. The adrenalin was completely drained. He went to his cave and lay down on his side. Fergath had followed him, probably to talk about the hunt. Hero opened his right eye, the yellow one, and saw Fergath gazing at him. Not really him, but his eye, as though wondering why Hero had these mismatched eyes. When a wolf with blue eyes and a wolf with yellow eyes had a pup, the pup usually inherited the father's eyes.

"It's because of Serval," Hero finally said.

"What do you mean?" he demanded.

"My burning desires to prove myself. You told me that she put herself in mortal peril to show she was the toughest wolf in all of Verinaul. I know I wasn't in mortal peril against the deer, but you know what I mean," Hero said.

"Oh," Fergath replied. "Yes, I suppose I do."

Hero looked at him, puzzled. Fergath just shook his head and walked out of the cave. Hero shrugged and lay his head down, merciful sleep overtaking him.

Winter passed and fresh patches of green could be seen popping out of the snow. Many wolves basked in the sun on top of their caves. Wolves celebrated spring, as it came quickly or not at all. Hero made his way into the center of the clearing; many wolves nodded their heads in greeting.

He looked around at the blossoming trees and wondered when his turn to rule over the network of caves and its inhabitants would come. Hopefully not for a long time yet, he thought. He hated the idea of being the Leader of the pack.

"Finally awake, huh?" a voice asked.

Hero turned to see a white wolf behind him—Nakoomu. He smiled at her, and she returned the gesture.

"Hello, Nakoomu," was all he could think of to say.

"Want to go on a walk with me?" she asked.

"I guess so," Hero said.

Nakoomu started off toward the woods. Hero followed. She seemed to be some kind of angel as they drifted through the blossoming flowers and trees. She looked back occasionally, blue eyes telling him something he couldn't comprehend. Deep pools of blue described her eyes, while his contorted eyes held no beauty.

"Remember what you asked me?" she said suddenly.

"Huh? What do you mean?" he asked.

"Mates, I believe the subject was," she smiled. "I've decided, Hero."

Hero held his breath, staggering forward slightly. What did she choose? The way she looked at him explained her answer quite clearly.

"I choose to spend my life with you and bear your pups," she said formally.

Hero let out a deep breath. He closed his eyes and smiled, letting her words soak through his mind and body. Nakoomu had accepted. She was his forever, never to be separated. It wasn't long until he would be old enough to have a mate.

"I will spend my life with you and look after the pups you give me," Hero said, equally as formally.

Nakoomu beamed at him and rushed toward him, nuzzling his neck with her face. Hero rubbed her head briefly and then stepped back to admire her. She was truly beautiful. She winked at him and then walked off back to the caves. Hero followed and watched her disappear into her cave. Hero turned and found himself suddenly face-to-face with Swift Paw.

"Congratulations," he said, beaming.

"What?" Hero exclaimed.

"You and Nakoomu finally chose each other. I thought I'd have to play matchmaker or something," Swift Paw laughed.

"What are you talking about?" Hero demanded.

"Oh come off it. You've been drooling after Nakoomu for years. It's about time you two finally figured it out," Swift Paw chuckled.

"Swift Paw, thank you. You always try to help me with everything. You are, without a doubt, the best friend a wolf could have," Hero smiled lightly.

Swift Paw blushed slightly, then scampered back to tell Shira the news. Hero watched them for a while. Shira jumped into the air and barked happily, ending her antics with a short howl. Hero smiled.

That night, Hero told Fergath of his choice for mate. He expected Fergath to congratulate him as well, but his father's mouth turned into a grimace, and he didn't look at Hero.

"Is something the matter?" Hero asked uncertainly.

"Nakoomu is not a good choice for a mate, Hero," Fergath answered slowly, as if measuring his words.

"What do you mean? Nakoomu is a wonderful choice. She's nice, open minded and my best friend," Hero snarled.

"Exactly. Best friends don't make good mates. At first they seem devoted to each other, but after a short period of time, they become distant, wishing their relationship was how it had been before they chose to be mates," Fergath explained.

"You don't know what you're talking about!" Hero snapped.

"I don't want to see you hurt, Hero. That's all," Fergath admitted.

"I won't be hurt by Nakoomu. She would never hurt me, and I would never hurt her," Hero said icily.

"I forbid it. You will *not* be joined with Nakoomu. It is not meant to be," Fergath snarled, trying to remain calm.

"Well, you can just forget it!" Hero bellowed.

"Don't you dare speak to me like that!" Fergath roared above Hero's voice.

"You don't like me and Nakoomu together? Well that's too bad. Either we join, or we leave, and you can find a new future Leader," Hero growled.

"I forbid it still. You wouldn't have the courage to leave. A wolf away from his pack is a dead wolf. You should know. Remember Rasco?" Fergath sneered.

"We'll see," Hero whispered as Fergath left his cave.

Late that night, Hero snuck away from his cave. He traveled down to Nakoomu's and crept inside. He nudged Nakoomu awake with his snout.

"Hero?" Nakoomu asked softly. "What are you doing here?"

"Follow me," Hero whispered.

He left her cave, and she followed. Hero led her right to the meeting cave and sat down. She also sat and looked at him with a questioning expression on her face.

"Nakoomu, we have to run away," Hero said bluntly.

"Run away?" Nakoomu asked. "Why? What are you talking about?"

"I talked to Leader earlier today. He said he would forbid us being mates," Hero explained.

"But why?" Nakoomu asked.

"Some nonsense about how best friends shouldn't be mates," Hero spat. "So we're going to run away."

"But Hero," Nakoomu said uncertainly.

"What is it?" Hero asked rather harshly.

"Our place is here," Nakoomu said wisely. "We are not meant to run. When something doesn't go our way at first, we keep trying and trying. We don't give up and leave."

"Believe me, Fergath will never allow our union," Hero said bitterly.

"Then we must follow his judgment," Nakoomu said painfully.

"What?" Hero gasped. "You'd give up being my mate because of Fergath?"

"Hero, he's still the Leader. His word is still law. We must listen to him," Nakoomu sobbed.

"This can't be what you want," Hero said sadly.

"Of course it isn't," Nakoomu cried. "I want to be with you."

"Then come with me, Nakoomu," Hero urged. "Please don't say that you won't."

"Hero," Nakoomu said, looking at him with tears flowing down her face. "I can't leave. We can't leave."

"But, Nakoomu," Hero pleaded.

"No, Hero," Nakoomu said urgently.

Hero's expression hardened. "Whether you come or not, I'm leaving. I hoped you would follow your heart."

"Please don't leave me, Hero," Nakoomu cried.

"I'm not," Hero said. "You're the one leaving me."

Nakoomu shook her head. "I will follow my responsibilities and remain here. You should too," she said, trying to sound firm.

Hero shook his head sadly and walked past her.

"Hero, wait...don't..." Nakoomu called to him.

"Good bye," Hero whispered in her ear.

He rubbed his head against her shoulder and ran out into the night. Nakoomu froze for a minute, unable to move at the shock she just felt. Hero had really left her. She let out a sob and ran out of the cave.

"Hero!" she called into the night. "Hero, come back!"

But Hero ignored her pleading voice and kept running.

Chapter 4

Many years later, far away from a network of caves buried in the heart of an ancient forest, a lone wolf walked to the edge of a cliff. He looked up into the ominous black clouds that filled the entire sky. It was going to be a big storm, and it was a long way back to his den.

He shook himself as the oppressive feeling that weighed him down his entire life increased. He walked briskly down the steep cliff path, having only gone to the cliff in the first place because he heard thunder. Now he understood that a much bigger event loomed on the horizon.

His surroundings did not resemble the home of his youth. Here, he lived among small scraggly trees and red sand for ground. He had never even seen a desert before; now he lived on the outskirts of one near many animals that he had never seen before, like vultures and snakes.

"It is different, but it is home," he said yet again. "I still do not regret my decision."

He looked at the clouds that covered most of the eastern sky. He growled rather sharply. He would have trouble finding food if the storm lasted too long. He quickened his pace as he felt a fat drop hit his head. His den was in sight now, and he rushed inside.

Hero had grown into a very strong wolf. The scarce food kept him a little thin, but he was fit and lean. His hair wasn't as full because of the hot weather in the desert. He went to the edge of his den and saw rain plummeting down to the parched earth. It would be good to have some wetness compared to the continual dryness. He stretched happily, closed his mismatched eyes and fell asleep.

"Curse this rain," Hero said silently.

He was trying to stay calm as he saw his prey walking closer to him. The thin desert rabbit wouldn't keep him full long, but Hero didn't care. The rabbit flicked back its wet ears and shook its body, splashing water everywhere.

It unsuspectingly made another step toward Hero, who stiffened expectantly.

A crash of thunder sounded, and the rabbit started. Hero lunged and clamped his jaws around the small animal's throat, crushing the tiny bones. He ate his meal and prepared to return to his cave when he felt a deep pang of sorrow. He was thinking about Swift Paw's first privileged hunt, the one where his friend had caught the rabbit. He remembered asking Nakoomu to be his mate, and how her sly eyes sparkled with delight. He remembered Fergath placing his trust in him to stop that "storm" from killing them all.

Suddenly Hero looked up at the purpled sky. The storm! Was this the dreaded Storm of Tears that the bear had warned them of so long ago? Hero shook his head and snapped his jaws. That was another life, one he couldn't return to and one to which he didn't want to go back.

After three weeks of nothing but rain, with no break in the torrent of wet sheets, Hero began to think more and more about the bear that had come. It wasn't impossible that the Storm of Endless Tears was real. Evidence existed that it could happen, the main source being Nazberath. If that were true, then Hero knew the only way to stop it was to find the hero called Lone Wolf, who would go to the human world. Hero also knew that the one way to get to Nazberath was the Pond of Change. A harsh voice interrupted his thoughts.

"Oh look, the little loner," the voice said mockingly.

It was a vulture that Hero had seen several times before. The vulture looked at him, expecting Hero to answer or to do something. Hero just peered at the large bird.

"What happened to you, I wonder," sneered the vulture. "I imagine you were exiled. A wolf doesn't really *choose* to leave the pack now does he?"

"You are wrong. I am Hero Red Eye. Son of Serval and Fergath. I was to be the next Leader but things happened and I left," Hero explained.

"So you ran away when things got tough, eh? What a coward. The little lone wolf who couldn't face his responsibility," the vulture chuckled.

"You had better stop now if you want to live," Hero snapped. "You are a pathetic liar who knows nothing of my past."

"I can say this for you though, you are indeed a coward. Even after all these years of living in this desert you refuse to return," the bird replied, flapping its sodden wings and flying off.

Hero stared after the bird for a long while and was about to shake off the meeting entirely, but he couldn't because he knew the vulture spoke the truth. He, Hero, had run away, and he had also refused to return. He knew that it didn't matter now, because he would never be allowed in again. But the time had come, he realized, to go back—not back to his caves, but back to the pond to see if he were truly the one to leave. Another thing about the vulture's remarks rang in his ears. The vulture had called him "Lone Wolf."

Hero gazed around at the trees surrounding him. He was home, back where everything started. He lifted his nose to the air and sniffed the familiar scents of pine that he had missed for so long. He made his way down the old path to the pond. How he longed to see that green water once again.

As soon as he saw the water, he felt its power flow through him. He almost didn't notice that he was not alone. He looked to the bank and saw another wolf sitting alone. This wolf looked as though she had been ill. Her eyes were dull and lifeless, and her fur, scraggly and gray. Her ears drooped, and her tail sagged. She looked extremely thin and so frail that it seemed as though a strong wind could blow her over.

Hero took a step back when those haunted eyes met his own.

"Hero," the wolf whispered longingly.

Hero's ears pricked up. He knew that voice, but it couldn't be her. It couldn't be…

"Nakoomu?" Hero asked.

Nakoomu stood up and stumbled over to him.

"Oh Hero, Hero! I made the wrong choice. Not a single day has passed that I have not dreamed about you. I should have gone with you. I needed you," she cried.

"Nakoomu, what happened to you?" Hero asked.

"I just gave up living after you left. Swift Paw and Shira helped me, but it was you. The thoughts I had of you kept me alive," Nakoomu breathed.

"Oh, Nakoomu," Hero said painfully. "I'm so sorry I made you suffer. I should have listened to you. I never should have left."

"What made you come back?" Nakoomu asked.

"The Storm of Endless Tears," Hero replied.

Nakoomu smiled. "I knew you would be the one to save us, Hero. I always knew."

"Nakoomu, would you please run and fetch my father?" Hero asked.

"Just don't leave without saying good bye," Nakoomu said.

"I won't. I promise," Hero said.

Hero walked into the water a little and looked at the sky. Nothing happened. He knew that he would have to go deeper, but he wanted to see his father before he did. He heard rustling and saw three wolves appear— Nakoomu, Fergath and Swift Paw. Sitting on Fergath's shoulder was the Wise One Hero he had spoken to long ago.

"Hero," Fergath said, as though he thought this meeting would never happen.

"I can't believe it's you," Swift Paw said.

"You are the one known as Lone Wolf, the one to end this cursed storm," said the Wise One, watching him with her large eyes.

"How do you even know that?" Hero asked.

"You know it too. Why else are you here?" the owl asked slyly.

"Hero, I'm so sorry. I always regretted my choice from the moment you left us," Fergath said, stepping to the water's edge. "If you could ever forgive me, I would be able to die in peace."

"Father, I forgive you. I'm sorry I wasn't as strong as I should have been. But I must tell you that I will return one day, and I will become Nakoomu's mate," Hero said.

"You may choose her as your mate. I should have seen the bond between you two sooner," Fergath said.

"Hero, thanks for coming back," Swift Paw murmured.

"Thanks for coming. I'll be back, and we can go hunting together," Hero answered. "Nakoomu, forgive me for everything. Please just wait a little longer."

"I will wait for you forever. I love you," Nakoomu replied gravely.

"Hero," the Wise One said. "If you are the chosen one, we will find out now. The Lone Wolf will be called to Nazberath on the second month of the storm in about two minutes. Be ready. You won't change the same way as the others. You will remain your age, and you will not disappear into the pond. Good Luck. Our fate rests on your shoulders."

Hero swam out into the middle of the pond and was about to respond, but a sudden bolt of lightning stopped him. He heard the owl yell, "It begins!" He heard no more than that. The lighting bolt hit the water next to Hero, and he believed he would die, but instead the pond began to swirl around and around. Hero thought he would be sucked into a whirlpool, but the water lifted into the air, making a column of green that stretched to the sky. Hero felt his body lift with it, and knew he was being carried toward the storm-heavy sky.

Chapter 5

Hero awoke and felt that he must have been dreaming. He was still in his den, and it was still raining. He was even wet like always. He opened his eyes and cried out in alarm.

A pale arm with long fingers attached to his body. He scrambled to his feet and realized that he had been lying in a gray pond. He looked down at his reflection and almost toppled backwards.

His long snout had shrunk, and he no longer had sharp teeth. Instead of fur wrapping his body, he saw only shaggy brown hair hanging from his head down to his hips. His stomach was bare, and his body's shape, changed. No tail. No rounded ears. He recognized only his one red and one yellow eye from his former self. He gasped. He had become a human.

Hero shivered as a cold wind swept over his naked body. Without his thick fur he had no idea how to survive the night. He looked at the sky expecting to see clouds, but to his relief it was a cold blue. But the sun held no warmth, and patches of snow covered the ground, not to mention the ice surrounding the pond's edge. Hero tried to walk, but found that his front "legs" were shorter than his back legs, and that his back wasn't shaped as it used to be. He then remembered the Wise Ones saying that humans walked on their back legs, like the bears sometimes did.

Hero used his arms to push himself to his legs. He tried to stand but found it so awkward that he fell into the frigid water. He quickly crawled out and tried again. This time he remained shakily on his legs. He tried to take a step forward and nearly fell flat on his face. He took another hesitant step, and this time he did fall.

Hero concentrated so hard on walking that he ignored his freezing body. However, once he learned to walk and run, he felt the cold cling to his bare skin, and he rubbed his arms with numb hands to try to warm himself. It didn't work, and he knew that the only way to get warm was to find a human and ask how. He then remembered that he couldn't speak in the human tongue.

"I am Hero," he said experimentally.

It sounded like a different language than wolves spoke, yet he could still understand it. Was it the human language though? He shrugged and continued on. If he couldn't find heat soon, he'd probably die. He gazed ahead and tried to ignore his freezing limbs. He was about to give up hope when he heard a loud noise behind him.

Hero turned. Two monstrous beasts trotted toward him. They had powerful chests, large heads, long and muscular legs and small pointed ears. They had hooves instead of paws. A piece of metal connected to leather wound about their heads. A long rope attached to the leather and was used to pull and yank on the metal in the beasts' mouths. Their dark hair tossed in the sudden breeze.

The beasts dragged a strange contraption made of wood. Square in shape, it rested on wheels. Hero peered at the strange thing and noticed that two people sat in it. They gaped at Hero with fear in their eyes.

"What are those?" Hero asked, pointing at the two beasts.

"Have you never seen horses before?" the smaller human asked.

Hero knew it was a girl, and that the older one with the ropes was a man.

"And the things wrapped around their heads?" Hero asked curiously.

"That would be a bridle," the man answered.

"The rope?"

"Reins."

"And what are you sitting on?" Hero continued, heedless of their bewildered stares.

"It's just a wagon," the girl said, the shock plain in her voice.

"Listen son, you must have hit your head or something. You look like an icicle too. Come here," the man said gruffly.

"Thank you," Hero said.

He stopped at the wagon and gave it a quizzical look before hopping in. The man undid a piece of cloth covering his torso and handed it to Hero. Hero struggled with it for a while until he put it on correctly.

"What is this?" he asked touching the soft substance that covered his skin. "Is it some sort of fur that can be removed?"

"It's a shirt. You know, those things made from cotton or wool. They keep us warm and give us dignity," the girl replied.

"You humans are rather smart," Hero murmured.

"What?" the man gasped, pulling on the reins. "Are you some sort of Carthafell demon?"

"Demon? I don't even know what a demon is," Hero replied truthfully.

"You have a lot of explaining to do once we reach the farm," the man said, shaking the reins and urging the horses forward.

Hero shook his head. Humans were stranger than he thought they would be. The wagon jolted on the rough ground, and Hero felt a little sick by the time they slowed down. What he saw made his jaw drop.

Huge wooden dens surrounded him. They were not made naturally, and they stood straight up and came in different sizes and slightly different shapes, but Hero knew they all must have a name. He pointed and before he could speak, the girl said sharply, "Those are houses, where we live, and this is called a town."

"Thank you for the information. This is really wonderful. I thought caves were the new thing, but I guess I was wrong," Hero said truthfully.

"Come with us," the man sighed, cutting off the girl's next words.

Hero happily followed, gazing at the other humans as they walked in the town. The townspeople shifted their eyes and pretended they didn't see him. Hero wished he could find a place to warm up. The shirt left his lower legs bare and sharp rocks jabbed painfully into his feet. The man and the girl stopped in front of a simple house that was at least a mile from the village. They opened a long wooden plank, and Hero stepped inside.

"Close the door would you?" the girl asked.

"The what?" Hero asked.

The girl sighed impatiently and pushed past him, closing the wooden plank. The man disappeared through another door and came back holding more clothes. He presented them to Hero who, by looking at the man, figured out how to put the clothes on in the rightful place.

"Sit down," the man said, seating himself on a strange piece of wood.

"And this is?" Hero asked, sitting across from him.

"It's a chair," the man answered incredulously. "We need to talk. What is your name first of all?"

"Hero," said Hero, "and you are?"

"Hank, Hank Weatherfields. Listen, Hero. What happened to you? You look like you're about 23 years old, yet you know less than a two-year-old child. Who are you really?"

"You really want the truth?" Hero asked, slightly perplexed by Hank's comparison. "Alright then."

"I don't know if you know of Verinaul, but it's the world of animals. Have you ever heard of it?" Hero asked.

"Yes I have. There are many stories about the world of animals, none of which I believe," said Hank.

"Start believing, because there is a world of animals, and that's where I am from. Until today, I used to be a wolf, the son of the famous Serval Red Eyes and the brave Fergath. I was supposed to be named Leader and rule over the pack when Fergath grew incapable of the job. My mother died when I was a pup, and my father was too busy for me, so I became friends with the other wolf pups. My best friend was Nakoomu. She was very nice.

"Anyway, after my father and I fought, I ran away and didn't see him for eight years. However, the Storm of Endless Tears had begun, and it was my duty as Lone Wolf to come here. You see, the storm started because of problems here in Nazberath, and the only way to end the storm is to end the problems here.

"So I returned home, leapt into the Pond of Change and ended up here," Hero explained.

"You are completely mad," Hank stammered. "But you sound so sure of yourself..."

"Wait a minute! You *still* think I'm lying?" Hero cried out.

"Well come on, you used to be a wolf? That is very hard to believe. And that storm story is one of the most famous legends of our time. You can hear it from all the storytellers, and they'll tell you it isn't real. It's just a fairy tale," Hank argued.

"It is not! I tell the truth. Tell me, do a lot of humans have yellow eyes? Or red ones for that matter?" Hero growled.

Hank looked into Hero's eyes for the first time and gasped. "Oh my goodness."

Hero sat back smugly as Hank called the girl to him. The girl entered the room and shot Hero a suspicious glare. He gave her a smile and a wave.

"What is it, father?" the girl asked.

"Jacquelyn, this man says that he is from Verinaul. He has come to help us and to save his world," Hank explained.

"Father you can't be serious. Has he seduced you to his insanity? This man needs help as soon as possible," Jacquelyn snapped.

"I am not 'mad' as you say. I tell the truth. I am a wolf, or I used to be," Hero said, gazing into her face until she saw his eyes.

"You *are* a demon! No human could possess such eyes," she shrieked.

"I am no demon," Hero roared, "If you humans are as stupid as I've heard, I should let you be wiped out, and I should return to Verinaul."

With that he went to the door and tried to open it, but he had no idea how. He gave a frustrated growl and sank to the floor. He had no hope of saving Verinaul. The humans thought him insane, and he had no idea what anything was. How was he supposed to learn all about humans and their weird devices and save them from a threat he hadn't even seen yet? He felt an arm wrap around his shoulders and looked up. Hank gently lifted him to his feet.

Hero hadn't really looked at Hank or Jacquelyn before now. Hank was a large man with messy blond hair. His chest was huge and his arms, like tree trunks. He obviously worked hard, for there were lines in his face that didn't belong there. He had a large nose and a long mouth; his eyes were a steely green.

Jacquelyn was a very pretty girl about a year younger than Hero. Her long black hair fell to the small of her back in an intricate braid. She had a thin body, but looked rather formidable. Her face was smooth and her lips, red. Her nose was slightly too long, and she looked at Hero with bright blue eyes. She wore a very long shirt that reached the floor. Hero would have asked about it, but Hank led him to another room.

The small room had a long white thing in the corner with a large square piece of wood on the far wall and another square that was transparent.

"That there is a bed. You sleep on it," Hank explained, pointing to the white thing. "That's a bureau," he added pointing to the square wood. "And that's a window," he finished pointing at the transparent square.

"How am I going to get around if I don't know what anything is?" Hero asked sadly.

"Don't worry. I know someone who could help. I'll go out to find him tomorrow, so I won't be back for a few days. My advice to you is to stay indoors until I find this person," Hank said.

He stepped out of the room and closed the door, leaving Hero alone. The former wolf crawled into bed and lay there. The door opened again, and Jacquelyn stepped in carrying a thin stick that was on fire.

"What is that?" Hero exclaimed.

"A candle," Jacquelyn replied quickly. She sat on the edge of his bed. "Hero, you've convinced my father to help you, and he usually doesn't care about strangers. I'll believe you until he comes back, but if this 'help' finds you are lying, I shall curse you until you die."

"Okay," Hero replied. He shivered with the cold. "Is there any way to get warm?"

"Don't you have blankets?" Jacquelyn asked.

"Blankets?" Hero asked, mystified.

Jacquelyn groaned and moved closer. She made Hero stand up and pulled back the white cloth, revealing more white. Hero climbed in after Jacquelyn's instructions, and she pulled the blankets over him. Hero immediately felt the warmth seep into his skin.

"You're as helpless as a babe," Jacquelyn whispered, shifting a soft round thing under Hero's head. "So I'm going to have to act as your mother until father returns."

Hero didn't hear what else she said for he was fast asleep.

Over the next few days, Jacquelyn warmed up to Hero, and they became good friends. The young woman tried to teach Hero all about humans and the stuff they used. Hero couldn't get the concept of using weapons when he asked the purpose of the long pointed piece of metal hanging over the fireplace.

"That is a sword. You use a sword to defend yourself," said Jacquelyn, taking hold of the sword. "You slash people like this, and they get cut and maybe even die if you put enough force into it."

"I don't understand. You humans don't just use your teeth and claws?" Hero asked.

"Well, our teeth aren't really designed for such things, so we use swords or other weapons to do it for us," Jacquelyn explained.

"If you say so," Hero sighed. "Being a human sure is tough. I don't see what problem you guys are having though. So far, I've seen no trouble."

"Oh, there's trouble all right," Jacquelyn said darkly. "The evil Queen of Carthafell is sending her soldiers across her borders. Our King Dervik's father made a peace treaty with her mother when she was in power. The former Queen desired peace, but her daughter Arlyn desires power and land."

"Go on." Hero encouraged.

"About fifty years ago, there was a great war between Carthafell and our Kingdom of Hasrath. Confusion reigned as bribes and threats dragged other nations into the war. Eventually, the countries of Feruh, Gelda and Zenbin allied with Carthafell and Jurik; Olkina and Ya'tach joined with Hasrath.

"The bloody 'War of Tears' lasted for five years. Finally, the Carthafell alliance fell apart, and Hasrath warriors beat the Carthafell warriors, sending them back to their country. There has been hatred within the country of Carthafell and those who were allied with them. But Queen Luna agreed to the peace treaty with King David, King Dervik's father.

"However, Luna passed away recently and her daughter, Arlyn, holds the power now and has ignored King Dervik's pleas to keep the treaty. She is massing her troops as we speak. There will be another war, and there will be more tears shed."

"That is pretty bad," Hero agreed. "Why doesn't anyone try to stop her before she's ready?"

"Queen Arlyn had already set up defense units around her borders, including demons and goblins," Jacquelyn sighed.

Hero gazed out of a window. So the trouble of war brewed in Nazberath, and he was somehow destined to end it. He was about to voice his question as to how he could help, but the front door opened suddenly, and Hank stepped in, leading a very frail figure in with him.

"Father, you've returned," Jacquelyn exclaimed hugging him.

"Yes I have, and I brought help for Hero," Hank replied, seating the frail figure on the nearest chair.

The figure wore a brown cloak—Jacquelyn had taught Hero the names of all the various types of clothing—and a hood covered his face. Once this figure removed his cloak, Hero saw the wrinkled face of a very old man. Bald with wrinkles on his brow, the old man had a nose shaped like a mushroom, and he was missing most of his teeth. His bony fingers scratched at his ears, which were full of white, fluffy hair. He gave them all a smile before cracking his knuckles and shaking snow off his shoulders.

"Hello all," he said, "Brand has come to help."

"Master Brand. We beg you listen to this man's story," Hank said, gesturing toward Hero.

Brand sat back and made a steeple with his fingers. Hero gulped at the strange man and began his story about his trip from Verinaul. He told Brand all the details he could think to tell. Brand sat motionless as Hero told his tale. His brown eyes remained fixed upon Hero's. When Hero finally finished, it took Brand several minutes to say anything.

"You doubt the word of this young man?" he asked Hank. Hank glanced at Hero before he nodded jerkily. "All you had to do was watch his eyes to know he tells the truth," Brand said sourly.

"You believe me?" Hero asked.

"Of course, I believe you, boy. Why would you lie to us?" Brand sniffed.

"So you really are from Verinaul?" Jacquelyn asked softly.

Hero nodded as Brand stood up on shaky legs. He moved over to the closest window and sighed heavily.

"I'm old, Hank. I don't know if I'm strong enough to help him, but since our future rests in his hands I suppose I'll have to try," he said.

"Help me? How?" Hero replied.

"I'm going to use my magic to help you understand humans and everything about them. You can't possibly save us if you don't even know what a horse and wagon is," Brand smiled.

"It would take weeks to teach him everything about us," Jacquelyn exclaimed.

"Not if I use my magic to jam it in his head at once. Soon he'll be as much a human as you or I," the old man wheezed.

"I am ready," Hero stated.

"You'd better be. It may be a little painful to have all this knowledge introduced at once into your feeble brain," Brand said seriously.

Hero ignored the part about the feeble brain and got ready to receive the knowledge he needed. He just hoped that it would be enough.

Chapter 6

Brand refused to work indoors, so he and Hero went outside toward the barn. The horses lifted their heads over the stall doors and watched them curiously. Brand didn't stop walking until he was past the barn and into the woods behind the house.

"Okay, this is good. Nothing to break your concentration here," Brand said.

"What will this do to me?" Hero asked nervously.

"My magic will allow you to have the knowledge we humans have. You will no longer have to ask about everything you see, unless I don't know what it is," Brand explained.

"Why wouldn't I know it if you didn't know it?" Hero asked.

"Because it is my knowledge that you will receive. Everything I know—and that's quite a lot—will be passed on to you. So we will share the same knowledge. Get it?" Brand asked quickly.

"I guess so," Hero sighed. "Might as well try it."

Brand told him to close his eyes, so Hero did. He felt Brand's cracked fingers touch his temple. The old man began to chant words of an unknown language. Hero felt incredibly calm as the chant continued. He felt warmth flowing from the wrinkled fingers. Suddenly, he felt a slight discomfort in the back of his head. He tried to shake off the feeling, but it grew stronger.

Hero gritted his teeth together as the discomfort turned to pain. His head felt as though squeezed in a vise. He felt tears stream down his face as the pain doubled. Brand kept his fingers on Hero's temple and began to chant louder. Hero tried to push the old man away, but he couldn't.

The unbearable pain lasted for about ten minutes, until the fingers broke the connection. Hero fell to his knees and clasped his head with his hands. Panting hard, he felt sweat on the back of his neck.

"I told you it would hurt, but now you have knowledge, and if you ask me the pain was worth it," Brand said slowly.

Hero looked up at Brand. The old man looked exhausted. Hero got to his feet and led him to the house where Jacquelyn waited expectantly.

"Did you..."

"Yes, I got it," Hero said, his head still throbbing painfully.

He assisted Brand onto the couch and flopped into the nearby armchair, hand pressed to his forehead. Hank walked in carrying a goblet of liquid. He handed it to Hero who took one gulp and began to cough.

"Is this mead?" he cried in dismay. "It tastes awful."

"Well, you knew what it was," Hank laughed. "I'll get you a different drink if you dislike it that much."

"Don't bother. I've just never had anything like this before," Hero said, taking a smaller sip.

Hank inspected Brand and chuckled as the old man let out a soft snore. "You tuckered him right out," he said.

"My head must have been really empty," Hero grinned, drinking more mead.

Hank gave him a friendly smile before going out to milk the cow. Hero went into his room and jumped onto the bed. His head still hurt from Brand's magic. He heard his door open and saw Jacquelyn standing there.

"Hello, Miss Jacquelyn, how are you?" Hero asked politely.

"I am well, Hero. Are you feeling all right?" she replied.

"Brand's magic has left me with a terrific headache," Hero admitted.

"Then I shall boil some herbs for you. It will quell the pain," Jacquelyn smiled sweetly.

"Thank you, Miss Jacquelyn," Hero whispered as the woman left the room.

Hero waited patiently and was about to go ask what was taking her so long when he heard Hank shouting.

"Curses, Jacquelyn! How many times do I have to tell you not to brew herbs? You'll be accused of witchcraft soon!"

"But father, it's for Hero," Jacquelyn cried.

"I don't care. You're not to do this anymore. Do you understand?" Hank roared.

"Yes father," Jacquelyn said weakly. "I just wanted to be useful."

"Hero must learn to endure this pain for that is part of the magic. If you heal him now, he will lose valuable knowledge," Brand explained.

"I want you to practice your knitting in your room," Hank said coldly.

Hero heard hurried footsteps pass his door, and then the unmistakable sounds of a door slamming. He heard Hank curse loudly and dump some sort of liquid outside. Hero assumed it was Jacquelyn's herbs and wished Hank hadn't disposed of it. His head hurt very badly. He decided the best thing to do was to sleep until the pain faded away.

The next day, Hero felt much better. His head was a little fuzzy, but the pain had gone. He walked out of his room in high spirits to see Hank escorting Brand to the door.

"Are you leaving, Master Brand?" Hero asked.

"Yes, young wolf. I have business elsewhere, and I have nothing else to teach you," Brand said.

"Thank you, Master Brand. I have learned much," Hero said bowing.

"Including some manners I see. Fair travel to you, Hero," Brand laughed.

Hank waved and led Brand down the icy path. It only then hit Hero that he would have to leave Hank and Jacquelyn soon. He liked the small family and wanted to stay with them, but he knew that he couldn't. It pained him, but he knew that they needed him to fulfill his destiny.

"Is he gone?" a sorrowful voice asked.

Hero turned and saw Jacquelyn standing behind him. "Who? Hank?" he asked.

Jacquelyn nodded and said, "I hate how he never lets me help. He claims my knowledge of herbs is witchcraft, but I learned it all from Mother."

"Where is your Mother?" Hero asked gently.

"She's dead. Father says that she was gathering herbs one day during a blizzard. He found her a day later, frozen and clutching Poison Root, a plant strongly related to witchcraft," Jacquelyn explained.

"Oh I see," Hero answered. "Well, I don't think it's my place to tell you what to do or say. I wish I could be of more help, but Hank seems to stick to his own path and is rather stubborn when it comes to his being right or wrong."

"Stay with us, Hero," Jacquelyn said suddenly. "I know that if Father had a son he might ignore what I do. You are a year older than I, so he'll want to settle the land inheritance and money."

"B-but, Miss Jacquelyn. I *can't* stay here with you. I have to find a way to save Verinaul," Hero stammered.

"Oh yes, Verinaul. That is more important to you than staying here," Jacquelyn said sadly. She turned around to stare out a window. "Maybe you can visit after you're done," she added.

"I'll try to, Miss Jacquelyn, but I can't guarantee it," Hero replied truthfully.

They sat silently in the dining room, awkwardly picking at unwanted food. Hero opened his mouth several times to start a conversation, but couldn't think of anything to say. He had lived with Hank and Jacquelyn for about a month now and had grown very comfortable.

"I must go to town for a while," Jacquelyn said. "Please look after the farm for me. The cow will need milking in an hour."

"Okay. Hey, you know what's strange?" Hero asked.

"What?" Jacquelyn replied slowly.

"There were no cows or horses in Verinaul. There were also no sheep or house cats, and some of the birds here aren't there," Hero declared.

"That is strange. Maybe Verinaul is only for animals that are wild and free. All the animals here have been domesticated for as long as anyone can remember," Jacquelyn said.

She got out of her chair, reminding Hero about the cow and walked into the gathering snowstorm. Hero called for her to be careful, and she answered with a sly smile and a quick wink. The door clicked shut, and Hero was alone.

He passed the time by polishing the sword hanging over the fireplace. When an hour had passed, he ventured out into the small blizzard and forced a path to the barn. One of the horses whinnied shrilly at his intrusion, and it took Hero awhile to calm the mare down.

He walked up to the large cow and smiled. "Okay, Bess, let's get this done quickly."

He set up the milking stool and began his small task. An insistent creaking made him look up suddenly. The barn door slowly open and just as slowly, closed. A figure in black crept into the barn. Hero crouched by the cow and watched to see the figure's intentions.

The hooded figure stopped in front of the white mare. She tossed her head nervously as the figure began to slide the stall door open. Hero jumped out of hiding, and the figure jumped with fright.

"What are you doing in here?" Hero demanded.

"I-I was just looking," the figure stammered.

"Just looking, huh?" Hero sneered. "Do you always come sneaking into barns dressed in black to look at people's horses?"

"N-no. I'm a friend of the Weatherfields. Please don't harm me," the figure said in a high voice.

"Remove your cloak," Hero ordered.

The figure removed the hood, and Hero saw a young girl. She was about sixteen and had high cheekbones. Her blond hair was dirty, and her eyes were round and feverish. She was shaking from head to toe.

"I want you to leave, little girl. I never want to see your face around this house again," Hero sighed.

"Yes sir, thank you sir," the girl whispered with a bow.

She rushed out the door, while Hero finished milking Bess. He made sure to lock the barn securely before returning to the house. He'd be in an awful amount of trouble if a horse thief succeeded in taking one of the horses.

Hero stayed with the Weatherfields for another week until he finally knew it was time to leave. The house had gloom in the air, and Hero couldn't find the words he wanted to say. He stood in the bright, cold sunshine with a large pack on his back, a walking stick and a sword buckled at his side. Hank and Jacquelyn stood in the doorway.

"I hope you succeed in your journey, Hero," Hank said, clapping a hand to Hero's shoulder.

"Come and visit us as soon as you can, okay Hero?" Jacquelyn asked mournfully.

"As soon as I can, indeed, Miss Jacquelyn," Hero answered. "I can't thank you enough for everything you've both done for me. Tell Master Brand that I'm deeply grateful if you see him again."

He turned around and walked down the snowy path.

Chapter 7

Hero made great time as he stepped across a fallen tree. The snow wasn't too deep any more, and it wasn't as cold as it had been a little while back. He started to whistle a song Hank had taught him, and he slowed his pace slightly. He knew it would be unwise to wear himself out early on in his quest.

Hero approached the town of Ra'sah cautiously. People rushed in various directions. A group gathered at the center of the town, and Hero knew they were the cause of the sudden evacuation. Inspecting them closely, Hero saw that they were demons. Their hair color was unnatural, like red, blue, green or purple. Their faces looked human at first glance, but further study revealed them as having larger than normal eyes that matched their hair color. Their lips were too thin, and their teeth, too long. Their ears pointed slightly at the top, and their skin color was much too pale for any human. Thin rapiers, painted to match their hair and eyes, hung at their sides. One red-haired demon, larger than the others, addressed the group with definite authority in his voice.

Hero crept closer to hear, but it all sounded like rambling to him.

"*Raz bethra uni yerht,*" the large one was saying. "*Okana uhnr gythr julent kelyerb.*"

Hero cocked his ear closer to the demons, fearing that he had lost the ability to understand the human tongue. Then it hit him. The demons couldn't speak in the human language. Hero had never learned how to speak the demon's language.

"*Zexven qwethren histanka lolop ferant,*" a dark blue-haired demon remarked.

The redhead took out his sword and quickly severed the blue-haired demon's head from its neck. Black blood gushed from the wound as the body hit the ground with a muffled thump. Hero backed away from the demons. They were ruthless! If he could only understand what the exchange of words had meant. He felt a hand grab his shoulder and another cover his mouth before he could let out a yelp of surprise.

He turned his head and saw Brand with a finger pressed to his lips. He indicated that Hero should follow him, and he began to crawl away at an alarming speed. Hero shook his head and followed, not daring to look back as he heard the harsh demon language start up again.

Brand led Hero to an old shack just outside the town. Hero peered out the only window and could see the faint outline of the pack of demons. Brand only allowed him to look for a minute before covering the window with a black curtain. He made sure to light only one candle, and then he sat down on the cold floor. Hero sat across from him.

"Hero, those demons are looking for you," Brand said, cutting right to the point.

"Wh-what?" Hero asked.

"They've been looking for you for about a year now. The Queen believes in the myth about the Lone Wolf coming to stop her. She wants you found and killed," Brand explained rapidly.

"Wait a minute. How did she know I came to Nazberath?" Hero sniffed.

"The Queen has many spies in any shape, size or age," Brand said darkly.

"The little horse thief," Hero said slowly. "She must have seen my eyes."

"Aye, your eyes give you away," Brand sighed.

"So now the demons know I'm around, and that means that the Queen must know it too," Hero said.

"I'm afraid so. Not a trick passes Queen Arlyn without her knowledge. I'm afraid you are running out of time," Brand replied.

"But I haven't even started yet. I still don't have any idea on how I'm going to stop Arlyn," Hero muttered angrily.

"I know. That's why you must hurry. Here," Brand said, handing him a small bag. "In that pouch is some magic dust I had Jacquelyn make. It will freeze anyone pursuing you for about a day. Use it wisely for there is not a lot."

"Jacquelyn made this?" Hero asked, holding up the pouch. "When?"

"That day she went to the town," Brand said with a sly wink. "She didn't go near the town. She made the dust, ran ahead of me and Hank and dropped it on the path, leaving my name on it."

Hero smiled and gazed at the pouch fondly. He placed it in his pack where it would be easy to reach. Brand glanced out the covered window and cursed, ducking low.

"Follow me," he hissed.

He ran to the back of the shack and opened a hidden door. He and Hero ran outside, and Brand ducked under the shack. He removed a stone slab and revealed a small stairway. He rushed down the stairs with Hero following, after making sure the slab was firmly in place.

The stairs descended into a small underground room. Brand ordered Hero not to ask him questions and pressed his ear to the earthen ceiling. Hero sat on the damp ground, confusion in his mind. What happened? Were the demons approaching? Hero shook his head and kept his mouth clamped shut. Brand glistened with sweat as he slowly squatted down next to Hero.

"Demons?" Hero asked very quietly.

Brand nodded in reply and indicated for Hero to stay silent. They heard loud feet stomping on the floor above them. The demons were searching the shack. Hero suddenly realized something. The girl would have told them that he, Hero, was staying at the Weatherfields' house. He attempted to leave, but Brand caught his arm and held on with surprising strength. The footsteps receded.

"What are you doing?" Hero hissed.

"Stopping you from getting yourself killed," Brand whispered sharply.

"You old fool. Those demons will head straight to Hank and Jacquelyn. It's my fault the demons are here, and I won't allow my friends to be hurt because of me," Hero argued.

"Hank and his daughter will be fine," Brand said calmly. "I've sent a message to them to get out and hide."

"You better not be lying," Hero snapped.

"What reason do I have to lie? I like that family as much as you do," Brand continued.

"I know that," Hero said. "You don't have to shout at me."

"Keep it down," Brand snarled quietly. "Or do you want to get us both killed?"

Hero grumbled to himself and got to his feet as Brand moved to the stairs. They climbed out of the secret room and looked around cautiously. They could see demon footsteps in the snow. They were making their way to Hank's house. Brand grabbed his shoulder again.

"It is time for you to go Lone Wolf," he said. "Make your way to Vernan River and cross it. Then follow it south until you reach Sesamare Gate.

Present this gate card, and the guard will let you into the country of Jurik. Olkina may no longer be safe," he explained, handing Hero the card.

"Very well. Thank you, Master Brand. You've been most helpful," Hero said, bowing low.

"I'm glad I was useful. Oh yes, one last thing. Go to *The Lady Light Inn* in Herzeen. My good friend, Keelo, is the inn master. Tell him that I sent you, and he'll know what to do," Brand said.

Hero promised he would go to the inn and hurried out of the town toward the Vernan River. He made sure the demons were gone before running across the road to a dense forest where he would be hard to find. He hoped with all his heart that Hank and Jacquelyn escaped from their farm unharmed.

Hero ducked low as he heard the steady footsteps of a horse. He ignored the sharp branch that poked his temple as the horse came into view. It was a large horse with a symbol of two swords forming an "X" with a blue oval behind them painted on its flank. From Brand's knowledge, Hero knew it was the symbol of Queen Arlyn.

The rider turned out to be the red-haired demon; his pace was very slow as if looking for someone. Hero heard another horse and saw an armored man riding up to the demon. Hero listened hard as the soldier saluted.

"Sir, I've checked the Vernan and found no sign of the man with red and yellow eyes," the soldier stated firmly.

"No sign, hm?" the demon said. "I made sure that girl described every detail about him. He can't be far, and I am convinced he doesn't know about us yet."

Hero smiled at that. If they thought he was still ignorant to their presence then he had the advantage.

"Shall I broaden the search in case, sir?" the soldier asked.

"Yes, that will be good. Tell your soldiers to keep a couple of guards at the Vernan, Captain," the demon smiled cruelly.

"Yes, Sir Hynraz," the soldier said, tipping his helmet to the demon before galloping back toward the river.

"*Bazra kinok iliy,*" Hynraz growled.

He turned his horse and headed back to the town. Hero breathed a sigh of relief. He would have to find a way to make it past those guards. If he set out now, the soldiers wouldn't have time to organize, and he would have a better chance of passing undetected. He set out and listened carefully for any noise that might prove dangerous. He jumped a foot when a squirrel cut across his path and leapt into a nearby tree, chattering angrily at something. Hero quickened his pace, afraid that someone would inspect the noise.

He crept along at a faster pace, nervous that the soldiers would be in place by now. He ducked under a thorn bush when he heard a thunderous noise approaching. He peeked through an opening and saw the same soldier followed by at least thirty men. Most rode horses, but some ran behind on foot. Hero pressed himself to the ground as they passed, fear racing through his heart. He suddenly missed being a wolf very much, considering that wolves never had to worry about being hunted by thirty beasts.

Once the last foot soldier passed from view, Hero made his way deeper into the woods and began to run. Those soldiers only meant one thing. The guard had been established and he would have to cross now, before they gained complete control. He ignored the stinging pain in his cheek as a branch cut into his flesh, causing a trickle of blood to flow down his face. He leapt over a hole in the ground and stopped suddenly. The trees were thinning out and the sound of rushing water could be heard.

Hero crawled forward and saw that the road ended at the river and continued on the other side. He spotted a bridge a few paces away, but guards were stationed there. He looked to his left and to his right and saw that the soldiers would make sure no one could go down either road. Hero was at a loss as to what to do. He couldn't use the bridge; he couldn't turn down the right or left road. He knew his only chance was to use Jacquelyn's powder and then jump into the river and hope it flowed south. Once he cleared the soldiers, he could climb out and run until he came to the Sesamare Gate.

Hero glanced at all the soldiers to make sure they weren't looking his way, and he took out the magic powder. Then, he stiffened his shoulders and broke from the cover of the trees. He rushed forward despite the sudden yells from the soldiers. An arrow whizzed by his head, and he ducked lower. The water came closer and closer. Hero threw the powder, and most of the guards froze like statues. The ground fell away, and Hero jumped. He fell for about three feet before hitting the icy water with a loud splash. To his delight, the river flowed south at an incredible rate.

Hero thought himself free from danger as he swam with the current. However, a lucky shot from one of the soldiers who had not been hit by the powder found its mark. Hero yelped as the arrow burrowed into his arm. He ducked under the water as more arrows followed him. When he could hold his breath no longer, he broke through the surface and saw that, although the few remaining unfrozen soldiers tried to pursue him, they fell farther and farther behind. Hero still swam as fast as he could, using his right arm while his left hung limply at his side, leaving a bloody trail in the water. He was freezing but knew that it would be his death if he tried to crawl out of the river with the soldiers running behind him. He kicked his legs feebly and hoped that the Sesamare Gate wasn't too far.

Chapter 8

Hero climbed out of the Vernan River only after the light had faded from the sky. The soldiers were far behind him, and he was too cold to stay in the water any longer. Fighting his way into the woods, Hero dug a fire pit and gathered some thick branches and some twigs. He removed his soaking clothes and started the fire, laying his clothes out to dry. He reached in his pack and pulled out fresh clothes, hurriedly put them on to fight the cold, and huddled next to the small flames, hanging a piece of dried meat over the fire. As soon as the meat sizzled, he took it away and gnawed at it hungrily. Once he finished, he knew the time had come to remove the remainder of the arrow.

He had been able to break off the head and tail of the arrow, but he had not removed the middle of the wooden shaft, which still pierced his arm. He rolled back his sleeve, prepared a bandage, and grasped the longest part of the shaft. Hero tugged at it gently, but the pain was excruciating. He closed his eyes, ground his teeth together and yanked at the arrow. It moved an inch or so forward. Excited, Hero pulled harder and felt the arrow slide out of his arm. As he expected, the pain increased and a fresh flow of blood trickled down his arm.

He took a cup of water from the fire and dipped some rags into it. After cleaning the blood from his arm, he wrapped rags round the wound. He then tried to move his arm but found that it was too painful, so he doused his fire, wrapped himself in his cloak and went to sleep.

The next morning Hero tested his arm again. It didn't hurt as much, but it felt very stiff. He gathered his things and set out again. The road was long, but Hero was confident that he had out run the soldiers for the time being. He kept a steady pace as he made his way to the gate.

With the sun high in the sky, Hero stopped to eat and wash his bandages. After eating more meat and taking a swig of water, he rested. A short time later, he packed his things and made his way to the road again, thankful he was fit. After all, thirty miles running was nothing to him when he was a wolf.

Hero looked behind him occasionally to make sure that the soldiers weren't close. He made his way into the woods to camp at night, wishing he had asked Brand the distance to the Sesamare Gate. Tired of looking over his shoulders for soldiers, Hero began to lose patience with this strenuous journey. He wasn't accustomed to being hunted; he was supposed to be the predator. But there were more soldiers, and he had no idea how to fight with his sword. He sighed as he dug another fire pit and started his cooking fire.

He did notice a couple of things that made his spirits rise. The weather wasn't as cold, and less snow covered the ground. The night air wasn't a harsh bite on his face as he wrapped himself in his cloak to sleep.

Hero opened his eyes the next morning in time to see the sun rise. It was slightly warmer than the day before, and he set out, spirits soaring. The Vernan River flowed happily along side him, and he slowed his pace to admire the beauty of the budding leaves and flowers. Spring was on the way, and that meant that traveling would be easier. He glanced up as a small bird fluttered above his head.

Hero stopped for a minute to unsling his walking stick from his back as he viewed hills in the distance. Jacquelyn had given him the best of the sticks in the house. It was made of oak and polished to a gleam. The top was thick and could be used as a weapon, but it was light and felt pleasant in his hand. He tried to carry it with his left arm, but his wound had not healed enough to hold anything.

Hero reached the first hill at noon. It was largest of them all and very steep. He leaned forward and tried to move quickly. It would be easy for the soldiers to spot him if he were still climbing when they arrived. He didn't know if they would pursue him this far, but he didn't want to take chances. If they had seen his face, then they would know his identity. Thinking about all of those soldiers and their demon leaders made him quicken his pace even more.

By the time Hero reached the top of the hill, he suffered from a small cramp in his side and panted heavily. He wiped away the sweat on his forehead and continued down the hill. Pleased with his achievement, he sighed with relief at the sight of the other hills, which were dwarfed by the first one and not nearly as steep. He allowed himself a short break at the bottom of the hill and took a gulp of water. The hills blocked the view of the Vernan River, but Hero could still hear it.

When he felt refreshed, Hero stood up and began to climb the next hill. He dug his walking stick into the ground and pushed himself forward. His left arm stung a bit with the strain in his muscles, but he didn't let it bother him. When he topped the second hill, he saw the Vernan glistening innocently in the sun. Hero couldn't help but feel that the river had a life of its own.

At the end of the fifth day, Hero saw a long wall in the not-to-far distance. It stretched on as far as he could see, and he knew it had to be the border wall between Olkina and Jurik, which meant that the Sesamare Gate was located somewhere along the border. Hero smiled brightly as he set up camp yet again.

It was dusk by the time Hero reached his destination. The wall, made completely of stone, was about forty feet tall, except for the gate, which was metal and only twenty feet high. Hero made his way to the guard window and grabbed the gate card from his bag. He strode boldly up to the window and placed the card on a wooden counter.

The guard inspected the card carefully and asked for Hero's name. Hero answered and the guard yelled up to the gatekeepers. Hero heard many men yell orders, and he gasped as two giants stepped out from the wall. Each took a chain attached to either side of the gate and began to pull, lifting the gate slowly from the ground. Hero thanked the guard and walked beneath the gate. Looking up, he saw that the gate points were very sharp.

As soon as he cleared the wall, the giants gave the chain more and more slack, and the gate slowly closed. He whispered a silent "wow" before turning his back to the gate. To his left in a large field, Hero saw a farm with a sign advertising horses for sale. Hoping to find a good horse, he went to the farm and followed another sign that pointed to the stables. Approaching the door, he knocked politely.

"Come on in," a warm voice called.

Hero opened the door and saw a large woman and a rather skinny man sitting in rocking chairs. He walked up to them, and the woman stood up and held out her hand. Hero took it, and they greeted each other.

"My name is Sarah, and this is my husband, Bobby," she said in a voice that was rather deep.

"I am Hero, and I've come to buy a horse," Hero replied.

"Oh wonderful! What type of horse are you looking to buy?" the woman asked, giving him a grateful look. "Work horse, race horse? What?"

"Well, I want a horse that I can ride for a long distance. So I don't have to walk everywhere," Hero said.

"Oh I see," said Bobby getting up and walking to a golden horse with a snow-colored mane and tail. "Then you'll be wanting Phoebus."

"What a beautiful horse," Hero said admiringly. "How much?"

"Well, he's our best horse, so I can't let him go too cheaply," Bobby replied craftily. "But I'd let you take him for about a hundred."

Hero's jaw dropped. Bobby and Sarah must not have known much in the ways of money. He knew he should have negotiated a better price for them. Phoebus was worth a lot more than a hundred, but he didn't have the money to pay fully. He handed the happy farmers their hundred coins and led Phoebus out of the barn.

"Wait a minute. Don't you want his tack?" Sarah asked.

"Yes, thank you," Hero said, quickly throwing on the saddle and reins.

He jumped onto Phoebus and dug his heels into the golden stallion's stomach. Phoebus jumped forward and set off at a brisk trot. Hero was very grateful for the rest, as Phoebus crossed distances in half the time he could have. Before long, a bustling town appeared in front of him. He looked at a sign and recognized the name of the town Brand had told him about, Herzeen.

Herzeen was a very busy town. Hero had never seen anything like it in his life. People rushed by on the dirt-filled roads, while salesmen hawked their goods. Hero noted that this town was nothing like the quiet town of Ra'sah. He slowed Phoebus to a steady walk and ignored the calling salesmen who waved meats and jewels heatedly in front of them.

Hero had to jerk his stallion's reins more than once to avoid hitting anyone as he moved through the twisting, narrow roads. He kept his eye out for *The Lady Light Inn*, but he couldn't find it, even though there seemed to be nothing but inns in Herzeen. Finally growing impatient, Hero jumped from Phoebus and led the stallion on foot. He paused when he saw an obviously wealthy lady stepping gingerly over a puddle.

"Excuse me, ma'am," Hero said, walking over to her. "May I ask you a question?"

"What is it, boy?" the woman asked sharply.

"Could you direct me to the inn called the *Lady Light?*" Hero asked hopefully.

The woman's face visibly softened. "I thought you were going to beg for money like all the others. The inn is down that road," she explained, pointing to a road that turned sharply to the left.

"Thank you very much, ma'am," Hero said, bowing slightly.

He turned down the road, leading Phoebus along behind him. There he saw a rather nice building made of wood with a red-slated roof. It was three stories high with a stable just behind it. Hero looked up and saw a sign with a picture on it. *The Lady Light Inn* was printed on the sign with a picture of a noble woman holding light in her palm. Hero walked toward the stables and approached a large woman standing just inside.

"Hello there," she said. "Taking out a room? There's an empty stall toward the back of the stable."

"Thanks," Hero replied.

He led Phoebus to an empty stall and almost cried out. The red-haired demon's black horse stood drinking from a deep bucket of water. Hero hid his face behind Phoebus' and hurriedly put his horse into the stall. He averted his eyes as he passed the demon's horse, as if it were Hynraz himself. He almost bolted out when the black horse jerked its head up.

The woman was about to enter the inn, but Hero called her back to him. "Did someone named Hynraz check in here?" he asked.

"Hynraz? No," the woman said. "Why, you meeting someone?"

"Not exactly. Was there a man with red hair and red eyes?"

"We don't give shelter to demons, sir. I suggest you find a room and not mention anything about those beasts," the woman said darkly.

Hero sighed and walked into the inn. A round-faced man with graying hair and a thick mustache sat at a desk. His eyes were narrow and black, and he wore a leather jerkin and a belt that stretched across his thick middle. He looked up as the door closed, and he placed a well-practiced smile on his face.

"Good day, young master. Will you be taking a room at our fine inn?" he asked.

"Yes please," Hero answered. "I'm also looking for a man named Keelo. Are you the man?"

"Yes, I am Keelo, the inn master here. What do you need?" the large man asked.

"Well, Master Brand told me you could help," Hero said, looking Keelo full in the face for the first time. Jacquelyn had warned him to hide his odd eyes as much as he could. "I have a slight problem," he added.

"I see. Well, rest first. Room 13 is vacant," Keelo whispered, handing Hero a rusty key. "That will be fifteen coins."

Hero handed Keelo the coins, picked up his bag and headed toward the stairs with great hesitation. Was the horse in the stables really Hynraz's? The demon's horse had looked like no horse Hero had ever seen. It had sharp teeth and ember-colored eyes, but he couldn't see the horse clearly as the stable had been dimly lit. He shook his head slightly and walked up the creaky stairs.

Room 13 was plainly furnished, but perfect for Hero. He threw his bag in the corner and looked into the mirror hanging over a washbasin. Those eyes, one burned like the sun; the other was the color of fresh blood. He closed them tight, but when he opened them nothing had changed. He never expected it to. Walking away from the washstand, he sat down wearily on the bed. It had been a while since he had been in a bed. He was asleep before he realized he had climbed under the covers.

Hero walked down the stairs and looked out a window. It was early evening, and he was hungry. Keelo motioned him toward a private dining room and then disappeared into the room himself, carrying plates of food. Hero followed and closed the door as instructed.

"You must be the one from the stories. Lone Wolf, our savior," Keelo said, uncovering meats and vegetables for them to eat.

"Yes, I suppose. However, I have no idea what I'm supposed to do. Do I kill a woman I don't even know? Or do I try to talk the world out of war?" Hero asked.

"There is only one way you are going to end this, Lone Wolf. You have to kill Arlyn and Muryn," Keelo said.

"Muryn? Who is Muryn?" Hero asked indignantly.

"General Muryn is Queen Arlyn's brother. He is also the most precious thing to her. You hurt Muryn, you bring her wrath on the world," Keelo explained. "So you have to think this out."

"What do you all expect me to do? Walk into Carthafell and kill Queen Arlyn, then turn around and kill her brother?" Hero demanded.

"Well, sort of," Keelo sighed. "You can't walk into Carthafell from the south, north or west sides. The only place not guarded as heavily is the east."

"Is there a reason for that?" Hero asked.

"How'd you guess? The east is guarded by the Jilok Mountains, which just happen to be the highest and steepest mountains in all of Nazberath. Especially Mt. Wervyn." Keelo smiled, not at all amused.

"Great," Hero sighed. "Nothing to it. Unless you add the fact that demons are chasing me, and war is about to break out again."

"Listen, Lone Wolf. I know this sounds impossible. But I believe you can do this. You just need to hide those eyes for one thing. And also, a little confidence never hurt anyone," Keelo said.

"My name is Hero, and I've tried to rid myself of these eyes. Unless you want me to cut them out, I think I'm stuck with them," Hero replied.

Keelo smiled as he pulled out a small bottle. He handed it to Hero. "Just put in three drops and your eyes will turn blue. You have to do it every morning and every night," he explained.

"Really? This is great!" Hero exclaimed. "Can I put it in now?"

"Knock yourself out," Keelo said, cutting into his third piece of steak.

Hero tilted his head as far back as it could go. He carefully let three drops fall into his left eye, and then did the same for his right eye. He blinked tearfully for a few seconds and then lowered his head to look at Keelo who nodded in approval and passed him a hand mirror. Hero looked into it and saw bright blue eyes shining back at him. His face split into a grin.

"Now on to business," Keelo said. "Brand trusted you to me for awhile, so I'm going to help you as best as I can."

"I need to get clear of all these demons. I need to get anywhere that I could do some good," Hero said.

"I suggest you go to the capital, Delring, in Hasrath. You really should meet the King and tell him who you are," Keelo decided.

"What if he doesn't believe me because my eyes are now blue?" Hero asked.

"Make sure you take out a room and stay a few days without using the dye. Your eyes will return to normal, and you can meet him then," Keelo explained.

"How do I get to Hasrath?" Hero asked. "Isn't it far from Jurik?"

"Oh my yes. I'll give you a map to keep you off main roads and get you there a little quicker," Keelo offered.

"You've been very kind to me," Hero smiled. "I will repay you personally some day."

"Getting rid of that Queen will be payment enough," Keelo said gruffly, but a slight tinge of pink crept into his face.

"Well, I think I need to sleep. I shall leave tomorrow morning," Hero said.

He stood up and walked to the door. Keelo stopped him with a quick tap on the shoulder. Hero turned and saw Keelo holding out a rolled piece of parchment. "The map," he said needlessly. Hero took it, thanked the elderly man and walked back upstairs. He stood to one side as he saw a tall man walking down the stairs. Even pressed against the wall, there was little room, and the man brushed by him rather roughly.

"Sorry," he muttered in a familiar voice. It was Hynraz.

But it didn't look like the Hynraz Hero had seen before. This Hynraz had short black hair and steely gray eyes. His skin was dark, and he was unarmed. Hero hurried up the stairs before realizing Hynraz could only recognize him by his eyes, which were now blue. That didn't stop him from walking quickly into his room.

The next morning, Hero woke to the fresh breeze of a promising spring day that drifted lazily into his room from the open window. He stretched and walked over to the basin. Grabbing the eye dye, he tilted back his head and put in the three drops again. He gazed at himself for a minute with a satisfied smile. He really liked the deep blue color his eyes had become.

He changed his clothes and pulled on his boots. Stuffing his heavy cloak into his bag, Hero grabbed it and the map and left the room. Keelo waited by the door.

"Here," he said, handing Hero a small bundle. "Some extra food."

"Thank you, Keelo. I will always remember your kindness. Good bye," Hero replied.

"Good bye, Hero," Keelo said, opening the door for him.

Hero walked to the stable and grabbed Phoebus' tack. He put it on the horse and looked around for Hynraz's black horse. It was gone. Hero shivered despite the warm weather and led Phoebus outside. He climbed into the saddle and started off again.

People looked up at him as he passed, allowing Phoebus to release his energy and frisk about for a while. Spotting some Carthafell soldiers on the next road, he sped up a little. Glancing at his map for a minute, he turned Phoebus to the northwest. His next goal would be Gilyn, a large city situated a few miles from the Uilik River, which he needed to follow for a few days until he reached Satlin, another city. From there, he'd have to cross the Uilik Mountains and pass through the Hurith Gate. Then he'd have to navigate his way through Feruh.

Hero put away the map as Herzeen came to an end at a wooden gate. He passed through it and looked back one last time, saying another silent thanks to Keelo. Phoebus trotted along the dirt road that led into a thick forest. Hero sighed and thought about his mission. Kill an evil Queen and her brother, stop the world from entering war, and somehow keep his head throughout the whole thing. Phoebus snorted, as if feeling Hero's discomfort, and Hero patted the horse's strong neck. He tried to keep his attention on the road ahead of him and decided it would be foolish to think about the future until the future was upon him.

Hero stopped Phoebus after only ten steps into the forest. Another rider followed the same road. His horse looked about to drop, and its gray coat looked patched and scruffy. The horse hung its head to the ground and frothed slightly from exhaustion. The man rubbed the horse's neck and bent over, whispering to it. The horse seemed to ignore him and kept on trekking. Hero didn't know why the man didn't get off until he saw that he was tightly tied to the horse's worn saddle. He nudged Phoebus in the ribs and the golden stallion cantered toward the mysterious man.

"Do you need help?" Hero asked, looking at the thick ropes that held the man in place.

"No," the man said, straightening his back.

"Are you sure?" Hero continued. "If you haven't noticed, your horse is about to collapse."

"I know," the man said warily. "What's it to you?"

Hero felt his jaw drop. "W-well I thought you might have gotten into trouble. You are tied to the horse rather tightly, as are your hands," he said, noticing the man's hands were tied at the wrists.

The man just stared at him. Hero felt uneasy. The man would have been very handsome had it not been for the rough black eye-patch covering his right eye. The long, ragged scar that ran from his eyebrow to his jaw did nothing to help hide the right side of his face. The other eye was a deep chocolate brown. His hair was blond and touched his shoulders. It was ragged and thick. The man's tunic was frayed and his pants, ripped. His traveling cloak was dirty and had been patched up sloppily. Hero tried to think of what to say, but the man's one-eyed stare left him speechless.

"Don't mind Merrick. He's a fool," the tired gray horse suddenly said.

"What the...?" Hero yelped.

"Who's the fool? You refuse to stop, and you're close to death," the man snapped at the horse.

"Oh quiet," the mare sighed. "Excuse him, sir, but he has become mistrustful ever since...Well no need to say more."

"You can talk?" Hero gasped.

"Hm? Oh yes. You've noticed. My name is Isabell, and I am no regular horse. I am a unicorn who lost my horn. Thanks to that Queen," the mare snorted.

"A unicorn? But I thought unicorns were white and immortal," Hero whispered.

"Usually," Isabell stated. "But when the horn goes, the color and the immortality go."

"How come you're tied to each other?" Hero asked, intrigued by this odd pair.

"Oh, well...er...we'd rather not tell people at the moment, but we would be grateful if you untied him. Merrick weighs more then he did a week ago. Or maybe I'm just getting tired," Isabell sighed sadly.

"You've said quite enough," Merrick said sourly, looking away from Hero.

Hero didn't mind Merrick's personality at the moment. The man looked about to drop, and patches of dried blood seeped through his clothes where the ropes cut in. Hero took out his hunting knife and cut the ropes binding Merrick to Isabell. The man dropped from the saddle, and Hero barely caught him. He had passed out cold. Hero gently cut the ropes binding his hands and laid him slowly on the ground.

"Poor fool. It's an awful fate to be hunted, especially when you're only twenty-seven years old," Isabell said, nuzzling Merrick.

"I know. I'm being hunted too," Hero replied.

"By whom?" the former unicorn asked.

"Queen Arlyn's demons," Hero said. "I can't tell you why at the moment. We have to see to Merrick. I suppose we should take him back to Herzeen."

"No! We cannot linger in any one spot, or we'll be found and brought back to Carthafell," Isabell whinnied.

"You, you're from Carthafell?" Hero whispered.

"Yes. Don't tell Merrick I told you this, but Queen Arlyn is his sister," Isabell whispered.

Hero stared at Isabell for a full minute before he could even think of replying. Queen Arlyn's brother? He shook his head as if that would make it untrue, then he thought of something.

"I thought Queen Arlyn only had one brother, General Muryn," he pointed out.

"That is what most people think. However, Merrick is indeed their brother, or half brother at least. Arlyn and Muryn share the same father, but Queen Luna married a noble Lord from Zenbin, and that Lord was Merrick's father. Arlyn and Muryn hated both the Lord and Merrick for it," Isabell explained.

She was about to continue, but Merrick suddenly stirred and sat up. He pushed Hero's hand away from him and stood up on shaky legs. Hero stood beside him, trying not to look prepared to catch the man again. Merrick gave Isabell an accusing look.

"How much did you tell him?" he demanded.

"I told him nothing, Merrick," Isabell sighed.

"She really hasn't said a word," Hero added.

"Humph. Well I suppose we should be off," Merrick grumbled. "Unless you want to wait around for Carthafell soldiers."

Hero urged Merrick to ride Phoebus as he walked alongside of Isabell. Merrick stubbornly refused, until Isabell gave him a sharp nip on the shoulder. Cursing softly, Merrick climbed onto the stallion, and Hero placed a hand on Isabell's neck. They agreed to stop at the next farm they could find. Merrick gently prodded Phoebus in the side, and the stallion walked along at a fast pace. Hero told Merrick that he and Isabell would catch up with him.

"You're very kind," Isabell commented. "I thank you for your patience."

"Well, I've never seen a unicorn before, and I'll never leave anyone behind for Carthafell soldiers," Hero replied.

"You are not a real human are you, Hero? I can sense it," Isabell suddenly said.

"Not really. I'm a wolf from Verinaul," Hero admitted.

"Lone Wolf?" the unicorn exclaimed. "The one to save us all? We're saved!"

Hero blushed with embarrassment and admitted that it would be very hard to do. Especially since he had no idea how to fight with a sword. "I'll end up throwing the thing down and biting my opponent," he said sheepishly.

"So what? A little foul play never hurt anyone. Besides, Merrick is a master at sword fighting. I'm sure we can talk him into giving you some lessons," Isabell chuckled.

They walked in silence after that, Hero wondering how to approach the ill tempered Merrick, while Isabell hummed a lively tune. Hero also thought about everyone he had met in Nazberath. He felt the weight of their faith as they looked to him to stop a war that seemed almost impossible to stop. He sighed and concentrated on the matter at hand. Learning how to fight would be harder than anything he had done so far.

Chapter 9

Hero and Isabell caught up to Merrick at nightfall. They had reached an abandoned farm that would be perfect for hiding out for a little while. Hero waited until after dinner to ask Merrick anything at all. The man's temper seemed to have cooled down a bit, so it was now or never.

"Merrick," Hero began. The one-eyed man looked over at him. "Have you ever used a sword before?"

Merrick's eye narrowed as he draped his faded green cloak over his black tunic and brown pants. Then he said quite simply, "I have."

"Do you think you could teach me?" Hero asked.

"Why?" Merrick asked. "You planning on killing someone?"

"I suppose you could say that," Hero answered slowly. "The point is I need to learn, and I need to be taught by someone good."

"Who says I'm any good?" Merrick smirked. "I could be awful for all you know."

"Are you bad?" Hero asked coldly.

"No, not really," Merrick answered carelessly.

Hero wished that Isabell hadn't gone to sleep. Merrick was impossible to convince. Merrick looked toward the night sky, studying the constellations. Hero cleared his throat loudly, and Merrick gave him another glance to show he was listening.

"Can we make a deal?" Hero asked. Merrick raised his eyebrows. "If I tell you all about me, you have to teach me how to use the sword."

"All about you, huh?" Merrick considered. "Oh what the heck. Talk away. If what you say is interesting, I will teach you."

So Hero again told his tale about Verinaul. He was pleased to see Merrick's eye open wider and wider in surprise. Indeed, when he finished, Merrick was goggling at him. As though realizing what he was doing, Merrick coughed and looked away.

"So, will you teach me now?" Hero pleaded.

"Sure," Merrick whispered. "Don't expect anything else though. Once you learn how to fight, I'm leaving."

"Fair enough," Hero grinned. "So, you do have a sword, right?"

For an answer, Merrick walked over to his saddlebags and pulled out a long broad sword. Hero nodded admiringly, and Merrick actually smiled. "I got this from my father," he said. Then his face reddened, and he mumbled something under his breath. He stared at Hero, sword in hand, and Hero realized that he meant to start his education that very night.

Hero dug his long sword out of its sheath and walked over to Merrick.

"Isn't this dangerous?" he asked, glancing at the sharp edges.

Merrick pulled out two long rubber tubes in the shape of the blades. He slipped one over his sword and handed the other to Hero. Hero pulled the rubber tube over his sword and nodded in satisfaction. Merrick clasped the handle of his sword in both hands and told Hero to do the same. He then planted his feet shoulder-width apart, but with the left foot slightly behind the right one. Hero copied his stance.

"Just blocking basic swings will do for tonight," Merrick instructed.

He swung his sword above his head and then brought it down slowly, aiming at Hero's head. Hero got the message and brought his sword up horizontally. Merrick's sword hit into Hero's sword with a dull thud. Merrick brought his sword back in front of him. Hero again copied him. Merrick slowly thrust the sword at Hero's heart, while telling Hero to move his body to the side and let his sword catch the thrusting blade. Hero sidestepped and let Merrick's sword slide along his own.

By the time Merrick decided to stop, Hero's arms felt like lead. Merrick never swung his sword fast enough to unbalance Hero, but the weight was unfamiliar to the former wolf. Merrick taught him how to block all kinds of swings, thrusts and sweeps. He also taught Hero a little bit of footwork, though not enough to keep him alive versus a demon or general. Hero looked over at the man and felt a deep gratitude that he had met him. Thanking him silently, he crawled onto a sagging mattress and fell asleep.

The next morning, Hero awoke to the smell of fresh bacon. He opened his eyes and looked over at the fire pit in the middle of the floor. Merrick held a long stick impaled with pieces of bacon over the fire. Hero walked over to him, rubbing his aching arms. Isabell walked into the farm from the back, where a large hole had appeared some time ago. She gave them a quizzical look but didn't say anything.

"We'll stay here until we finish with you," Merrick said suddenly, taking the bacon away from the fire. "Then we'll have to go our separate ways."

"That's as good a plan as any," Hero agreed.

"So you're actually doing some good, Merrick?" Isabell chuckled.

"Hey, none of that," Merrick growled, handing Hero some bacon strips.

Hero smiled to himself as Merrick and Isabell began arguing again. He couldn't see how the two managed to stay hidden with all the shouting. They might have ignored the fact that they belonged to two different species, but they acted like siblings. Hero looked up in time to see Isabell sticking her chin up indignantly, which just looked plain silly coming from a horse. She walked out soon after. Merrick grimaced as he finished his bacon. He then pulled out his sword again. Hero got the message and grabbed his own.

"We'll practice footwork today," he said. He stood on his toes and bounced up and down lightly for a minute.

Hero did the same and felt his legs loosen quite a bit. Merrick put his legs in the same stance as the previous night, but this time he stayed on his toes and kept shifting his weight from the front leg to the back leg. Hero did too and knew that he would be able to move a lot easier now.

"Let's do some exercises," Merrick said.

He grabbed a fistful of rocks from outside and came back. He told Hero to dodge them as best he could, telling him to imagine them as sword thrusts. Hero nodded and got ready. Merrick whipped a rock at his mid-section, and Hero barely jumped away in time. He was completely off balance as the next rock came whizzing by and hit him in the arm. He regained his footing and successfully dodged another. However, the slightly large pebble that came out of nowhere smacked him dead between the eyes, and he toppled over backward.

"Are you okay?" Merrick asked, pulling him to his feet.

Hero wiped away the small trickle of blood running down his face and nodded. Merrick stepped back and got ready to throw more stones. Hero managed to dodge a couple more, but most found their target.

It took Hero about a week to master all the fancy footwork that Merrick had learned during his life. Hero took pleasure in hearing that Merrick thought him ready to learn how to actually strike. He was also pleased to hear that striking was the easiest to learn, until he heard that it was the hardest to do. Merrick taught him the main areas to strike and some tricky moves that would take the enemy by surprise. Hero enjoyed himself at the farm as he learned new moves and added in all the footwork. By the time he put it all together, it was like a dance.

"Well, I can't rightly let you take off before a match," Merrick said.

He had become friendlier toward Hero as time passed between them, though he still never revealed anything about himself. Hero didn't mind as long as they could train together and talk about other things. Hero got his rubber-covered blade ready as Merrick covered his own blade.

"Ready?" Merrick asked.

As soon as Hero nodded, Merrick thrust at him so quickly that Hero couldn't move. Hero's arm took the full blast of Merrick's thrust, and he stumbled. He caught himself before he fell and countered Merrick's next blow. He thought about everything he learned for a second and then charged at Merrick. The two exchanged blow for blow, one occasionally slipping and getting hit. Merrick was indeed a master, Hero decided, as he parried more thrusts. He remembered a tricky sweeping move Merrick taught him, so he dropped down and swept his sword into Merrick's shin. Merrick yelped and fell. Hero rushed forward and tried to put his sword to Merrick's throat, which would signify the winner, but Merrick was already on his feet. He swung his sword at Hero, who blocked with his sword, but the older man changed the swing into a thrust and jabbed Hero in the stomach. Hero buckled over and saw Merrick swinging his sword down toward his neck for a mock beheading. Hero stepped back and blocked the sword with the back of his hand, rushing forward and placing his sword against Merrick's neck.

"It seems your wolf came out there," Merrick panted, looking at Hero's reddening hand.

"I suppose so," Hero agreed taking his sword away. He drank deeply from his canteen, while wiping away the sweat on his forehead. The late spring air had grown hot as the morning melted into early afternoon. Merrick studied his sword as if wondering how he lost. Hero walked over to him.

"Well, it looks like we shall go our separate ways," Merrick said slowly.

"Oh, right," Hero said hesitantly.

Isabell walked over to them. "I can't believe how foolish people can be," she sighed. "If you want to stick together, you should just stay together."

"What?" Hero asked. "I have no objection if Merrick wishes to go his own way."

"Of course you have no objections, but you would rather have him with you. I hear you guys talking to each other until the sun comes up, like you're old friends. You won't be able to find each other if you split up, and then who would you talk to?" the wise unicorn scoffed.

Merrick and Hero exchanged looks of surprise. The graying unicorn laughed gruffly and walked back to where Phoebus was tethered. Merrick shrugged and said that it was up to Hero.

"Would you mind if I tagged along?" Hero asked hopefully.

"No, but I am being chased," Merrick pointed out.

"So am I," Hero said. "I suppose it would give them a harder time if they tried to take two at once."

Merrick nodded and grinned at the thought of having someone else to fight with him. They packed their bags and climbed onto their horses. Isabell was now refreshed and ready to move, and the ever-ready Phoebus frisked his head impatiently. They set off at a slow trot and never noticed the two sets of eyes watching them from the shadows.

Hero tugged out his map and looked for the hidden path that would lead him to Gilyn. The path lay two miles up the road, so he and Merrick quickened the horses, eager to be off a main road. Isabell looked behind them as they turned onto a path hidden by brush and leaves. She thought she heard something following, but she saw nothing. Grumbling to herself, she followed Hero and Phoebus as they followed the unknown path.

Hero could tell that Isabell couldn't shake the feeling that they were being followed. She stopped suddenly and turned around.

"What's wrong?" Merrick whispered.

"Something's out there," she replied just as softly.

Hero turned Phoebus and waited quietly with them. A sudden snort from a horse sounded to their left, and Hero swirled around in his saddle. A demon sat on a great black horse. It wasn't Hynraz, but he looked just as deadly. The sun glinted off his blue hair, and he smiled showing pointed teeth.

"How do they know it's me?" Hero thought. Then he realized why they pursued them. Merrick.

Another snort from their right showed a green-haired demon had followed them too. Merrick placed a hand on his sword, but the blue-haired demon cut him off with a growl. The two demons pulled out blackened bows and notched barbed arrows, aiming at the two humans.

"*Ish no kin. Habeth uut nesva?*" the green-haired demon asked the other.

"*Cien fya, Kinop,*" the blue-haired one chuckled.

The only thing Hero understood was that the green-haired one was named Kinop, while the blue-haired one was called Habeth. Judging by Kinop's sour face, Habeth was the leader. He fingered his sword, and the two demons pulled back their arrows more. Habeth indicated for them to raise their hands above their heads.

"Do it," Merrick hissed. "More are hiding in the trees."

Hero glanced around and knew Merrick spoke the truth. He could make out wild colors hidden among the greens and browns of the forest. Habeth rode toward them and waved his right hand in the air. The dozen or more demons hiding came into full view. Hero felt his heart start to race. He couldn't be killed now.

Habeth grabbed his chin and forced his face up so he could see it. Hero used the dye everyday so glistening blue eyes, not mismatched ones, met Habeth's stare. Habeth snorted and moved over to Merrick. He grabbed the man's chin and looked into his face as well. Habeth sneered and looked to his companions, who had formed a tight circle around them.

"*Juza onday meer. Uda techa honda. Yulay Merrick dodompo lusfar Arlyn foy Muryn,*" he exclaimed.

The other demons cheered evilly. Merrick gave Hero a sad look as if he felt it was his fault. Hero shook his head and gave him a small smile. Merrick managed a smile too, but it dropped quickly off his face. Habeth slung his bow across his back and produced the same ropes that had bound Merrick before, and Hero realized that Merrick must have recently escaped from these demons, which was why he was bound when they had met. Habeth grabbed Merrick's arms and twisted them behind his back, nearly pulling the man onto the demonic horse. Once Merrick's hands were behind his back, Habeth shoved him back onto Isabell. Kinop grabbed Hero's arms and tied them in a similar fashion. The green-haired demon then took Phoebus' reins, while Habeth grabbed Isabell's. The demons would lead them back to Herzeen.

Habeth sent two demons running ahead once the town came into view. Hero tried to run once and now had a large welt across his back. Merrick's head just dropped lower and lower as the town gates came into clearer view. Habeth laughed cruelly and spurred his horse into a gallop, forcing Merrick to clench Isabell with his knees. Kinop followed his leader's example and soon the whole group of demons galloped toward Herzeen. Hero knew who waited for them there—the leader of all these demons, even over Habeth. Hynraz would be pleased with his captives.

Hero thought that the demons might actually bring them to Keelo's inn, but he was not that lucky. They went to another inn across town called the *Executioner's Lodge*. It did not look friendly. Habeth leapt from his horse and dragged Merrick with him. Kinop also grabbed Hero, and Hero saw the rest of the demons take the horses.

As he was dropped painfully to the floor, Hero was not surprised to see Hynraz. Habeth and Kinop backed out of the room as Hynraz stood up. He examined Merrick first, and a smile lit his face.

"Welcome back, Merrick. I haven't seen you for a while. I suppose you won't find it too surprising that I'm to bring you and that 'unicorn' back to Carthafell," the red-haired demon said.

Merrick groaned and looked away from the piercing eyes. Hynraz turned his attention to Hero. "You just happen to be traveling with traitors. Make sure you learn everything you can about your new friends," he smiled.

Hero looked into those cold red eyes with defiance. Hynraz looked back, and surprise filled his face.

"Didn't I bump into you at the *Lady Light*?" he asked. "I could have sworn it was you."

"It was indeed," Hero answered. "But you certainly looked different."

"Who are you? I don't like it when I run into someone twice. It usually means he's up to something," Hynraz said softly.

Hero paused. If he told Hynraz who he was, he would be dragged off to Carthafell. However, if Hynraz thought he was unimportant, he might just kill him and be done with it. Hero suppressed a growl of frustration. He had hardly started to figure out a plan, and he was already neck deep in trouble.

"I am Hero, from Verinaul, the world of animals," Hero said.

Hynraz laughed out loud. "You are not the Lone Wolf from the stories. You don't look like a hero, and you don't even have the eyes that mark the hero."

"Look in my pocket, and you will find eye dye. I got it from a friend," Hero said, not wanting to mention Keelo. "It was to hide my identity from the likes of you."

"I see," Hynraz sneered, pulling out the dye. "This doesn't prove a thing you know."

"Just wait for a few days. Without the dye, my eyes will return to normal," Hero argued.

"Very well. I was told to bring the Queen the hero, and it wouldn't do to let you slip through my fingers. We shall wait for three days. If your eyes remain blue, I shall kill you slowly and make you wish you had never mentioned Lone Wolf," Hynraz threatened. "Oh, and Merrick, they'll be *very* happy to see you."

With that the demon left the room and locked them in. Merrick buried his face into the musty carpet and groaned again. Hero crawled his way over to him and sat on his knees in front of him.

"You shouldn't have told them who you were," Merrick grumbled. "Now they'll know even if you change your eyes."

"I know, but they would have killed me here if I had lied to them," Hero replied. "Besides, the two of us may find a way to escape on the way to Carthafell."

"Are you crazy?" Merrick demanded, raising his head. "Demons are known for their cleverness. Anything you or I can think of they already know."

"Well, that's a problem, but we can overcome it. There has to be a way, Merrick. I refuse to be taken to that awful woman!" Hero snarled.

"Listen, I want out as much as you do. I can't let Arlyn see me. She'll torture me again...I mean..." Merrick stumbled.

"Again? Why did she torture you?" Hero asked, though he thought he could guess the answer.

"I don't want to talk about it," the man mumbled.

"Merrick, we may not have another chance to talk. I want to know about you," Hero pleaded.

"Well, I guess it couldn't hurt. We are going to die after all," Merrick sighed, ignoring Hero's indignant sniff. "I'm Arlyn and Muryn's brother. Somehow I think you heard this from Isabell, but whatever. My father was from Zenbin, while their father was from Carthafell. For some reason they hated me for sharing their...our mother.

"I never bothered them, but they bothered me. Arlyn always made me do her chores, calling Muryn over if I refused. Arlyn is skilled with magic, and I'll tell you now she can think of really horrible ways to use it. So she would torture me with magic, while Muryn beat me with his fists. Mother tried to stop them, but they grew angry with her too. When she died, Arlyn assumed the throne. By then she was twenty, and gaining all that power stirred more evil within her.

"She had me tied to one of the columns in her throne room. That way she could do what she wanted with me if things didn't go her way. Muryn would join in sometimes, when he wasn't off directing defenses at the borders. I thought I would die, but somehow I lived.

"It was raining the day I ran. Muryn rode me down on his horse and tried to bring me back. But I had stolen a sword from one of the guards, and I fought him. He managed to give me this scar and take out my right eye. I still managed to run though, using the dark night to hide myself. I was twenty five then, and, in these two years, they haven't stopped hunting me."

Hero gazed at Merrick and saw that his eye had become very shiny, as though he was on the verge of tears. Hero wished he could have said some comforting words, but he was so shocked at the ruthless Queen and her brother that he couldn't say a word. Merrick stretched out his legs and rolled onto his back. He forced his hands down to his thighs and began to struggle to bring his hands forward. In a few minutes, his hands rested on his stomach, tied but at least in a more comfortable way. Hero did the same, realizing that he could hold a sword this way.

"Merrick, we can fight like this," he said standing up.

"I suppose we could," Merrick agreed.

"When the next demon comes in, we should surprise it. We can jump it from both sides of the door," Hero said excited for the first time that day.

Merrick only sighed, "Hero, when you found me in the forest, I was still trying to escape the demons. They do not let you rest or eat a full meal. As you saw, I didn't even have time to untie myself. These demons are ruthless."

"Just because they're ruthless doesn't mean a thing!" Hero snarled. "If you want to let them drag you to your sister then go ahead, but I'm not coming!"

"You act as if I *want* to go back," Merrick said coldly.

"Well, when you act like this, I find it hard to think otherwise. I thought you had stronger will power then this, Merrick," Hero replied.

"Just shut up, Hero. You haven't got a clue how much will power I've had to use in the last two years. You don't know anything of danger, of glowing eyes hunting you in the night, of nightmares you can't awaken from no matter how hard you try. I have no patience for fools who act as if they can take on the world!" Merrick yelled.

"I'm supposed to take on the world, remember?" Hero shouted back. "That's why I'm here. If I give up, both Nazberath and Verinaul will be destroyed. You have to wake up, Merrick. You have to find something to fight for."

"I don't have anything to fight for," Merrick said weakly.

"I can name two things right now. Isabell and revenge. You should stand up to your brother and sister and let them feel your pain. As for Isabell, she's like family to you. That should be enough to make you fight," Hero urged.

The key rattled in the lock, and they fell silent. Kinop stepped in with two trays of food. He set them down and watched the two humans eat. Once they finished, Kinop pointed to Merrick and indicated that he should follow him. Merrick shook his head stubbornly. Kinop growled and grabbed him by the scruff of his neck. He then dragged Merrick with him, ignoring the punches and kicks to his body.

Hero tried to follow them, but Kinop slammed the door in his face, locking it behind him. Hero pounded on the door with his bound hands and shouted for freedom. He slumped against a wall once the sounds of footsteps fell away. His hands were bloody from his meaningless effort, but he didn't care. He had to save Merrick. If the demons decided to bring him to Carthafell first, Hero would be doomed. He closed his eyes and tried to think, never really noticing that he had fallen asleep.

When Hero woke up, he saw a dark mound beside him. It was late in the night, and he could see stars from the small window near the ceiling. The mound turned out to be Merrick. Hero rolled him over and saw that Merrick had been beaten. He shook him awake, and Merrick's eye opened in panic. Hero calmed him down and helped him sit up.

"What did they do?" Hero asked.

"Just following Arlyn's orders. 'Once you find him give him a beating for leaving his dear sister to worry about his whereabouts,'" Merrick recited, rubbing a swollen jaw.

"Curse them," Hero said. "We have to get out of here before my eyes change. That window is our only chance."

"Hero, did you not notice that the window is too high to reach and probably too small to fit through?" Merrick asked.

"We can force ourselves through. But we'll need each other to reach it. I'll let you stand on my hands so I can lift you up. Once you get to the window, you can break it open and climb through. Then you'll have to grab me and pull me up," Hero explained.

Merrick studied the window for a minute before saying, "I guess it's a good thing I lost all that weight during those two years."

Hero grinned and walked over to the window. He braced himself against the wall and held his hands out for Merrick to step on. Merrick placed one foot on the bound hands, and Hero lifted him toward the window, marveling at how light Merrick was. Merrick began pushing at the glass window, trying not to cause too much noise.

"Just break it," Hero hissed, as his hands started to throb.

Merrick shrugged and smashed the window open with his hands. He made sure the window ledge was free of glass before trying to crawl through. He had to squeeze his chest and shoulders, but the rest of him went out smoothly. He skillfully turned around and draped his hands down to Hero. Hero grabbed them and Merrick pulled him up.

The drop to the ground would sting their legs, but it was worth it. However, before Merrick could even jump, the door opened again and Hynraz appeared. He gave one look at the scene and rushed forward.

"Go!" Hero yelled.

Merrick tried to protest, but Hero shoved him and caused him to fall to the ground. He jumped away from the window just as Hynraz's sword stabbed where he was only a second ago. The demon's eyes blazed with hate.

"You foolish little human," he spat, charging with his sword again.

Hero dodged it and tried to make for the open door, but Hynraz antici-pated his moves and lunged with his blood red blade. Hero moved out of the way, but felt the demonic sword glance off his arm. The wound instantly felt as if it were on fire. He clenched his teeth and dodged the sword again.

"You will die!" Hynraz shouted, swinging his sword at Hero's head.

Hero dropped to the floor in order to dodge the blow. He knew he didn't have a chance fighting like a human, so he decided it was time to fight like a wolf. He lunged at Hynraz from the floor, trying to get to the demon's neck. Hynraz wasn't expecting the leap and cried out as Hero landed on him.

Hero snapped his jaws at the surprised demon's neck, but Hynraz fended him off with his arm. His eyes narrowed, and he threw Hero to the floor. Hero stayed crouched down and again leapt at Hynraz, this time going for his shins. He caught the left shin with his teeth and bit down hard. Hynraz growled in pain and disgust and began kicking Hero with his free leg. When this didn't work, he stabbed down with his sword. Hero was too quick for the sword to find its mark. He spat out some of Hynraz's blood and prepared for another onslaught.

Hynraz gave him a cocky smile that enraged Hero. He jumped at the red-haired demon's throat again, but Hynraz produced a hidden dagger and threw it at Hero. Not able to dodge in mid-jump, Hero took the dagger in the shoulder. He fell heavily to the floor, blood seeping into the carpet. Hynraz laughed and reclaimed his dagger, giving Hero a harsh kick as he did so. Then, thinking Hero was about to die, he left the room, not bothering to lock the door.

"Find Merrick and bring him to me!" the demon shouted.

Hero struggled to his feet and stumbled to the window again. He grabbed a long piece of glass that had fallen to the floor and cut through the ropes that bound him. The sharp glass cut into his skin whenever he missed the ropes, and it took him several painful minutes to remove them. He found a musty blanket in the corner and tore it into strips, which he tied around his bleeding hands. He covered the more serious wound on his shoulder with the rest of the blanket. Then he jumped up toward the win-dow, knowing it was his only means of escape.

Try as he might, Hero couldn't reach the window. He needed another person to help him. He tried one more time and nearly cried out as a hand wrapped around his own and pulled him out the window. Hero fell to the ground. When he looked up, he was surprised to see Merrick.

"Why didn't you run away?" Hero demanded.

"Couldn't just leave you to die now could I?" Merrick asked with a roguish grin.

Hero smiled in thanks and they stood up, hiding in the shadows. Hero looked around for Phoebus and Isabell, but he couldn't see the stables.

"This way," Merrick said, leading Hero toward a grove of trees.

"What about the horses?" Hero asked softly.

Merrick told him to keep quiet and led him to the grove. Isabell and Phoebus stood tethered to a tree, swords tied to their saddles. Hero grabbed Phoebus' reins, swung up into the saddle and nudged the golden stallion to a gallop. They rode off into the night, the sounds of the yelling demons falling farther and farther behind. Hero glanced around once and saw them heading in the opposite direction. Clearly none of them had seen them ride off.

They rode throughout the night, not daring to stop and only slowing down to a trot after sunrise. They hid in a large cave covered with vines. Herzeen lay far in the distance, but they had ridden too far west. They'd have to head east until they came to the forest again. Hero let out a sigh as he sat down on a rock.

"Let me see that wound," Merrick said, looking at his bloody shoulder.

"Sure," Hero replied. "I don't think it's too deep."

He removed his tunic and unwrapped the blanket. Merrick took the blanket and dipped it into hot water. He washed away the dried blood and examined the wound. It was deeper than Hero thought and large enough to be stitched up. Merrick dug into his saddlebags and produced a needle and thread. Hero stiffened his shoulder as Merrick slid the needle in.

As Merrick stitched the wound up, Hero told of the battle he had endured the previous night. Merrick congratulated him on surviving versus a highly trained demon, and Hero couldn't help but feel a small bubble of pride. He also felt very grateful that Merrick knew how to stitch well. They decided to rest for a few hours and then move on. Hero hoped that the demons never found them again.

Chapter 10

After the two felt rested enough, they started to make their way toward Gilyn again. They stayed far from Herzeen and circled around the forest until they found the hidden path. Cutting through branches was hard, but they did not dare show their faces on the main roads.

Once they found the path, they made sure no demons lurked. Hero decided it would be best to run awhile just in case. Merrick agreed heartily. So they dug their heels into their horses and galloped down the overgrown path, heedless of branches whipping at their faces.

They kept moving for the whole day, eating in their saddles so they could stay ahead of Hynraz and his men. When night fell, Isabell found another well-hidden cave. It was very cramped, but that didn't bother any of them, not even Phoebus. Merrick began to dig out food as soon as he sat down, grimacing when he mentioned they would have to have a cold dinner so that the firelight didn't attract unwanted guests. Hero took a piece of meat and welcomed the coldness of it. He had eaten raw meat as a wolf all his life.

"How far do you think Gilyn is?" Merrick asked softly.

"Let's see," Hero answered, pulling out his map. "I'd say another day at the most."

"Good, Gilyn is a large city so we should be able to hide there for a day or two. Where are you going anyway?" Merrick asked.

"I'm heading to Delring so I can speak to King Dervik," Hero replied.

"King Dervik, huh? Well good luck with that. His soldiers don't let anyone near him anymore. They're afraid some Carthafell men will sneak in and slip a dagger in his ribs," Merrick sighed.

"Every time I think something will be easy, it turns out to be hard. I can't wait to return to the simplicity of being a wolf," Hero muttered.

"Can you go back?" Merrick suddenly asked.

"I should hope so," Hero said, suddenly nervous. He had never thought about that. "I'll find a way home. No problem."

Merrick didn't say anything, and soon he curled up to sleep. Hero wasn't tired though. What if he couldn't get back to Verinaul? It was a dumb question. Of course he would be able to return. He put all doubts of being stuck in Nazberath out of his mind and tried to fall asleep. It took him a good two hours.

The next day dawned cloudy, and by early afternoon it began to rain. Hero and Merrick kept their cloaks over their heads and spurred the horses on through the mud. Phoebus nearly slipped once or twice, but Hero managed to balance him out before the stallion fell. Isabell muttered about the dampness and the pace from time to time, but she never slowed down. By the time the gray clouds turned black, Gilyn's gates were in view.

"Listen, if those demons are here we have got to take on new names," Merrick whispered. "I'll be Marcus and you can be my brother Lucius."

"Fine by me. What about a last name?" Hero asked.

"How about Carro?" Merrick replied uncertainly.

Hero shrugged, and they decided on Carro. Once they reached the gate, an older man stopped them. He was bald but had a great black beard that stretched down to his stomach.

"What is your purpose here?" he asked, making it very clear that he carried a large spear.

"Just come to stay and rest, sir," Merrick said warmly.

"Your names?" the gate man asked.

"I am Marcus Carro, and this is my younger brother Lucius," Merrick answered with a slight smile.

"I see. Traveling a bit late aren't ye?" the man asked.

Hero took over as he saw impatience flash in Merrick's eye. "We didn't wish to camp out again, sir, that's all."

"Alright, you're clean. If you cause any trouble, you'll be thrown out though," the man sighed, opening the gate.

Hero felt his breath escape in a gasp of surprise. He had never seen anything as confusing as a city. Buildings were everywhere, and people crowded the streets, heedless of the rain and night. The roads themselves were a marvel. They were cobblestone, and the horses' hooves clattered upon them. The buildings were also a sight, taller than any Hero had ever laid eyes on. The walls were plastered down, and Hero saw that they were made of better wood than the buildings in Herzeen. It was a true wonder to someone who had lived in a cave all his life.

Merrick led the way to side streets where people seemed to appear out of nowhere. Inns lined the streets along with herb shops and bakeries. Merrick stopped outside an inn with a large sign showing a dragon. It was called the *Dragon Heart*. The innkeeper was a skinny old man with eyes that were too large for his thin face. He greeted them kindly enough and had his son bring the horses to the stable.

"Room 20 is free. Two large beds and a bath right down the hall," the innkeeper said.

"How much?" Merrick asked.

"That would be thirty coins a night," the innkeeper replied.

Hero's jaw dropped. Thirty coins was expensive! Then he realized that he was in a city, and that prices would undoubtedly be higher and match competitors. Merrick pulled out thirty coins and handed them to the eager innkeeper.

"Very nice. My name is John, by the way, and you are?" the thin man encouraged.

"Marcus Carro," Merrick said, while Hero added, "Lucius Carro."

John smiled, and, as he gave Hero the key, he mentioned how rare it was to see siblings traveling together. They thanked him and climbed the broad stairs. They found their room easily enough and found it to their liking. Hero was delighted with the size of the room. It had two full-sized beds with silken sheets, and he felt it would suit them very comfortably.

"If you'll excuse me," Merrick began, "I think I'll take a bath."

"I think I'll do the same after you're done," Hero said.

"It's not just one tub you know. I've seen baths in these types of places. There's always more then one tub. And don't worry about intruding on someone's privacy. They hang curtains around your tub," Merrick explained with a small smile.

"Oh. Okay then," Hero replied sheepishly. "Lead the way, Marcus."

Merrick grumbled something under his breath as he opened the door. The bath was at the end of the hall, and Hero was pleased to see steam coming from under the door. Still soaked from the rain, he was rather cold. Merrick opened the door and a woman exited at the same moment, hair damp from the bath. Hero cried out and leapt away.

"What's wrong?" Merrick asked.

"There are *women* in there too?" Hero asked indignantly.

"Yeah, so?" Merrick shrugged. "You cannot see anyone. Okay Lucius?"

Hero gulped and walked hesitantly into the room. It was very large with curtains everywhere. Hero looked down at the floor, not wanting to chance a glance at anyone. Merrick rolled his eye and approached a servant.

"Two baths and make them next to each other," Merrick said.

"Yes sir. This way sirs," the servant replied, walking over to two empty brass tubs.

Once they entered, more servants appeared with buckets of steaming water. They poured the water in the tub until it reached the top. They bowed themselves away as two more servants pulled the curtains around them. Hero thanked the servants as they left him to himself. He undressed and sat down in the water, sighing in relaxation as steam drifted lazily toward the ceiling. He definitely needed this.

After about thirty minutes, Hero stood up and dried himself off with a fluffy white towel. His wet clothes had been taken, and, in their place, was a white robe. Hero slipped the robe over his shoulders and tied it closed. He pushed through the curtains and looked over at Merrick's closed bath. A servant stepped in front of him and handed him his clothes, which had been dried and cleaned.

"Thank you," Hero said.

"Your welcome, sir," the woman answered as two more servants pulled back the curtains.

Another pair started to fill buckets up with the bath water and walked into another room to dispose of it. Hero thanked them again and made his way to the door. A voice stopped him.

"I don't believe it," the voice exclaimed.

Hero turned and saw Jacquelyn standing next to a servant. Her dark hair hung loosely around her, falling down to the small of her back. Her blue eyes filled with surprise and happiness. She held a green riding dress in her arms. She also wore a white robe, and her hair was damp. Hero stared at her as she made her way over to him.

"Hero," she whispered.

"Hush. My name is Lucius Carro for now," he hissed in her ear.

"Okay, Lucius what are you doing here?" Jacquelyn asked.

"I'm making my way to Delring so I can speak to the King," Hero replied.

Servants began to look at them, and the room fell into silence. Hero closed his mouth before he could say anything about demons.

"Let's go to my room," he said quietly.

Jacquelyn agreed, and the two left the steamy room. Hero locked the bedroom door and sat down on his bed. Jacquelyn stood by the other and looked at Hero expectantly.

"I'm being chased by demons," Hero said.

"I know. They came to the farm," Jacquelyn replied sadly.

"Are you both okay?" Hero exclaimed. "Is Hank here with you?"

"We're both fine. Father isn't here though. We thought it would be better to separate so they wouldn't be able to find us so easily," Jacquelyn sighed.

"Listen Jacquelyn. I think you should get as far away from me as possible. I was captured by the demons so they know my face. If you stay with me, you'll be hurt," Hero suddenly said.

"Who said I was going to go with you in the first place?" the young woman asked, but pink tinged her cheeks.

"I can see it in your eyes, and I'm telling you now that you can't come with me," Hero replied.

"Why not? I've dealt with danger before, Hero! You can't tell me where to go! If you leave me behind those demons will find me and kill me, but you don't care do you?" Jacquelyn spat.

"Of course I care, Jacquelyn. Listen to me would you? The demons will be looking for me more than they'll be looking for you," Hero pleaded.

"I want to meet them," Jacquelyn said darkly.

"What are you talking about?" Hero demanded.

"Those demons burned the farm, Hero. They killed all our livestock except for one horse! Our fields are nothing but ash, and Father lost his right arm trying to keep me safe, but I didn't escape unscathed in the end," Jacquelyn explained.

She pushed the robe down so that Hero could see her left shoulder. A long pink scar stretched diagonally down her chest until the folds of the robe hid it. Positive that Hero had seen the wound, she pulled the robe back onto her shoulder.

Hero stared at her for the longest time. He had a million things to say to her, but nothing came out. In the end, he was only able to say two words, "I'm sorry."

"Hero, it wasn't your fault. Father and I knew the consequences the moment we took you in," said Jacquelyn. "I have no regrets."

"Please, Jacquelyn, please do not come with me. You will be killed," Hero said.

"Hero," Jacquelyn began, planting her fists on her hips. "I'm coming, and if you say one more word I swear I'll slap some sense into you."

Hero gaped at her as she finally sat down on Merrick's bed. A sudden knock at the door caused him to jump, and he got up to answer the door. He opened it a crack to see Merrick standing there, blond hair still slightly messy. Hero opened the door the rest of the way and stepped out of his friend's way. Merrick took two steps into the room before he noticed Jacquelyn.

"Lucius, you can't just bring in women. There is another place and time for that," he sighed.

"Excuse me?" Jacquelyn shrieked. She stormed up to Merrick and jabbed a finger in his chest. "You listen here mister! I'm a friend of Lucius.'"

"Huh?" Merrick asked.

Jacquelyn prodded with her finger again and added, "I don't know who you are, but I don't appreciate your comments."

Merrick seemed completely speechless at Jacquelyn's little outburst. But almost instantly his dark temper flared. He pushed her away from him rather roughly and growled threateningly.

"You watch your mouth, wench," he said, cocking his head in an almost arrogant manner, showing a touch of royalty.

"Stop this," Hero interrupted. "I won't let you two kill each other. Merrick this is Jacquelyn Weatherfields. Remember the woman I told you about. Jacquelyn, this is my friend, Merrick Thanos. We've been through a lot together," he explained.

Jacquelyn and Merrick shook hands rather reluctantly, but it was a greeting nonetheless. Introductions complete, Hero invited Jacquelyn to sit at the end of his bed so that the three of them could plan their next course of action.

"You are trying to cross Feruh?" Jacquelyn asked incredulously.

"It's the quickest way," Hero pointed out.

"Yes, but it's also allied with Carthafell. They don't speak English well, and I think they probably know your face by now, Hero," Jacquelyn explained.

"What would you have us do?" Merrick asked coldly. "Cross the Ocean of Mist into Gelda where we will most certainly meet death?"

"I never said a thing about Gelda. I know that it's the only country bordering Carthafell, and that Hero would be killed in a second," Jacquelyn sniffed.

Hero sighed as the two of them exchanged insolent stares that dared the other to say one more word. He was going to have to work on building teamwork between the two.

"Anyway," he said, clearing his throat loudly, "I think that we should maintain our chosen path. Feruh isn't as bad as crossing the Ocean of Mist and a country of murderers."

"You are absolutely right," Merrick said, that arrogant nobility coming through again.

Hero guessed that he intended to impress, or intimidate, Jacquelyn. He had grown up with a King and Queen and had been around his brother and sister constantly. He must have been an arrogant child and never lost that side of himself. Jacquelyn paid no attention to it though.

"I think I better go back to my own room and get some sleep," she said. "Good night, Hero."

With that she stood up and walked out the door, giving Merrick a stern glance as she closed the oak door with a slight snap. Merrick shook his head and muttered about women with too much spirit before crawling under his covers. Hero was about to say something to defend Jacquelyn, but his friend had already turned his back to Hero and feigned sleep. Hero sighed and blew out the candles that had illuminated their room.

When Hero woke up, Merrick was already gone. He stretched and made his way down the stairs to the dining hall. As he opened the glass doors, people gave him a glance before turning back to their meals. He saw Merrick and Jacquelyn sitting at the same table, having a silent, but heated, argument.

"Good morning all," Hero began. "Nice to see you fighting already."

"Lucius, Marcus is being very stubborn and foolish," Jacquelyn said in a tight voice.

"How so?" Merrick snapped. "*You're* the one with no common sense. Leave the thinking to those who can, farm girl."

"Don't talk to me like that you mangy haired oaf," Jacquelyn hissed angrily.

"Both of you stop right now and tell me why you're acting like two children," Hero ordered.

"I was just saying that it would be better to ride right through Satlin to save us some time," Jacquelyn sniffed.

"And I was telling her that was a rash action that would surely kill us all seeing how Satlin is probably filled with demons," Merrick added.

"And I told him that it couldn't be, because if Carthafell had started to occupy countries under King Dervik's control, it would start the war," Jacquelyn argued.

"I see." Hero pondered. "I think we should consider this carefully. I would like to reach Delring as soon as possible, but I really don't want to fall into the hands of those demons again."

"Then our path is clear. We pass through the slums of Satlin to avoid them," Merrick said triumphantly.

"What if the demons anticipate this?" Jacquelyn demanded. "They wouldn't think that you'd go through the main city, but it's obvious that you'd go through the slums."

"Excuse me, sir?" a serving girl asked. "Would you like something to eat?"

"Oh, yes. I'll have rabbit soup please," Hero said, hankering for some meat.

"Very well. I'll be back soon. Would you care for more sir and lady?" the woman asked looking at Merrick and Jacquelyn.

"No thank you," they answered at the same time.

The serving woman nodded her head and went to the kitchens. Hero was glad the fighting was on hold. It didn't last long though because Jacquelyn found her second wind. But instead of trying to prove her point she said, "Hero, what do you think we should do?"

"You ask me?" Hero stammered. "I have no idea. I haven't really been here long enough."

"Oh shut it," Merrick growled. "It all depends on whether you want to risk meeting those demons or not."

"Then I must say that it would be less likely to see demons in the slums," Hero replied with a slight pause.

Jacquelyn's lips pursed together, but she only nodded in agreement. Merrick gave Hero a smile that said he thought Hero made the right choice. Hero wanted to say something to Jacquelyn, but the serving woman had returned carrying a steaming bowl of soup.

"I hope you're happy, Marcus," Jacquelyn snarled as they left the inn.

The people of Gilyn were already up and about. They glanced at the three of them, and Hero couldn't blame them. Luckily his eyes were still blue from his eye dye so they didn't stand out too much. However, Merrick and Jacquelyn's constant quarreling made people curious.

"I am happy, thanks for asking, farm girl," Merrick said, amusement in his voice.

"You call me that again, and I swear I'll slap you, you arrogant pig," Jacquelyn flushed.

"Whatever you say, farm girl," Merrick chortled.

Hero sighed as Jacquelyn gave Merrick a harsh slap across the cheek. She strode toward the stable before another word escaped his lips. Hero stopped Merrick from following her, knowing that Merrick had an awful temper when in a foul mood. He started to complain to Hero about how Jacquelyn was going to be a burden, and that she should be left behind. Hero stopped listening within five minutes.

By the time the two men reached the stables, Jacquelyn's black mare was saddled and ready to go. Hero had never seen it before and guessed that she had bought her while Hank took the one from the farm. She gave Hero a slight smile and scowled at Merrick as he passed her. He only gave her an identical stare.

"Let's hurry shall we?" Hero said. "Before you two throttle each other."

He brought out Phoebus' tack and got his golden stallion ready. He heard Isabell murmur something to Merrick in the next stall, but couldn't catch what she said.

Once they were all ready, they rode at a swift walk through the city. They had enough food and water to last them for a while. Hero told them that they would have to follow the Uilik River until they reached Satlin. The river was a few miles from Gilyn.

"Once we get through Satlin, we have to cross the Uilik Mountains to reach Hurith Gate," Hero reminded them.

"I hope you can handle it, Marcus. Your horse looks a little worn out," Jacquelyn said.

"Well, I think she can manage a few mountains. If you're looking for someone to worry over, look to yourself. You do realize that you will probably slow us down. I can't imagine that you can fight or anything," Merrick sighed.

Hero looked at his map once more before stuffing it into his tunic. He wondered if they could manage to stay out of danger the whole way. As if to say "no" to the thought, an arrow whizzed by Hero's head and buried itself into the ground.

"We're under attack!" Hero roared.

He turned Phoebus around and saw five soldiers galloping toward them. They were not from Carthafell, the insignia on their armor being different. A white tiger decorated the chest of their steel breastplates. Hero had no idea where they were from.

"They're from Feruh," Merrick answered as soon as Hero asked about them.

"We must fight them," he said. "Jacquelyn stay back."

"Are you kidding? I came to fight, Hero," the woman replied firmly, drawing a short sword.

"Charge," Merrick shouted.

All three spurred their mounts and raced toward the soldiers of Feruh. To their surprise the soldiers stopped and raised hands in the signal that they wished to talk. The three slowed their mounts reluctantly.

"We are looking for two fugitives who have an arrest warrant on their heads," said one of the soldiers.

"Well what do they look like?" Hero demanded.

"The reports describe two men who look exactly like the two of you," another soldier sneered, fingering his sword hilt.

"Don't be ridiculous," Jacquelyn laughed. "These two men can't be those you seek."

"And why is that?" the first soldier asked.

"This man here is my husband," Jacquelyn said, laying a hand on Merrick's arm. "And this here is my husband's brother."

"What are your names then?" the rear soldier ordered, actually drawing his sword.

"My name is Marcus Carro, and my brother is Lucius Carro. My wife's name is Shara," Merrick said, laying his arm around Jacquelyn's shoulders.

"How long have you two been married?" one of the soldiers asked, disbelief heavy in his voice.

"Only a year," Jacquelyn said, practically falling off her horse to lightly kiss Merrick on the cheek.

"Humph. The papers say they are warriors. These people make me sick with their weakness. Let's go men!" the first soldier yelled.

He galloped past them with the rest following close behind. As soon as they vanished from sight, Merrick removed his arm from around Jacquelyn, and she firmly pushed away from him.

"Why didn't you say Hero was your husband?" Merrick demanded, wiping at his cheek.

"You were closer. So stop whining about it. I would gladly take Hero over you," Jacquelyn sniffed.

"Would you two stop fighting for a minute," Hero shouted.

He nudged Phoebus and headed for the river. Merrick and Jacquelyn rode behind him, hanging their heads rather sheepishly. Isabell chuckled to herself as they made their way to the Uilik River and whatever lay beyond.

Chapter 11

The journey was rather pleasant, except for the occasional spats between Merrick and Jacquelyn. The two argued over almost everything. Hero and Isabell would snap at them constantly, growing tired of their bickering.

It didn't take long to reach the Uilik River. The swift water churned around the many boulders. Seeing a bridge down the path, Hero glanced at his map to see if they had to cross it. He signaled to the others that they did, indeed, have to cross over the bridge.

Hero felt slightly nervous about passing over the gray water. He remembered his past experience with rivers, and had decided that he never wanted to go in any water again, except for bath water. He shuddered slightly as Phoebus' step caused the bridge to creak slightly. He looked back and saw that neither Merrick nor Jacquelyn was bothered, which made him realize how silly he was.

"So which way do we go?" Jacquelyn asked. "You said follow the river, but the river branches off into three different directions."

"We have to head west," Hero said, pointing to the smallest branch of the river.

"The west sure is going to be hot this time of year. In between spring and summer, that's the worst," Isabell groaned.

"We can deal with it," Merrick answered. "We've done it before," he murmured.

"When was that?" Jacquelyn asked curiously.

"None of your business," Merrick snapped.

Jacquelyn raised her eyebrows but said nothing. Hero realized he would have to warn her about speaking to Merrick about his past. He glanced at Merrick and saw him scowling at no one in particular. He reined in beside him and asked if he was okay. He mumbled something under his breath, but Hero couldn't hear what.

"How long are we going to follow this river?" Jacquelyn asked.

"A few days. I'm not sure how many, but our path looks free of hills or anything," Hero answered.

"Great. We get to be out in the open for anyone to see," Merrick muttered.

"Are you always in a foul mood?" Jacquelyn asked.

"Hey, none of that. I am so sick of hearing you bark at each other. Shut up for a minute will you? Or we really will be caught," Hero sighed.

"I agree. You two are like senseless children the way you go at it," Isabell nodded.

So they continued on. The horses' hooves plodding along the dirt path made the only sound. Hero was thankful for the momentary peace. When Merrick and Jacquelyn started they didn't stop for a few hours. It really did grow tiresome for him and Isabell. As if sensing his thoughts, Phoebus shook his head, and Hero smiled. It looked like it annoyed the stallion, too.

That night, they found a grove of trees that would make a great camp. It had started to rain, and the leaves formed a natural roof, which the thick drops couldn't penetrate. Jacquelyn was about to start a fire, but the two men warned her against it. If any demons were around, they would be able to see the light a mile away.

"Well, I'm going to be of *some* help then," Jacquelyn sniffed, picking up the bow she had brought along.

"Where are you going?" Hero asked.

"Hunting. I'm going to find us some food," she snapped.

"But we have food," Hero pointed out.

"Well, then I'm going for fun, okay?" she asked.

"Don't get yourself lost," Merrick said. "Or caught by the enemy."

Jacquelyn didn't answer him. She just went off into the woods. Hero heard her curse and then a loud rustling of bushes. Hero wondered if she was really going hunting, or whether she left to gather herbs. Hero wanted to know how Merrick felt about herb gathering so he decided to bring the subject up.

"Do you believe in witches?" Hero asked.

"What?" Merrick replied, looking at him.

"Witches. Do you believe in them?" Hero asked again.

"Of course I do. Arlyn is a witch," Merrick answered giving him a quizzical look.

"She is? How so? Does she gather herbs and things?" Hero continued, eyes widening.

"Herbs? People who gather herbs just know things about medicines. I mean that she is a real witch. She can put you under a spell by just speaking to you, or by looking at you in a special way. She can also use magic to kill. Didn't I tell you that?" Merrick explained.

"I remember now. I must have not grasped the knowledge when you first told me. I was kind of focused on escaping," Hero gulped.

"How else do you think she controls all those demons and beasts?" Merrick asked darkly.

Hero gazed down at the food Merrick handed him. He felt sick. So now she was a witch who could entrance him with a single word? How was he supposed to win against her? Did that mean that Muryn was also skilled with magic? Was Merrick? He was about to ask, but a sudden scream pierced through the night air.

"Damn that foolish girl," Merrick cursed, rushing off in the direction of the scream.

Hero followed, grabbing his and Merrick's sword. He caught up to his friend and handed him his weapon. Merrick nodded thanks and sped up with Hero trying to keep pace. However, Hero hadn't ever run on two legs for such a distance. He growled a curse and forced himself to run faster. He soon caught up to Merrick.

They broke free of the trees and saw nothing. Jacquelyn was nowhere to be seen.

"Where is she?" Hero asked desperately.

"How should I know?" Merrick snapped. "I *knew* something like this would happen."

Hero sniffed the air, forgetting that he didn't have his keen wolf senses for a minute. He stomped the ground in frustration. Why had he let her go off on her own? A sudden commotion in the high grasses near him made him jump. He rushed over and nearly cried out.

Jacquelyn was flat on her back, trying to fight off a man who had a dagger held to her throat. His garments suggested that he was a thief and thought that Jacquelyn would just hand him the money peacefully.

"Get off of her," Hero demanded, drawing his sword.

The man leapt up and stepped away from Jacquelyn, who stood up and notched an arrow to her bow.

"What is the meaning of this?" Hero asked, blue eyes starting to fade to yellow and red.

"You. You're the one with an arrest warrant on your head," the man exclaimed.

Hero placed the sword against the man's throat. "I believe I asked you a question," he said, emotionless.

"I just wanted some money, but she wouldn't give me any!" the man complained.

"Humph. A petty thief," Merrick sighed, replacing his sword.

The thief gave him one look and cried out, "I don't believe it. You have an arrest warrant on your head too. And you're the Queen's—"

"Shut your mouth," Merrick warned, redrawing his sword.

"You better get out of our sight before I count to twenty," Hero said, pressing the sword harder. "Or else we're going to see what a beheading looks like."

The thief gave them all one last look before running as fast as his legs would go. Hero watched him for a while before turning to Jacquelyn.

"Are you okay, Jacquelyn?" he asked gently.

"I am. Thanks," Jacquelyn answered, a slight blush creeping up her face.

"For that I am thankful," Hero sighed. "Don't you ever make us worry again."

"Right. Sorry," Jacquelyn murmured.

"That is why you don't go running off alone," Merrick said, placing his sword where it belonged.

"And I suppose it was agonizing for you to come after a farm girl like me, huh?" Jacquelyn hissed.

Hero cut Merrick off before he could retaliate. "Actually, Merrick was the first to respond. He was in such a rush that he left his sword behind."

Merrick gave Hero a disgusted look, while Jacquelyn just looked highly affronted. The one-eyed man strode back to the camp and left Hero alone with Jacquelyn. Hero was about to follow Merrick, but Jacquelyn called him back.

"Hero, I really want to thank you for coming to help," she said.

"It was no problem. I wouldn't let a friend get hurt now, would I?" Hero grinned.

For some reason, Jacquelyn looked hurt. As if she didn't want him to be funny about the whole thing. Hero was about to open his mouth to correct himself, but Jacquelyn turned around and walked toward the camp. Hero sighed. He still didn't quite understand the human mind. He was clueless when it came to emotions and the like. Shrugging his shoulders, he followed the path his two friends had taken.

He half expected to find the camp under attack by thieves or demons, but fortunately he found only Merrick, Jacquelyn and the horses. He slumped down onto the ground and gazed into the darkening sky. He began to have serious doubts about all this. How was one man supposed to stop the world from waging a war? He then thought about Verinaul and all his friends there, including a very special white wolf named Nakoomu. He suddenly felt a pang of homesickness in his chest. He wanted to leave this world of uncertainties and return to a simple life. He wanted to be Leader, wanted to go hunting with Swift Paw and Shira and, of course, have a pup to take over for him when he passed on.

"You okay, Hero?" a whispered voice asked.

Hero turned his head and saw that Merrick was next to him on the ground.

"Just thinking of Verinaul," Hero answered truthfully.

"You must miss it, huh?" Merrick asked. "But don't worry. I'm sure you'll see it again real soon."

"What if I can't ever go home, Merrick? Who says that I can return once I kill Arlyn? I've got no proof that I can! And besides that, who says I can beat a highly trained General and a magical Queen and stop a war from ever starting?" Hero's voice grew louder.

"Hero..." Merrick began, unsure how to answer.

"It's too big." Hero trailed off, burying his face in his hands.

"I know," Merrick replied. "But you will succeed, Hero. I can feel it in my heart."

"I guess you would know how it feels, huh?" Hero said, not bothering to lift his head. "Being who you are."

Merrick didn't answer, and when Hero looked into his face, he saw that his friend had an expression that said all too well that he knew how Hero felt. Jacquelyn suddenly came over and lay down on Hero's other side, wrapping herself up in a blanket to keep the dirt off of her.

"Good night, Hero," Jacquelyn yawned.

"Sleep tight," Hero responded.

"Oh yeah, Merrick...thanks for coming to save me," Jacquelyn stammered.

"You're welcome," Merrick said after a slight pause.

They all woke up with the sun the next morning. The ground was slightly wet with dew, and a light rain continued to fall. Hero yawned as he saddled Phoebus. As soon as the other two had mounted, they started off again. Finding the Uilik River, they followed it west to what they hoped was a short journey to Satlin.

Hero thought something was missing by midday and realized that Merrick and Jacquelyn had not argued since yesterday. He figured that they were on friendly terms for the time being, after the misadventure with the thief.

Hero was about to comment on this but saw someone on horseback ahead. Luckily the rider's back was turned, or else there would have been trouble. There was no mistaking the meaning of bright purple hair. Hero signaled the others to get off the road before the demon turned. They quickly dodged to the side; the horses' usually thudding hooves were mysteriously quiet. Nevertheless, the demon did glance behind him and gaze at the spot where they had stood moments before. He then kicked his horse into action and galloped away.

"Twenty coins says he saw us," Merrick muttered.

"Oh, I don't know," Jacquelyn began, "I think he might have overlooked us."

"Can you explain why he galloped off like that then?" Merrick asked, while Isabell and Hero shared a disgruntled look.

"Who knows what goes through a demon's head," Jacquelyn sighed. "However, he might have had orders to be in a certain place at a certain time."

Merrick nodded in reluctant agreement and walked back to the road. Isabell whispered something, and he gave her a sour look. Hero knew she must have commented on the length of the argument, which had been incredibly short compared to all the rest.

Hero wished he could believe Jacquelyn's assured explanation that the demon had other business, but he couldn't trust himself to relax. Whatever anyone said, a demon was bad news, especially if you had to debate on whether it had seen you or not. He kept his eyes focused on the road stretching ahead of him and noticed that Merrick glanced rather uneasily at the trees. Jacquelyn, however, made a point of riding easily with no fear, which Hero found rather foolish.

That night, their camp was a little more open than before. The rain had stopped, but a heavy fog covered the land in a white haze. Hero checked around for any signs of danger and finding none, he returned to the others. Merrick had already divided the food into three small piles. They had plenty left, he assured them, but there really was no reason to eat a lot if Satlin lay only a few days away.

Hero considered himself lucky that he slept lightly that night. His eyes snapped open when he heard a low whistle. He glanced above his head and saw a dark figure in a scraggly bush. He slowly reached for his sword and glanced around to see how many there were. Only four, he breathed. They had a chance if he could surprise them.

"Wake up. We're under attack!" He roared.

Merrick and Jacquelyn quickly rose and grabbed their weapons. The four figures leapt from their cover. They were, as Hero suspected, four demons. Two had blue hair, while the other two had pink. The pink-haired ones caught Hero's interest the most for he had never seen demon women before. They looked almost exactly like the men, only with slimmer features. And, unlike the men, they carried two long knives, the blades matching their eyes and hair color, of course.

Hero charged at the smaller of the blue-haired demons. It parried and thrust his own blade at Hero, who blocked the blow. He glanced over and saw Merrick and Jacquelyn fighting the women. The last blue-haired one stayed out of the fighting.

The demon Hero fought against must have been inexperienced, because Hero wounded him relatively quickly. He repeated all the forms Merrick had taught him and soon had the demon backing away rather fearfully. He thrust at the last minute and his sword plunged into the evil creature's stomach.

Jacquelyn's short sword flashed all over the place. The demon women seemed to be dancing not fighting. Their moves flowed like a river, one following the next without pause. Jacquelyn thrust at her opponent, but the demon flipped backwards and avoided the blow. As the demon regained her feet, Jacquelyn threw her sword at the pink-haired devil and caught it off guard. The female demon clutched at the sword as it pierced through her neck.

The second demon woman seemed more experienced than the first. Merrick was having some problems but looked under control. The demon noticed this and tried to catch him by surprise. She ducked down low and swung at his feet, but Merrick jumped over the two knives and kicked the demon in the face. The demon growled and stood up, spitting out a mouthful of black blood. She smiled and charged again. Merrick sidestepped and sliced her back. The demon toppled forward, black blood staining the ground.

When he had witnessed the killing of all of his comrades, the last male demon did not flee. He gazed at the three humans with utter hate, and then got his weapon to the ready.

"*Hiiza thath eian,*" he snarled.

With that said, he charged at Hero who anticipated this and prepared to block the blow. But at the last minute, the demon jumped away and struck at Jacquelyn! Jacquelyn cried out in alarm and fell backwards, landing heavily to the ground.

"Jacquelyn," Hero growled, rushing forward.

The demon saw him coming and raised his sword over his head, prepared to bring it down on the helpless woman's skull. Hero felt his animal instincts stir again. He clenched the handle of his sword with his teeth, ran and lunged as if he were a wolf. The demon let out a cry of surprise as Hero launched himself on top of him. As they fell, he took his sword in hand and tried to stab the demon. But the demon was skilled and managed to knock his sword away. Hero bit the demon's hand, causing him to drop his blue-edged blade.

Hero was more used to fighting like this than the demon. He clawed at the demon with non-existent claws. The demon tried to fend him off, but before long Hero found his throat and chomped down on it. He managed to pierce it and felt the blood flow into his mouth. He stood up, spitting out the blood and turned to face his friends.

They stared at him with a mixture of amazement and fear. Jacquelyn hadn't even bothered to stand up, so Hero walked over to her and offered her his hand. A slight blush crept up her face as she grabbed it and allowed him to pull her up.

"Thank you, Hero. You saved my life again," she whispered.

"Of course. You are my friend," Hero replied with a smile.

"I hate to break this up, but we shouldn't stay here," Merrick cut in.

"You're right," Hero said. "Let us ride from this place."

They got their horses ready. Isabell mumbled about not being able to get a good night sleep, and it seemed Phoebus and Jacquelyn's black mare, Moon Dance, nodded their heads in agreement. Jacquelyn gave the large mare a pat on the neck to soothe the affronted animal.

"You know, I think Satlin may only be a couple of more miles," Hero said, trying to picture the map in his mind.

"I suggest we just ride until we get there then. Satlin is even busier then Gilyn, so the gates will be opened for travelers," Merrick replied.

"Sounds as good a plan as any, though I still say we should stay out of the slums," Jacquelyn muttered.

They reached Satlin's gates in a few hours. Merrick was right, the city was a lot larger than Gilyn. The gates themselves were more impressive. They were made of heavy stone with doors of fine oak with carved gold leaves. The gatekeeper's clothes spoke of wealth, which led them to believe that Satlin was a very prosperous city. After the routine questions every gate-keeper asks, they received permission to enter the city.

It was dark as could be, but people lingered in the streets. Jugglers and dancers paraded everywhere. Lights shone out of huge glass windows on all the lords' manors. Vendors were still out and about, shouting about their half price wares and competing with the cart next to their own. It was loud and busy, even though it was the dead of night.

"This is amazing," Hero exclaimed.

"Yes, it's a pity we'll be spending our time in the slums," Jacquelyn complained, gazing at all the clothes vendors.

One of the vendors caught her eye and hurriedly rushed over, jumping in their way and forcing them to stop.

"Would you like to buy something my lady?" he asked sweetly.

"Well, I suppose it wouldn't hurt to look," Jacquelyn blushed.

"This dress here would show your eye color nicely. It would be fitting for such a beautiful lady," the vendor bowed, raising a bundle in his arms.

It turned out to be a dress the color of sapphires. It was very beautiful. The sleeves had cuffs of white frill matching the frill that circled the hem. The front was embroidered with white jewels that ran in stripes to the waist. The neck hung a little low, but not too much so. It was made out of a very fine silken material that shimmered in the light.

"How much is this dress?" Jacquelyn asked eyes alight.

"For you, beautiful lady, I will lower the price to twenty-five coins," the vendor smiled.

Jacquelyn turned to Hero and Merrick with a pleading look in her eyes.

"Well, it is really pretty," Hero ventured.

"But do you really need to spend so much on clothes. This isn't really a vacation," Merrick sighed.

"Can't we have a little pleasure to keep our spirits up though?" Jacquelyn asked earnestly.

"She's got a point. But I'll buy it for you instead, okay?" Hero asked with a large grin.

He dug into his pouch and counted out twenty-five coins, handing them to the vendor as he put the dress in a large bag. The vendor thanked him and handed the dress to Jacquelyn, who beamed.

"Thank you, thank you, thank you," Jacquelyn cried happily as they made their way to the slums.

"No problem really," Hero said modestly.

"Well isn't that something, Hero. I think you may be falling for her," Isabell said slyly.

"I just wanted to give her a gift for all the things she and her father did for me when I first got here," Hero argued.

"Right," Merrick said in a voice of disbelief.

Isabell and Merrick stifled snickers as Jacquelyn and Hero blushed deeply. Hero did like Jacquelyn a lot, but he had already found his mate. He couldn't possibly have two, even if they lived in different worlds. Nakoomu was the one for him. He gave Jacquelyn a quick glance and saw that she had a small smile on her face. He couldn't fathom why, but he certainly hoped she didn't believe Isabell and Merrick.

Chapter 12

Satlin was a very clean city until they reached the slums, which just seemed to start at a certain point. At one point, the three companions wandered in a bustling street with wealthy lords and their ladies watching the people from balconies. The next minute, they found themselves in a dirty alleyway with no lights and almost no sound.

The slums were definitely scary. Dirty, scrawny people looked at the three companions as though ready to jump them. The eyes of the slum dwellers were unusually bright, and they held their tattered clothing close to their frail bodies. The ones with hair had a stringy, matted mess hanging down their heads. Jacquelyn murmured something about going back, but Hero didn't pay much mind.

Glancing at his map, Hero saw an inn positioned within a small section of the slums. Once they arrived, they saw that the inn stood two stories high and looked rather dilapidated. They entered anyway, hoping to escape the many eyes that watched them from the dark.

"Excuse me," Hero said to a frail old man sitting behind the desk.

"Yeah, what?" he asked grumpily.

"Any rooms available?" Hero asked kindly.

"No, go away!" the man snarled, reaching down for what might have been a weapon.

The three quickly left and untethered the horses from a fallen fence. They climbed on and cantered out of the slums.

"There is no way we are staying there. We have just as much a chance of being murdered in our sleep by the people without worrying about demons," Hero breathed.

"I hate to say I told you so, but, I told you so," Jacquelyn argued.

"Enough childish comments. We must find an inn," Isabell replied.

They walked at a quick pace, still a little unnerved by the slum dwellers. They chose an inn rather larger than they wanted, but it was smaller than any of the other places. It was called the *Eclipse* and looked rather inviting.

The first floor had a bar with many tables, and a pretty lady was singing a song at the back of the room. Soldiers from everywhere occupied the many tables. The room seemed to be split down the middle. The soldiers on the right had various insignias claiming allegiance to King Dervik, while the other half seemed to be allied with the Queen. They weren't fighting, but they cast many wary glances from one side to the other.

"What can I get you sirs and lady?" a voice asked.

It was a serving lady.

"Two rooms for the night and a place to keep the horses," Merrick answered.

"The horses will be taken to the stable in the back. You may have Rooms 16 and 17. I'll have some men bring up your belongings so relax yourselves in the bar," the woman said, pointing to an empty table.

"Well, this is a great place," Merrick murmured, glancing at the Carthafell allies.

"Don't worry about it. They won't bother us," Hero said encouragingly.

"May I take your order?" the serving woman asked.

"Just get us a roast and salad with wine all around," Hero replied.

The serving lady curtsied and disappeared into a door that led to the kitchens. The singer sang a slightly faster song, and couples began to dance.

"Let's dance, Hero," Jacquelyn exclaimed.

"I cannot dance," Hero replied firmly.

"Merrick?" Jacquelyn asked eagerly.

"No way," Merrick answered.

"You two are no fun," Jacquelyn complained, slumping down in her seat.

"May I have this dance?" a rich voice asked.

Jacquelyn turned around and saw a Carthafell soldier behind her. He had long blond hair brushed to either side of his face. He had a small shadow of a beard on his handsome face, and he wore full armor. He sported a red breastplate with the double sword sign of Carthafell; the armor fell down to his knees with a black belt to hold his sword at his waist. He wore black riding pants and heavy black boots. Merrick choked on the water he was drinking.

"Sure," Jacquelyn said nervously.

She took his hand, and he led her to the floor, giving both Merrick and Hero a slight smile that Hero didn't like.

"We have got to get out of here!" Merrick whispered urgently.

"Huh? Why?" Hero asked.

"Because that soldier with Jacquelyn happens to be Muryn," Merrick whispered.

"You mean General Muryn, as in your brother?" Hero gasped.

Merrick nodded his head in despair. Hero stood up and tried to find Jacquelyn. She was at the other end of the room, dancing with the General.

"You stay here, I'll tell her we have to go," Hero offered.

He didn't wait to hear any complaints from his friend. He stomped firmly over to the pair and was about to say something when an older woman swooped him up and began to lead him into the dance.

"What are doing?" Hero demanded.

"I thought you was lookin' fer a partner," she said in an odd accent.

"No, I was trying to get to her," he answered, pointing to Jacquelyn, who was again on the other side of the room.

The woman let go of him. "Humph! Guess I ain't good enough fer ya!"

Hero shook his head and made his way to Jacquelyn again. However, before he could get to them, they stopped at his table and sat down. Hero gulped, they were both trapped. On either side of their table sat Carthafell soldiers. He snuck closer so as to hear the conversation.

"You're a wonderful dancer, miss," Muryn said.

"Thank you, sir," Jacquelyn said.

"Are you staying here long?" the General asked, seeming to ignore Merrick.

"I don't believe so," Jacquelyn answered, clueless to the danger she was in. "Will we be here long, Lucius?"

"No," Merrick answered, staring into his goblet.

"Lucius? Is this your brother or something?" Muryn asked, eyes glinting.

"No, he's my husband," Jacquelyn lied. "We're on a trip to see the world together."

"Well, that's nice," Muryn smiled.

"Will you get to it already?" Merrick suddenly snapped, punching the table.

"What are you so upset about?" Jacquelyn asked sourly.

"Yes do tell," Muryn said cruelly.

"Well, if you're going to be like that," Merrick began.

He stood up and made to run, but Muryn caught him by the shoulder and dragged him back. Merrick whipped out his sword and tried to slice his older brother's face. Muryn stepped back and drew his own sword. He and Merrick started a furious fight, with the rest of the customers looking eagerly on. Hero tried to get through to help, but the circle of people prevented him.

"Why are you fighting him, Lucius?" Jacquelyn demanded.

Merrick didn't answer her. He just kept swinging at Muryn, who blocked his every blow. Finally, Muryn made a lunging move and knocked the weapon from Merrick's hand, bringing his sword up against Merrick's throat at the same time.

"Do it. See if I care," Merrick growled.

"Those are not my orders," Muryn replied. He snapped his fingers and the other Carthafell soldiers came over and bound Merrick's hands behind him.

"What are you doing to my husband?" Jacquelyn snarled.

"Your husband? He isn't your husband. Lucius isn't even his real name," Muryn replied, glaring at Jacquelyn.

"I think I know my husband better then you do, sir," the young woman replied defiantly.

"I don't think you do. If you did, you would know that his name is Merrick, and he happens to be my younger brother," the General replied, turning his back to her.

"Br-brother?" Jacquelyn gasped.

Muryn forced Merrick's head up and gazed into his face. "Well, you've kept yourself alive," he said. "Good boy."

"You're going to regret this," Merrick spat.

Muryn punched him in the stomach, leaving his sibling winded. He looked around the room as the soldiers led Merrick out, and his eyes rested on Hero. He strode over to him, and Hero fingered his sword.

"You must be the other one on the wanted list," Muryn sneered. "Are you going to come quietly? Or do I have to defeat you as well?"

For an answer, Hero drew his sword and lunged for Muryn's face. The Queen's General blocked the thrust and swept his sword low to the ground, trying to take out Hero's feet. Hero leaped over the sword and as he came down from the air, brought his sword straight down toward the top of

Muryn's head. Muryn leapt backwards and avoided the blow. Hero charged forward, but Muryn sidestepped him and kicked him in the chest, sending him flying.

Hero stood up immediately and prepared for an attack. Muryn ran at him, sword-pointing straight toward the former wolf's stomach. Hero blocked the blow and stepped to the side, slashing at his friend's older brother. Muryn leaned his head back and avoided the slash, a smile playing around his lips.

"This can't be your best," he smirked.

"You just wait. I would have thought that a General would know not to underestimate his opponent," Hero growled.

Muryn shook his head and struck again, narrowly missing Hero's left arm. Hero saw a figure running toward them, as though ready to stop the fight. It was Jacquelyn. Hero turned away from Muryn and met her half way across the room.

"Jacquelyn, you have to run now," Hero demanded.

"No, I can't," Jacquelyn protested, flinging herself into his arms.

"Go! Or I'll never forgive you," Hero said coldly.

Jacquelyn gave him a startled look, then gasped and looked over his shoulder. "Look out!" she screamed.

Hero turned around and as he did, a sword plunged into his stomach, missing the fatal spots, but still shooting pain throughout Hero's body. He looked up and saw Muryn holding the blade, a triumphant glow in his cold eyes. Hero pulled the sword out and clasped a hand to his stomach, trying to catch the blood flowing out of his body. There was too much, he decided, as he let the blood stream over his hands. He collapsed onto the floor. The last thing he saw was Jacquelyn on her knees beside him, crying her eyes out.

When Hero next opened his eyes, he knew he was on a wagon. His hands were tied up behind his back, but he didn't have the strength to even try to break free. His wound had been bound, but not stitched, making him afraid to move. He lifted his head slowly and saw Merrick sitting up beside him, and Muryn close by.

"Wh-where are we going?" Hero demanded weakly.

"To Carthafell," Muryn answered. He was sharpening a knife in a foreboding way.

"Why?" Hero continued, feeling that he already knew the answer.

"Queen Arlyn is just dying to meet you, Lone Wolf," the General replied.

Hero didn't respond. He just tried to see out the back of the wagon. But a large canvas covered the opening. He tried to catch Merrick's attention, but Merrick just stared at the floor. He looked around to see if Jacquelyn was anywhere, but she wasn't.

"Where is she?" he demanded.

"Who? My brother's 'wife'?" Muryn asked. When Hero nodded he answered simply, "She is irrelevant."

Hero almost sighed in relief. Then he caught himself. What if they had just killed her? Irrelevant meant she wasn't of any use. And they were Carthafell soldiers. They wouldn't care about killing women. Hero considered asking if they had spared her, but Muryn was too busy with his knife, and Hero didn't want to give the man a reason to use it.

"No matter how many times you catch me, I'll always find a way to escape," Merrick suddenly said.

Muryn stopped sharpening his knife and let out a chuckle of cruel amusement.

"I'd like to see you try. Next time I won't hit your eye, I'll hit your legs," he sneered.

"Then I'll just run faster so you won't be able to," Merrick snapped.

Muryn reached over and grabbed him by the collar of his shirt. He waved the knife in front of his face in a very threatening manner.

"You try to do anything, and I'll kill you, my dear little brother," he taunted.

Merrick clenched his teeth in frustration and tried to throw his body into Muryn's. But Muryn was too strong. He simply held Merrick away by the shoulders and pushed him down. When Merrick got to his knees again, Muryn slashed with the knife and made a shallow cut on Merrick's chest. He then kicked his brother back down on his back.

"Stop it," Hero ordered, sitting up and ignoring his own pain.

Muryn threw the knife, and it hit the side of the wagon, a hair's breath away from Hero's face.

"That's enough chatter for now boys," Muryn said, climbing to the front of the wagon.

Jacquelyn was exhausted. She had been riding bareback throughout the night and could still see the wagon faintly. Isabell's breath was labored, but the former unicorn refused to stop. Phoebus and Moon Dance tried to keep up. When Jacquelyn told her to rest, the stubborn animal said she would leave the girl behind if she dismounted.

"You need to stop," Jacquelyn pleaded, as Isabell stumbled.

"No. I can't let them reclaim my master or Hero," Isabell snorted, straining herself beyond her limit.

"If you refuse to rest, then at least tell me about Merrick. Why did that General call him his brother?" Jacquelyn asked.

"General Muryn," Isabell started.

That was General Muryn? Queen Arlyn's brother?" Jacquelyn exclaimed.

"Yes, you impatient girl," Isabell snapped. "Merrick is Muryn's, and, therefore, the Queen's, younger brother."

"All this time, and I never knew," Jacquelyn whispered.

"Don't tell him I told you," Isabell murmured.

"I won't. But we have to hurry. Hero's been wounded, and I can't imagine those awful soldiers took care of him," Jacquelyn said earnestly.

"You're in love with Hero, aren't you, Jacquelyn?" Isabell suddenly asked.

"I have no idea what you're talking about," Jacquelyn replied, blushing crimson.

"Oh come off it," Isabell chuckled. "It's rather obvious that you are."

"No it isn't. I mean...uh...I don't love Hero, end of story," Jacquelyn argued.

Isabell just laughed and the young woman gave an indignant sniff.

"Any ideas?" Merrick asked as the wagon halted for the night.

"Not really. I can't move because of my wound. I think it's getting infected or something," Hero replied weakly.

"That's it! We can use the sick prisoner routine!" Merrick exclaimed softly.

"The sick what?" Hero asked.

"Since you're sick, I'll call out to the guards, and they'll come in to see if you're all right. Then I attack them and—"

"Merrick?"

"Yes?"

"I can't run like this, and you can't carry me because your arms are tied."

"Oh yeah."

They sat in silence, trying to think of ways to escape. Suddenly, the canvas was ripped down and about ten soldiers entered the wagon. They grabbed the prisoners, brought them to a small tent and shoved them inside. The guards circled around the tent, making sure a mouse couldn't get through.

"I'm so sick of being captured. First Hynraz and now Muryn. I don't think escaping these soldiers will be as easy," Hero sighed.

"I did it before, and I'll make sure we can do it again," Merrick whispered.

"Merrick, I want you to leave without me," Hero replied suddenly.

"What? Are you crazy? I'd never do that," Merrick argued.

"Please, Merrick. I'll only slow you down with this wound, and it'll be easier if we each escape at different times," Hero explained.

"No it won't. If I escape, then they'll double the guard around you," Merrick muttered.

"Merrick, I'm a wolf. No matter what I look like I'll never lose my spirit as a wolf, and a wounded wolf is the most dangerous of animals," Hero answered.

"I don't see where you're going with this," Merrick sighed.

"Wolves are meant to survive, Merrick. I will survive, and I will complete my mission. I will stop this approaching war and dispose of Arlyn," Hero explained gravely.

"But what if I can't find you again? I want to help kill Arlyn and Muryn too," Merrick complained.

Hero looked at Merrick and gave him a broad smile. He would have hugged him if his hands were not bound. He never expected Merrick to want to stay with him. He thought he would leave as soon as he could. But after everything they had been through, they had become the closest friends imaginable.

"Just go, Merrick. I'm sure we'll see each other again. Don't worry about me," Hero said.

"Hero, you are the bravest man I've ever met. Don't get yourself killed...okay?" Merrick asked sadly.

"I promise I won't get killed. I know you're just going to try to get to Carthafell yourself, so wait for me at the Uilik Mountains," Hero replied.

"You read my mind," Merrick smiled. "Once you reach the mountain's base, head to the east until you reach a pond, I'll wait for you there."

"Give me nine days. If I don't come, then go on without me. Got it?" Hero asked.

"Got it," Merrick answered.

The tent door opened, and Muryn stepped in. He carried two bowls of water.

"Excuse me, but I can't drink without using my hands to lift the bowl," Merrick said, before Muryn had even set the bowls down.

"Then drink like the dog that you are," Muryn said.

He put the bowls in front of them and then turned on his heel. He strode from the tent, and Hero heard a soldier murmuring that his General shouldn't be serving the prisoners water at all. Hero didn't care about drinking like an animal. He hunched down on his stomach and drank from the bowl, his face nearly submerged in the musty water. Merrick shrugged and followed suit. They wouldn't be able to escape if they died of thirst.

"I don't see how they manage to keep ahead of us when they stop for the night, and we do not," Jacquelyn grumbled.

She had dismounted from Isabell and walked beside the silver horse. Isabell had tried to argue that she didn't mind carrying Jacquelyn, but the young woman refused when Isabell fell to her knees for a fourth time that afternoon.

"Shall we step it up a bit then? I think the campfires are a little closer," Isabell suggested.

"You mean run? But we're both exhausted," Jacquelyn complained.

"Do you want to save Hero or not?" Isabell snapped.

"I'm not only trying to save Hero you know. Rude as he is, I can't possibly leave Merrick behind. Especially since he came to help with that thief a while back," Jacquelyn mumbled.

"Yeah right. Hurry up," Isabell ordered, breaking into a slow trot.

Jacquelyn sighed, hitched up her skirts and jogged beside the horse. She wore the blue dress that Hero bought her. It was beautiful, and she hoped that Hero would think the same. Not that she'd ever tell anyone that.

"Okay, so how are you going to escape?" Hero asked.

"I'm going to rip a hole in this tent. It isn't nearly as strong as it looks," Merrick explained.

"What are you going to rip it with?" Hero continued.

"My teeth?" Merrick suggested.

Hero rolled his eyes, now back to their original colors, and gave Merrick a look of disapproval.

"What? I'm sure if I really tore at it," his voice trailed off. "You think of something then."

"How about you...nope...never mind," Hero blushed. "That would just be embarrassing."

"What is it?" Merrick asked.

"You could pretend you really had to go to the bathroom, but since your arms are tied up behind you, you couldn't, well, get your pants down," Hero stammered.

Merrick looked at him for a minute and then said, "I think that may actually work. Oy, a little help in here!"

Two soldiers came in, spears at the ready. "What is it?" they demanded sharply.

"I need to go to the bathroom," Merrick replied.

"And?" one soldier asked.

"Since my hands are bound behind my back, I can't quite..."

"Wait here," the second one said.

"Why? You don't have to discuss everything do you?" Merrick shouted.

"Shut up, Merrick. Yell at them, and they'll never let you go," Hero hissed.

They waited for about five minutes until Muryn reappeared, looking for the first time since Hero saw him, in a foul temper.

"What are you complaining about?" he snarled, grabbing Merrick by the collar of his shirt and forcing him to his feet. "Do you know what time it is?"

Hero saw that Muryn indeed looked ready for bed. He had thrown his cloak over his small clothes. He suppressed a snicker.

"I just need to use the bathroom. I don't know why you would need to be told that," Merrick sighed.

"I was told, because I told the soldiers to alert me if you started anything. I'm sure you can hold it in anyway so shut up," the general snarled.

"Hold it in? I've been holding it in all bloody day," Merrick argued, trying to back away from his enraged brother, who still had a firm grip on Merrick's shirt.

"You watch your mouth," Muryn snapped, punching Merrick in the face with his free hand.

"But Muryn, I need to go to the bathroom," Merrick complained.

Hero thought that Merrick must have been going for the whiney younger brother approach, which suggested that at one point in time the two brothers got along better than Merrick had let on.

"Come on then," Muryn snapped.

He grabbed Merrick by an ear and dragged him out of the tent, Merrick yelping when Muryn gave a sharp tug on his ear. Hero couldn't help but smile. Merrick was getting exactly what he wanted.

Muryn took out a knife and cut Merrick's bonds.

"Hey, my hands feel better now that blood is circulating again," Merrick sighed.

"Just shut up and go," Muryn replied dangerously. "And if you even *think* of running I'll kill you and your friend!"

"I wouldn't leave Hero behind anyway so stop worrying about it. You'll get wrinkles before your time otherwise," Merrick taunted.

"*Shut up,*" Muryn roared, kicking Merrick in the back.

Merrick gave an exaggerated jump and tumbled down a hill. It was his opportunity. He rolled to his feet and started to run for his life.

"After him!" Muryn bellowed.

Merrick sped up as the sound of many footsteps began to come after him. He heard the pounding of hooves and dove for cover in a large brush. He crawled forward on his belly, hoping that he wouldn't be noticed. He looked behind him once to see if they followed and gave a smile when he saw the soldiers heading in the completely opposite direction. The smile was wiped from his face, however, when he felt a hand grab a fistful of his hair and force him up.

"Muryn," he exclaimed.

"The same tricks won't work twice you little fool," Muryn sneered.

He took out his sword and smacked Merrick in the head with the flat of the blade. Merrick fell to the ground unconscious. Muryn hoisted his younger brother onto his horse and mounted behind him. He rode back to the camp, telling one of his Lieutenants to alert the soldiers that the fugitive had been recaptured and to return to camp.

Hero listened to the many soldiers returning and thought that Merrick must have escaped. He smiled happily and began to plan for his own. Suddenly the tent's door opened, and a soldier entered. He had Merrick slung across his shoulders. He threw the man on the ground and left. Hero crawled over to him.

"Merrick, Merrick wake up!" he urged.

Merrick opened his eye and looked at Hero's face slowly. It took him about a minute to register where he was. When he did remember, he shot right up and shook his head.

"What happened?" he groaned.

"I don't know. You were thrown in here about three minutes ago," Hero replied. "Why didn't you run away?"

"I tried to Hero, I really did," Merrick answered sadly. "But Muryn found me and knocked me out. I guess he brought me back here."

"I guess we won't be able to escape then," Hero muttered.

"I'm sorry, Hero. I shouldn't have made any mistakes," Merrick sighed.

"Don't blame yourself, Merrick. I'm not mad at you or anything, and you shouldn't be mad at yourself either," Hero said with a small grin.

"Thanks, Hero," Merrick replied softly.

"I suppose we ought to get some sleep then," Hero said. "I'm sure we'll think of something by tomorrow."

Jacquelyn stumbled and would have fallen, but Isabell grabbed the back of her dress with her teeth and pulled her upright. They could see the pale light of dawn climbing over the distant mountains. Jacquelyn rubbed her eyes. They still had not taken a single break since the two men had been captured, and it was starting to affect them both. Jacquelyn regretted leaving Phoebus and Moon Dance behind, but they had stopped following a while ago and Jacquelyn couldn't wait for them.

"Look," Isabell snorted.

The Carthafell soldiers' camp loomed up suddenly. Jacquelyn and Isabell darted for cover. They watched as two soldiers walked by, guarding the camp from intruders.

"How do we get closer?" Isabell wondered.

"With this," Jacquelyn whispered, holding a large pouch. "These herbs will make a sleeping solution. All I have to do is launch it into the camp, and everyone will fall asleep."

"How will we get those two oafs to wake up though?" Isabell asked, growing more interested in the herbs.

"I have the antidote right here," Jacquelyn replied, pointing to a small pouch tied around her neck.

"Let's try it," Isabell murmured. "How long will they be out?"

"At least two hours, and they'll wake up with horrendous headaches," Jacquelyn sniggered.

"All right then. Do you need to get closer?"

"Yeah, a little bit," Jacquelyn said.

She started to creep forward, but her dress was catching on to bushes and roots. Isabell called her back. She walked to the unicorn who told her to unpack one of the saddlebags. Jacquelyn did so and pulled out some of Hero's clothes.

"Put them on," Isabell ordered.

"But they're for men," Jacquelyn argued. "And they belong to Hero."

"Do you want to be caught by those soldiers and executed, or do you want to save your friends?" Isabell snapped.

Jacquelyn sighed and slipped out of her dress. She put it on Isabell's broad back and reluctantly put on the black breeches and green tunic. She ignored Isabell, who was chuckling under her breath, and started to creep forward again. She did have to admit that these clothes were a lot easier to move around in.

Once she was actually in the camp, she tied a heavy cloth around her mouth and nose, reached into the pouch and grabbed all the herbs. Quickly and quietly she crunched them all together, forming them into a ball. Once she was ready, she took some of her water and sprinkled it over the herb bomb. It instantly started to send off green smoke. Jacquelyn threw the herb ball to the center of the camp and it exploded, sending a green haze throughout the camp. Jacquelyn retreated into the safety of the woods until the haze completely saturated the camp.

She heard the heavy clank of armor as soldiers hit the ground in a sleep as heavy as if they were dead. She crept into the camp and began to check the tents. Soldiers slept in the first cluster of tents, which smelled like sweat and beer. She quickly went on to a very fancy tent, wondering if her friends would be kept in such luxury. All she saw was the man she had danced with sleeping in a large cot fit for a King. She ducked away, remembering that he just happened to be Merrick's brother and the leader of this camp.

She sighed as she looked in and out of the many tents. Finally she saw one with many guards asleep around it. She entered and clapped in delight. Hero and Merrick were sound asleep. She took out her short sword and cut their bonds. She rubbed their hands for a moment to help the blood start circulating again. Then she grabbed her small pouch of herbs and ground them together quickly, making them into a thick, chunky liquid.

As Jacquelyn leaned over Hero to put some of the antidote in his mouth she paused. Isabell's words rang through her head. Was she really in love with Hero? She hadn't even known him for that long. She looked into his face and noticed that he did have certain wolfish characteristics to him—slightly bushy eyebrows, a nose that might have been a touch too long on any other face, and his shaggy hair. She brought her hand to his face and, trembling slightly, brushed his hair away. She shook herself mentally and poured some of the herbal antidote into his mouth. He began to stir.

Before he was fully awake, Jacquelyn moved on to Merrick and poured some into his mouth. By this time Hero was sitting up and staring at her with amazement.

"Jacquelyn, you came to rescue us?" he asked.

"Yes," Jacquelyn answered softly. "I mean, I couldn't exactly carry out our mission by myself could I?"

"Huh? Our mission? You're coming the whole way too?" Hero asked, rubbing his stomach.

"What's that suppose to mean?" she demanded.

"Not so loud or the guards will hear you," Hero warned.

"Not a chance. The guards are sleeping like babies. Now let's go. We have about an hour and fifteen minutes until they wake up," Jacquelyn exclaimed.

"I'm so confused," Merrick sighed.

"That's not surprising," Jacquelyn said impatiently. "Let's go."

They ran from the tent, not bothering to step over the guards on the ground. Merrick suggested killing them all, but Jacquelyn and Hero utterly refused to kill helpless men. Instead they simply reclaimed their weapons from the guards and moved on. They quickly started for the woods so they could put a lot of distance between themselves and the camp.

Isabell was waiting in the clearing where Jacquelyn had left her. She was nudging Phoebus and Moon Dance affectionately and explained that they had caught up while Jacquelyn was in the camp. Once Merrick entered the clearing, Isabell pranced up to him, and he wrapped his arms around her neck and snuggled his face into her mane.

"I thought I'd never see you again," he muttered.

"Oh, come off it. Even when you're sick to death of me, I'll come after you," Isabell joked.

Jacquelyn walked up to Isabell and took her blue dress off the former unicorn's back. When she walked past Merrick, he grasped her shoulder.

"Thank you, Jacquelyn," he said seriously. "I was wrong about you all this time. You will never be a burden, and it is an honor to travel with you."

"Thank you Merrick. That means a lot to me. I'm glad to have met you, and I should never have doubted you. And I am a farm girl," Jacquelyn replied.

"Something you should be most proud of," Merrick smiled.

Jacquelyn gazed into his face for a second and started to laugh. He joined in and soon was joined by Hero and Isabell. Even Phoebus and Moon Dance snickered in amusement. Jacquelyn gave Merrick's cheek a quick pat and moved away to Hero.

"Thanks Jacquelyn. We'd be dead without you," he said.

"My pleasure. Anything for a friend, right?" she asked with a grin.

"Right," Hero replied. "And hey, those are some fancy clothes you're wearing. Where on earth did you get such trendy clothes?"

"Oh, you're terrible," Jacquelyn snapped with mock anger. "I think these clothes are just awful. Whoever owns them must have found them on the side of the road."

"Or in your house," Hero added innocently.

Jacquelyn laughed and slapped him playfully on the shoulder. She walked on into the forest to change, but not without threatening the life of anyone who peeked at her.

Chapter 13

The three companions set out as quickly as possible. They passed by the camp at a distance and saw with relief that no one had stirred yet. It took them about half an hour to reach the base of the Uilik Mountains. The mountains were steep, and the path was nearly covered with brush and rock. The peaks rose into the sky, where the tops disappeared into the clouds. It would be heavy travel for the next few days.

Almost immediately after stepping foot on the mountain path, Hero felt the land incline softly. He gazed up ahead and saw that within minutes the trail would lead almost straight up. He gave Phoebus an encouraging pat and leaned forward slightly, so that he wouldn't slip off his back.

"This is too hard for the horses," Merrick said after an hour.

They had barely made any progress. The start of the path was still clearly visible. The horses panted and strained their muscles.

"What should we do then?" Jacquelyn asked. "Go back down and go around the mountains?"

"No, that'd take too long," Hero said, looking at his map. "This mountain range serves as the border wall of Feruh. According to the map, the Hurith Gate lies somewhere on the other side of Demon's Peak."

"Demon's Peak, huh?" Jacquelyn shuddered. "I don't like the sound of that."

"Don't worry. It's only called that because of the Demon-Human War that occurred there a thousand years ago. It was there that the demons made their last stand," Merrick explained.

"The question still remains though, what do we do about the horses?" Hero asked.

"Nothing. We can handle this," Isabell snorted, pulling herself up the steep path.

"No way, this is ridiculous. I say we dismount and walk beside them," Jacquelyn suggested.

The two men agreed to this and dismounted, ignoring Isabell's shrill arguments that they would be fine. Hero almost wished they had listened to her. Within fifteen minutes he was drenched with sweat and his legs felt like lead. He had never climbed anything so challenging in his life.

Jacquelyn stumbled on her dress and grabbed on to Moon Dance's neck to keep herself from falling.

"Jacquelyn, maybe you should wear my clothes again," Hero said. "You'd be surprised at how much simpler it would be."

"Well, I guess so," Jacquelyn sighed.

They stopped, and she took out the green tunic and black breeches again. Then she ducked behind a large boulder and changed. She smiled sheepishly as Hero and Merrick gave approving nods. They started out as soon as Jacquelyn had packed her dress into one of her saddlebags.

Hero felt a sudden drop land on his head. He looked into the sky and saw stormy gray clouds. He signaled for a halt and pointed up. Merrick and Jacquelyn peered at the sky as it began to rain heavily.

"I don't think we should try to climb during a storm," Hero explained. "It'd be too easy to lose our footing."

"But Hero, those Carthafell soldiers are probably coming after us. They won't stop for the rain, and I don't think we should either," Merrick replied.

"And the rain will keep us cool and maybe provide cover if those soldiers catch up," Jacquelyn added.

"I guess you're right," Hero sighed. He didn't like rain.

Phoebus whinnied as his foot slipped from under him on a wet rock. Hero cursed and pushed himself against the stallion's side, forcing him upright. They had been making slow progress through the mountain path; it was dark, and the rain was coming down harder than ever. Hero could barely see the outline of his two friends as they struggled behind him.

"Watch out up here! There's a slippery rock!" he called.

"Thanks!" Merrick shouted back.

Jacquelyn tugged Moon Dance along. The mare was growing stubborn. Suddenly she saw a large cave loom up in the rock face.

"Hey, you guys, I think we should stop for the night!" she yelled above the howling wind.

The two men doubled back and looked in the cave. They gave the tempest one last look before agreeing to this plan. They rushed into the large cave and sighed with relief when they found it was completely dry.

"How much longer do you think we'll have to travel like this?" Jacquelyn asked, stabbing at her barely cooked piece of meat.

"If the storm keeps up, at least another six days. Without a storm, maybe three to four," Merrick replied.

"Three to six days, huh? All depending on the weather," Hero murmured. "I'll have been in the human world for three months."

"I guess you miss Verinaul," Jacquelyn whispered.

"Of course I do. I left my father, my friends, my title...and Nakoomu," Hero replied dully.

"Who's Nakoomu?" Merrick asked.

"She's going to be my mate, if I ever get back," Hero answered, a small smile lifting his lips. "She's the most beautiful wolf you could ever see. Her fur is like the purest snow and her eyes like the sky. I could spend my life looking in her eyes, and it wouldn't be a waste."

"Sounds like you really love her," Isabell said from the shadows.

"Yes. Nakoomu means the world to me. I guess she's one of the main reasons I even agreed to do this mission. I was so concerned that the Storm of Endless Tears would destroy her, that I rushed here as fast as I could," Hero explained.

"Oh, are we going to have story time?" Isabell chuckled.

"Yeah, tell us about being a wolf, Hero. I'm sure it must be interesting. And a lot different than being a human," Merrick exclaimed.

"I guess I could. Jacquelyn? Would you like to hear too?" Hero asked politely, moving a bit closer to her.

"I suppose...I mean...why not?" Jacquelyn replied rather sadly.

"Well, being a wolf is very different from being a human, as you can probably imagine. I would wake up with the sun and leave my cave. Oh, the sun would climb above the tree line slowly as if wondering whether to come up that day. I am the son of Fergath, the Leader of our pack. Being Leader means that you are responsible for the well being of our pack. I was never too thrilled to learn that I'd have the job one day.

"I loved to go off in the woods with Nakoomu, even when we were younger and forbidden to do so. I remember showing her a green pond once. I didn't know it was special. That pond is actually a gateway from

Verinaul to Nazberath. Anyway, we were discovered and punished. I guess we were kind of like human children in a way.

"I remember that I also got in a fight with Fergath. He said that Nakoomu wouldn't be right for me, and that I couldn't be her mate. So I left the pack. I know that sounds weird and all, because wolves don't usually go out on their own. Hence the name Lone Wolf, I guess. Anyway, I wandered around for a few years, and then the Storm started. I remembered that when I was a pup, a bear came to our caves, telling Fergath about the legendary Storm of Endless Tears. I didn't pay too much heed to it then, but once the Storm started, I rushed back to the caves.

"I ran into Nakoomu at the pond. She looked very sad when I saw her. She must have missed me greatly. I asked her to fetch my father before I left, so I could say farewell. They came back, and we talked briefly. I went in the pond, a whirlpool tossed me around, and I woke up in a lake in Nazberath."

"That's when we found you," Jacquelyn put in. "And you didn't have a clue about anything."

"Yep. I had no idea about wagons or horses or anything," Hero laughed.

"Wait a minute. Don't they have horses in Verinaul? They're animals," Merrick wondered.

"Yes, I wondered that too for a time," Hero answered. "But I found that domesticated animals like horses, cats and dogs do not live in Verinaul. Only wild animals."

"So, you said your father didn't want you to mate with Nakoomu. When you get back are you going to go against his word?" Jacquelyn asked slowly.

"No. Before I left, he said he recognized his mistake. He said that he would allow us to be mates. I forgave him that night, and I now look forward to returning to my Nakoomu," Hero replied rather dreamily.

"That's always a great goal to fight for," Merrick said slyly. "Fighting for the girl of your dreams."

"I-I think I need to sleep," Jacquelyn said hastily.

She hurried into the corner with the horses. Merrick and Hero watched her, blinking in surprise. They looked to one another and shrugged.

"Hey, Hero, do you think that you'd ever be able to come back here after you go home?" Merrick asked suddenly.

"Huh? You mean jump back and forth between the worlds?" Hero replied. "I'm not sure."

"It'd be great if you could. Then we could get together without the threat of war looming over us. I could bring you to the best places, and we could have a blast. I could show you the advantages of being a human," Merrick explained.

"The advantages, eh? Sounds like fun. I hope I can do it. If not, then I guess—" Hero didn't finish.

He didn't need to either. If he couldn't return, then he'd never see Merrick or Jacquelyn again. Hero glanced over to Jacquelyn again. She seemed upset after his tale. He couldn't understand why. He shook his head and curled up to sleep.

Hero had the oddest dream that night. It felt so real that he wondered if he were awake. But what was said just couldn't be true. He lay with his eyes closed, reliving the vivid dream.

Jacquelyn sniffed silently. She couldn't stop the tears from slipping down her face. Moon Dance nudged her gently with her nose, trying to cheer her up, but it didn't help. Jacquelyn sniffed again as she heard the two men settle down to sleep. She heard a heavy foot come closer and saw that Isabell had made her way over.

"Leave me alone," Jacquelyn sniffed.

"I'm sorry, Jacquelyn. I truly am," Isabell sighed.

"Why? I'm just really tired," Jacquelyn lied. "It's not your fault that I'm tired now is it?"

"I know how you feel about him," Isabell whispered. "And I feel bad that he already has someone."

"Go away," Jacquelyn hissed.

"Very well. I just thought you might want someone to talk to," the former unicorn sighed.

She walked away, leaving Jacquelyn feeling worse than ever. She sat up and checked to see if Merrick was sleeping. Once assured that he was, she crawled over to Hero.

Hero paused in his thoughts. Had that been a dream? But there had been more. He struggled to recall the rest of it. She gazed at his face, half hidden by shadow. She sighed and walked to the mouth of the cave. The rain was still coming down, but not as heavily as before.

"Can't sleep?" a sudden voice asked.

She looked around startled. It was Merrick. He was sitting up and looking at her with his one eye. She walked over and sat down next to him.

"You can't sleep either?" she asked.

"Well I could, but I heard someone walking around and decided to investigate," Merrick replied softly.

"Oh, I see," Jacquelyn answered. "Merrick, can I tell you something?"

"Go ahead," Merrick replied.

"First you have to promise not to tell Hero," Jacquelyn muttered. "Okay?"

"You have my word. I won't tell Hero," Merrick replied.

"I'm in love with him," the young woman blurted out.

Merrick just stared at her, the light of their small fire making his eye glisten.

"Oh," he said lamely. "Well, that was unexpected. When did you figure this out?"

"I think I knew ever since I first met him three months ago," Jacquelyn sighed.

"Why don't you tell him?" Merrick wondered.

"Why?" Jacquelyn repeated incredulously. "Did you not hear a single word he said tonight? He's already in love. It's like he's engaged to be married."

"Oh, right," Merrick agreed. "But you could still tell him. I bet it would make you feel better."

"No, I don't think so," Jacquelyn answered coolly.

"Suit yourself, but you'll regret it forever if you don't tell him eventually," Merrick yawned, stretching himself out.

"Wait a minute," Jacquelyn hissed. "Don't go to sleep!"

"Why not?" Merrick asked.

"Because I-I need someone to talk to."

"What on earth do you want to talk about at this hour?" Merrick mumbled, still laying flat on his back.

"I don't know, you could tell me about yourself. If we're to be friends, I want to know about you," Jacquelyn suggested.

"I don't think so," Merrick said darkly.

"Why won't you tell me? I'm sure you've told Hero already," Jacquelyn sniffed.

"You wouldn't want to hear my story. It's not for women," Merrick sighed.

"Oh, get over yourself," Jacquelyn scoffed. "I'm not some rich merchant's daughter. I think I can handle a story."

Merrick looked up at her eager face and sighed with vexation. He sat up and began to tell her why he was on the run from Carthafell soldiers. By the time he finished, Jacquelyn's mouth hung open in disgust. Merrick shrugged and lay down again. This time, Jacquelyn didn't ask him to stay awake. She did lie down on the spot though, so that his shoulder lightly brushed against her own. He didn't really care. If he had learned the one he loved already had chosen another, he wouldn't want to sleep alone either.

Hero finally opened his eyes. He looked around and saw that everyone else was sleeping. He smiled when he saw Jacquelyn and Merrick sleeping back to back with one another. He froze when he realized the scene from the night had been no dream. He stood up and stretched, trying to loosen his aching muscles and relax. It wasn't bad knowing. The idea that Jacquelyn liked him made him feel happy.

He walked to the mouth of the cave and looked up at the winding path. It still led straight up. He sighed, wondering if he'd ever see level ground again. He peered down the mountain as well, trying to catch a glimpse of the Carthafell soldiers. He saw no trace, which bothered him slightly.

"Good morning," a voice said. It was Isabell.

"Morning," Hero yawned.

"Should we wake these two up?" Isabell asked, nodding toward the others.

"No, let them sleep until sunrise at least. We have a long road ahead of us," Hero replied.

"We could carry you again," Isabell offered.

"I won't allow that. You horses have a hard enough time without lugging us around," Hero smiled.

Isabell shook her head and turned away. Hero dug into one of his saddlebags and took out some dried meat. It wasn't too fresh, but it was the best thing for breakfast at the moment. He separated the meat into three equal portions and set two aside. He saw Merrick stirring and sat down close by.

"What an uncomfortable place to sleep," Merrick groaned.

He looked over his shoulder at Jacquelyn and sighed with slight annoyance. He rolled away from her and then joined Hero, who handed him the meat.

"When are we heading out?" Merrick asked, ripping the meat into smaller pieces.

"At first light," Hero answered. "I haven't seen a trace of the Carthafell soldiers. That makes me uneasy."

"Hm...they would have had a harder time in the storm than we did, carrying all that luggage with them," Merrick offered.

Hero remained doubtful. He had dealt with too many enemies to trust that they didn't have a plan. He couldn't see how they could possibly have passed them, but there was always a chance. He would play it safe in order to keep the others alive.

"Hello? Wake up, Hero," Merrick called.

Hero snapped out of his thinking. "Huh?" he stammered. "What?"

"I was *saying* that we should probably move on now just in case those guys are up to something," Merrick declared impatiently.

"Oh yeah, my thoughts exactly," Hero replied. "I'll wake up Jacquelyn if you get the horses ready."

Merrick walked toward the horses without complaining, and Hero made his way to Jacquelyn. He placed a hand on her shoulder and shook her, deciding that he would pretend that he hadn't heard her secret.

"W-What?" she murmured sleepily.

"We're going to move out now," Hero replied. He handed her some meat. "I think you'll need to eat this before we go though."

Jacquelyn nodded and sat up, taking the meat and chewing it slowly. Hero joined Merrick and started to throw Phoebus' tack on. He looked out the cave mouth to check the weather and saw with pleasure that it was mainly sunny with a few clouds dotting the sky.

Within the hour, they started making their way up the steep mountain pass. The going was getting harder the higher they climbed. After an hour, Hero called a stop so they could rest on a large ledge.

"Hey look, we can see the top," Jacquelyn exclaimed pointing.

"Good, that means we'll be able to head downhill until the next mountain," Merrick said.

"Once we get to the bottom of the other side, we'll rest for a while. Maybe even two days since it's been so hard," Hero suggested.

"Even with the threat of the Carthafell soldiers, I'm willing to stay the extra day," Jacquelyn sighed with relief.

"I suppose it wouldn't hurt. They do have wagons to bring over, and that will certainly slow them down quite a bit," Merrick agreed.

"So then, let's go. To motivate you, just think of the nice long rest at the other side!" Hero exclaimed enthusiastically.

"Yeah," Merrick and Jacquelyn replied in unison.

"I'm ready for a nice rest," Isabell said as she started to climb the path once more.

The path twisted near the very top of the mountain, and it was hard to follow. Hero didn't mind this. The peak loomed in front of them. He strained himself forward, pulling Phoebus along with him. The stallion tossed his head but kept going. Nearer and nearer the peak came, until Hero stopped dead in his tracks. There was a crevice in the middle of the path; its depth seemed unfathomable.

"What do we do?" he asked in despair. "How do we reach the top with this hole in the way?"

"We have to jump across," Merrick replied.

"I can't jump that far!" Jacquelyn argued.

"That's why we're going to mount our horses because they can jump that easily," Merrick explained. "Now back up and mount your horse."

They all backed up and climbed onto their horses. Hero and Jacquelyn were extremely nervous about the whole thing. Merrick offered to go first. "Look straight ahead when you're going over, and it ain't bad," he said.

"I'm ready," Isabell declared.

Merrick dug his heels in, and Isabell started to canter toward the gaping crevice. It was at least nine feet across. As Isabell drew nearer, she sped up a bit, and then she sailed through the air. Hero found himself holding his breath, while Jacquelyn prayed furiously. With a clank of hooves and a spray of dirt and pebbles, Isabell landed on the other side. Merrick looked back triumphantly and gave Isabell a thankful pat on the head.

Once he had moved far away, Hero faced up against the crevice. He gave Phoebus an encouraging pat on the side of the neck before kicking the stallion into action. Phoebus galloped to the crevice. Hero followed Merrick's advice and looked straight ahead to the other side. He had faith in Phoebus; he knew the golden stallion could do it. He felt a lifting motion and the unsettling feeling of having nothing but air beneath him, and then a large jolt as Phoebus landed on the safe side. He actually whooped out loud and leaned down, hugging Phoebus.

Jacquelyn gulped before kicking Moon Dance into a canter. The black mare looked edgy about jumping. But Jacquelyn spurred her on. Once they got to the crevice, however, Moon Dance stopped. Jacquelyn nearly flew over the mare's head into the crevice, but luckily she grabbed a fistful of mane in time.

"Come on Moon Dance," Jacquelyn snarled, backing the horse up.

She kicked the mare harder this time, so that the stubborn animal charged in a full gallop. As they neared the edge, Moon Dance slowed down a bit, but still jumped. Jacquelyn couldn't help but look down. When she did, she saw that sharp stones lined the bottom and would impale anyone who fell. She tugged fearfully on the reins midway across the crevice and Moon Dance shook her head in annoyance. When Moon Dance's front legs hit the ground, they fell from underneath her, and her head slammed into the ground face first. Jacquelyn was thrown off and hit her own head against a large boulder. Both lay quite still.

When Hero and Merrick heard the noise, they rushed back to the crevice. They saw Moon Dance trying to get up, her chest and knees scraped rather badly, blood dripping from the wounds. Jacquelyn lay against a boulder, her head resting on it. When Hero drew closer he saw that the left side of her face, the side against the rock face, was covered with blood.

"Jacquelyn!" he cried.

He pulled her gently from the boulder and set her down on her back. He looked at her face for any sign of a cut, but found blood flowing from her head. He separated the strands of her hair to look at the skin. A nasty cut right above her ear stretched down within two inches of her forehead.

"Merrick, she's hurt badly!" Hero called.

Merrick rushed away from Moon Dance and knelt down beside Hero. He took one look at her head and cursed.

"We have to do something about this quickly. Hero, go get some water and bandages, and we may need my stitching tools," Merrick ordered.

"Okay," Hero said, running off to reach Isabell and Phoebus, who walked toward them.

Merrick examined Jacquelyn closely. He had to make sure she didn't have a serious concussion. Hero ran back and gave Merrick the supplies. Merrick ripped off his tunic and started to drench it with water. He used this to press against the wound. Every few minutes he lifted it up to see if the bleeding had stopped. When it finally did, he washed the blood from her face and hair.

"That looks pretty bad," Hero said, now able to see the whole cut without hair and blood in the way.

"Yes, but not as bad as I thought," Merrick replied. "She'll definitely need stitches."

He set about readying his equipment. Hero walked over to Moon Dance and looked over her wounds. They weren't serious.

"Why did you do that?" he whispered.

Moon Dance seemed to hang her head. She nudged Hero in the shoulder. He patted her on the forehead, but couldn't help to feel a little resentful toward the animal. He looked over to Merrick and saw that he had already begun stitching up the wound. He looked over Moon Dance's cuts again, but they had already stopped bleeding.

That night Hero and Merrick watched over Jacquelyn to see if she woke. She groaned occasionally, but that was all. Hero began to feel very worried, what if she didn't wake up at all?

"Merrick, will Jacquelyn be okay?" Hero asked softly.

"I don't know, Hero. I thought she'd be awake by now. The injury must be worse than I imagined," Merrick replied.

"What are we to do?" Hero asked. "We can't sit around for too long or else those soldiers will catch us."

"I know, I know. But we can't exactly carry her over the mountain can we?" Merrick snapped.

"What if we put her on one of the horses?" Hero suggested.

"I guess we could try, but we shouldn't move her at all tonight," Merrick sighed.

They fell into a deep silence, hoping their friend would wake up some time soon. Hero gazed at the star-filled sky and hoped that they wouldn't be discovered. Merrick seemed to read his mind for in a moment he sighed and said, "I don't think they'd try to jump the crevice during the night."

"Huh? Oh yeah, you're probably right," Hero replied.

They took turns guarding anyway, Hero volunteered to do the first shift, so Merrick curled up and went to sleep. Hero sighed. Guard duty certainly was boring, he decided, leaning back against a rock.

It was morning when Hero opened his eyes. He stood up and looked around. The others still slept, and there were no signs of danger. He shook his head and cursed himself for falling asleep. He walked over to Merrick and shook him awake.

"My turn to guard?" Merrick asked sleepily.

"No need. I kind of fell asleep," Hero replied sheepishly. "It's already late morning."

"Oh well, can't be helped," Merrick groaned, sitting up and rubbing a sore arm.

"Should I try to wake Jacquelyn up?" Hero asked.

Merrick nodded and got out fresh bandages. Hero walked over to Jacquelyn. She hadn't moved since the previous night and that worried him. He sat down and shook her gently. Jacquelyn groaned but didn't wake up.

"Wake up, Jacquelyn!" Hero said firmly, shaking her a little harder.

Jacquelyn's eyes snapped open, and she sat up. Almost immediately, she cried out in pain and grasped her head. Hero laid her back down and gave her a sip of water.

"H-Hero? What happened?" she asked shakily.

"You took a fall. Well, Moon Dance fell when you landed, and you hit a rock," Hero explained.

"Will I be okay?" Jacquelyn asked, fear filling her blue eyes.

"You? You'll be fine. It's the rock we're worried about," Hero joked.

Jacquelyn smiled and shook her head slowly. Merrick came over with the new bandages and asked Hero to prop Jacquelyn into a sitting position.

"What are you doing?" she asked.

"Changing the bandages and checking to see how that gash in your head is doing," Merrick answered.

He gently removed the used bandages and pushed her hair out of the way. Merrick had stitched the cut very well, and it wasn't infected. The skin around it was black and blue, but Merrick said it was only slightly bruised.

"Can you see clearly?" Merrick asked.

"Yeah, except when I turn my head quickly," Jacquelyn answered truthfully.

"You let me know if your vision starts clouding up. If so we may have to find a doctor," Merrick told her.

Jacquelyn nodded in consent. Hero stood up and dug out some food for their breakfast. They had a silent meal, each thinking private thoughts.

When they finished their meal, Hero helped Jacquelyn onto Phoebus, ignoring her demand to walk. He assured her that Phoebus wouldn't mind carrying her at all, and that it might be dangerous for her to walk while still feeling the affects of her fall. It marked the first time they had argued over anything for a prolonged period of time, and Hero was losing patience.

"Just ride the horse," he yelled.

"I don't need to ride the horse! I'm not going to be a burden," Jacquelyn roared.

"But if you're off the horse, you will be a burden," Merrick pointed out.

She rounded on him, "You stay out of this," she snarled.

"Jacquelyn, we just don't want to see you get more hurt. It's not that big a deal. Just ride him until we start the descent, okay?" Hero sighed.

"I guess so, but if Phoebus starts to get really tired I'm getting off," Jacquelyn replied.

"Fair enough. Now let's go," Merrick muttered.

They finally started out, noting that they had lost a lot of time because of the argument.

Chapter 14

Before night fell, the top of the mountain appeared into view. They faced a hard decision then, whether to keep going or to rest. Finally they decided that Merrick would scout ahead and leave Hero and Jacquelyn to find a place to sleep just in case they decided to stay. Once Merrick disappeared from sight, they searched around and saw a nice open area with scraggly trees for cover. They sat down to wait for Merrick's return.

"Hero, I'm really sorry about fighting with you earlier," Jacquelyn whispered. "I just wanted to show you that I could be strong too."

"It's okay, Jacquelyn. I know you're strong. But even I would ride a horse if I sustained an injury like yours," Hero replied.

"The accident was my fault," Jacquelyn explained. "I looked down and became frightened. I tugged on Moon Dance's reins, and she obviously couldn't stop. She was all disoriented when she landed and that's how I fell. I was weak."

"Hey, don't say that. Anyone would have freaked if they had looked down. It could have happened to anyone," Hero said firmly.

"Hero, I need to tell you something," Jacquelyn suddenly declared.

"Oh yeah? What's that?" Hero asked, wondering if she was going to admit her feelings.

"I love...how you make me feel better when I'm down. I admire your skill at cheering people up," Jacquelyn sighed, cursing herself mentally for avoiding what she really wanted to say.

"Oh well, guess I learned good manners," Hero blushed.

"Yeah," Jacquelyn replied.

They heard a rustling sound and saw Merrick force himself between the trees.

"Keep your voices down. We have demons on our tail," he whispered.

"What? How did they find us?" Hero hissed.

"Muryn must have ordered them to go after us instead of climbing himself. It seems that it's our old pal Hynraz," Merrick mumbled darkly.

"Good," Jacquelyn said coldly.

"What's good?" Merrick asked.

"I can get my revenge. Those wretched demons destroyed everything I loved and scarred me in more ways than one," Jacquelyn growled.

"They destroyed her home, cut open her chest and made her father lose his arm," Hero whispered to Merrick.

Jacquelyn stood up and drew her short sword. Hero and Merrick grabbed her and pulled her back down.

"Let me go," she hissed dangerously.

"No, you can't beat them in your condition," Hero backfired.

"And besides," Merrick added. "They're way behind us. I saw their camp from the top of the mountain."

"We have a decision to make," Hero said, still holding Jacquelyn back. "Should we continue to climb or not?"

Merrick shook his head and told them that the path turned very rocky and steep. He had nearly slipped on a loose boulder and fell off. So they settled down for the night, hoping that they would stay clear of the demons.

They had a restless sleep and began walking well before dawn. Shivering in the cold mist of the mountain, they looked toward the east, trying to catch a glimpse of the sun. They reached the top of the mountain late morning and looked back to see if they could see the demons.

Alarmed, they saw them, not too far off riding horses that seemed darker than darkness itself. Hero thought that the leader looked a lot like Hynraz, but then again, many of the demons were hard to tell apart. He did see at least two with white hair, which surprised him because he thought demons didn't have natural hair color.

"They must be incredibly old," Merrick replied after Hero asked him about the hair.

"How old do demons usually get?" Hero asked with interest.

"Hm…let's see…I think they live to about 500 years old if they aren't killed first," Merrick recalled.

"F-five hundred?" Hero and Jacquelyn exclaimed.

"I think that's what Arlyn said," Merrick replied.

"That's discouraging," Jacquelyn sighed.

"Why? It's not like they're immortal. They can still be slain," Merrick explained.

"Well, I don't think we should wait here for them. Let's move," Hero suggested.

They walked at a swifter pace, finally beginning to descend the large mountain. Isabell refused to let the humans walk another inch on foot, so they mounted their steeds and trotted carefully down the path. Hero checked to see how Moon Dance was coping with her wounds and was pleased to see her trotting smoothly, even though Jacquelyn looked ready to bail at any moment.

By dusk they had reached a small river with a natural bridge of rocks barring their path. Hero suggested that they camp there for the night, and the others had no objections at all.

"Let's go swimming," Jacquelyn exclaimed.

She dove into the river and began to play around. Hero shrugged and removed his red tunic. He put a toe in the water, found it warm enough and jumped in after his friend. Merrick sighed and soon followed suit.

"You know…I don't think we've had a bit of fun on this journey so far. No breaks, no swimming, no playing. This is just what we needed," Jacquelyn laughed.

"You're right. This is fun," Hero exclaimed. "I used to swim when I was a wolf too."

"Really? That's interesting," Merrick smiled. "To tell the truth I've never gone swimming in my life."

"Never? Boy did you miss out," Jacquelyn joked, splashing him with water.

"Oh, so that's how it is then, eh?" Merrick smiled.

He splashed water back at her. Jacquelyn screeched with joy and splashed water at Hero, who splashed her back and then got hit by Merrick.

"I'll never be taken alive," he yelled, pretending to be severely wounded.

He dove under the water and swam over to Merrick. He then resurfaced and tackled his startled friend. Merrick poked his head back out of the water and laughed. Hero dove again and went after Jacquelyn who started to run but, weighed down by Hero's clothes, was caught. She laughed as she stood up, wringing out her hair.

They played around for a good hour, until their stomachs started to grumble.

"Well, that was entertaining to watch. You behaved like children," Isabell chuckled.

"You should come in next time, Isabell," Merrick teased.

"I will then," the former unicorn snorted with mock anger.

Hero sat down next to Jacquelyn. She gave him a smile, which he returned.

"How's your head?" he asked.

"I think the water actually helped, if you can believe it," Jacquelyn replied.

"Mind if I take a look at it in case?" Hero continued.

"Not at all, I'd be pleased," Jacquelyn blushed.

Hero carefully unwrapped the wet bandages and examined the cut. It did look better. It wouldn't be completely healed for about a week, but there didn't seem to be any danger of the stitching coming loose. He got dry bandages and rewrapped her head.

"Well, I better change," Jacquelyn sighed rather dreamily.

She walked over to her saddlebags and grabbed her favorite green riding dress. It was an emerald green with a white design over the abdomen. The front had a large wide white strip down to the hem. She disappeared into the trees to change.

"Hey, dinner's ready," Merrick called.

"Okay," Hero replied walking over.

Jacquelyn strode over from the trees, in a dress once more. Her hair flowed freely down her back. She sat in between the two men and accepted her meal eagerly. Merrick made their first real feast tonight—a large steak, chicken, fresh salad with carrots and cucumbers, cheese and wheat bread, goblets of white wine, strawberry muffins, and a vanilla cake to finish it all off.

"Whoa," Hero murmured after the meal. "It's been so long since I've been really full."

"I know what you mean," Merrick replied, rubbing his stomach.

"That was so delicious. I don't think I've ever had such a fine meal," Jacquelyn added.

"And you know what's really good after a big dinner?" Hero asked.

"What?" Merrick replied.

"A nap," Hero finished, flopping down on a bed of grass.

Merrick and Jacquelyn heartily agreed and found their own places to sleep. The horses wandered a bit to where the grass was longer and began to graze. All in all, it was the best day they had had together, and they all felt closer than ever.

The next morning was dull and cloudy, which dampened the companions' spirits as they started out once more. With heavy hearts, they crossed over the river they had played in the day before. All wondered when they'd be able to cut loose like that again.

Hero suggested that they speed up, in case the demons had not stopped. The others agreed, not wanting to chance an encounter. The horses forced themselves into a trot, and they moved with haste down the mountain.

"Hero," Jacquelyn said at midday. "How much longer until we reach the next mountain?"

Hero pulled out his map. He looked it over carefully. "I'd say another hour at least," he answered.

"I just want to get over Demon's Peak and go through Hurith Gate. Then squeeze our way through an enemy country and somehow get an audience with the King," Jacquelyn sighed, noting their many tasks.

"Well, sorry to break it to you, but we have to cross at least three more mountains before we get to Demon's Peak," Merrick said.

"Three?" Jacquelyn shrieked. "Are they all as big as this one?"

"No, not at all. The next mountain is pretty big, but an easy climb; the next one is steep but small, and the last one is like the second one, tall but easy," Merrick explained.

"Well good," Hero said cheerfully. "We can handle anything after this mountain, right?"

"I know I can. I've done it before," Merrick mumbled.

"I guess so," Jacquelyn sighed, rubbing her head thoughtfully.

"Then no more frowning. We're almost through the mountains, and we'll handle Feruh when the time comes," Hero encouraged.

The others agreed with non-committal nods of their heads. Hero sighed. It was hard being cheerful when everyone else looked so gloomy. However, an hour later, when the base of the mountain came into view, all sighed with relief.

"Can we actually rest now?" Jacquelyn asked as they dismounted.

"Yes, we can. Merrick and I used a cave that is well hidden the last time we came through here," Isabell answered. "There's a small stream nearby, and hot spring a little farther than the stream."

"All right. Let's get to the cave first," Hero said with a large grin.

"A hot spring here? Oh what luck," Jacquelyn laughed.

With spirits soaring, the companions made their way to the cave. Isabell was right; it was well hidden and rather hard to get to. However, once inside, they sat down to rest. The cave was large enough for the horses to stand straight and walk around. The entrance was a tight squeeze for them, but it was better than having an obvious opening.

"I'll go refill our water flasks," Merrick offered, walking to the cave's entrance.

"I'm going to go check out that hot spring," Jacquelyn exclaimed happily.

She ran from the cave. Hero stretched and pulled out all the food to see how much they had left. It looked like enough food to last a week, which meant conserving their meals from now on. He sighed. Traveling wasn't all adventure and sword fighting. It was learning how to survive in the wild. He left some food out for dinner, but packed the rest away.

"I'm going to go see if I can find a rabbit or something," Hero said to Isabell and the other horses.

"Okay, be careful and don't wander too far," Isabell warned.

"I won't," Hero replied leaving the cave.

He circled to the back of the cave and climbed up to the top of it. He stood up slowly and looked around the landscape. There was no sign of life back the way they came, so he looked forward, to the next mountain. About a mile away, he saw a small forest and felt that something must live there, so he climbed from the cave and started to jog toward the forest.

As Hero snuck into the forest, he began to feel more like a wolf again. He was alone for the first time in months, hunting in a forest, and it was quiet with no sounds of human interference. He stopped suddenly as a deer entered a small meadow warily. She was a grand doe, fat and with a wounded leg as well. Hero crouched on all fours and crawled forward. He remembered the feeling of his first hunt when he caught a deer, and the thought made him feel homesick again. He mentally shook it off and continued to stalk his unknowing prey.

Hero pulled a large hunting knife from his belt. The deer stood in front of him, just a leap away. Hero sat back on his haunches, and then flung himself on the deer. He wrapped his arm around her neck and plunged the knife into her shoulder, causing her to stumble. He then raised the knife again and prepared to stab her neck, but the deer bucked up with her hind legs, and Hero dropped the knife. He couldn't hold on long with the wounded deer bucking like a rodeo ride, so he did the only thing he could.

It felt good to sink his teeth into flesh again. Hero held onto the deer with both hands, leaned down and bit into the side of her neck. He hadn't pierced the skin yet, so he released and then bit her again, harder. He forced his jaws to bite harder, and soon blood poured into his mouth. The deer fell, so Hero leapt off her back, never letting his mouth off her neck.

Hero pulled away after five minutes. The deer was dead, with a gaping wound in her neck. Hero panted with exhilaration, looking around at his true home, happy that he found his true nature once again. He grabbed the deer and slung it over his shoulders, and to keep from alarming the others, he reclaimed his knife and washed the blood from his face. It was slow going, carrying the heavy deer after so many days of harsh climbing, but he didn't quit.

"Hero, when did you go hunting?" Jacquelyn asked as Hero reemerged at the cave.

"Just now. Weren't you going to the spring?" Hero replied.

"I was going to eat first," she answered.

"Okay, well, I'm going to make the deer travel size," Hero smiled, retreating behind the cave.

"Travel size?" Jacquelyn mumbled. "What does that mean?"

"It means he's going to skin it and then chop it up to fit in the saddlebags so you have more food," Isabell explained.

Hero grinned as he heard Jacquelyn's outburst of disgust. He took out his knife again and began his messy job.

"Okay, now that we've eaten, let's go to the spring," Jacquelyn suggested.

"Right. So are you going in with a dress or do you need my clothes?" Hero asked.

"Well, you see, there are two springs. So I am going in one, and you two will go in the other. The bushes separate them, so it'll be private,' Jacquelyn explained, blushing.

"Huh?" Hero asked.

"Hero, just don't go to the spring Jacquelyn is in, okay?" Merrick said.

"Uh, okay?" Hero replied, more confused than ever.

Once they got to the hot springs, Jacquelyn rushed over to the one surrounded by bushes. Merrick and Hero stripped to their small clothes and jumped in. Hero finally understood why he couldn't see Jacquelyn now.

"Well, I'm embarrassed," he sighed.

"Hey, don't worry about it," Merrick laughed. "You have an excuse, being a former wolf and all."

"Still, she's going to think I'm some kind of creep," Hero sighed.

"I doubt it," Merrick exclaimed. "If you knew the things I did."

"Huh? What do you mean? What things?" Hero demanded, who had forgotten all about the conversation he had heard.

"No way. I'm not telling you. That's for her to do," Merrick taunted.

Hero swam across the small spring and tried to look menacing. "I want to know now," he said quietly.

Merrick looked at him for a few seconds, and then started laughing so hard that he shook. Hero sniffed indignantly and went back to the other side. He folded his arms across his chest and looked at the bushes. Was Jacquelyn listening to them as he watched?

"You have to practice that face of yours," Merrick smiled. "You looked like you had stomach pain or something."

"Oh shut up. Maybe I just don't like to look mean," Hero sniffed.

"You couldn't look mean if you wanted to," Merrick pointed out. "Well, no, I guess you can be pretty scary looking at times."

"Like when I rip out a demon's throat using my teeth?" Hero smiled.

"Yeah, like that," Merrick said.

Hero lunged across the spring and grabbed Merrick by the shoulders. He bared his teeth and said, "I demand to know what Jacquelyn said to you."

"Oh really?" Merrick said calmly. "What if I did this?"

With that said, Merrick kicked Hero's legs out from under him, and Hero fell into the water. He resurfaced, coughing and wiping the hair away from his face. He returned again to his side of the hot spring.

"I'll remember that," he said, wringing out his hair.

"Go ahead," Merrick smiled. "I'll just do it again."

Hero smiled back and began to chuckle. They really were acting quite childish, but he didn't care. What was wrong with a little fun? He heard a splash from nearby and knew that Jacquelyn must have been peeking while they were busy.

"Hey, we can't peek at you, but you can peek at us?" Hero called.

"Peeking? I don't know what you're talking about," Jacquelyn called from the other side of the bushes.

"Sure you don't," Merrick sighed, pointing at Hero and then pointing at the bushes. "How would you feel if we looked in on you?"

"You better not. I'm in nothing but a shift here," Jacquelyn warned.

"So? We're in nothing but our small clothes," Merrick pointed out.

"I didn't look at you," Jacquelyn insisted.

By this time, Hero had successfully crept to the bushes unnoticed. Merrick gave him a signal that obviously meant he wanted Hero to jump out and scare Jacquelyn. Hero grinned and got ready. He leapt from the bushes, slipped and fell headfirst into the hot water. When he poked his head back up, a hand whipped across his face with a resounding slap.

"*How dare you*?" Jacquelyn shrieked.

Merrick appeared, "Jacquelyn, calm down...easy, eaaassssyyyy," he said, trying not to laugh.

"What do you all think you're doing?" she demanded.

Jacquelyn picked up a nearby rock and threw it at Merrick, who in dodging it lost his balance and fell into the spring on top of Jacquelyn. Then, spluttering with outrage, Jacquelyn resurfaced, facing the two guilty men.

"I'm gonna eat you alive," she threatened.

She charged at them, and they scattered to the other side of the spring.

"She's gone crazy!" Hero gulped, dodging the incoming hand.

"I'll show you crazy," Jacquelyn declared, swinging her other hand.

Hero caught it and Jacquelyn lost her footing on the slippery bottom. She fell against Hero's chest and grabbed his shoulder to keep from falling.

"Now you want to dance?" Hero asked with a grin.

"You're going to get it puppy dog," she said.

Jacquelyn pushed away from him and smacked into Merrick, who twirled her around and started to do a little jig with her, until she freed her hand and slapped him. Merrick stumbled back, and Jacquelyn started toward him, but Hero came from behind and placed his hands over her eyes.

"Guess who," he laughed.

"Dead man," Jacquelyn said, trying to sound angry but failing miserably.

"Wrong answer, Missy," Hero laughed.

He turned her around and smiled. She smiled too, and Hero sighed in relief.

"Are we safe?" Merrick asked.

Suddenly, Hero winked at Jacquelyn, who in turn nodded back to him.

"We are, but you aren't," they said.

"What?" Merrick gulped.

"Get him!" Jacquelyn ordered.

They both rushed at their one-eyed friend and attacked. Hero got behind him and held his arms back, while Jacquelyn contemplated what to do.

"Do your worse," Merrick said boldly.

"As you wish," Jacquelyn answered with a smile.

She walked up to him and started to tickle him. Merrick laughed and tried to escape the relentless attack, but Hero held him fast.

"N-no, hahahaha...Stop! Hahahaha...I-I give up," Merrick pleaded between laughs.

"No mercy," Jacquelyn replied, continuing the torture.

"Hahahah! P-please I give. Haha...Mercy! M-E-R-C-Y," Merrick exclaimed.

Jacquelyn stopped, and Hero let him go. Merrick rubbed his sides, complaining that laughing was a painful exercise. They all got out of the spring and wrapped their cloaks about them, because the towels were soaked.

When they got back to the caves, Isabell raised her head and stared at them with a bemused smile.

"What? We slipped," Hero said.

"I guess so," she replied.

"Hey, what's that suppose to mean?" Jacquelyn asked.

"Hm, I was just acknowledging the fact that all three of you slipped," Isabell said with a nod. "So how was the water?"

"Hot," Hero said.

"And slippery apparently. Tell me, how is it that all of you managed to make it this far when you can't even sit in a spring?" the unicorn asked.

"Oh shut up," the three companions laughed.

They stayed in the cave for three days. They did see the demons and were thrilled when they just passed them by, though it seemed that Hynraz sensed their presence. Merrick and Hero had to hold Jacquelyn back again, because apparently Hynraz was the one who wounded her. Once the demons were a good distance away, the three companions packed up their belongings and mounted their horses. The deer meat was much appreciated, because it increased their food supply to about two weeks if they ate sparingly.

It was raining when they started out, but they didn't dare stay any longer. They all bid farewell to the place and wondered if they would ever return. Hero sighed and looked at the mountains ahead. Merrick spoke the truth about the mountain that loomed in the distance. It was large, but the path was smooth, not too steep, and it went downhill as well as up.

They reached this mountain mid-afternoon and took a little break to renew their energy. Jacquelyn gathered some herbs to make a great seasoning and other plants to use for cuts and burns. Her head had healed, and only a scar remained to show that anything had ever happened. Moon Dance also had a small scar on her chest, but it didn't hinder her.

"Well, I suppose we should start up the mountain again," Hero suggested.

"Yes. I'm ready," Jacquelyn said.

"Let's do it then," Merrick agreed.

They mounted their horses again and started to climb. It was actually rather pleasant, walking up the dirt path, the soft rain making music on the leaves. Hero breathed in the air deeply. It smelled like fresh pine and clear air. He loved that smell. He even heard a bird chirping, which was odd because they were already pretty high up on the mountain with the trees far behind them.

"Anyone know what kind of birds those are?" he asked as he heard another to his left.

"Birds?" Merrick asked.

"Yeah, just listen," Hero whispered, so he wouldn't scare it away.

They paused for a minute and heard the strange chirp again to the right. Another came from the left and a third from behind them.

"Those aren't birds," Merrick yelled. "They're demon signals!"

Sure enough, the demons that had been following them leapt out on all sides and surrounded them, except for straight ahead. Hero was about to spur Phoebus to the opening, but Hynraz stepped into view, completing the circle of demons.

"Well, well, it has been awhile," he said with a smile. "Ah, I see you have a new companion. Haven't we met before?"

"You better believe we have, monster. You did this to me," Jacquelyn snarled, pulling her dress out of the way to show the top half of her scar.

"Oh yes, the little farm girl who harbored Lone Wolf. I guess you really are Lone Wolf. Good thing I found you again, Queen Arlyn was upset that I let you escape," Hynraz smiled.

"Then she's going to be more upset. I will not fall into your hands again," Hero growled.

"I'm afraid you have no choice. And since you escaped once, I'm going to have to be more rough this time around," the red-haired demon sneered, drawing his sword.

The rest of the demons drew their own swords. There were at least fifteen of them. There were still the two old ones, but they looked as scary as the others, still broad shouldered and with heavy lines in their faces.

"We're a little out-numbered," Merrick whispered.

"I don't care. They're dead," Jacquelyn replied softly.

"We fight. Do not let them capture you. Be killed if that's what it takes," Hero said.

He drew his sword and charged at the nearest demon. Jacquelyn grabbed her short sword and went right after Hynraz. Merrick charged at the demons to the left and began hacking away at them.

Hero was surrounded by demons. They all jabbed at him and Phoebus, trying to force him to the ground. Then Hero realized something. The demons had orders not to kill him. He could use that to his advantage. He rushed at one demon, and, sure enough, it avoided stabbing him. Hero was not so merciful. He cut the demon's head off and then turned to the next one.

Merrick caught on to Hero's idea and decided to copy it. Isabell bit at the other horses, while Merrick killed the demons left and right. A demon crept up behind him, but Isabell swung around, knocking it out with her heavy flank.

"Hold on," she said, rearing up on her hind legs.

She landed on the fallen demon and split another one's skull with it. Merrick patted her neck before going back to the battle.

"Are you that angry with me?" Hynraz asked with a bemused smile.

"I'll make sure you're dead, even if I go with you," Jacquelyn answered.

"And if I just kill you?" the demon asked, nudging his horse closer.

"That is not possible," Jacquelyn growled.

She leapt forward and her sword bounced off Hynraz's with a clang. The demon lashed out with a fist and caught her on the jaw. Jacquelyn spit out a mouthful of her own blood and swung at the demon again. Hynraz easily deflected the blow.

"Do you even know how to use that sword?" he taunted.

"Shut up!" Jacquelyn bellowed.

She jumped from Moon Dance's saddle and landed behind Hynraz. She put her sword against his throat.

"Not so tough now are you?" she smirked.

As she was about to bring the sword across his throat, Hynraz grabbed the blade with his bare hands. He tugged it out of the woman's hand and backhanded her off his horse. Jacquelyn hit the ground and sank into the mud a little. The rain made it hard for her to see Hynraz above her because drops kept falling in her eyes.

"Nice try, little girl," Hynraz said.

He threw her sword at her, and Jacquelyn barely dodged it. It buried itself into the ground, trapping some of her dress with it. In an instant, two demons stood over her, ready to end her life.

"No!" a voice yelled.

It was Hero. He urged Phoebus into a gallop and rode into the first demon, and then he leapt from the saddle and landed on the other one's back, stabbing it in the back of its neck. He tugged Jacquelyn's sword free and helped her up. Jacquelyn hugged him in gratitude.

Only five demons remained: the two old ones, a purple-haired one, a blue-haired one and, of course, Hynraz.

"*Okasvi yadak culde,*" Hynraz ordered. The other demons started to flee down the mountain.

Hynraz raised his left arm to the sky. The rain poured down harder, and thunder crashed in the sky. His arm glowed blue and suddenly a bolt of lightning tore from the sky and hit his raised arm. Hynraz smiled evilly and pointed his fingers toward the three companions. From each of his five long fingers, small arrows of lightning shot toward Hero. Without waiting to see if he had hit him, Hynraz galloped off after the remaining demons.

The lightning came closer and closer, but Hero couldn't move. He hadn't noticed that the mud had formed around his feet and hardened to keep him in place. Those arrows would kill him, and he wouldn't be able to save Nakoomu.

A flash of gold appeared in front of him before the arrows could strike. He heard a high-pitched whinny and a thud. Hero had closed his eyes against the blinding light, and was now afraid of what he would see. When he opened them, his fear came true.

The mud had softened again and the lightning had stopped, but Hero cried out in agony. Phoebus, his noble and beloved stallion, had taken the arrows for him. The poor horse barely held on to life. Hero knelt beside him, while Jacquelyn and Merrick looked on at a distance.

"Phoebus, thank you," Hero cried softly. "You were always there for me. I wish I could be there for you."

Phoebus nudged his hand with his nose, licking it feebly. Hero bent down and wrapped his arms gently around the stallion's bleeding neck, crying into the mane.

"You will always be my friend. I'll always remember you," he whispered.

Phoebus let out a small neigh filled with gratitude. Hero looked at his wounds and knew he could do nothing. The lightning arrows had struck his neck, stomach, legs and flank. Hero hugged him again, and Phoebus tried to stand.

"No, stay down my friend. Rest up a while okay?" Hero said with a sad smile.

Phoebus closed his large eyes and breathed deeply. Hero stroked his head slowly, trying to help him relax. After about a minute, Phoebus' chest heaved no more.

"*Damn you, Hynraz!*" Hero roared at the dark sky.

They buried Phoebus in a small clearing surrounded by boulders. Hero and Merrick placed a boulder over the ground where the horse lay. Then

Jacquelyn picked some mountain flowers and laced them together, placing them around the boulder like a necklace.

"Let's go," Hero said after a while.

"Okay," Jacquelyn said softly.

Hero got on Moon Dance and Jacquelyn climbed up behind him. Hero looked over his shoulder one last time. He had never before experienced the loss of a good friend.

Chapter 15

They climbed to the top of the second mountain in two days. The descent proved as easy as the climb. Hero felt depressed the whole time. Merrick and Jacquelyn just left him alone, for which he felt grateful. He didn't really feel like talking about it.

"You know, Hero," Isabell said as the base of the mountain came into view. "We don't have too much to do. I'm sure King Dervik will handle everything once you show up."

"Why does it matter?" Hero wondered. "What am I supposed to do that will stop a war?"

"We'll see when we get there," Isabell replied.

"No. I want to know why I'm putting myself in danger for humans! How will King Dervik use my presence as an asset? 'Hey, Queen Arlyn, we have Lone Wolf here so don't you start that war'? What kind of solution is that?" Hero snapped.

"Hero, we don't know why you were sent here either. The stories say that Lone Wolf will come and save us," Merrick explained.

"Save you? I'm just one person, just in case you all haven't realized. I can't beat an army. I bleed like a normal human. I have feelings like a human. I'm no different from you. Why not send in someone who is really skilled with a sword or something?" Hero demanded.

"Hero, stop doubting yourself. You know somewhere in your heart that you can do it. Somewhere in your heart is the answer to this war. I don't know how you can stop it myself, but that's for you to figure out," Jacquelyn said softly.

"Oh sure, like that'll do it. What am I supposed to say to King Dervik so that he doesn't think I'm some kind of lunatic? 'I swear I can stop the war,'" Hero asked.

"Why don't we wait until we reach the capital?" Merrick asked firmly.

"Why don't we just go to Carthafell, murder your sister and then go after Muryn? A chicken can run without its head only for a few moments. Kill those two and the war will stop before it starts," Hero said.

"Do you know how hard it is to get into Carthafell?" Merrick questioned. "Huge demons live there, like Minotaurs and Cyclopes that eat humans alive. Then add the normal demons like Hynraz, and then the army, then Muryn, then Arlyn. Plus, the only way to get into Carthafell is to go through Gelda or through the neutral, but violent, Randaar and get through the Reenith Gate, or cross the Jilok Mountains from the east or enter from the sea," Merrick explained.

"Well that just makes me feel a lot better," Hero groaned.

"Let's just handle one thing at a time, like this upcoming mountain. I can see the top of it from here, but it really is steep," Jacquelyn said.

They started up the small but difficult mountain. Hero's bad mood persisted throughout the day. It increased when Jacquelyn suggested that they buy him another horse as soon as they could.

"Hero, Phoebus was a great horse, and you probably won't find better. But you have to let go and live on," Jacquelyn pleaded.

"Nice speech," Hero mumbled. "I think I'll decide what I want to do, thank you."

Merrick and Isabell sighed as Jacquelyn started to yell at Hero some more. They plodded along slowly, the steep path becoming more and more difficult. Within the hour, they had to dismount. Hero looked at Moon Dance and Isabell and felt another stab of pain. Why couldn't it have been the mare? Jacquelyn had no love for it, and it certainly wasn't as good as Phoebus. So why Phoebus?

"Because he loved you, and he didn't want to see you hurt," Isabell whispered in his ear.

"Huh?" Hero gasped.

"I could see the question in your eye, Lone Wolf. Please let Phoebus rest in peace. He didn't sacrifice himself so that you could rot in self pity," the former unicorn replied.

"Isabell, that's not...hm, I guess that is what I'm doing, huh?" Hero admitted. "I should be ashamed"

"No, you should be happy. That's what Phoebus wanted. That's what we all want—for you to smile again," Isabell chuckled.

"Smile? I'd almost forgotten how. Thank you, Isabell," Hero said.

He forced his lips in a small smile and did feel a lot better.

"Let's rest for the night," Hero said lightly.

The others agreed and started to pull out some food. Hero started a fire and offered to cook the meat himself. When Merrick asked him why, he answered simply that it made him feel useful. Merrick shrugged and handed him the food.

"Okay, here we go," Hero smiled. "Hey, are there any hot springs around here?"

"Nope. There is a really big one half way up Demon's Peak. You'll love that one," Merrick replied.

"A big one? How big?" Jacquelyn demanded.

"Big enough to swim in, and deep enough in the middle for the water to get up to your chin," Merrick smiled.

"Yes. Let's hurry up and get there," Jacquelyn laughed, beaming with the thought of another spring.

They all sat around the small fire. Hero placed the meat on flat rocks and put it directly on the flames. Then he stretched and yawned, poking at the meat with a stick. He silently watched his two friends out of the corner of his eye. Did they really believe he could do it? Or did they follow him on false hope? In the time that Hero had known them, both had been through dangers that threatened their very lives. He didn't expect people to be that brave. The Wise Ones described humans as arrogant and power hungry. But neither Jacquelyn nor Merrick, nor even other people he had met, like Hank and Brand, possessed those traits.

"What's wrong?" Jacquelyn asked, staring at him.

"I was just thinking," Hero replied truthfully. "We've been through a lot together. I just want to say thanks for sticking with me."

"We're your friends, Hero. We'll always stick with you," Jacquelyn said.

"She's right. No matter what," Merrick added.

"I'm really glad I met you both. I don't think I would have been able to make it this far without you," Hero smiled.

"I'm glad I met you too," Merrick replied. "I would have been captured if you hadn't helped me back then."

"I've been filled with happiness ever since I met you guys. I couldn't bear to leave either of your sides," Jacquelyn said, wiping away a tear of emotion.

Hero leaned over and wrapped an arm around her shoulders. She buried her head in his chest and smiled deeply. Merrick smiled and gave a cough. He tugged on Isabell's bridle and asked if she would like to go look for water with him.

"Jacquelyn, thank you for taking care of me," Hero said, moving away.

"Hero, I...you're welcome," Jacquelyn said.

"I'm serious though. You were the first person to become my friend in Nazberath. When I left your farm, I felt really sad because I thought that I'd never see you again," Hero admitted.

"I felt sad too. Being with you made me happy," Jacquelyn breathed. "I'm just so scared sometimes."

"Scared? Scared of what?" Hero asked.

"That once you fix everything and go back to Verinaul, I'll never see you again," Jacquelyn whispered.

Hero couldn't think of anything to say. He gazed up at the dark sky. Jacquelyn watched his eyes; they reflected the starlight in a beautiful way. Hero returned his gaze to her. He felt so sad, so torn up. Like he was fighting something inside, fighting his feelings.

"I'm sorry," he said. "I probably won't be able to come back."

Jacquelyn burst into tears. Hero walked over to her and leaned in close. Jacquelyn looked into his mismatched eyes. Tears slipped from her blue eyes as he stared back at her.

"I don't want to hurt you anymore. I'm going to go on ahead of you guys. Tell Merrick that I'll miss him, and that he'll always be in my heart. And to you, Jacquelyn, I'm sorry I can't be there for you," Hero said. "I'm really going to miss you. Please return home and forget about me. Only then will you feel true happiness. Staying with me will only cause you more pain."

"Hero, no. You can't do this alone," Jacquelyn whispered.

"My name is Lone Wolf, Jacquelyn. I have to be alone. Otherwise, you two will get in trouble," Hero said.

"But we've done well together for so long," Jacquelyn argued.

"Listen. You both are growing closer and closer to me. If we stay together, we'll just build a stronger bond, and if I can't return then it'll hurt so much more," Hero explained. "I have to go now."

Jacquelyn felt more and more hot tears slip down her face. Hero leaned forward and hugged her briefly. Before breaking away, he gave her a light kiss on the forehead. As soon as he let her go, Jacquelyn sank to her knees weakly. She put her face in her hands and wept uncontrollably. Hero whispered another apology and disappeared into the darkness.

Chapter 16

"What do you mean he's gone? Gone where?" Merrick demanded.

"He said he didn't want to hurt us anymore, so he left," Jacquelyn replied, her voice numb with sadness.

"Hurt us? What does he think leaving us is doing? We were all supposed to face this threat together," Merrick snarled.

"He said that he didn't want to get to know us so well that it would be unbearable to leave us when he went back to Verinaul," Jacquelyn explained.

"But what if he can come back here?" Merrick argued.

"We don't know if he can," Jacquelyn whispered. "I don't think we're ever going to see him again, Merrick."

She started to cry again. Merrick sat down and looked to the sky, which was starting to become light. He felt betrayed. Hero was his best friend, someone he relied on and could trust. He punched the ground in anger.

"Merrick," Jacquelyn said, face still in her hands. "Let's go to Delring anyway. Maybe we can meet up with him there."

"Why should we? He obviously doesn't want us to go with him," Merrick grumbled.

"Then you can go where you want, but I'm going. There's a chance that Hero will need our help in Delring, and I won't abandon him," Jacquelyn snapped.

She stood up and saddled Moon Dance. Merrick watched her and then sighed with weariness.

"I guess I'll go. I'd rather not be alone with those demons running around," he said.

"Thanks Merrick. Now let's ride. We may end up getting there first on horses," Jacquelyn replied.

"Right. Okay Isabell, I know this won't be easy for you, but let's ride," Merrick exclaimed.

"I can take on a steep path once in a while you know. This'll be no sweat," the unicorn said, walking briskly up the mountain.

"Sorry Hero, but friends stick together," Jacquelyn said.

"No matter what," Merrick added.

Hero was running up the mountain practically on all fours. He had to reach Delring quickly. He could not predict when the war would finally break out. He wished desperately that he was a wolf for the moment. It would be much easier going, but he kept running and running, never slowing down.

He did feel horrible about leaving the others behind, but it would be much easier for them to go somewhere else. He realized that he couldn't think that they'd go home, seeing how Jacquelyn's home had been destroyed and Merrick's was a living hell, but they could go somewhere nice and forget all about Lone Wolf.

"Hero?" a voice asked out of nowhere.

Hero stopped short and looked around. There in the trees stood a young boy by a very small cottage. The cottage blended with the trees so well that he wouldn't have noticed it if the boy hadn't called out.

"How do you know my name?" Hero asked.

"It's me, Jeru. Remember? I died about eleven years ago. But then I was reborn as a human. You and Swift Paw were the last to see me," the boy laughed.

"Jeru, the old wolf who was like a hero to us. I remember now," Hero said in awe.

"Come in and have some tea with me," Jeru laughed.

Hero walked into the cottage in a stupor. Another former wolf, but he was completely different from Hero. He had died and been reborn, while Hero had just been transported here, remaining the same age. He remembered the transformation Jeru went through after he had died. How he had turned into a human baby right before his eyes.

"So how come you're older than me?" Jeru asked, handing Hero a mug of hot tea.

"Do you know about the Storm of Endless Tears?" Hero asked.

"Yeah, a little...all that rain that's supposed to drown our world?" Jeru replied.

"Right. Well it has started, and I turned out to be Lone Wolf. So I didn't die, I just came here," Hero explained.

"Oh, I see. That's very interesting. So you know what you're doing here?" Jeru asked.

"I'm supposed to stop the upcoming war between Carthafell and Hasrath. I have no idea how to do that," Hero sighed.

"Stop the war, eh? That's a tough one. Why don't you just let the war happen? That way Carthafell will be weakened, and you can easily slip in and kill that Queen," Jeru suggested.

"Are you insane? I can't just let the war happen," Hero exclaimed.

"Well, you're never going to be able to enter Carthafell as you are now," Jeru said.

"I can't just change into a wolf at random now can I?" Hero snarled.

"No. But I've heard of something that allows such a power. It's called the Desert's Rose, and it grants the one who finds it one wish," Jeru explained.

"Well, I don't have time to find a rose in a desert," Hero grumbled. "I should probably go. Time is running out."

"I'll go with you," Jeru said.

"But you're just a kid, no older than eleven," Hero gasped.

"So what? I'm a lot smarter than some pup. Obviously I kept my wolf mind when I came here," Jeru scoffed.

"Are you sure? There's a chance that we'll be killed, and I am supposed to do this alone," Hero pointed out.

"Alone? Wolves don't travel alone, Hero. I can keep up with you. I saw how fast you are, and I'll tell you now that I can keep up," Jeru said impatiently.

Hero glanced at the wolf he had admired as a pup. He didn't look a thing like that wolf. His face was slightly round, and his skin was tanned. He had short hair that fell in a mess to his ear lobes. Although he had the face of a young boy, his eyes and hair betrayed him. His hair was silver and his eyes seemed normal at first glance, but if you looked into the bright blue irises for long, they seemed to be filled with a wild spirit that had experienced much toil.

"You know, I miss talking to a wolf. We can talk about Verinaul together, and you can tell me some of your adventures," Hero smiled.

"All right," Jeru shouted with joy.

Hero raised his eyebrows.

"Sometimes my childish nature takes control of me," Jeru explained sheepishly.

"Okay," Hero said.

Jeru rolled up the sleeves of his long-sleeved tunic. It was blue and a couple of sizes too big for the boy. He wore brown breeches and black boots that reached his knees. He cracked his knuckles, opened the door and prepared to run. Hero stood with him, and they both smiled. The tree branches swayed, and they were off—two former wolves in a strange land, hoping to achieve the impossible.

"You think you can keep this up?" Merrick asked as Isabell strained herself to the top of the mountain.

"I'm pretty positive. Now stop distracting me!" Isabell snapped.

Merrick shrugged and looked to see how Jacquelyn fared. She was a few feet behind him, urging Moon Dance forward with encouraging words and pats. The black mare snorted as she forced herself up the steep path. Merrick looked to the top of the mountain; it was only about an hour's ride away.

"Merrick, I don't know if Moon Dance can go any farther," Jacquelyn called.

Merrick turned his gaze to them and saw that Moon Dance could not move anymore. "We'll let her rest for a while then," he said.

Once they had dismounted and relieved the horses of their tack and saddlebags, they sat down on a large boulder. Jacquelyn sighed and lay down on her back, gazing at the blue sky. It was summer time and climbing the mountain in summer's heat was terrible. Merrick glanced at Jacquelyn and saw a glazed look in her eyes.

"You okay?" Merrick asked.

"Yes…just thinking about Hero again," Jacquelyn replied. "You were right as usual. I wish I had just told him how I felt."

"We'll see him in Delring so you can tell him then," Merrick smiled.

"Thank you. You know, when we first met, I thought I would never grow to like you," Jacquelyn admitted.

"Well, I have problems trusting anyone, so I apologize if I sounded rude. Hero was the one who changed that for me. There was something about him, maybe his eyes, that just told me I could trust him," Merrick said.

"I think that's true. I felt the same way the first time I looked into his eyes." Jacquelyn sighed dreamily.

"Quiet," Merrick whispered suddenly.

Jacquelyn almost retaliated, but Merrick was serious. He was watching the path where they had come from. Jacquelyn watched too, and thought she spied red with the greens and grays of leaves and rocks.

"*Hynraz*," She shouted with rage, jumping from the boulder.

"You idiot," Merrick snarled, going after her.

Jacquelyn didn't bother with him. She charged to where she had seen the red, but no one was there. Did she just imagine it? A sudden pain shot through her lower leg. She fell to her knees and looked at her right leg. A large arrow shaft was embedded in her flesh. Five demons stepped from cover. Hynraz smiled at her, tossing the bow aside and drawing his sword.

Just as Hynraz raised his sword to deliver the final blow, Merrick burst to the scene and rammed into the demon. Hynraz dropped his sword and barked a command to the other demons. They drew their swords and started toward the injured woman.

Jacquelyn forced herself upright and grabbed her own blade. The purple-haired demon that Jacquelyn recognized from the previous encounter, stepped forward. The demon rushed at Jacquelyn who swung her sword. The demon dodged easily and jumped behind her, kicking her to the ground.

Merrick scrambled up from the ground and rushed forward to help his friend, but an arm wrapped around his neck from behind and stopped him short. He looked behind his shoulder and saw that one of the older demons had grabbed him. Hynraz stepped in front of him, holding his sword in a menacing way.

"Since you have taken the lives of so many of my demons, you get the pleasure of watching your little girl die, nice and slowly," he sneered.

The three remaining demons circled around Jacquelyn, who was still on her knees but swinging her sword at the demons' legs.

"*Higei mienth*!" Hynraz yelled. "And for those who can't speak demon, that means kill her," he whispered to Merrick.

The demons laughed with crazed delight as they brought their swords up to kill the wounded woman.

"No," Merrick snarled.

He forced his head back and head-butted the demon holding him, slamming the back of his head into the old one's face. The demon let go, clutching a broken nose. Merrick shoved past Hynraz and grabbed his sword from the ground. He threw it at the blue-haired demon and hit it right in the back of the throat. The two other demons turned to attack this greater threat. As they lunged for him, Merrick rolled past them and retrieved his sword.

"Come on. Let's see what you've got," Merrick taunted.

The purple-haired demon dashed ahead and cut at his face, ripping the eye patch from his face. Merrick stabbed the demon and saw with dismay that the old one stood ready. A sudden short sword stabbed into the demon's thigh, and Merrick cut his head off. Hynraz and the remaining old one retreated.

"Thank you for the help," Merrick said, grabbing the short sword from the dead demon's leg.

"No. Thank you for saving my life again," Jacquelyn said, leaning against a tree.

Merrick turned, and Jacquelyn gasped. She had never seen him without his eye patch. His eye closed over nothing. Another scar crossed horizontally across the eye, so that the two scars formed a mangled cross. He stared at her with an almost blank stare that frightened her.

"Merrick," she whispered.

"Yeah, I know it's pretty bad," Merrick said, his voice seemed cold and without emotion.

"How could your brother do that to you?" Jacquelyn asked softly.

"My brother has no love for me, and I none for him. He had no problem doing this to me," Merrick replied.

Jacquelyn limped over and traced the scars with her index finger. She had a look of pity in her eyes, but Merrick ignored it.

"It looks as if we are both wounded." She smiled sadly, placing her hand on her chest.

"Yes," Merrick replied. "Now, come on. We have to keep going if we're going to stay ahead of Hynraz."

"Why don't we just wait for him to come? We've beaten him two times already, and now he only has that old one with him," Jacquelyn pointed out.

"I've heard strange things about those old ones. I've heard that they can twist the turn of events to their favor somehow," Merrick said.

"Twist...in their favor?" Jacquelyn asked.

"Yes. There are stories that a man can stab an old one, and, if the demon lives, the wound disappears and reappears on the man," Merrick explained.

"Okay, let's go," Jacquelyn gulped, looking at the dead body of the demon with white hair.

Hero and Jeru only stopped to rest after they had reached the mountain's summit. At Jeru's request, Hero explained everything that had happened to him, feeling a sting of sadness as he recounted his departure from his friends.

"You should have stayed with them then," Jeru pointed out, seeing Hero's saddened face.

"No. It's better this way. I don't want to have to feel the pain whenever I think of leaving," Hero sighed. "Besides, Arlyn is mainly after me, so they'll be safer without me."

"You told me you ran away from your responsibilities of being Leader. Forgive me, but isn't leaving your friends kind of the same?" Jeru asked cautiously.

"How do you mean?" Hero asked coldly.

"Well, they were counting on you to stick with them to the end. That's what friends are for, right? In a way, you ran away from the responsibilities of being a good friend," Jeru explained slowly.

"What?" Hero roared. "So I'm a bad friend because I want to protect them from feeling hurt?"

"Think about it," Jeru said, eyes hardening. "Wouldn't it hurt them for you to have abandoned them in the middle of this quest?"

"I-well...not as much," Hero snapped.

"How do you know? What if these two friends of yours go on to Delring without you, fail to convince the King about you, and then go off to Carthafell themselves?" Jeru asked.

"They wouldn't be that stupid," Hero said bluntly.

"Oh no? They're humans, Hero. They don't think the way wolves do. Humans seem to have a tendency to seek out danger so they can become legendary heroes in the future," Jeru said.

"Not Jacquelyn or Merrick. They aren't like the others. In fact, a lot of humans aren't like that," Hero backfired.

"You wait and see. I'll bet anything they're heading to Delring as we speak," Jeru sighed, stretching out and closing his eyes.

Hero watched him, but soon the young boy slept heavily. It was strange to see someone who used to be so much older than he, now younger. He sighed and lay down himself. He thought about what the wise old wolf had said. Jacquelyn and Merrick couldn't be going on with the journey. He had told Jacquelyn not to worry about it, didn't he? But then he thought of something else. Neither had homes to go to, so where would they go?

The next morning, Hero and Jeru ate a light breakfast and then started down the mountain.

"You know, this would be a lot easier if we did this," Jeru said.

He stood up and then dove. He landed on his stomach and began to slide down the steep slope, whooping with joy. Hero shook his head, but it did look like fun. He lifted his tunic and looked at the scar, the gift from Muryn's blade. It was completely healed. He ran a few steps and then jumped.

The two former wolves landed in a heap at the edge of a ledge that dropped straight to the base of the mountain.

"Any ideas?" Jeru asked.

Hero looked around and saw a large lake to their right.

"We could jump in there," he suggested.

"What if there are rocks or it isn't deep enough?" Jeru demanded.

"Well, it's more fun when there's more risk," Hero smiled.

He grabbed the boy around the middle and ran to the edge of the ledge. He chucked the boy and jumped after him. Jeru screamed in pure terror, but Hero just yelled for the thrill. They were flying! He gazed at the water as it started to rise up to meet him. He forced his body into a diving position and hit the water a little painfully.

He resurfaced and looked around for Jeru. The boy was spluttering and swimming toward shore. Hero laughed and followed him. Once they reached shore, Jeru turned around and raised a threatening finger at Hero.

"If you ever throw me again, I'll break your arm," he snarled.

"Sure you will, shorty," Hero smiled.

"S-shorty?" Jeru cried out indignantly.

"Well, you are rather small," Hero pointed out, putting a hand on top of Jeru's head.

"I see you haven't really changed much, you young rascal," Jeru pouted.

"Who are you calling young?" Hero snickered.

Jeru punched him in the gut. Hero doubled over wheezing.

"I still have the strength to beat *pups* like you." Jeru smirked as Hero coughed.

"Oh yeah?" Hero spat, leaping at his small companion.

They grappled about on the ground, each trying to out match the other in strength. After a few minutes of intense wrestling, Hero won. He laughed with pride as Jeru sulked.

"You're lucky, you're older. That's the only reason you won," he sniffed.

"Oh sure, stop being a poor sport," Hero laughed ruffling Jeru's silver hair.

Jeru smiled and stood up. He stretched and started to run toward the very base of the mountain. Hero let out a bark and ran after him. They reached the spot in no time, tongues lolling. It was if they really were wolves again.

"I think it's safe to rest for a while," Hero smiled.

"Yeah," Jeru agreed.

They found some huge bushes and climbed through the branches, inside little huts of leaves. Hero stretched out and smiled. He had missed running around like a wolf. Jeru was exactly like himself, and that made the going a little easier, though he had to admit that he missed Jacquelyn, Merrick and Isabell greatly. He sighed. Sometimes being a hero was a rough path, littered with danger and pains, but suddenly he knew that he could do it. Jacquelyn was right. He would find a way.

Chapter 17

"Hey, we made it," Jacquelyn panted, tugging a reluctant Moon Dance with her to the top of the mountain.

They had just broken camp half an hour ago, and had already reached their goal. Jacquelyn gazed down the grassy path, surprised to see two heavy trails that looked very new. She went over to examine them.

"Merrick," She called. "I think these are human trails."

"Huh?" Merrick asked, walking over to her. "I think you may be right."

They studied the trail a little more and decided that whoever made them must have fallen and slid all the way down the mountain.

"Wouldn't that have been painful?" Jacquelyn asked.

"I don't think so. This grass is really soft. Maybe Hero made the trail," Merrick guessed.

"But there are two," Jacquelyn pointed out.

"Well, maybe he thought it was so much fun that he climbed back up here and did it again," Merrick replied.

Jacquelyn shook her head and said that she doubted Hero would have wasted time to slide down a mountain again. Merrick shrugged and started to lead Isabell down the mountain. Jacquelyn sighed and followed him. She wanted desperately to catch up to Hero again. He couldn't possibly do this on his own.

About thirty minutes later, Jacquelyn and Merrick were forced to stop. They had come across a steep ledge.

"What do we do now?" Jacquelyn asked eagerly.

"There's a path to the east a bit. It goes down. It was difficult to climb, but it'll be harder to go down. It's the steepest part of this mountain," Merrick explained.

"How long is this path?" Jacquelyn gulped.

"Only about ten to twelve feet. Just make sure you don't slip and be sure to stay ahead of your horse," Merrick instructed, walking off to the east.

Jacquelyn glanced at Moon Dance and nervously rubbed her head where the cut had been. What if the fool horse made another blunder? She shook her head, remembering that accident was her fault. She nearly bumped into Merrick, who stopped suddenly to examine a bush. She was about to ask what he was doing, but he simply drew his sword and hacked at the bush until only the roots remained.

With the bush out of the way, Jacquelyn could see a small path. She could see where it ended, but it was very steep and very narrow.

"I'll go first," Merrick offered.

He stepped onto the path, and Isabell stepped behind him. He edged his way down slowly, very slowly. He stopped with every step and made sure to push against Isabell's chest so the horse's weight couldn't force him down. When Isabell nearly slipped, he stopped and braced himself as the horse crashed into him. Jacquelyn knew that if Isabell fell, Merrick would fall with her.

Once Merrick and Isabell had negotiated the path safely, he returned to help Jacquelyn. She tried to protest, but she was grateful anyway. Merrick allowed her to keep Moon Dance balanced, but he stayed ahead of her, making sure that both were safe.

Moon Dance slid a little, and Jacquelyn dug her heels into the ground, pushing back against the heavy animal. When the mare regained her footing, they set off again. Jacquelyn could see the end of the path. She wanted to just run, but she knew that it would be foolish to risk injury with the end in sight. Then, dripping with sweat from her efforts to keep the horse safe, she reached level ground and flopped down onto the grass.

Merrick decided it would be good to let the horses graze here, since both were tired. They could see a lake nearby, and Merrick explained that they had to swim across it if they wanted to stay on the right track. Jacquelyn looked at the large lake and sighed. Nothing seemed easy at all. She lay down on her back and gazed at the perfect blue sky. Hero might be looking at the sky as well. Merrick sighed and lay down a little way off.

"You know, this has been quite the adventure," Jacquelyn said. "Before I met you and Hero, I just lived on a farm. My only adventure was collecting herbs and trying to hide them from Father."

"Really? Why didn't he want you to gather herbs?" Merrick asked.

"Father thinks skill with herbs is connected to witchcraft," Jacquelyn explained, a small smile on her lips. "If only I had been able to use my herbs for him."

"He's dead?" Merrick asked bluntly.

"No. But his arm is completely useless, severed just below the elbow. But before all that turmoil and confusion, we lived a quiet, but happy, life together," Jacquelyn sighed.

"Do you ever regret meeting Hero?" Merrick asked.

"Not at all. It's just that I wish I could go back to that life every once in a while, but I know that it cannot be," she replied.

"At least you have some happy memories. For me, life was always dark and filled with pain," Merrick said coldly.

"Did your mother not do anything?" Jacquelyn asked gently.

"Well, when she was alive, I tried to stay with her always, but whenever she had to go away, Arlyn and Muryn came after me," Merrick explained.

"And your father?" Jacquelyn urged.

"My father was murdered when I was nine. He was killed right before my eyes by a renegade demon tribe," Merrick answered.

"Oh, I'm sorry," Jacquelyn began.

"Don't worry about it," Merrick said rather impatiently. "I can't stand it when people give me sympathy."

"Well, you can't expect them not to," Jacquelyn mumbled.

Merrick glared at her, but she just returned her gaze to the sky. The grass felt like a fresh bed, and flowers swayed lazily with the light breeze. Jacquelyn could spend her whole life in a place like this. Maybe when this was all over, she would build a small house here, and she could return to being a farm girl.

She glanced over at Merrick and saw that he, too, studied the sky. He had both his hands behind his head and his legs stretched out to the fullest. They hadn't been able to find a replacement eye patch for him, and she felt a sting of hurt whenever she saw the scarred eye. She put a hand to her hip and felt her own scar. She hated this scar; it just reminded her of her awful experience.

A large cloud floated above her head, and she smiled when she realized that it looked like a badly disfigured wolf. She watched it and watched it, hoping it would continue floating in the sky. But, as with most clouds that form a truly identifiable shape, it soon lost the look of a wolf and became distorted beyond recognition.

"I think we should move on now, if you're ready," Merrick said after another minute.

"Yes, maybe we'll catch up to Hero," Jacquelyn put in hopefully.

"Okay, time to swim," Jacquelyn sighed. "How deep is this lake, Merrick?"

"It's really deep in the middle, so don't take Moon Dance over there. Just follow me and it'll be fine, though the water may go over our heads for a few steps," Merrick explained, walking into the water.

Jacquelyn gulped and followed him. She was starting to get tired of all these risky paths they had to take. She set one foot in the water and jumped back.

"This water is like ice," she gasped.

"Well, it comes directly down from the mountains. I don't think it ever gets warm," Merrick replied.

"Perfect," Jacquelyn thought, stepping into the water again.

"I think it's rather refreshing," Isabell said, as the water soaked into her fur.

"Well, of course, you would like it. You have a built-in fur coat," Jacquelyn said.

"Let's just get this over with," Merrick sighed.

Jacquelyn shivered as the water closed around her waist. Moon Dance dipped her nose into the water and took a gulp. She nodded her head as the fresh water hit her tongue. Jacquelyn tugged on the reins, and Moon Dance snorted as she was forced forward. Merrick was already up to his chest in water, and Jacquelyn realized that the ground beneath her feet was slowly declining.

"This is really nice," Isabell sighed peacefully, stepping over a large rock.

"Sorry that we have to hurry then," Merrick replied, teeth chattering. "But this water is numbing my legs."

"Right, let's go," the former unicorn sighed sadly.

Jacquelyn cried out as the water got high enough to submerge her completely. She kicked her legs and started to swim, keeping a firm hand on Moon Dance's reins. The horse could still touch the bottom, but she had to keep her head up to do so.

Jacquelyn just stared at the other side of the lake as she swam. It was getting very close now. Her foot hit a boulder, and she rested on it for a second. Merrick climbed out of the freezing water and began to rub his arms for warmth. Jacquelyn took a deep breath and stepped off her boulder. The ground had risen again, and she no longer had to swim. However, Moon Dance stopped short when Jacquelyn was still waist deep in the water.

"Come on you foolish animal," she snapped, giving the reins a sharp jerk.

Moon Dance stepped forward reluctantly and looked to her right and stopped again.

"What the heck is the matter now?" Jacquelyn demanded, looking at the black mare.

Moon Dance began to shiver with fright. Jacquelyn walked over to her and started to stroke her forehead and whisper encouragingly to her. Moon Dance looked to her right again and tried to rear up on her hind legs, but the ground was too uneven and she tipped over backwards, splashing Jacquelyn with the icy water.

Merrick saw the commotion and grumbled as he returned to the water. Jacquelyn tried to right the struggling horse, but Moon Dance had lost her wits completely.

"What's going on?" Merrick yelled as he started to draw nearer.

"I don't know. Something is upsetting her!" Jacquelyn answered.

Merrick scanned the water and saw a dark shape circling around the horse. He drew his sword and leapt at it. Jacquelyn cried out as more water splashed into her face. Moon Dance continued to struggle, and she let out piercing shrieks of fear. Jacquelyn felt something brush against her leg and she yelled too.

Merrick saw the shape to his left, and he dove at it again. He grabbed a slimy tail and held on as the thing thrashed about. Merrick dug his heels behind a boulder and yanked the tail toward him. He raised the creature out of the water and got his first clear look at it.

It was a very large eel, about six feet long and green with black spikes on its slippery back. Its teeth were long and dangerous and about five inches long. The eel had a square head and a hard skull that could easily break a bone if it rammed into someone fast enough. It bent around and tried to head-butt Merrick in the stomach, but he drew away.

Seeing the threat neutralized for the moment settled Moon Dance down a bit. She was still scared enough to try to canter out of the water, dragging Jacquelyn painfully along. Once they reached shore, Isabell headed Moon Dance off and stood in her way whenever she tried to run. Soon, the black mare had settled down and stood still, shivering occasionally. Merrick stepped out of the water, eel still in hand. Once he was far enough from the water, he tossed it back in. He walked toward Jacquelyn, examining a light wound on his arm made by the spikes on the eel's back.

"You okay?" he asked.

"Yeah, thanks," Jacquelyn replied. "I'm sorry. I seem to always get into this sort of trouble."

"There's nothing to apologize over. It happens," Merrick replied.

"Yes, but this is the second time. What if next time you get hurt trying to save me from one of my blunders?" Jacquelyn asked sadly.

"Better that I get hurt than you die. Anyone could have made those mistakes. And besides, you can't expect Moon Dance not to scare when a six-foot-long eel comes at her," Merrick smiled.

"I guess so. I just wish that it didn't always happen," she sighed.

"I think we should probably change into dry clothes now," Merrick answered, walking to Isabell and his saddlebags.

Jacquelyn opened her own and pulled out a plain wool riding dress with a white top and a brown skirt. Not fancy, but it was comfortable and had belonged to Jacquelyn's mother. She found a private place and changed, and Merrick did the same. She certainly felt a lot better in warm, dry clothes. She stuffed the wet clothes into an empty saddlebag and mounted her horse.

"Merrick," Jacquelyn said after they had entered a large forest.

"Yes?" Merrick asked.

"I'm sorry for prying, but I just can't believe that your siblings could have hated you from the moment you were born," Jacquelyn said hesitantly.

"I can't stand people who nag," Merrick sighed. "But I guess I could tell you. My brother didn't hate me at first. When I was about five, he always played with me. We would take out our wooden swords and practice in the grove behind the castle. He always won, but it was all in fun. He even let me win sometimes. However, Arlyn never did like me, and Muryn got along with her better than he did with me, so whenever she was around he was very nasty to me.

"I never asked him why he did that. As soon as Arlyn left, he would dig out the training swords, and we would continue our games. But soon, he really did start to resent me. It was all Arlyn's fault, of course, but it was a scar that never healed. Well, I told you that he liked her better and believe me they got along really well. That was why Muryn took this so heavily.

"Arlyn had asked me to take her for a ride out to the woods. I didn't want to, of course, because she hated me, but I thought maybe I could change her point of view. Anyway, we went off and were attacked by bandits. Arlyn could have dealt with them easily, but she refused and pleaded for me to help. Well, there were five bandits and I was still young, so naturally they overpowered me and knocked me out. When I woke up, Arlyn lay next to me. She had been stabbed in the stomach.

"I carried her back to the castle, and mother took her from me. Had I known that saving her would cause so much grief, I would have finished her off in that forest. But Muryn saw her and learned that I hadn't protected her. He also knew that I didn't like her. So he assumed two things: one, that I was so weak I couldn't protect her and, two, I meant for her to be wounded.

"Needless to say he hated me from that point on…for being weak I suppose," Merrick explained.

"That must have been really hard," Jacquelyn replied.

"I've gotten over it," Merrick sighed.

Hero looked around. A fork in the path branched off into four different directions. Jeru stood beside him and began to study them.

"You *do* know which way to go, right?" Hero demanded.

"Sure, sure. I just need to sort out my memory a bit so be patient," Jeru replied.

Hero slumped onto the ground as Jeru peered down each of the paths. Since none pointed straight, it was very hard to pick one. Jeru walked down the paths for a few feet and tried to remember which one he had traveled before. When he returned, he had a sheepish expression on his face.

"Well, I know the one farthest to the right leads to Mathwen, the City of Scholars, and that the one farthest to the left leads to Shiboo, a small farming town in the mountains," he smiled.

"Well that's informative. Which one leads to Demon's Peak?" Hero asked.

"I don't know. I do know the wrong path doubles back to the beginning of the mountain range," Jeru said softly.

"So we either get to Demon's Peak or have to do this all over again," Hero mumbled. "How far away is Shiboo?"

"Hm…about a good day's walk from here," Jeru replied.

"And Mathwen?" Hero urged.

"Oh, a week at least," Jeru sighed.

"Then we shall go to Shiboo and ask for the right directions to Demon's Peak," Hero said.

"That's a good idea. I wish I could remember, but it's been a really long time since I climbed up the mountain," Jeru complained.

Hero shook his head and started to walk down the left path. Too tired to run, he was glad Jeru hadn't suggested it. Since it was already late afternoon, Hero knew they wouldn't reach the town until after dark. He asked Jeru if they should just stop for the night or keep going. His young companion thought for a minute and suggested that they just keep going until they reached the town. Hero nodded in agreement, and they continued at a faster pace.

Night fell in a few hours, and Hero was just glad that the path was straight and not very rocky. He gazed at the sky and saw the moon half covered by clouds. He hoped they would see the town soon. Jeru stumbled behind him and cursed as he fell flat on his face.

"You okay?" Hero asked, helping him up.

"Yeah, I guess so," Jeru replied.

"You want to stop for the night?" Hero asked.

"No. The town should be just beyond that hill," Jeru said, pointing to the dark mass in front of them.

Hero nodded and started to hurry up the large hill, panting with exhaustion by the time he made it to the top. He turned around and offered Jeru his hand, but the boy swatted it away and forced himself to the top without any help. They stared at the large valley spread out before them. Lights shown from the houses and the sound of voices drifted toward them. Hero let out a yell of joy and ran down the hill, Jeru on his heels.

The town of Shiboo was having a festival that night, so people crowded the streets. Hero and Jeru burst into sight. Many yelled out in surprise, while others claimed they were demons.

"Sorry about that," Jeru laughed. "But we have been wandering the mountains and are so glad that we have found a town."

"Oh you poor things. Let me go fetch the town's chief for you," an old woman clucked.

She hobbled off to the largest house. Hero looked beyond the houses and saw many dark shapes, the barns he gathered. He could see fields with crops growing. His gaze was interrupted when a short, fat man with graying hair appeared before him.

"What do you want?" he asked with a squeaky voice.

"Just to stay in your town for the night, sir. We've been wandering the mountains for weeks and haven't seen anybody," Hero answered with a broad smile.

"Who are you then?" the chief asked.

"I am Jeru. Pleased to meet you," Jeru smiled.

"My name is Lucius," Hero lied, deciding that it might be dangerous for these people if they knew who he was.

Jeru gave him a questioning glance but said nothing. The town chief introduced himself as Peter and welcomed them to stay as long as they liked. The Festival of Good Harvest was in full swing, so the chief invited them to enjoy themselves.

"What's with the name?" Jeru whispered once Peter moved away.

"If any demons happen across this place, it's best if the townspeople didn't know I was here," Hero replied.

"Got it," Jeru nodded.

They walked over to where everyone danced to the tune of a fast song. The musicians played reed flutes, violins and small drums. It was a cheerful atmosphere. A woman about a year or two older than Hero approached him.

"You want to dance, sir?" she asked.

"I can't really dance, sorry," Hero replied truthfully.

"Well, I could teach you," the woman said with a smile.

She had green eyes, thick red hair and a face tanned from working in the sun, but she was very pretty. She wore a plain blue dress with white cuffs at the sleeves.

"Go on and enjoy yourself. I'm going to go dance with that little pretty over there," Jeru said, nudging Hero before walking over to a girl his age who stood clapping on the sidelines.

She had blond hair and blue eyes and wore her hair in pigtails. Her dress was violet but rather plain. Freckles dotted her face and red cheeks. When Jeru offered her a hand, she blushed furiously but accepted the invitation. As they circled past Hero, Jeru gave his friend a wink.

"Well, you want to dance or not?" the woman asked.

"I suppose so," Hero said nervously.

"I'm Cassandra, by the way. Pleased to meet you." The woman smiled, leading Hero into the fast dance.

"I'm Lucius," Hero said, watching her feet.

She led him around and around in circles. He watched the other guys to see what to do, and found he rather enjoyed dancing. Cassandra laughed as he twirled her around. She gasped for breath once the song ended.

"You want a drink?" she asked.

"Okay," Hero replied.

They walked over to a table and poured themselves some mead. Cassandra was quite unpredictable. She offered to have a chugging contest with Hero who declined, saying that he never really drank too much. She shrugged and chugged it down herself.

"Let's get back to it," she exclaimed as the music picked up again in another bouncy melody.

"All right," Hero replied, feeling the excitement flow throughout his body.

They danced and danced for about three hours. When the musicians put their instruments away, and the festival drew to a close, Cassandra separated herself from Hero.

"Thanks for letting me have so much fun," she smiled, kissing him lightly.

"Your welcome," he replied, blushing.

She started to run back to her house.

Jeru joined him, breathing heavily from the night's activities.

"That Molly sure was a good dancer. I could hardly keep up," he laughed. "Gave me a big kiss at the last moment too."

"Cassandra kissed me too. I completely froze. I know she didn't mean it to be anything. Darn it, I'm bad with women, but that's a good thing since I love a wolf," Hero sighed.

"You do? Who is it?" Jeru asked slyly.

"Nakoomu, of course. Once I get back to Verinaul she's going to be my mate," Hero said proudly.

"You can go back?" Jeru asked blankly.

"I should hope so. I'm not coming to live with the humans, just save them," Hero said quickly.

He walked off to the inn, while Jeru just stared at him. He had to believe in a way back. If not, then poor Nakoomu would wait the rest of her days for him. He could picture her sitting at the green pond, watching the sky, heedless of the rain that drenched her to the skin. He didn't realize that he had tears in his eyes when he got to his room.

Chapter 18

When Hero woke the next morning, he smelled the fresh aroma of breakfast. He dressed quickly and went downstairs. Large pieces of bread and cheese, bacon, steak and eggs and fresh pancakes filled the table. Hero helped himself to a little of everything, devouring the excellent food hungrily. Jeru joined him soon after and began to eat in a similar fashion. Both shoveled the food down their throats as fast as they could, not noticing how the innkeeper and her husband stared.

"Well I'll be darned. You boys must have been in them mountains forever," the man laughed as Hero and Jeru finished up the heaping meal.

"It was just so delicious," Jeru complimented, wiping his mouth with a cloth napkin.

"I just love when people appreciate my food," the innkeeper beamed. "I could sit in the kitchen all day listening to people compliment it."

"Maybe we could take some with us when we go," Hero suggested.

"Well that's a fine idea," the innkeeper smiled.

"You can take all the food ya need from good ol' Charlotte here. She'd be much obliged to help anyone in need," Charlotte's husband added.

"Hey, Lucius, maybe we should stay here one more day. It couldn't hurt," Jeru pleaded.

"I was going to say the same. We could use the break," Hero agreed.

"Our doors are always open," Charlotte said as they left the inn.

"Jeru...Jeru!" a high voice called out.

The two former wolves turned around to see Molly running over to them. Her hair was in one braid today, and she wore a brown dress that fell to her knees. Jeru grinned and walked over to her with Hero following.

"Hello Molly, what do you need?" Jeru asked proudly puffing out his chest.

"I want to show you to the magic willow," Molly smiled. "It's an old willow tree not far from here, but I believe, and so do others, that some fairies have nested there."

"I would love to," Jeru replied. "Before we go, I'd like to introduce you to my friend, Lucius."

"Hi there," Hero said.

Molly looked into his eyes and grew pale.

"Please don't eat me. I'm sure a wolf like you could find better food," Molly cried.

She ran off toward the fields. Jeru gave one frightened look at Hero and ran after her, calling out to her that she must be ill. Hero just scratched his head in confusion. How did she know he was a wolf?

"Don't worry about her," a voice said. "She's always been a little strange."

"Cassandra, why does she think I'm a wolf? There are no wolves in Nazberath," Hero said a little shakily.

"Because of your eyes," Cassandra explained. "You have the eyes of the legendary Lone Wolf. She thinks you are Lone Wolf, and that you are evil."

"Evil? But Lone Wolf is suppose to be good isn't he?" Hero spluttered.

"For most of the world yes, and I guess this means you're with King Dervik," Cassandra sighed.

"Huh?" Hero asked.

"We're with Feruh, and therefore with the great Queen Arlyn. While everyone in King Dervik's realm sits spouting the fantasy about the Lone Wolf, we do realistic things such as farming to supply our troops," Cassandra smiled.

"Troops? You mean to tell me that Feruh is heading off to war?" Hero gulped.

"Of course. Feruh is going to Zenbin to join the army massed at the border. We attack Delring in one month. Queen Arlyn has decided it would be a heavy blow to King Dervik if we take out his capital city," Cassandra explained, a smile on her lips.

"I don't understand. You all seem such nice people," Hero murmured.

"That's what I hate about people like you," Cassandra snarled. "You think just because we support Queen Arlyn we have to be savages who want nothing but destruction. Queen Arlyn only wants to grow her empire. She would do this through negotiation, but that selfish King of yours refuses.

King Dervik is the bad guy here. He has his vast empire, while ours is so much smaller, but he will not allow us to expand to fit our empire's needs."

"And what does your empire need more land for?" Hero demanded firmly.

"We need land for our growing population. Queen Arlyn does not fight this war out of hate. She fights it to help us," Cassandra sighed.

"Oh really? From what I hear, she's a sadistic witch who enjoys torturing people for fun," Hero snarled.

"Yet you hear this from people who were taught that she is evil," Cassandra pointed out.

"No, I heard it from a man who lived in Carthafell," Hero said with a smirk.

"A thief, no doubt," Cassandra argued. "Who only hated her because she threw him in prison for breaking the law."

"Wrong again. This man was her younger brother, Merrick," Hero finished triumphantly.

Surprisingly, Cassandra started to laugh. She patted him on the cheek as if he were a clueless child. He waited impatiently for her to stop laughing, which took her longer than he thought necessary.

"You poor man," she cooed. "Of course, Merrick would say that. He's a traitor to Carthafell."

"Explain yourself now," Hero snapped.

"Two years ago Merrick started a small rebel group to try to take down the royal house. He wanted to be King, and so he decided he would murder Queen Arlyn and General Muryn," Cassandra explained. "But they caught the little fool and brought him before Queen Arlyn.

"Now Arlyn could've had him killed for treason, but she spared him, announcing to the country that she couldn't possibly hurt her own brother, even though he was only her half-brother. Merrick escaped from prison and tried to kill Arlyn in her sleep, but she used her magic to hold him at bay. Still she didn't use her full strength because she thought she could help him.

"Again Merrick escaped, but General Muryn captured him this time. He was not so merciful. He blinded Merrick in the right eye, but he escaped yet again. Queen Arlyn has not abandoned the search, hoping to find him and straighten the hate he has for her."

"That's a lie," Hero snarled. "You're lying. Merrick would never do such a thing."

"Oh really? How long have you known him?" Cassandra asked, a smile on her lips.

"I've known him long enough to know that everything he told me was the truth," Hero fired back. "You heard your story from Arlyn and, of course, she would bend the details to her favor!"

"You better watch what you say around here, Lucius," Cassandra said. "We of Shiboo support Queen Arlyn's every decision, and if you declare yourself her enemy, then we are also your enemy."

She walked away after giving him one last smile. Hero's eyes blazed with rage. He knew that she had lied, that Merrick was the man he knew. People stared at him as they passed, wondering why he looked ready to kill someone. Hero stormed off in the direction of the woods. It was high time he and Jeru left, before Arlyn could order the attack on Delring. He found the young boy and Molly staring up at a willow.

"Jeru we're leaving," Hero said gruffly.

He saw small lights dancing through the willow's branches. They must have been the fairies.

"Right now? Why?" Jeru asked.

"Maybe he is hungry," Molly said slyly.

"Shut up," Hero ordered. "This is not the town for us," he added to Jeru.

"Huh? Why not?" Jeru asked.

"Because you two support the King, and we support the Queen," Molly smiled.

"What?" Jeru exclaimed.

"These people are with Queen Arlyn. I guess they're a part of Feruh. We need to go now. I have some bad news to tell you," Hero explained quickly.

"Lone Wolf," Molly cried as they turned to go.

"What?" Hero snapped.

"Take the path to the left, neither of the right paths lead the right way," Molly finished, turning back to the willow tree.

Hero nodded and hurried back to the inn where he had stashed their remaining food. Charlotte handed them both a big bag and waved them farewell, clueless to their anxious expressions.

"So what's the bad news?" Jeru asked as they walked out the door.

"I'll tell you when we're out of here," Hero whispered. He saw the townspeople approaching.

"Now, now Lucius, we can't have you leaving and telling King Dervik about our plans. Not that you'll ever reach Delring in a month anyway," a voice sang.

It was Cassandra again. She led the townspeople in an effort to block the two men from leaving. Hero felt nothing but a burning hate for the woman and the people standing behind her. He saw Molly from the corner of his eye, but she refused to join in. She just watched him with a smile.

"You get out of my way," Hero warned, baring his teeth.

"There are only two of you, if you hadn't noticed," Cassandra smirked.

"Good," Jeru smiled, pulling out a large knife.

The townspeople raised all sorts of farming tools and charged. Hero drew his sword and started to hack through weapon and flesh alike. He had to make it to Delring and warn the King about the upcoming war. A large man knocked his sword from his hand, and Hero lunged, fighting like a wolf again. He ripped out the man's throat with surprising ease.

He felt his teeth, and found that they had returned to his wolf teeth. He laughed and lunged for the next opponent. Soon the people ran away, but Hero had to finish one off. Cassandra backed away, holding the fragments of a hoe in her left hand. Hero walked forward slowly. Cassandra gave a frightened squeak and ran, but Hero pounced and killed her.

"Hero, what happened to you?" Jeru asked, as Hero's teeth returned to their human form.

"I don't know," Hero replied truthfully.

"I knew it was you, Lone Wolf," Molly said cheerfully, as if the pile of dead bodies in front of her just didn't exist. "Did you like my trick with your teeth?"

"Who are you really?" Jeru asked. "You can't be normal."

"You're right. I'm the Fairy Queen and fairies can see people in the forms as they should be. You, Lone Wolf, I see you as a wolf, not a human like all the others. You have such a beautiful coloration in your fur. And your eyes, simply amazing," Molly laughed as her pupils turned pink and the whites of her eyes, purple.

"You mean you see me as a wolf?" Hero asked.

"Yes, and I must say you are very beautiful," Molly smiled. "Jeru, I also sense a wolf's spirit within you, but you are still a human, why?"

"I used to be a wolf. Then I died and was reborn as a human," Jeru explained proudly.

"I see," Molly mused. "Many things exist in this world that even I do not understand. Please come visit me again when you have more time."

"You can count on it. Even though you're a Queen, you're still going to be my dance partner," Jeru laughed.

"Let's go," Hero exclaimed, running toward the woods once more.

"Good luck, Lone Wolf. And you, too, Jeru," Molly called after them.

"That was very strange," Jeru said once they turned down the inner left path.

"Yes, we must hurry Jeru. Cassandra told me that Queen Arlyn will launch an all out war on the city of Delring in a month," Hero said earnestly.

"A month? We'll never make it in time," Jeru wailed. "It'll take at least a month to get across Feruh!"

"Well, we have to try, Jeru," Hero snapped. "We can't turn back at this point! Our only option is to go forward, so let's go."

"Right...you're right," Jeru murmured, picking up his pace.

They started to run, but their food bags weighed them down, so they progressed a little more slowly than usual.

"We need horses," Jeru panted.

"I know. Maybe we'll pass a farm up ahead," Hero hoped.

Breathing heavily, Jeru couldn't answer; he didn't like running with heavy bags on his back. Hero also knew that his young friend probably thought they had no chance of finding a horse before crossing Demon's Peak, and that finding one in Feruh could prove to be a very dangerous thing. He sighed and, not for the first time, wished that Phoebus had not died.

They stopped early that night, exhausted from the day's events. Hero unpacked some of their older food so it wouldn't go bad. He and Jeru ate in silence, both thinking over the new dangers that awaited them. Hero knew that if they couldn't get into Delring on time, they would probably run into a full-fledged war. He also couldn't stop thinking about Molly. He almost wished she had joined them. She had seen him for who he truly was, and he liked that. He wanted to be a wolf again, and at least he now knew that someone knew his secret without him having to explain it. He sighed as he thought about her, wondering if he would ever see her again so that he could ask her questions about her vast knowledge.

"She was awfully pretty," Jeru murmured, and Hero knew he was thinking about the Fairy Queen too.

"Too bad she didn't come," Hero sighed.

"Hey, she's my girl," Jeru said playfully. "You said you were in love with Nakoomu."

"Oh right, must have slipped my mind," Hero grinned. "No, I just wanted to ask her some questions."

"Me too," Jeru agreed.

"Well, we better get some sleep. We'll have to get up earlier and stop later if we want to make it in…well, to get there as fast as we can," Hero said, curling up.

"Okay," Jeru said quietly, stretching himself out on his back. "Hey Hero, what's going to happen if we don't get there in time?"

"I don't know. We may have to try to stop a war," Hero said softly.

"Stop the war? I guess I better sharpen my knife," Jeru muttered to himself.

Hero heard him, but decided not to answer. Jeru was right. It was going to be almost impossible to stop the attack on Delring with words. They would have to talk with their weapons. But how could two extra people make any difference. He thought about what Cassandra had told him about Arlyn. Was she really the innocent one in all of this? He shook his head and remembered what Merrick had told him about the Queen of Carthafell. She was evil, and the evil in Nazberath had to be destroyed in order to save Verinaul.

Chapter 19

Jacquelyn and Merrick had passed Hero and Jeru without knowing it. Since they hadn't stopped in Shiboo and since Merrick knew the right way to Demon's Peak, they were a good day ahead of the former wolves, though they still believed they trailed behind.

"Do you think he knew which path to take?" Jacquelyn asked.

"I'm not sure. I hope he took this one," Merrick replied. "Otherwise he'll never make it to the Hurith Gate."

"I'm so sick of this mountain range," Jacquelyn complained. "I just want to get into Feruh and be done with it."

"Once we get into Feruh, you'll be singing a different tune. That country is full of danger, especially to outsiders," Merrick explained. "There will be a lot of fighting before we're out of there."

"Oh wonderful," Jacquelyn said sarcastically. "That's exactly how I want to spend my visit to a foreign country—killing the natives."

Merrick rolled his eyes as Isabell let out a chuckle. Then they saw a mountain rise in front of them.

"Is that Demon's Peak?" Jacquelyn asked.

"No. That's the last mountain before Demon's Peak. Don't worry. It's an easy climb," Merrick explained. He pointed to a dark smudge against the sky. "That's Demon's Peak."

"But it practically reaches the heavens," Jacquelyn exclaimed.

"It is beautiful, in its own way," Merrick admitted. "Though after we climb it, you may think a little differently."

Jacquelyn sighed. She really wished they could cut a break occasionally. The smaller mountain's foothills loomed up out of nowhere, and soon they found themselves climbing up the rocky path. It wasn't steep, but it was a very big mountain. Jacquelyn looked up at the sky and saw the peak staring down at her. She sighed again; she never wanted to see another mountain after this trip.

"We should rest," Merrick said as night fell upon them.

They had made it up quite far, in Jacquelyn's opinion. She could still see the bottom of the path, but it was far below them. She helped Merrick prepare some food and then started a small fire to cook their dinner.

"You know, I think we may have to find some more food before we climb Demon's Peak. That mountain will take at least a week to climb, and we're going to need a lot of food to restore our energy," Merrick said, looking at the remaining food. Jacquelyn suggested that she make a special drink from some of her herbs. It would revitalize them after a long day of hard travel.

"What kind of herbs do you need?" Merrick asked.

"I have them already," Jacquelyn smiled. "I figured we would need them to climb Demon's Peak, so I saved them. I'll mix the herbs with some water and make the drink now. The longer it sits before we drink it, the stronger it becomes."

"That's amazing. So, by the top, when we're really tired, it will make us feel like new?" Merrick asked.

"Yes, my mother created the drink. She just called it an energy potion, but I'm going to name it Clara's Elixir," Jacquelyn smiled.

"Clara was your mother's name?" Merrick guessed.

"Yes, she was a wonderful woman. Always so kind and gentle, but when she needed to be she was as strong as an ox. Mother always helped me out of trouble, like when I went in the woods and some mean men tried to steal me, she came out of nowhere and fought them off," Jacquelyn said, a small tear of emotion sliding down her cheek. "I told her not to go out that winter. She already had a cold, but she went anyway, saying she was going to heal herself. When she didn't come back, I knew that she couldn't have made it.

"Father found her the next day, frozen solid in the snow. She was caught in an unexpected storm that night. My father said it was the Divine Punishment, to make mother repent for her 'witchcraft.' We were never as close from that moment on.

"I just wish that she hadn't gone. I wish that she had just waited for daylight and then gone into town to buy medicine from the doctor. I think about it every time I gather herbs, and it never stops hurting."

By now, Jacquelyn was sobbing. She had never talked about her mother so much before, and she found it rather painful. Merrick stared at her sympathetically but couldn't think of anything to say. Jacquelyn wiped her eyes furiously. She didn't want Merrick to think she was weak.

"It's all right to let it out, you know," he smiled. "Crying doesn't mean you're weak or anything. When you have a good reason, which you do, then there is nothing to be ashamed of."

"Thank you, but she probably wouldn't want me to cry about her every time I talk or think of her," Jacquelyn said, forcing herself to smile.

"Oh I don't know. She's probably very happy that you care for her so much," Merrick replied.

Jacquelyn nodded and took a small bite of her food. She thought about what Merrick had said. She appreciated him being so nice, but she didn't really know how to let him know. She glanced over and saw him touch his scarred eye lightly, a scowl on his face. She knew then what to do.

Once she made sure he was asleep, she and Isabell rummaged through some of the clothes they had. They found a black tunic that belonged to Hero, and since he wasn't with them, Jacquelyn decided to use that. She then went into the forest and gathered some stiff herbs and flexible tree bark.

She slit the tree bark in half and stuffed the herbs in between. Then she forced the tree bark back together. Isabell leaned her head down, and Jacquelyn cut a few hairs from her mane. She sewed the back of the homemade pouch closed to keep the herbs in. Then she cut the bark into a patch shape. After she completed that step, she took the tunic and cut it into the patch's shape. She took more hair from Isabell's tail and sewed the tunic over the bark. She looked at her handiwork, and Isabell swore it was better than his other one.

"Almost done," Jacquelyn smiled.

She went back to the small grove of trees and found some stringy vines. She went back to the camp and rolled them together into a fine, but sturdy, rope. She cut more of the tunic and wrapped it around the vines. She then attached the rope to the patch so that it was finally complete.

"Thanks for the help," Jacquelyn said.

"No problem. I was glad to," Isabell replied.

"I hope it fits. You did judge the length right, didn't you?" Jacquelyn asked nervously.

"Well, I do know almost everything about him," Isabell said proudly.

Jacquelyn smiled and lay down to sleep. She would give him the gift tomorrow morning before they rode out. She looked at it once more and smiled; it really was quite good.

"Merrick," Jacquelyn said as they started to head out again. "I made you a gift."

"Huh? What for?" Merrick asked.

"Well, for being there for me when I've made all those mistakes, and for cheering me up when I was sad about mother," Jacquelyn explained.

She held out the eye-patch she had made the previous night. Merrick took it and examined it. His face blossomed to a smile, and he ruffled Jacquelyn's hair playfully.

"Thanks Jackie," he grinned. "This is really something. I love it."

He put it over his scarred eye, and Jacquelyn made sure it fit snugly. Merrick thanked her again, and she blushed with pride. They mounted their horses and started up the large mountain again.

"You know, this has been a great journey when I think about it," Merrick said after an hour of riding. "If I hadn't met you and Hero, then I would probably be back in Carthafell by now."

"I suppose when you look at it from a positive view, it really has been great. I've had a lot of fun since meeting you and Hero. Although we've experienced hardships, we've dealt with them together and have grown really close," Jacquelyn mused. "I mean, I think of you as an older brother and well, Hero you know about. Even you, Isabell, I think of you as part of my family."

"That's really sweet, considering I'm a few species removed," Isabell said. "Thanks Jacquelyn."

"When I think about it, I realize how much beauty Nazberath has. All the people, plants, and animals...all of it...is just so precious," Jacquelyn whispered.

"Unless you count the people who are trying to destroy that beauty," Merrick pointed out.

"That's why we have to stop them," Jacquelyn decided. "We have to make them understand what a perfect world this would be if they stopped fighting."

"Maybe that's Hero's task," Isabell guessed. "Maybe he is supposed to talk to the people."

"Well, he may have taken a wrong path and therefore be behind us. If that is so, then we will have to carry out the message in his name," Merrick declared.

"Yes, we can tell them all that Hero, the Lone Wolf, is among us," Jacquelyn laughed. "Unless we meet up with him in Delring," she added hopefully.

They were silent after that. Jacquelyn wished now that she had told Hero how she felt. She wanted to see him again and hold him in her arms. She loved him with all her heart, but knew that he waited for Nakoomu. Maybe she could convince him that she loved him more than the wolf, and maybe Nakoomu had already found another mate.

She shook herself mentally; she just couldn't do that to him. If she really loved him, she would tell him and support him in any way he needed. Even if that meant supporting his love for Nakoomu. She sighed and looked up at the mountain path in front of her. The peak loomed in the distance.

As they continued up the mountain, Jacquelyn thought she heard a faint cracking noise, as if a twig were snapped in half. She looked around in the boulders and scraggly trees but saw no sign of danger. So she tried to ignore it, but she couldn't shake the feeling that they were being watched. She shifted uncomfortably and looked around at the surroundings again. There was nothing.

After ten minutes of riding, Jacquelyn figured that she had just heard a small animal so she stopped worrying about it. She settled back in her saddle to the comfort of Moon Dance, who had begun to catch her mood and had turned skittish. Once Jacquelyn relaxed, the mare followed suit. The sun started to set as they walked on and on. Finally, Merrick stopped and turned around in his saddle.

"I think we should stop here," he began, but couldn't finish.

As he spoke, a large arrow pierced through his chest and almost hit his heart dead on. He toppled off of Isabell, who whinnied with fright. Jacquelyn cried out and jumped off of Moon Dance as another arrow hit the horse in the flank. Moon Dance fell to her side and thrashed about, landing a painful blow to Jacquelyn's shoulder. But she didn't care; she crawled forward to try to get to Merrick, who was guarded by Isabell. Before she could reach him, two familiar figures emerged from cover—Hynraz and the other old one who had escaped with him.

"Well, now that the threat is eliminated, we shouldn't have any problems. Nice shot Waylien," Hynraz sneered.

The older demon laughed and brandished his long oak bow arrogantly. Jacquelyn stood up and drew her short sword.

"I swear I will kill you demons," she snarled.

"You're out-numbered, and you are no warrior. You should give up, or I may have to scar that lovely face of yours," Hynraz smiled.

"You've scarred me enough," Jacquelyn growled. "How about we have a duel. Waylien can't help you, and we fight to the death."

"Master, forgive me, but wouldn't it be better to just finish this quickly. Queen Arlyn is growing impatient," Waylien pointed out.

"I guess you're right. Sorry little lady, but I'm just going to have to have my comrade kill you. Make sure you do it nice and quick now," Hynraz laughed.

"I got it," Waylien smiled, notching another barbed arrow onto his bowstring.

Jacquelyn froze; she didn't want to give any hints on her movement. As soon as the arrow was loosed she would dive to the left, closer to Merrick. She tensed her body and got ready. Waylien released his grip slightly and Jacquelyn dove to the ground. But the demon hadn't let the arrow fly. He had predicted her move, and now she was flat on her stomach with no way of getting up.

"Good bye, beautiful," Hynraz sneered as Waylien got the arrow ready again.

Waylien readied to fire when a large stone hit him right between the eyes. He stumbled back and fell down the path for a few feet, smacking his head against a rock. The blow knocked him out, and a small pool of blood spread slowly around his head like a halo.

Jacquelyn and Hynraz looked around for the assailant and saw Merrick, leaning heavily against Isabell and clutching at the arrow in his chest. He was bleeding heavily, and Jacquelyn knew he needed medical care as soon as possible.

"You really are amazing, I'll give you that," the red-headed demon sighed, shaking his head.

"Merrick, stay down," Jacquelyn exclaimed.

"I'm going to kill you now. I'm sick of seeing you around," Merrick said in a low voice, gasping for breath.

"I'd like to see you try, in your condition," Hynraz taunted.

Merrick drew his sword and charged at the demon. Hynraz got his own red-colored blade ready and parried Merrick's blow, which was slow and sloppy. Merrick lashed out with his weapon again, but Hynraz dodged and kicked Merrick in the stomach. Merrick fell to his knees and sat, catching his breath. Jacquelyn rushed forward and blocked the demon's sword as he brought it down to strike Merrick.

Hynraz chuckled cruelly and brought his sword above his head, bringing it down on Jacquelyn's with all of his strength. Jacquelyn's sword snapped in half. She threw down the useless hilt and grabbed the blade, ignoring the pain as it cut into her skin. She drove the blade at Hynraz's heart, but the demon jumped behind her and raked his sword against her back. She felt her blood spill from the wound and stain her dress, but she ignored the pain. She turned around and threw her broken sword at him. Hynraz jumped again, but the sword buried itself into his leg. He yelped with shock and pain.

"You'll pay for that," he said, no amusement in his voice.

His eyes started to glow, as did his sword. The sword became encircled with a raging fire, the color of blood. He swung the sword in her direction and a blast of fire raced toward her. She dove to the ground, cringing as the heat touched her wounded back. She stood up only to face another jet of fire. She leapt behind a boulder and gulped as the fire hit where she had stood only moments before.

"You should pay more attention when you fight, little girl. Take in every aspect," came the demon's voice.

She peaked her head from around the boulder and looked at him. He pointed to Merrick who had collapsed. Jacquelyn was about to run to him, but Hynraz pointed the sword at the wounded man.

"What do you want?" Jacquelyn demanded, stepping into view.

"I want to carry out my Queen's orders. Round up this little vagabond and find the Lone Wolf. Bring both back to Carthafell and kill any who stand in the way. It must feel awful to be unwanted, hm? Now you have to die and can't join us on our trip," Hynraz smirked.

"I would much rather die than be in the presence of that monster you call a Queen!" Jacquelyn backfired.

"I don't take kindly to harsh words about my Queen," Hynraz snarled.

He rushed forward and punched Jacquelyn in the face. She fell back against the boulder and covered herself as more blows rained down on her. Once the demon relented, she sank down to her knees, feeling her swollen lip and blackened eyes. Hynraz looked at her for a minute and sighed.

"Such beauty wasted. You should have never joined this silly quest. You should have stayed home, or rebuilt it I should say, then you could have been safe," he said.

He brought his sword above her head and prepared to strike her down when Merrick regained consciousness and stood up. Hynraz turned to him with amusement in his eyes, as if it were all some great entertainment.

"First things first," Merrick muttered. "Have to get this arrow out."

"Ha! That arrow is barbed. You won't be able to just pull it out," Hynraz barked.

"I didn't say I was going to pull it out," Merrick spat.

The arrow was buried in his chest with most of the shaft sticking out in front. The tip of the arrow was still deep inside him, but he concentrated on the visible part. He snapped off the back where the feathers had been and breathed deeply for a second. Then he jumped and didn't put his hands in the way to block his fall. He landed on his chest, driving the arrow through his back and causing it to stick out there instead of in the front. He grunted in pain. After a moment, he gritted his teeth together and felt at the shaft. The arrowhead itself was out, so he grabbed it right below the stone and pulled. The thin wooden shaft slipped out of his body, covered with warm blood.

"Merrick," Jacquelyn gasped.

"Unbelievable," Hynraz said.

"Now that that's out of the way," Merrick panted. "We can have some fun."

He grabbed his sword and rushed at the demon. Hynraz just laughed and stepped away as soon as Merrick swung at him. Merrick turned and struck at Hynraz again, but the demon jumped in the air and drew a small knife from his belt. He threw it at Merrick, and it lodged itself into his left leg. Merrick fell to the ground with a growl.

"Merrick, please stop fighting," Jacquelyn cried. "You can't beat him when you're this wounded!"

"Quiet. This demon won't beat me," Merrick snarled, pulling the knife out of his flesh.

"Persistent little vermin aren't you?" Hynraz taunted. "You really should listen to the lady."

"*No way! You're dead!*" Merrick yelled, stumbling forward.

Hynraz rushed up to meet him and smashed his elbow into Merrick's forehead. The wounded man fell back a few steps, clutching his throbbing skull. He swung his sword at the demon, but Hynraz blocked it with his own and knocked the sword from Merrick's hand. Merrick sank down onto his knees.

"Time to go back to Carthafell," Hynraz smiled.

Jacquelyn ran to the fighters and placed herself between Merrick and Hynraz. Her arms held open wide, and her face, determined.

"I won't let you take him back there," she declared.

"As if you had the authority to tell me that," Hynraz laughed, stepping forward.

As he prepared to cut her down, Isabell galloped over and reared up on her hind legs. She brought her front hooves down on Hynraz as hard as she could. The demon threw his arm in the way to avoid being killed, but Jacquelyn heard the bones snap. Hynraz fell off the nearby ledge, cursing the unicorn with every vile word he could think of.

"Isabell, you did it. You killed Hynraz!" Jacquelyn exclaimed.

"I'm afraid not," the horse sighed. "Demons like Hynraz, who have a position of power, can't be killed so easily. I believe the only way is to separate the head from the neck or to stab them through the heart."

"That will at least get him off our trail for a long time though," Jacquelyn pointed out. "The most important thing is to tend to Merrick."

She sat down on her knees beside Merrick, who had by then fallen to his back. She examined the deep hole in his chest, and the smaller wound in his leg. Merrick was breathing hard, and he still bled rather heavily.

"I need to work very quickly. Isabell please fetch my bag of herbs," Jacquelyn said softly.

Isabell trotted over to Moon Dance, who had stood up and was trying to keep all her weight off her own wound. Isabell grabbed the bag of herbs with her teeth and brought it back over to Jacquelyn who set to work making a salve to clean the wound and stop the bleeding. Merrick had fallen unconscious by then and had grown very pale. Jacquelyn mixed the ingredients with shaking hands.

"I know this isn't the time, but do you now love Merrick?" Isabell asked tentatively.

Jacquelyn thought about it for a minute, never stopping in her task.

"You know," she said, "I don't. I feel strongly for him, but only as a really good friend. I know Merrick will always be there for me, and I'll be there for him. However, this feeling definitely isn't love. I think I just feel that he is like a brother to me."

"I see. So you love him, but not in a romantic way," Isabell replied.

"Exactly. I still love Hero, even though his mind is only focused on Nakoomu, and he will never love anyone else," Jacquelyn said sadly.

"If it doesn't work out between you two, then I'm sure you'll find a nice husband who will treat you well," Isabell smiled.

Jacquelyn smiled to herself as she boiled more herbs in water. While they brewed, Jacquelyn began to tear out strips from her dress to make bandages. Isabell put her muzzle to Merrick's face and nudged him gently. Merrick's eye opened slightly, and he groaned.

"Are you all right, Merrick?" Isabell asked softly.

"I don't know," Merrick answered truthfully.

"Don't worry, Merrick, I know what to do," Jacquelyn smiled. "You'll be better in no time."

"I think the arrow might have pierced my lung," Merrick rasped, coughing up some more blood.

"You'll be okay Merrick. Jacquelyn will make you okay," Isabell whispered anxiously.

"That's right. Just relax Merrick and I'll have you fixed up," Jacquelyn urged.

Merrick closed his eye and started to breathe deeply. Jacquelyn knew she had to work fast. She couldn't let Merrick die, not after all he had done for her. She took out the boiled herbs and gently rubbed them into a thick lather. She spread this over both wounds and then wrapped them up with the strips of cloth.

"Don't die, please," Jacquelyn whispered, while Isabell paced nervously nearby. "I can't do this alone."

Chapter 20

Hero and Jeru had been making good time. They had seen demons on the mountain, but Jeru knew a shortcut to the top. So they had been running up the large mountain for the main part of the day. When the sun started to sink to the west, Jeru suggested they stop since they had made such good time that day.

"I wonder what those two demons were doing around here," Jeru said as he prepared water for the dinner.

"Looking for me and my friends," Hero answered. "The Queen of Carthafell wants me and her younger brother."

"Do you think that they were tracking your friend?" Jeru asked.

"I hope not. If so, then I think Merrick would have noticed them and gone into hiding with Jacquelyn," Hero replied, hoping he was right.

"How were you and Jacquelyn connected?" Jeru asked slyly.

"As I said, she is my friend, that is all. Although she is very kind to me, I cannot share any love. I just love Nakoomu too much. I wouldn't even think of betraying her. Even if the woman lived in a whole different world," Hero replied sharply.

"Sorry, I was just fooling around though," Jeru sighed. "I know you wouldn't do that to your one true love. But what does Jacquelyn feel for you I wonder."

"From what I can tell, she just thinks of me as her best friend. Maybe even an older brother. Hopefully that's all, because I really don't want to hurt her," Hero said sadly.

The night he had heard Jacquelyn and Merrick talking about him had vanished from his memory after all that had happened. Besides, even if he did remember, it could have just been a dream.

"Okay, one last question," Jeru said as he threw rabbit meat into the boiling water. "What if Jacquelyn said she loved you?"

"Then I would have to tell her the truth. I would just tell her, gently, that I don't have those sorts of feelings toward her," Hero said.

"I see," Jeru smiled. "It must be hard following one's heart. Now me, I think I may be in love with Molly."

"Do you think it's possible for a former wolf to end up with the Queen of Fairies?" Hero asked with a grin.

"Hey, once I throw on the charm she'll be all over me," Jeru boasted. "You'll see."

"Maybe," Hero laughed. "All I want to see is this rabbit soup in my bowl."

Jeru laughed too and ladled some of the steaming soup into Hero's wooden bowl. Hero began to eat right away, ignoring how hot it was. He slurped up the rest, and Jeru offered him another bowl, which he didn't refuse.

"Phew. I was starving," Hero sighed after the meal.

He sat back and rubbed his full stomach. Jeru set his bowl aside and lay down on his back, gazing at the cloudy sky. Hero followed his gaze and saw the dim outline of the moon trying to break through the blackness that blocked its radiance. Hero heard Jeru sigh and looked over to see his young friend sitting up and staring at a nearby boulder.

"What are you looking at?" Hero asked.

"The boulder looks as if it has a face with the light catching it that way," Jeru explained, pointing the rock's face.

Hero looked, and, after a second, saw how the light caught the boulder in such a way that it did seem a rough and scraggly face stared back at them. Hero smiled and sat closer to the boulder.

"It's like the guardian of the mountain," Jeru smiled. "It watches all who come up to his lair."

"Oh really? And what about the people who climb the normal path?" Hero asked.

"He can see everything that happens on his mountain. He can jump from rock to rock in seconds, scouting his home and making sure nothing bad comes forth," Jeru replied.

"Those demons are pretty bad," Hero pointed out.

"Yes, but by now they are probably off the mountain and wounded," Jeru persisted.

"So are you a psychic now, or what?" Hero grinned.

"Laugh while you can, my friend. Pretty soon you'll learn that I'm excellent at guessing the future," Jeru bragged.

"Oh really? And what is in store for my future?" Hero asked with a smirk.

"Umm...I don't know. You are very confusing deep down inside. How would you like it if I told you that you would save the world and make it back to Verinaul?" Jeru asked sheepishly.

"I would like that very much," Hero laughed.

"All right then. That's your future. And for me, my future is to get a good night's sleep before tomorrow," Jeru yawned, stretching out on the ground.

Hero followed suit and was soon fast asleep.

Hero had a strange dream that night. He was running through a battlefield. The ground was soaked with blood, and he slipped in it as he ran. People stood above him and swung heavy weapons at him, narrowly missing. Hero leapt and bit their throats out, causing more blood to spill. He saw the flags of Carthafell waving in the wind and men in red armor advancing upon a city. He rushed forward, not knowing why it was so important to keep them from the city's walls.

He slid to a stop and nicked his paw on a sharp stone. He saw his claws stain red, and he could feel the blood of others in his mouth. He stood before the great gates of the city, alone against the charging army. Just a lone wolf protecting everything he had come to love. As soon as the army reached him, he vanished and slipped into a dark abyss, and nothing was all around him.

Suddenly, he heard footsteps. He looked back and saw Jacquelyn walking toward him with Merrick not far behind. They looked worn out, and both appeared wounded, but they smiled at him. He heard more steps and looked back over his shoulder at Jeru, who had returned to being a wolf also.

"Hero," Jacquelyn whispered.

"What is this?" Hero asked, but his voice was gone. He opened his mouth and a bark came forth.

"Hero Red Eye...Hurry to Delring...There is no time," Merrick pleaded, rubbing at his chest where a stain of dried blood could be seen.

"I'm trying to go as fast as I can," Hero tried to assure them, but he could only bark and growl like a wolf.

"Run Hero. Run until you drop," Jeru barked.

Hero woke with a start to the sound of a heavy wind. He sat up and saw that Jeru was also awake. The young boy was tying their supplies together to keep them from blowing away. Hero walked over to help him, but his mind wasn't really focused on his task.

"Are you okay?" Jeru asked. "You look really pale."

"I-I'm fine," Hero lied.

Jeru gave him a questioning look but said no more. They tied the bundle to the large boulder to make sure the wind wouldn't carry it away. Then they made their way back to sleep until dawn, though neither felt really sleepy any more.

"This isn't a natural wind," Jeru said suddenly. "Someone skilled with magic is causing it."

"What?" Hero exclaimed. "Who?"

"Me," a voice snarled.

Hero and Jeru leapt up and saw Hynraz step into view. His hand glowed red, and that, evidently, was how he gathered energy for the wind. His left arm was badly mangled, and Hero knew it was broken. Black blood oozed onto his face from a head wound. Behind him stood the old demon, Waylien, who was also bleeding from his head.

"No holding back for you. You're dead," Hynraz snarled.

For the first time, Hero felt really afraid of this demon. He knew that Hynraz had been pushed into a terrible rage, and that he would kill anyone in his path. The demon's red eyes blazed, and he fixed them on Hero's.

"Hero, catch!" Jeru shouted, tossing Hero his sword.

Hero caught it and drew it from its sheath. Hynraz grabbed his own sword, which was chipped but still dangerous, and he rushed at Hero with unmatchable speed. Hero dove from his path and saw that Jeru had engaged Waylien in battle as well. Hynraz let out a snarl of pure fury and launched himself at Hero again. Hero picked up a rock and hurled it at the demon's broken arm. The rock smashed into the arm, and Hynraz stumbled.

Hero rushed up and kicked the demon in the jaw. Hynraz growled and swung his sword at Hero. Hero jumped back, but wasn't expecting the wave of fire that shot from the red blade. He felt his skin crawl as the flames surrounded him and forced him into the air. He slammed against a tree and sank to the ground. Panting, he stood up and quickly felt his body for any major burns. He found only a few, and the more serious ones were small. He bared his teeth and charged at the sneering demon.

"I won't let you hinder us any longer!" Hero yelled.

Hynraz snarled and blocked Hero's sword. Not missing a beat, Hero kicked out and hit the demon in the chest. Hynraz cried out, but the kick didn't stop him from punching Hero in the jaw. Hero fell back a step and spit the blood from his mouth.

"You know, I'm going to leave you dead. Just like your one-eyed friend," Hynraz sneered.

"What? You killed Merrick?" Hero gasped.

"Pretty much. Getting hit in the chest with an arrow must be very painful," the red-headed demon smiled.

"Curse you!" Hero shouted.

He lunged forward and slashed Hynraz across the stomach. Hynraz bellowed in agony, but had enough strength to stab at Hero's arm. The red blade pierced through Hero's arm causing him to grit his teeth in pain. Hynraz grinned evilly as he pulled his sword out of Hero's arm and backed away, clutching at his own bleeding stomach. Hero felt the blood that poured from both ends of his arm and growled.

He walked slowly toward Hynraz, and the demon prepared for an attack. Hero remembered his dream, how both Jacquelyn and Merrick appeared wounded and knew that those wounds must have come from Hynraz and the old demon. He used this to his advantage, his anger growing and causing him to forget the throbbing pain of his arm. He narrowed his eyes and charged.

Both Hero and Hynraz lashed out at the same moment. However, Hero's blade penetrated Hynraz's chest, while the demon's blade plunged into Hero's side. Both withdrew their swords and collapsed to their knees. Hero was panting and knew that the wounds he had inflicted upon his enemy should at least slow him down. He got back up and saw Hynraz do the same.

"I will kill you," Hero threatened.

"I don't think so. Even if the Queen wants you alive, I will make sure you are dead," Hynraz replied darkly.

Hero smirked and ran forward, ignoring the intense pain of his injuries. Hynraz let out a battle cry and charged as well. The demon swung his sword at Hero's neck, but Hero dropped down quickly to avoid the fatal blow. He straightened up and slashed at Hynraz's head, but the demon leapt back. Hero rushed forward and pretended to aim for the head again, but as soon as Hynraz raised his sword to block the blow, Hero dropped his sword lower and stabbed the demon through the heart. Hynraz cried out and fell. Hero smirked and turned his back to the dying demon.

"You will not live through the night, Hynraz," he said.

"Maybe so, but you won't either!" Hynraz shouted.

He launched himself forward and slashed Hero across the back. Hero felt the sword penetrate the skin from the left shoulder to his right. Hynraz then brought the sword diagonally across Hero's back, causing a wound that looked like half a "Z." It wasn't a shallow wound either. Hero fell to the ground and saw Hynraz fall nearby.

"It looks like we'll be going to hell together, Lone Wolf," Hynraz sneered.

"At least I brought you with me," Hero smirked.

Hynraz chuckled and closed his blazing red eyes. He breathed heavily for a few minutes, but then he exhaled one last time. Hero watched to make sure, but when the demon's chest didn't rise again, he relaxed and closed his own eyes.

"*Hero, don't' close your eyes! Stay awake!*" a voice screamed.

Hero opened his eyes half way and saw Jeru kneeling beside him. He had a cut on his forehead, and his side was soaked with blood too. Hero smiled, and Jeru sighed with some relief to find him alive.

"You're bleeding all over the place," Jeru whispered.

"I know," Hero panted. "I doubt I'm going to last the night like this."

"Come on now, you can't die here. What about Nakoomu?" Jeru cried.

"I hope she doesn't wait her whole life for me," Hero whispered. "She deserves happiness, not misery."

"If you don't want her to be miserable, then you will get up and live. You hear me, Hero? You have to *live!*" Jeru exclaimed.

"But I've got so many wounds," Hero said weakly.

"Let me see," Jeru replied, removing his friend's shirt gently. He gasped at the long gashes. "Small burns here and there. The main worry is your arm, side and this gash on your back."

"I feel numb...and drowsy," Hero whispered.

"Don't you dare give in, Hero. Think about anything that will keep you alive. Tell me about something that happened to you or something," Jeru pleaded.

"Very well," Hero said weakly. "I remember I felt this way once before. It was on my first hunt…I remember the first month when I left the pack. I ran until I knew the pack couldn't find me. I found myself in a desert.

"It was so harsh where I lived…and empty. I thought about a lot of things, mainly about Nakoomu. I remembered all the times we spent together and all trouble we managed to cause.

"Living in the desert was horrid. It made me bitter and resentful, because I figured the pack had just forgotten me and didn't care about my fate. I think I expected them to come after me, to find me. I was convinced that I would meet one of them who would beg me to return to the pack. To tell me that I was needed.

"Then I went home briefly, before I came here. And Nakoomu, Father and Swift Paw were so happy to see me. I didn't know anyone cared so much."

"Hero, you still have people who care for you. Not just in Verinaul, but in Nazberath too. All the people you have become friends with—Jacquelyn and Merrick and anyone else you might have met beforehand. They are counting on you, Lone Wolf. They have placed their trust and hope in you, because they believe you have the power to make a difference," Jeru explained determinedly.

"To make a difference…That's right," Hero smiled warmly.

"I believe this too, Hero. I believe that you have the strength to change the mistakes of this world and make it better," Jeru replied.

"Then I can't die here tonight. I won't join those demons," Hero said firmly.

"Hold on, and I'll find some herbs for those wounds. Stay awake Hero," Jeru ordered.

"I will stay alive," Hero reassured him.

The younger boy smiled and raced off to find anything that might help. Hero grimaced as he shifted slightly. The wound on his back made it very difficult to move. He placed a hand gingerly on his wounded side and felt the deep gash. He couldn't help but let out a small whimper at the pain. His blood stained the ground around him, and he felt drowsier, and his body felt like it was filled with lead. He was finding it very hard to keep his eyes open.

Chapter 21

Jeru worked all night on Hero's wounded body. He mixed herbs together to make a thick paste, and he rubbed it gently over the long gashes. Hero winced and growled when the sting of the herbs reached him, but he sat as still as he could.

By morning, Jeru had bound all the wounds with bandages he had grabbed from Shiboo. Hero felt stiff and in pain. He tried to walk so they wouldn't waste time, but Jeru quickly told him to sit back down.

"We can't risk those wounds opening again and bleeding. You've lost enough blood as it is, and you need to rest," the boy declared.

So Hero agreed to sit, while Jeru made a big feast to help Hero get some of his strength back. Hero also had to sit while Jeru buried both dead demons. Hero wouldn't hear of it when Jeru told him to stay back from Hynraz's grave.

"I just have to do something," Hero growled, shoving Jeru away from him.

Jeru sighed with annoyance and stepped away to give Hero privacy. Hero glanced to make sure his friend wasn't watching before he started to think of something to say.

"We would never be allies, and despite what I may have said during our battle, I want you to know that I respect you," he said softly. "You were on the wrong side, but you fought for what you believed in, and I can't take that pride away from you. You were a loyal soldier for your Queen, and she must have been proud of you.

"I guess what I'm saying is that even though we were enemies, I want to say that you were a great warrior, and that I had a great challenge whenever our swords met. So thank you."

With that said, Hero bowed slightly and stumbled back to the small fire Jeru had built to cook the meal. Jeru gave him a slight smile and a nod that told Hero that the boy thought he had done the right thing. Hero nodded in return before looking at the blue sky. His wounds pained him and when he voiced this to Jeru, the boy proceeded to apply more herbs on them.

"Tonight I will have to stitch them up. These herbs are cleaning them, and they are also a pain reliever. So whenever your wounds start to hurt, tell me so I can apply more. That way the stitching won't hurt so much," Jeru said.

"I just can't wait for tonight then," Hero sighed.

Jeru smiled and started preparing the small feast they would soon enjoy. Hero watched him for a few minutes, but then he curled up and took a nap.

He was awakened by Jeru shaking him. The boy looked anxious when Hero snapped his eyes open.

"Phew, I thought you were dying or something. I've been shaking you for ten minutes," he breathed.

"Sorry," Hero replied.

He groaned as he sat up. He felt the skin break open on his wounds as he did so. He grunted and looked at the bandages, which started to stain red.

"My wounds have opened," he muttered.

"What? Oh shoot. Okay relax, I'll fix you right up again," Jeru replied.

He unwrapped the bandages and took a tunic from his bags. He dipped it into the boiling water and pressed it to Hero's wounds until they stopped bleeding. Then he rubbed more of the herb paste onto the wounds and re-wrapped the bandages. Hero sighed in relief, and Jeru wiped sweat from his brow. There was going to be a lot of stress for the next few days.

"Time for food," Jeru said, trying to sound cheery.

He brought forth bowls of various meats and salads and a pot of soup. Hero smiled with delight and started to dig in. He was so hungry that the food quickly disappeared from his plate.

"Go on, take as much as you want. I already ate," Jeru smiled. "Eat until you pop."

"Thanks," Hero exclaimed.

He set upon the food as if it were the last meal he would ever eat. Jeru watched with a small smile. By the time Hero finished, all the food was almost gone. Jeru offered to clean everything up, while Hero got ready for the stitching. He hoped it would take Jeru a long time to wash the dishes and pots.

Too soon, the boy came back with the stitching gear he had grabbed before they had left his house together. He decided to start with the back, since it was the deepest wound. Hero gritted his teeth as the needle glided smoothly through his skin, closing the gaping wound.

It took a very long time for Jeru to finish. Not as skilled as Merrick, Jeru took longer to work the needle. He had to make sure he made no mistakes. He examined his handiwork and sighed with relief.

"There we go. That will help," he said happily.

"Thank you, Jeru. I feel better all ready, so let's go," Hero exclaimed.

"Dusk will fall soon. We can go tomorrow. You get some sleep, and I'll go hunting now," Jeru said.

At any other time, Hero would have joined him, but he felt tired again, so he decided to sleep. He had a dream of running through a field of flowers with Nakoomu at his side. When Jeru returned dragging a slain deer, he found Hero smiling broadly in a deep sleep. The boy laughed to himself and curled up to sleep. He tried to ignore his rumbling stomach. He didn't even have a bite of the meal he had spent so long preparing, knowing that Hero needed all the energy he could get.

"Hey, let's go," Hero said enthusiastically the next morning.

"Okay, we'll have to walk because running would only open those wounds again," Jeru told him.

"Better than waiting for my wounds to heal," Hero pointed out. "We'll just walk longer into the night."

Jeru agreed, though he was prepared to stop much earlier. Hero would not be able to climb very long after suffering such blows. After only half hour, Hero started to slow down. Jeru waited for him to catch up before moving out again. Hero grimaced and held his wounded side with his uninjured arm.

"You need to rest?" Jeru asked as his own stomach growled greedily.

"No, not yet," Hero answered.

Jeru sighed and took two apples from his bag, He threw one to Hero who caught it and tucked it away. He would eat it later in the afternoon, so he wouldn't have to stop for dinner until late that night.

However, it still was a long way until nightfall when they decided to stop and rest. Hero could barely move because of the pain of his injuries, and Jeru decided he shouldn't walk another step, or else the wounds might split open again. Hero sat down slowly and leaned against a large rock. They had a long way to go and not nearly enough time. It would take about a week to cross over Demon's Peak and then another month to get through Feruh. By that time, the Queen's army would have been at war with the King's for more than a month. He sighed and watched as Jeru prepared dinner.

"Jeru, this is impossible," Hero said after they had eaten.

"What is?" Jeru asked.

"This mission. In my condition, it'll take even longer to reach Delring than we thought it would. How are we going to make it in time?" Hero asked.

"I don't know," Jeru murmured. "All we can do is try."

"I just wish we had more time. If the city is destroyed, then everything I've done amounts to nothing," Hero replied sourly.

"Don't give up, Hero. Something's bound to happen to increase our luck," Jeru said cheerfully.

"The glass is always half full with you, isn't it?" Hero asked with a grim smile.

"I don't see why we should give up when there still may be a chance," Jeru replied sheepishly. "It won't do us any good to complain."

Hero nodded and curled up to sleep, even though the sun was still quite high in the sky. No matter what Jeru said though, Hero knew it was impossible to reach the capital city in time. All he could hope was for the King's soldiers to be ready for it and not be taken completely by surprise.

The next day when Hero woke, he felt very stiff. He knew he wouldn't be able to travel very far today either. Cursing himself silently, he stood up on shaky legs, took a step forward and fell to his knees. The pain seemed to have doubled in the night. He growled as his injuries throbbed in painful protest as he rose again.

Jeru blinked lazily and stretched. He yawned loudly and packed the bags. He slung his own pack and Hero's onto his back and suggested that they get a move on. Hero agreed, though he would have given anything to stay put.

"If only we could teleport or something," Hero exclaimed angrily, stumbling down the path.

They had reached the middle of the mountain and were relieved that the path Jeru had chosen led around the mountain, instead of over. It would save them a lot of time and energy.

"I know what you mean. There used to be dragons living around here. But I think Queen Arlyn had them all killed so they wouldn't stand against her empire," Jeru sighed.

"Do you think there might be some around who could give us a lift, maybe take us all the way to the Hurith Gate," Hero said.

"Even if they were around, they wouldn't take us anywhere near a gate. They might take us to the top of Demon's Peak though, and that would save us almost a whole week," Jeru replied excitedly.

"The only question is whether the Queen left anyone alive here," Hero said, looking around as if there might be a sign leading them to the right place.

"Well, if we wanted to find someone I suggest looking in the caves at the bottom of this mountain. We should reach them by the end of the day," Jeru said, though he sounded unsure.

Hero nodded, and they started walking again. Somewhere in his heart, Hero knew they would find something at the caves. He wished he knew whether that something was a dragon or not. If it were a dragon, then how would they ask it to help them? And even if they could, would a dragon consent?

As Jeru had anticipated, they arrived at the base of the mountain by dusk. The caves lay about twelve feet away, and when they reached them they found them large and dark. The mouths of the caves seemed to be waiting for unwary prey to come within their grasps. Hero gulped as they neared the ominous caves.

"Jeru," he said softly. "What if we find a dragon, and it tries to kill us?"

"It won't. Dragons are pretty smart. They aren't like normal animals. If you meet a dragon, it won't kill you outright unless you threaten it," Jeru explained.

"Is there any way for us to communicate with them?" Hero asked nervously.

"Yeah. Dragons can talk, Hero. Like I said, they're pretty smart, almost as smart as humans. They are also very powerful in magic and have an unbelievable amount of strength," Jeru chuckled.

"Let's hope we find one," Hero gulped.

Jeru nodded and led the way in. Since they didn't have a torch, they had to feel the walls in order not to trip. It was very difficult as the ground was full of holes and rises, just waiting to catch them unawares. Hero cursed as he slipped, and he slowly straightened as his wounds screamed at him yet again.

They crept farther into the cave, hands sliding on the now slimy walls in an attempt to keep their balance. Hero sighed and wondered if they should leave, when he saw a faint red glow in the distance. He stopped and Jeru bumped into him, colliding painfully with Hero's wounded back.

"Sorry," the young boy said.

"Don't worry about it," Hero grunted. "I see a glow up ahead, maybe someone's living down here."

"Hey, Hero that glow seems to be getting brighter," Jeru pointed out.

"And it seems to be getting hotter in here," Hero replied, shifting his feet.

They studied the glow a second longer and then yelled in surprised. The glow was a large wave of fire and it was coming right at them. They ran back up the path, heedless of hitting the walls or tripping in holes. Jeru saw a small opening and grabbed Hero by the arm, pulling him in after him. They sat hunched on the ground as the wave of fire passed by them.

"I thought you said they didn't just attack people," Hero panted.

"Well, I didn't really think there'd be one left," Jeru gasped. "Besides, the last people who tried to come down here were probably the Queen's soldiers."

"So it thinks we're here to butcher it or something?" Hero groaned.

"Maybe," Jeru sighed.

They peeked their heads around the corner, but only darkness filled their vision. Hero took a timid step forward and walked a little way down the path again. He stopped for a minute, then walked silently back to Jeru.

"I think if we're really quiet we can sneak up to it and show it we're not enemies," Hero whispered.

Jeru nodded, and they crept from the small opening and crawled down the path, trying not to make any noise. There was one tense moment when Jeru hit a loose stone from the path, and it tumbled loudly downhill. They waited for a minute and heard a low growl, but no fire came. Hero breathed with relief and continued crawling forward. Something was hidden there, and the fire suggested a dragon.

The cave floor eventually leveled out, and they saw a large underground chamber. It was made of old stones covered with soot and falling apart. A blast of heat emitted from the back of the chamber where Hero could see a large hulking beast. He couldn't make out any details save for two glowing eyes. Bright green with slit pupils like cats' eyes, they glowed brightly and scanned the chamber wildly.

Jeru stood up and approached it slowly, raising his arms to show that he had no weapons. The dragon reared up on its hind legs, amazing Hero with its size. The glowing eyes nearly brushed the ceiling.

"Do not fear us," Jeru said. "We are friends."

The dragon let out a low growl that turned into a disbelieving laugh. Hero saw the eyes close slightly as if the dragon pondered what to do.

"He's right," Hero stammered. "We don't want to hurt you."

"Why should I believe you?" the dragon asked in a voice too deep for any human, yet with a ringing clarity to it, as if a small child was speaking in time with the dragon.

"We've come unarmed and are fighting against your enemies as well," Jeru replied truthfully.

"Let me see you clearly," the dragon snarled.

He blew a small breath of fire and lit a huge candelabra that sat in the center of the room. Hero and Jeru stepped into the light as the dragon leaned his face close. Hero was amazed at the dragon. His face was large and lizard-like. He had a pointed nose and a long jaw with razor sharp fangs extending from his upper lips. Hanging from his chin, he had a wispy, black beard that stretched all the way to his chest. His cheeks were lined with small black spikes that stood out against his red, scaly skin. Two large horns protruded from his forehead; they were curved so the tips pointed at the back of his neck. A mane of black hair framed his massive head.

Hero was speechless. He couldn't see the rest of the dragon's body clearly, but he could make out enormous wings that spread out behind. He blinked and rubbed his eyes, as if imagining something that wasn't there. The dragon's large green eyes focused on Hero, and Hero's eyes locked with dragon's. The dragon's pupils widened, and he turned his head away quickly.

"Lone Wolf?" he asked, his features disappearing as he moved from the light.

"Yes. I am Lone Wolf, and I need your help badly," Hero replied. "You see, Carthafell is going to send troops from Feruh and Zenbin to attack Delring in a month. We need to get there in time."

"You expect me to show my face in the Queen's countries?" the dragon snorted.

"No, if you could maybe fly us over Demon's Peak and save us a lot of time that would be great," Jeru explained.

"Flying you over Demon's Peak would reveal myself to Hurith Gate," the dragon pointed out. "I am the last of my kind you see, and I must live to honor those who did not."

"What if you could fly us to the top of Demon's Peak? Or bring us half way down the other side?" Hero pleaded.

"That is a request which I must brood over." The dragon smiled grimly, and the light shone off his pearly white teeth.

"We shall leave you in peace, but we wish to remain in the caves if that's all right," Jeru said timidly.

"That is not a problem, but you have to promise not to reveal where I am no matter what I choose," the dragon answered.

"We would never tell that wretched woman where to find you," Hero reassured him.

"That is good, Lone Wolf. By the way, my name is Barudokai," the dragon said.

Hero and Jeru nodded and turned to camp out in a nearby cave. They found a rather small one that was at least dry and let in a little light. Hero stretched out painfully, his wounds aching again.

When Hero and Jeru woke up the next morning, they headed straight back to Barudokai's cave without bothering to eat breakfast. Neither of them felt very hungry, as they were extremely nervous. If the dragon refused to help, then they had wasted a lot of time only to achieve nothing.

They walked quickly down the dark cave and reached Barudokai's chamber. He was awake and waiting for them.

"Have you decided?" Hero asked earnestly.

"I have," Barudokai answered.

The two companions waited impatiently as Barudokai shifted his weight. Finally the dragon sighed and looked at them with his glowing green eyes.

"I have decided to take you over Demon's Peak and land you halfway down the mountain," he said.

"Thank you, Barudokai. You are most kind. When this is all over, we'll make sure you don't have to spend the rest of your life hiding," Hero exclaimed.

"That would be a worthy payment," Barudokai smiled. "Now come on. You better get out before me. Sometimes I knock boulders down, and it wouldn't do for you to be crushed."

Hero and Jeru ran from the cave with excitement. Hero didn't even care that his injuries pained him. Within minutes, they heard a loud thump, and Barudokai stepped from the cave. Hero gaped as the whole body came into the light.

Barudokai's body was as impressive as his head. Like his head, his skin glinted a deep red in the morning sun. He didn't have arms; instead he only had his wings where arms would have been. Though looking more closely, Hero realized that the long bones stretching nearly all the way to the tips of his wings were shaped like fingers. Barudokai had long legs that folded neatly beneath him when he sat down. His tail was very long and had black spikes at the end. His belly was black also and looked to be made of armor.

"So, you need me to fly you, or are you just going to sit there staring all day?" Barudokai asked with an amused expression.

Hero shook his head and walked up to Barudokai. The dragon lowered his wing and told Hero to grab hold of it. As soon as Hero did so, Barudokai lifted his wing and set Hero gently on his shoulders. He did the same with Jeru, and the small boy held onto Hero as the dragon stood to his full height.

"You better hold on or else you'll fall off," Barudokai said.

Hero and Jeru tightened their holds, and Barudokai spread his wings, which spanned about twenty feet across. He flapped twice and rose into the air. Hero thought it very odd. He felt as though he had become weightless. Barudokai leaned forward and flapped his wings, riding higher on the air currents.

"This is awesome," Jeru yelled over the wind as they sped through the air.

"Yeah," Hero agreed.

"You want to have some fun?" Barudokai asked. When they nodded yes, he smiled. "Hold on tight then," he grinned.

He flipped upside down and then pulled a loop. Hero and Jeru whooped with joy. They had never experienced anything like this before. Barudokai righted himself, and then did another roll for his own amusement.

"This is amazing," Hero exclaimed. "We're going to make sure that dragons' lives won't be taken, Barudokai. Then you can fly all throughout Nazberath."

"That would be fantastic," Barudokai said with a large grin. "Now hold on tight, Demon's Peak is coming up and I'm going to have to ascend."

"Okay," Jeru shouted as Barudokai started to flap his huge wings.

Hero gazed ahead and saw Demon's Peak rise before them like a rock temple. Its jagged spires and caves looked like blank windows. He imagined that demons must have really lived in the mountain a long time ago, before they all went into Carthafell. Barudokai flew straight up into the air, giving the two men the awful feeling of slipping right off his back. Hero grabbed onto the dragon's neck a little tighter while Jeru held onto Hero for dear life.

"You okay back there?" Barudokai asked.

"Yeah, it just feels a little disconcerting," Hero admitted. "But we're fine."

"Good. It'll take me at least ten hours to get to the top, and I'm going to have to take a break when we reach the half way mark," the dragon instructed.

"Hey, Hero, I hope you have warm clothes. No matter what the season, Demon's Peak is always cold as you near the top," Jeru said.

"I see your point. There's snow and ice up there. I think I have some warm clothes," Hero replied nervously.

"Don't worry, I'll light a fire big enough to keep you warm all night. If that doesn't work, you can sleep under my wing or mane," Barudokai chuckled.

Hero and Jeru thanked him for his offer and held on as he rose higher into the sky. They continued to fly up into an endless mist, growing miserable as the cloud vapor soaked them to the skin. Hero and Jeru shivered with cold as the water in their clothes and hair began to freeze.

"We're half way up the mountain. I've found a cave where we can sleep for the night," Barudokai informed them.

"Good. My cuts are starting to really bother me," Hero sighed, flexing his muscles.

Barudokai landed gently on a large ledge, and Hero and Jeru climbed down. They quickly ran into the cave, looked in their bags for dry clothes and quickly changed. Then they gathered what wood they could find, and Barudokai lit a fire. The two humans sat close to the blaze, holding out shivering hands.

"It feels like winter here," Hero said as Jeru prepared dinner.

"I know. It was even colder when I climbed it myself. I believe I did it in the fall," Jeru laughed.

"That's one reason I enjoy being a dragon," Barudokai said smugly. "It would have to be extremely cold for me feel it."

Hero and Jeru grumbled as Barudokai gave a loud laugh. They ate their small supper and decided to sleep. It was too cold away from the dragon, so they both snuggled up to his large stomach, while he draped his wing over them. Then he curled his head around to make sure no cold air could sneak in.

"Never thought I'd be sleeping under a dragon wing," Jeru said as he curled into a ball.

"I didn't even know there were dragons left," Hero admitted.

"It figures that it was the Queen's fault," Jeru muttered darkly. "Any piece of bad news you hear is caused by that witch."

"I know, and it was so strange that the people of Shiboo thought she was innocent and King Dervik was the devil," Hero mused.

"They were all crazy. I wouldn't believe any one of them except Molly. She was the only sane person there," Jeru said.

"Are you sure you're not just saying that because you fancy her?" Hero asked slyly.

"I could see it in her pretty pink eyes," Jeru smiled.

"Those were some powerful eyes. Pink pupils surrounded by purple. They were stranger than my eyes," Hero said.

"Yeah," Jeru said dreamily. "I think I'll try to sleep now while her image is so fresh in my mind. Good night."

"Good night, lover boy," Hero muttered, closing his eyes.

All around them they heard a soothing song and realized that Barudokai was singing softly in a strange language that neither of them understood. But the song sounded so beautiful and calming that they both fell asleep quickly, noting that the song also sounded very sad, like it was the last ballad of the dragons and would never be heard again.

Chapter 22

When Hero and Jeru woke the next morning, it was hot. Barudokai's wing still covered them, and they realized that the dragon had certainly kept in the heat. They were both sweating, which Hero didn't enjoy as the salty sweat irritated his wounds. Jeru gave the wing a slight push, and it immediately uncovered them.

Hero and Jeru threw hands over their eyes as a dazzling sun blinded them. The sky was pure blue and the air, brisk and refreshing.

"I wondered when you were going to wake up," Barudokai said. "I thought you might have died or something."

"We've been traveling for a long time now. In fact, I've been on the move since last winter," Hero said, remembering back to when he first arrived.

"You've been traveling for seven months nonstop?" Barudokai asked.

"Yes. I have to get to Delring. You know the legend of Lone Wolf, right? I've got to save the world," Hero said with a grim smile.

"So let's get moving you two. Come on," Jeru exclaimed.

They climbed onto the dragon's back and took off. Within fifteen minutes the cold penetrated Hero and Jeru's skin, but they tried not to complain. Barudokai knew they suffered so he tried to speed up to end their misery.

"I c-can't feel my fingers," Jeru moaned after two hours. "I th-think they're f-frozen."

"Let's switch places then. If you bury your fingers under his mane, they'll stay warm," Hero suggested.

They asked Barudokai to stop and float in midair while they changed places. Once Jeru had his hands securely under the black mane, Barudokai started up again. Hero stretched his back a few times as the wound started to ache. Barudokai strained as the air began to thin, and Hero could see his breath coming out in great white puffs. He asked the dragon if he'd like to take a break, but Barudokai stubbornly refused.

It took another three hours to reach the top. Barudokai had to stop or else he would have fallen from the sky. Nothing protected them from the harsh wind on the summit, and there were no trees or plants that they could use to light a fire. The snow was about three feet deep, and Hero and Jeru struggled to move in it. Once he had rested long enough, Barudokai blew a large pillar of fire that at least melted the snow into cold puddles, which froze about ten minutes afterwards.

"This is awful," Jeru groaned as the wind nearly pushed him to the ground.

"I know, but at least we have an excellent view. Look, we covered all of that ground. I can see so far. It's like I'm looking into the past you know? We started way back there, and now we're here," Hero said in amazement.

"I know what you mean," Barudokai smiled. "It's like we can see all the world stretched out below us."

"It is great," Jeru admitted. "But it would be better if it were warmer."

Barudokai laughed as Hero shook his head. No matter what the splendors, the boy completely ignored them. He tried to keep his dignity as the two laughed at his lack of enthusiasm.

By nightfall, Hero had to agree with Jeru about the weather. The temperature had dropped below zero, and even snuggling under Barudokai's wing didn't stop them from shivering. The night passed slowly and miserably, and neither Hero nor Jeru could sleep for more than an hour. The wind made eerie noises throughout the night, while flakes of snow sneaked in and hit their faces, making them shiver even more.

When the sun began to rise, Hero and Jeru looked puffy eyed and pale. They hadn't slept much, and they shivered with cold. The sun offered no warmth at all, and they were eager to be off the mountain.

"You ready Barudokai?" Hero said, his teeth chattering.

"Yes. This mountain air has even made my scales twitch once or twice," Barudokai murmured.

Hero let Jeru take the front as they climbed onto the dragon's broad back. Barudokai launched himself from the ground and flew quickly down the mountain, keeping low to the ground so the people stationed at Hurith Gate wouldn't see him.

Even going very fast and without taking breaks, it was mid-afternoon by the time they reached the halfway point of the mountain. Hero and Jeru climbed down from Barudokai for the last time.

"Thank you for everything," Jeru said, hugging the dragon.

"No problem. I needed to stretch my wings," Barudokai smiled.

"We couldn't have done it without you," Hero said truthfully. "Barudokai, when we stopped the first night, you were singing. What was that song?"

"The last dragon slain by Queen Arlyn created that song. It tells of the dragon's reign and the horror of the acts of violence done to us. It is the last tale of the dragons, one that I would have passed down to my children if they hadn't been killed," Barudokai answered sadly.

"I'm sorry," Jeru said solemnly.

"Barudokai, I promise I will make her pay for every one of them," Hero said, placing a hand on Barudokai's neck.

"Thank you, both of you. And please, be careful," Barudokai smiled.

"We will. Thanks again, Barudokai," Jeru replied.

"And don't worry. I'll keep my promise," Hero called as the dragon lifted himself into the air.

He circled over them twice before making his way back up the mountain. Hero and Jeru watched him until he disappeared into a mere speck in the sky. And then he was gone, the last dragon left on all of Nazberath was returning home.

"Look down there," Jeru pointed.

In the distance they could see the gate leading into Feruh, and the wall that marked the country's borders. Hero wondered if giants opened this one as well.

"Come on, we still have a long way to go," Hero said, walking down the rocky path.

Jeru agreed, and they made their way to the Hurith Gate. Hero wondered how long it would take them to get into Delring from here. He knew that the city was in Hasrath, which lay to the north of Feruh, but would they be able to get through Feruh? It was sympathetic to Carthafell and rumors of his coming must have reached the country by now. He gulped and tried not to think of it.

"You know what?" Jeru said after a while. "It's going to be really hard to move you through Feruh with your eyes so recognizable."

"I know. I wish I still had my eye dye. How am I to keep them hidden?" Hero asked.

"Well we could tie bandages around them and say you're blind. I could lead you through the country with your map," Jeru suggested.

"I suppose so," Hero replied reluctantly. "Though I'd feel safer if I could see."

"Think about it though," Jeru smiled. "No one will suspect you of anything. If we go tramping in there like we own the place, then they'll probably kill us."

"What a pleasant sounding country," Hero said sarcastically.

He sighed and shook his head. Being blind also meant missing a lot of sights that he'd never have the opportunity to see again. But with no other option, they decided to go for it. A few miles from the gate, Jeru wrapped up the last of the bandages around Hero's head, making sure his eyes were completely covered.

"Now hunch over so it looks like you're worn and crippled," Jeru whispered. "We'll have to say that you're my older brother, and I'm taking you back home."

Hero hunched over, which hurt his back a bit, and held out his hand blindly. Jeru grabbed it and guided him to the bottom of the mountain. He stumbled a bit on small rocks, but soon grew used to it. He found if he listened to the sound of Jeru's footsteps and breathing, he could guess what might happen next.

"Okay, the gate is in plain view. Another five minutes and we're in," Jeru whispered.

"All right," Hero replied. "Should I talk or not?"

"No, pretend that you got in a horrible accident in the mountain and are now blind and dumb," Jeru instructed.

"Blind and dumb it is then," Hero murmured. "Except at night."

He felt the ground finally level, and Jeru picked up his speed a bit. They agreed to walk only a little in the day and full out at night, when no one would be able to see his eyes anyway. Hero heard Jeru's feet stop and his breathing become less labored. They had arrived at the gate.

"Oy. What're you doin' 'ere?" a voice asked in a strange accent.

Hero remembered Jacquelyn telling him about that. He could barely distinguish one slurred word from the other.

"We're just humble travelers. My brother got in an awful accident on those mountains, and we're returning home," Jeru answered.

"Well, we ain't supposed to let no one in 'ere fer a time less you'm got a better story then tha'," the man chuckled.

"Why aren't you letting us in? We need to go home." Jeru pleaded.

"Tha's too bad ain't it? We're gettin' ready to attack and no un's gettin' through in case they be that there Lone Wolf," the man explained.

"Do we honestly look like that man?" Jeru asked angrily. "You think an eleven-year-old boy with his blind and dumb brother are the Lone Wolf?"

"I didn' say tha' now did I? You best be a gettin' out of my sight, before I beat ya abou' the head," the man snarled.

"Yoland, what're ya doin'? These people look harmless ya git. Now let 'em in ya twit," another voice ordered.

"Whot? Yes sir," the first man whimpered. "Oy. Open tha' gate you yeller-bellied oafs."

Hero heard a loud grinding sound as the earth began to tremble under his feet. The gate opened. He heard people panting and wondered if any giants lived around here.

"Get on in there then," the first man said sourly.

"Thank you," Jeru replied smugly.

He took Hero's hand and started to pull him forward again.

From what Hero could hear, Feruh sounded like a very dangerous place. They had entered a large city, and Hero heard coarse yells throughout the streets. He stumbled on debris more than once and took a firmer hold onto Jeru when he felt the crowd all around him. The city, Cuth, was over-populated and dirty. Hero wanted to get out as soon as possible, but he felt tired and his injuries still throbbed a bit.

"We'll rest at the next inn," Jeru whispered.

Hero nodded, fearing that no matter how low he made his voice, someone would hear him and end his charade. Jeru led him through a small doorway and stopped him at the front desk.

"Do you have any rooms available?" Jeru asked politely.

"Well tha depends on whot you're willin' ta pay," the woman at the desk said scornfully. "But by the looks o tha one I'd say ya better move on."

"We have enough money," Jeru said, handing her a small sack of coins. Hero heard the money hit the counter. Evidently it was enough, for Jeru soon led Hero up a rickety staircase that sounded as though it might collapse.

"Okay, we're safe." Jeru sighed in relief as Hero untied the bandages from his eyes.

"What a horrible place," he grumbled, sitting down on the slightly damp mattress.

"We'll be out of here by tomorrow morning so don't worry about it," Jeru smiled.

"You don't know how bad it is, being blind. I would hate it if I were," Hero mused. "I hate not being able to see."

"Feruh isn't a large country, so we'll be able to make it through relatively quickly," Jeru explained.

"I hope so. I just want to get to Delring and warn the King about the attack. If we make it in time," Hero said.

"Don't worry about it. We'll make it soon enough," Jeru replied.

Hero looked out the dirt-stained window and wondered how Jacquelyn and Merrick were doing. Had they returned home? He smiled humorlessly at that. Neither had a home to return to and wasn't this their journey as well? He had been selfish to decide that they couldn't come. Almost arrogant. Sure he told Jacquelyn that he didn't want their bonds to grow deeper for fear of having a broken heart when he left and that he wanted to protect them for himself. That was completely true, but he also felt that he wanted to be the one to save Nazberath. Wasn't he the Lone Wolf? Why had he turned them away, but allowed Jeru to remain? Was it because he knew Jeru from his world and wouldn't miss him as much? He liked Jeru a lot, but he knew in his heart they would never be as close as he was with Jacquelyn and Merrick.

He sighed as he wished for the impossible. He wished he could make it to King Dervik in time. He wished he could see Jacquelyn and Merrick again. But for the most part, he wished to go home and see Nakoomu once more. It had been too long since he had gazed upon her snow-white fur and bright blue eyes, the slight curve of her mouth whenever she was pleased and the twinkle in her eyes when she howled with joy. How he longed to see her. But, to his dismay, he felt the same pull to Jacquelyn. Was it possible that he had fallen in love with the woman? If so, how could he choose? He shook his head, knowing that Nakoomu was the one for him.

Why did it hurt so much when he thought about Jacquelyn then?

Chapter 23

Jacquelyn glanced over at Merrick. He still looked very pale, and his wound bled every night, no matter how much medicine she applied. She began to fear for his life. When he saw her looking, Merrick smiled lightly but said nothing. Isabell walked slowly, to make sure she didn't jostle him too much.

They had reached the top of Demon's Peak and had just stopped at the hot spring Merrick had talked about. Once they were in the large cavern, Merrick fell from his saddle.

"Merrick!" Jacquelyn cried, leaping from her saddle and running over to him.

"I think that arrow pierced my lung," he said softly.

"That's not the only problem. I think it was poisoned," Jacquelyn said breathlessly, removing Merrick's shirt to see the wound.

It was bleeding rather heavily again. Jacquelyn guessed that the poison must have been acidic, so that it burned Merrick from the inside, causing him to bleed anew every other day or so.

"We have to do something. You're losing too much blood," Isabell moaned nervously.

"I don't know what to do," Merrick replied sadly.

"Well, let's get you to the spring first. Maybe some warm water will help close the wound," Jacquelyn said, trying to sound cheerful.

She helped him up and led him to the spring. The cold air seemed to melt as they neared the water. She waited politely as Merrick undressed to his small clothes before helping him into the deep spring. She didn't bother to undress at all before stepping in after him.

"Does that feel better?" she asked.

"It does," Merrick said.

Isabell walked over and nuzzled Merrick's head from behind. He reached up with his arm and patted her on the jaw.

"Come on in here, Isabell," he said, smiling.

Isabell walked over to the other side and slipped in. She neighed contentedly as the warm water washed away her fatigue. She walked over to them and stood by Merrick. Jacquelyn noted that he was smiling again, always smiling recently.

"Merrick, are you sure you're all right?" she asked.

"I'll be fine. I bet this water is washing the wound nicely," Merrick said, looking at her.

She studied his deep brown eye and noticed a small glint there, as if he was holding back a tear. She gasped as she realized he was giving up hope of recovery. He looked at her curiously as she backed away, horrified. He couldn't die, not before they met up with Hero again.

"Oh Merrick, no," she whispered painfully.

"What are you talking about?" he asked playfully, though his eye had become sadder.

"You don't want to fight against the poison anymore. You're giving up," Jacquelyn yelped.

"Merrick is too strong for that," Isabell argued.

"No. She's right," Merrick admitted, sinking farther into the water.

"But Merrick," Isabell gasped.

"Muryn once told me about this poison that is now inside of me. It takes about two weeks to kill a fighting victim. However, that victim suffers from pain, drowsiness, nightmares and nausea. I can't deal with it anymore, and it's already been two weeks since I took the hit. I'm going to die tonight," Merrick muttered.

"But, there's a chance that I can save you," Jacquelyn pleaded.

"You've tried everything you know," Merrick pointed out.

"I noticed a plant that I haven't had before, growing at the edge of the spring. Let me try one more time to cure the poison," Jacquelyn replied determinedly.

"You have nothing to lose," Isabell said.

"You may try anything you want," Merrick sighed.

Jacquelyn swam over to the strange bluish plant and took some back to the others. She found a flat rock and placed the leaf on it. Then she found a fist-sized rock and used it to grind the plant into a mushy pulp. She returned to the plant and grabbed another leaf. Finally, she moved over to Merrick and applied the pulp to his wound, using the second leaf to cover the deep hole. She washed the bandages in the water and then replaced them on his chest.

"It feels like the plant and the poison are battling," Merrick said, sweating with discomfort. "Like they're both burning each other."

"This plant will hurt you. I should have said so in the beginning. But it will help in the end," Jacquelyn mumbled.

Merrick didn't reply. He just reached up and scratched Isabell in the nose. She closed her eyes with pleasure, and Jacquelyn couldn't help but smile at the two friends.

"How long have you known Isabell?" she asked.

"Since I was six. My father gave her to me," Merrick replied without facing her.

"How nice," Jacquelyn smiled.

"We've done everything together ever since," Isabell said. "That's why I won't let him die."

"We shall see if your skill works later tonight," Merrick said, glancing at Jacquelyn.

"Then let me get the place set up nicely for you," Jacquelyn smiled.

She got out of the spring and put on her warm wool dress. Then she gathered sticks and built a large fire by the water, gradually adding wood to increase the heat. She spread out the skin of a deer they had killed earlier and placed a worn but heavy blanket on top of it. She helped Merrick from the spring, and he dressed in his warmest clothes, throwing on his old coat and heavy boots as well. Jacquelyn helped him lie down on the skin, and she covered him with the blanket. He lay between the fire and the water, and with his heavy clothes on, he started to feel as if it were summer.

Isabell clambered out of the spring and stood near him, watching carefully to make sure he lived out the night. Jacquelyn watched too, occasionally wiping his sweating brow with a cool cloth.

"How are you feeling?" Isabell asked, leaning her head down to Merrick's ear.

"I feel strange," he replied.

Jacquelyn pushed his shirt up and examined the wound on his chest. The surrounding skin was tinged green, but it appeared to be returning to normal. She ran over to the blue plant and ground more up to spread on the wound. When she finished, she covered him with the blanket once more and sat back to watch.

She didn't realize that she had fallen asleep. But Isabell's loud whinny woke her up with a start. She glanced around and saw that the fire had gone out.

"Isabell what's wrong?" she exclaimed.

"The fire went out! Get it back!" the former unicorn bayed.

Jacquelyn hurriedly lit another fire, thoroughly confused at Isabell's fear. In the light of the fire, she saw what had scared the horse so. Merrick's eye was completely white, and he was gasping for breath.

"This is the final stage of the fight—his body against the poison," she said. "If he doesn't get air, he's not going to make it!"

"What do we do?" Isabell shrieked.

"I'll have to give him air," Jacquelyn replied.

She leaned down, and Isabell gasped as she kissed Merrick.

"This isn't the time for romance," the horse snapped.

"Don't think of it that way," Jacquelyn replied, now using her hands to push at Merrick's chest in a rhythmic way. "I'm blowing air into him. It's the only way."

"Oh, sorry," Isabell apologized.

But Jacquelyn didn't answer. She continued giving Merrick more air. When she drew away he gasped for more, but she pushed his chest again. Isabell soon realized that she pushed in time with a heartbeat. She watched anxiously as Jacquelyn repeated this again and again.

Finally, when she drew away once more, Merrick let out a deep cough and sat up, sweat drenching his body. He continued to cough as Isabell shouted with surprise and joy and gently rubbed her head against his shoulder. Jacquelyn sat back with relief and smiled broadly as Merrick wiped his brow and looked at her.

"You won, Merrick. The poison has dissipated," she whispered, still catching her own breath.

"Jacquelyn, you saved me," he said bluntly.

"Thank you, thank you so much," Isabell sobbed.

Jacquelyn stood up and hugged the horse. She buried her face in the gray mane and smiled happily. When she turned, Merrick stood right behind her.

"Thank you," he whispered.

She smiled and hugged him tightly. He hugged her in return, and she felt a teardrop hit the top of her head.

"I'd be lost without you," she admitted.

"And I'd be lost without you," he replied.

"This is great. Now we can all help Hero on his quest," Isabell whispered excitedly. "For a minute, I thought we'd lose you, Merrick."

Merrick pushed Jacquelyn away gently and gave them a cocky smile. "You won't be rid of me that easily," he laughed.

"For which we are ever grateful," Jacquelyn replied.

"I think we should all get some sleep now," Isabell said.

"Yeah, I'm exhausted," Merrick replied.

"Good night," Jacquelyn said, curling up by the fire.

The next morning cold air wrapped the top of Demon's Peak. Jacquelyn woke first. She made a small breakfast and noted that their food supply was running low. But nothing lived on this mountain. She sighed as she remembered that it would take at least two days to climb down the mountain. Then they had to go through Feruh until they finally reached Delring.

Once Merrick and Isabell had breakfast, they set out again. Moon Dance was a bit frisky with the cold, but Jacquelyn kept a short reign. The last thing she needed was to go teaming off the side of the mountain on the black mare. She checked on Merrick regularly. But he replied that he was fine each time, and she believed him. The wound on his chest hadn't bled at all that day, and he didn't have a look of pained calm on his face anymore.

"What a day," Isabell sighed. "You know, dragons used to live on this mountain with the demons."

"That is amazing," Jacquelyn replied. "Aren't dragons good creatures and demons evil?"

"Dragons aren't really good, nor are they really evil. They serve what side suits them. If dragons still lived and believed in Arlyn, they would side with her," Merrick explained.

"So they fight for their beliefs not for good or evil," Jacquelyn mused.

"All things fight for their beliefs, even Arlyn. She is evil, don't misunderstand me, but she believes what she is doing is right and so she fights for it," Isabell replied.

"I understand. I always thought that Nazberath was divided into good and evil," Jacquelyn admitted. "Since I grew up on a farm, I didn't get to read much about history. Just the basics."

"There is definitely more than good and evil," Merrick smiled. "Though sometimes the in-betweens are so close to the two that you can't tell the difference."

Jacquelyn smiled at her own naiveté on human nature. Of course there was more than good and evil. She shook her head and slowed Moon Dance down as the mare tried to pick up a trot. She swore the horse was suicidal.

It took two days to reach the base of the mountain. They didn't encounter anything of interest on the way, for which they remained forever grateful. They saw the Hurith Gate come ever closer. Soon one of the gatekeepers ordered them to halt.

"Who goes there?" he asked in the Feruh accent.

"Just some weary travelers who seek a town," Merrick answered.

"Whot? More travelers from tha' mountain? How many folks are comin' through tha' there pass?" the man asked with disbelief.

Jacquelyn's heart skipped a beat. Hero must have come through recently. She swallowed her questions as Merrick began to speak again.

"Well, we haven't seen any other people on the mountains. So, would you let us in?" he asked.

"No," the gatekeeper sneered. "You's got ta stay outta' Feruh fer a few days."

"Why?" Jacquelyn asked pleasantly.

"Cause we're lookin' fer that Lone Wolf fella' so you'm got to stay away," the man said.

"But we aren't Lone Wolf. Why do we have to stay out?" Merrick asked, puzzled.

"How do I know you ain't 'im?" the man demanded.

"Because I only have one eye and it's brown," Merrick pointed out.

"Oh yeah. Well, hurry up then. You get through there an' leave me alone," the man pouted.

They neared a large city with a sign saying 'Cuth' on it. Jacquelyn held her nose as the smell overwhelmed her.

"What an awful city," she whispered unhappily.

"Don't let the locals hear you," Isabell warned. "They'll tear you limb from limb."

Merrick glanced around as he saw a group of Feruh soldiers marching toward them. "This could be trouble," he said.

"'Scuse me, Lord an' Lady. Have ya seen a little boy and a blind man around?" one of them asked.

"No, why?" Merrick asked.

"Tha' ain't yer business!" the soldier snapped. "If yer see the pair, you better inform us okay?"

"Yes sir," Jacquelyn replied.

Once the soldiers marched off she looked at Merrick. "I wonder what a poor blind man and his friend, or son, could have done to deserve that," she said.

"They probably were poor and stole something from a noble," Merrick replied. "The punishment for stealing in Cuth is to have both your hands sawed off with a blunt sword."

"That's horrible," Jacquelyn gasped.

"I know," Merrick agreed. "So for their sake, I hope they got out of the city."

They rode through Cuth until they saw a small inn. They led Isabell and Moon Dance to the stables, where a large man stood watch.

"It costs ten coins ta bunk up ya horses in 'ere," he said.

Jacquelyn sniffed as she held out the coins. The man smiled and opened the doors. He led them to two empty stalls and left them to take care of the tack. Once the horses were settled, they walked into the inn, which was not very pleasant.

Low tables were everywhere, most of them filled with drunken men. Each table had a stub of a lit candle on it. Musicians played rowdy music, while women danced around the inn. Jacquelyn looked at the women with disgust, most wearing clothes that could hardly be called decent.

The innkeeper, a short woman with black hair that fell to her knees, flitted over to them. She wore a red dress that had too low a neckline and showed too much leg.

"Would you like a table?" she asked sweetly.

"Yes please," Merrick answered shortly.

She led them to a table in the corner and asked what they would like for dinner.

"I'll have that brought out to you shortly," she said when they had finished giving their order.

"Merrick, I don't like this place," Jacquelyn said sourly.

"I don't either. But it's cheap, and we don't have a lot of money left,"
Merrick replied softly.

A dancing woman came over and sat on Merrick's lap.

"Care fer a dance, handsome?" she asked.

"Uh, no, actually. I've got a hurt leg, and I shouldn't put unnecessary
weight on it," he lied.

"Which leg?" she asked sweetly.

"My left one," he replied.

She gave it a quick jab, and Merrick jumped in surprise. "All better?" she
asked.

"Not at all," he said quickly.

"I could make it better," she urged. "A good dance is all you need."

"Listen Blondie," Jacquelyn snapped, leaning her face in. "He said 'no,'
so get out of here."

"Well, I ain't never seen a girl so rude as ya before," the woman sniffed.

She jumped out of Merrick's lap and stalked off to a different table. Jacquelyn looked around to make sure no one had witnessed the scene, but
everyone was too occupied to notice.

"You saved my life again," Merrick laughed.

"The *nerve* of these people," Jacquelyn fumed. "If any more come over
and ask you to dance, I'll slap them!"

"Calm down, Jacquelyn," Merrick laughed. "It's their culture. They aren't
acting rude in their eyes. All the inns probably have these types of women
in them. When you're asked to dance, it's suppose to be an honor."

"How strange," Jacquelyn exclaimed.

"I know it seems strange to someone like you raised with proper manners,
but to them it's as natural as talking," Merrick explained.

"So will you dance with one if you're asked again?" Jacquelyn asked.

"Absolutely not," Merrick replied. "As I said, it may not seem rude to them
but to me, that's another story."

"Sir an' Miss, yer dinner," the innkeeper said, putting their food down on
the table.

"Thank you ma'am," Merrick said.

"Yes, thank you," Jacquelyn replied.

The woman bowed and then returned to serving food to the other guests. As Jacquelyn and Merrick spoke quietly about Hero, a hairy hand pounded on the table.

"'Ey you," the owner of the hand said.

They looked up to see a large, chubby man with small beady eyes and a thick mustache. He wore a silk vest and white riding pants and had a red sash tied around his enormous stomach. His head was bald and his nose seemed squashed into his pudgy face.

"Yes?" Merrick asked politely.

"Is tha' yer dancin' partner?" he asked drunkenly.

"Why?" Jacquelyn asked sharply.

"If ya ain't, then I wan' ta dance wit' ya," the man smiled, stroking his mustache.

"Yes, we're partners," Jacquelyn lied quickly.

"Then how come ya ain't dancin'?" the man asked dangerously.

"I hurt my leg. We were going to wait a bit longer so it isn't as stiff," Merrick replied smoothly.

"Huh, ya couldn' let me dance wit' her now then could ya?" the man implored.

"Not a chance," Merrick smiled.

The man cursed more before leaving the table. Jacquelyn breathed a sigh of relief. She shook her head as the man went to another woman, who was clearly married to the man sitting next to her. Surprisingly, the woman nodded, and the two began to dance while the husband clapped.

"Merrick, I want to go to my room," she whispered fearfully.

"All right," Merrick replied.

They got up and found the innkeeper standing near the door.

"Excuse me, ma'am? May we have a couple of rooms?" Merrick asked.

"Follow me, handsome," she smiled.

She led them upstairs to two rooms next to each other.

"Here ya go," she said, handing them their key. "I'll be downstairs if ya need somethin'," she finished.

Once she was out of sight, Merrick turned to Jacquelyn. "Make sure you lock your door okay?" he said.

"Merrick, I'm afraid of this place," Jacquelyn said quietly.

"You'll be fine. As long as you lock the door, you'll be fine," Merrick reassured her.

Jacquelyn nodded and walked into her room. She lit a candle and then turned to lock the door. Once she made sure it couldn't be opened, she lit all the candles in the room and sat on the bumpy mattress. This was going to be a long night. She knew she would get no sleep in such a place.

Jacquelyn must have fallen asleep sometime during the night. She sat up with a jolt when she heard the steady song of a large blade as it was drawn from its sheath. She reached over and grabbed her short sword and positioned herself in the darkest corner to take the intruder by surprise. The door was kicked open, and a man entered. He had a brown sack on his shoulder, and Jacquelyn realized he was a thief.

She let out a battle cry as she leapt from the shadows. The man turned too late, and Jacquelyn struck him down with the flat of her blade, knocking him out cold. The man sank to the floor, and she dragged him over to the musty-smelling closet and locked him in. She left her room and pounded on Merrick's door.

The door opened a crack, and she saw Merrick's eye peer out suspiciously. When he recognized her he let her in, glancing at her sword with puzzlement.

"What happened?" he asked.

"A thief broke into my room. After I locked it and everything," Jacquelyn complained loudly.

"Are you hurt?" Merrick asked, locking the door and shoving the dresser in the way for good measure.

"No. Luckily I got him before he saw me. I locked him in the closet," Jacquelyn grinned with pride.

Merrick smiled too, and Jacquelyn sat on the floor with a sigh. She looked around Merrick's room and saw that it looked exactly like her own. It seemed the inn didn't have a very creative builder. She smiled to herself at the thought.

"You still tired?" Merrick asked.

"Yes I am," Jacquelyn said. "How long until dawn?"

"A good five hours," Merrick answered. "You can have the bed if you want."

"I don't know if I do. I think the floor is softer," Jacquelyn chuckled. "So you can have it."

"I've been using the floor," Merrick said, pointing to the blankets on the floor.

"Then I will too. Are there any extra blankets in here?" Jacquelyn smiled.

Merrick pointed to the closet. Jacquelyn walked over and grabbed a couple of moth eaten blankets. She set them up against the wall opposite Merrick. Instead of putting her sword somewhere safe, she sheathed it and put it beside her. She grabbed one of the blankets, rolled it up and placed it under her head for a pillow. She was going to ask Merrick how much longer it would take to leave Feruh, but she fell asleep.

Chapter 24

At dawn, Jacquelyn and Merrick quickly rode from the small inn. In the street, soldiers talked in small groups about an upcoming war. Jacquelyn gave Merrick an inquisitive glance and led Moon Dance to one of the groups.

"Hello good sirs," she smiled. "I couldn't help but hear some of your conversation. I wonder who it is you are attacking."

"Well, tha' really ain't yer business. But we're attackin' Delring in two weeks," one of the men said.

"T-two weeks?" Jacquelyn stammered.

"Yeah," another said. "Whot's wrong wit yer? You one of Dervik's little followers?"

"No. I'm just happy that he is going to be crushed so soon," Jacquelyn lied, smiling lightly. "I'll be able to sleep in peace."

"Where are ya from girl? You ain't from Feruh," the first soldier demanded.

"I'm from Zenbin," Jacquelyn replied.

"Whot is wit all them Zenbinians travelin' around lately?" the second soldier muttered. "Tha's whot tha' little kid an' tha' blind guy said before we figured out they were up ta no good."

"We should go," Merrick whispered to Jacquelyn.

She nodded, and they turned to leave. The soldiers watched them with wary eyes. Merrick warned Jacquelyn not to speed up or turn around. She nodded again and kept her eyes straight ahead. Once they had crossed the city, she breathed a sigh of relief.

"What are we going to do, Merrick? They're going to attack the capital!" she cried.

"I don't know. We can only hope that Hero gets there in time," Merrick replied rather sadly.

"He will. He has to," Jacquelyn said to herself.

"Look, there's the exit," Isabell whispered as the streets started to fill up with people.

They rode to the gates, but two soldiers blocked their path. They pulled their mounts to a halt and waited for the soldiers to speak.

"Sorry to bother ya, but ya haven' seen a boy leadin' a blind man here have ya?" one of them asked.

"This again?" Merrick wondered. "No, sirs, we have not."

"Tha's too bad. They better not have slipped out durin' the night," the second one growled.

"We'll be sure to keep an eye out there," Jacquelyn said, pointing to the forest that stretched out beyond the gate.

"If ya find 'em, bring 'em back 'ere," the first one sighed.

"Yes sir," Merrick replied.

The guards stepped out of the way, while Jacquelyn and Merrick spurred their horses into a brisk trot. The forest was very old and overgrown with vines and moss. The trees seemed weighted down by the years. Overgrown bushes covered the path. The horses had to literally push against the many leaves and twigs that covered the road.

"This forest is amazing," Jacquelyn whispered.

"Except for in the middle," Merrick replied sourly. "In the middle, trees and plants let off a poisonous mist. If you get caught in it too long, you're dead."

"So how do we get through?" Jacquelyn asked.

"Easy, Merrick and I have gone through before. We know the path that goes around the heart of the forest," Isabell boasted.

"That's reassuring," Jacquelyn laughed.

They rode on in silence after that. The forest seemed to be a place of deep quiet. Chips of bark and leaves floated to the ground constantly, making it seem as though it was raining in the forest. Flowers of the wildest colors grew just off the path. Jacquelyn wanted to pick some, but Isabell told her most were poison. Jacquelyn sighed with disappointment.

"All the beautiful things are deadly," she sighed.

"You're not deadly," Merrick smiled slyly.

"Well, thank you for the compliment," Jacquelyn smiled.

"So, I'm deadly?" Isabell asked.

"Very deadly," Merrick said seriously.

"Excellent," Isabell smiled.

Jacquelyn and Merrick laughed, and even Moon Dance let out a quick snicker. They gazed around at the forest and saw that the path before them appeared disturbed, as if someone had recently gone through.

"You think it was the boy and the blind man the soldiers talked about?" Jacquelyn asked.

"It could be. I'm telling you now, I'm not bringing them back to that city. I'm going to find out what they did, if anything," Merrick replied.

"I agree. Those Feruh soldiers may act politely, but if they think you're up to no good, they'll execute you on the spot. Even if you weren't doing anything at all," Isabell said gravely.

"That's horrible," Jacquelyn answered darkly.

"We have to turn here," Merrick said. "Or else we'll end up in the heart of the forest."

"But there isn't even a path," Jacquelyn pointed out.

Merrick pointed to a tree and Jacquelyn inspected a deep gash in its side, obviously made by a sword. She figured that Merrick must have made the mark himself. She wondered why he would do that. Why would he ever go back the way he came when he was running? She voiced her question to him.

"I always planned to return to Carthafell one day," Merrick said. "Arlyn must be killed, and I want to be the one to do it."

Jacquelyn didn't reply. She wished that Merrick didn't feel such hatred for his own family, even if they had mistreated him. She wanted to ask him if he would ever warm up to them, but she didn't want to invade his personal feelings too much. She glanced around and saw that the branches of the bushes that hung out over their path were already broken. Whoever had come before them knew to go this way. She wondered how this could be when the only person who seemed to know about the 'path' was Merrick.

"Hey Merrick, how do the soldiers or other people get through here if they don't know where your path is?" she asked.

"They don't come through here," Merrick replied. "They go around to the east for about ten miles where the forest was cut to allow a trade route and a larger road for the soldiers."

"But someone came through here," Jacquelyn pointed out.

"So you noticed too, huh? Well, the person must have been pretty sharp. Either that or he saw the mist and turned back and happened to stumble across the path," Merrick answered.

"Maybe it was Hero," Isabell suggested. "That's what you're both wondering, isn't it?"

"Yeah," Jacquelyn and Merrick replied at the same time.

Isabell chuckled and forced her way through an overhanging tree branch. Jacquelyn ducked as another branch seemed to reach out for them. Moon Dance shook her head as a fly landed on her nose. Jacquelyn saw another fly land on a nearby tree, and three more land on some bushes. She glanced around rather fearfully; she hated flies. Soon, about ten more flies followed them.

"Merrick, have you noticed the increase of the fly population?" she asked.

"What?" Merrick asked, looking back over his shoulder.

He saw the flies and spurred Isabell into a gallop.

"Come on Jacquelyn, quick," he shouted.

Jacquelyn dug her heels into Moon Dance, and her black mare raced off after Isabell.

"What's going on?" Jacquelyn shouted.

"Those flies belong to Urtha," Merrick yelled. "A witch who lives in these woods and is the cause of the poison!"

"And?" Jacquelyn urged.

"If she finds us, we're dead," Merrick replied sharply, as Isabell jumped over a fallen tree.

Jacquelyn leaned closer to Moon Dance's neck, and the mare sped up. She could hear the buzzing of fly wings following her. She turned her head back and saw that the flies were flying in a frightening formation. They seemed to be making the shape of a human. She whipped her head back around and ducked under a tree branch. A fly landed on her shoulder, and she slapped it with a hand, causing it to fall to the ground.

"Turn right," Merrick shouted.

Jacquelyn followed him as he made a sharp turn, causing Isabell to nearly slip onto her flanks. Moon Dance snorted with displeasure, but made the turn. Jacquelyn saw that they would have run into a wall of flies had they continued.

"Are we going the wrong way?" she cried.

"No," Merrick called back to her. "Now ride as fast as you can, she's catching up to us!"

"Flies are coming at us from the left," Isabell whinnied.

Merrick cursed as a flock of flies crashed into Isabell and Moon Dance. The poor black mare reared up on her hind legs and bashed the flies with her hooves. More flies came from the right and attached themselves to the humans. Jacquelyn tried to draw her sword, but the flies had jammed themselves into her sheath, making it impossible.

"This is too gross!" she screamed.

She jumped up and down to try and get the flies off of her. She sobbed out in disgust as flies tangled into her hair and landed on her face and ears. She slapped at herself fiercely, crushing some of the flies but more replaced them. Pretty soon flies weighed her arms down so much that she couldn't lift them. She glanced over and saw that the flies were covering the horses and Merrick too.

She tried to take a step toward him but fell flat on her face from the weight of the flies. A black boot came into her view. It was shiny and had a sharp heel. She glanced up and saw a woman with a cruel smile on her face.

"Urtha," she whispered.

The woman nodded, and Jacquelyn gasped. She had expected the witch to be ugly, but the opposite was true. She was beautiful. She had flowing black hair that fell to her ankles. Her face was very pale and tinged green, but still pretty. She had black lips and purple eyes, and she wore a black gown with a black cape thrown over her shoulders. Black gloves covered her hands, and Jacquelyn saw that her fingers were strangely long.

Urtha bent down and examined Jacquelyn's face. She smiled again, showing slightly sharp teeth.

"Please get these flies off of me," Jacquelyn said softly.

Urtha stood up and snapped her fingers. The flies rose into the air with a great hum and flew off into the forest again. Jacquelyn walked over to Merrick and the horses and stood defiantly staring at the witch.

"What do you want?" she demanded.

"It has been a while since I've seen a human in these woods," the witch replied.

Her voice was like a soft breeze, but there was something horribly sinister in it.

"So what are you going to do with us?" Jacquelyn asked.

"I'm going to do to you what I do to all the people I catch," Urtha smiled cruelly.

"And that is?" Merrick growled.

Urtha stared at them for a minute before answering with a smirk. "I take them to my cave, drain their blood and throw them into the river. Don't worry about your blood. I promise to make it into very good wine for myself."

"You wouldn't. That's sick," Jacquelyn choked out.

"I am joking. I would never drink it. I'll use it for some new potions or poisons," Urtha chuckled.

"You're still sick," Merrick snarled.

Urtha shrugged and took a step forward. She held out her hand in an inviting way and gave them a sweet smile.

"Would it make you feel better if I gave you a sleeping draught so you won't feel anything?" she asked.

"It would make us feel better if you didn't kill us at all," Jacquelyn snapped, drawing her sword.

Urtha's eyes glowed, and Jacquelyn dropped the now red-hot sword. She waved her hand through the air, trying to cool her now burnt flesh. She glared at the witch with anger.

"You're just like Arlyn," Merrick growled. "And if I can't kill you, then I can't kill her, and I know I can kill her."

"You know Arlyn?" Urtha smiled. "How?"

"I'm her younger brother, Merrick," Merrick replied, putting a hand on his sword.

"Oh I see. I'm the one who gave her the power she now wields. She has rewarded me greatly, and I won't let anyone threaten her life," Urtha sneered.

"You gave her those powers?" Merrick exclaimed. "Then it was partly your fault that my life was a living hell!"

He charged at the witch with his sword drawn. Urtha sighed lazily and waved her hand. Merrick was picked up into the air and thrown backwards into a thick tree. Jacquelyn silently crept over to her sword and picked it up. She made sure that Urtha was busy before creeping back to the horses. She needed to wait for the right moment to attack.

Merrick cursed and faced Urtha again. She smirked and gave him a little wave. Merrick snarled and charged. But instead of charging straight at her, he jumped to the left at the same moment she pointed a finger at him. He swung his sword and seemed to hit her, but she somehow melted into the trees. She appeared behind him and smiled.

"Try again, boy," she sneered.

Merrick growled and quickly turned, swinging his sword with his turn. The momentum from his body caused his swing to be faster, but Urtha had risen into the air and landed near Moon Dance. The mare rammed into the witch, who was taken by surprise. Jacquelyn glanced at Moon Dance in awe. The horse had never attacked anyone before, no matter how mean.

Moon Dance snorted and reared up again. She tried to crush Urtha under her sharp hooves, but the witch threw her palm out before her and thrust the horse backwards. Moon Dance landed awkwardly on her back and thrashed around until she could get back up on her legs. Urtha walked toward the horse, eyes blazing. Merrick crept up behind her intending to cleave her head in two, but as soon as his sword got close to her, it bounced off an invisible wall, and he stumbled away from the witch.

Urtha turned to fight him again while Moon Dance bristled with anger. Jacquelyn ran over to the horse and mounted her.

"We'll attack together in a minute," Jacquelyn whispered.

Moon Dance snorted and laid her ears back, pawing the ground and baring her teeth. Jacquelyn saw Isabell getting ready to charge as well.

Urtha took out a whip and swung the deadly crop at Merrick. He blocked it, but it wrapped around his sword. Urtha tried to pull the weapon from Merrick, but he pulled back. For a second, Jacquelyn thought Urtha would succeed in wrenching the sword from Merrick, but Merrick dug his heels into the ground and yanked with all his might. Urtha's whip flew from her grasp and landed on the ground between them.

"Curse you," she snarled.

She held her hand over her head and the ground shook. Roots from the trees broke through the soil and coiled themselves around Merrick's arms, legs, chest and neck.

"You can only win using cheap tricks!" Merrick barked.

"Magic is my weapon you fool. You can't call it unfair," Urtha taunted.

She walked over to him and cupped his chin within her hand. She forced his head up and lifted her hand. A knife materialized in it and she prepared to end Merrick's life.

Jacquelyn kicked Moon Dance hard, and the mare seemed to fly across the ground. She slammed into the witch once more and sent her sprawling. Isabell had charged at the same time and succeeded in trampling the evil woman. Jacquelyn cut Merrick from the roots, and they ran over to Urtha who spluttered with rage.

"You filthy creatures," she bellowed. "I shall kill you all!"

She snapped her fingers and the flies returned. They melted into her body, causing her to grow bigger and to sprout wings. She grew two antennae on her forehead. Her eyes grew round and red, like a fly. She grew two more arms and stretched them out before her.

"Now you all die!" she screamed, her voice horribly loud.

She lifted herself into the air and flew at them. They barely had time to dodge as she whipped by them.

"How is she so fast?" Jacquelyn thought.

Urtha stood at least twelve feet tall and had to be carrying a lot more weight than before. So how could she be that fast? She pressed herself to the ground as Urtha passed over her again. She crawled over to Merrick and asked how to fight the witch.

"Wait until she passes over us and stab her stomach," Merrick instructed.

Urtha let out a fierce cry as she swooped above them again. Jacquelyn and Merrick prepared to stab her, but she flew high into the air instead of directly over them. They stood up and saw that Urtha was getting ready for something. She waved her hands in slow circles, and a purple light formed around her.

"This is going to be bad," Jacquelyn whispered as the purple light grew brighter.

Urtha cried out in triumph as she released a great purple flame from her hands and sent it shooting toward the companions. Jacquelyn threw herself to the ground and buried her face in her arms. She felt an enormous heat above her searing her skin. Suddenly, the heat dissipated, and she looked up to see a small boy attacking Urtha.

He had leapt from a tree onto her shoulders and stabbed the evil woman everywhere he could. Urtha screamed and grabbed the boy with one huge hand. The boy growled and slashed the hand with his knife. She dropped him, and the boy grabbed a nearby tree branch. He pulled himself up and placed his feet firmly on the branch. Urtha flew at him, swooping low to hit him. At the same time, Jacquelyn, Merrick and the boy thrust their weapons into her stomach. The witch soon fell dead, and the boy walked over to Jacquelyn and Merrick. He helped them to their feet and gave them a friendly smile.

"Thank you," Jacquelyn said.

"No problem. I couldn't let that nasty monster kill you," the boy replied with a grin.

"What are you doing in a forest like this alone?" Merrick asked. "Where are your parents?"

"I don't have any. I was just leading my blind brother through Feruh," the boy said. "Jeru's the name."

"The blind man and the boy? You're the ones those soldiers were asking people about?" Jacquelyn asked in surprise.

"They're asking about us, eh? Well they won't be able to find us," Jeru said with a smile.

"Why are they after you two?" Isabell asked.

"I have no idea. One minute we're checking into an inn, the next about thirty soldiers came to apprehend us," Jeru explained.

"You said you're from Zenbin, correct?" Merrick asked.

"Yeah," Jeru answered slowly.

"You should probably head back there so you're protected. The soldiers are anxious with the war so close," Merrick instructed.

"You're right, of course," Jeru smiled. "I shall be getting back to my brother now, before he wanders off somewhere."

"What is your brother's name?" Jacquelyn asked.

"Sorry, miss, but I'd rather not reveal it. He hates when I tell strangers his name. Good day to you both," Jeru said.

He walked off into the woods. Jacquelyn and Merrick stared after him. Jacquelyn felt something about the boy seemed familiar. Maybe he just reminded her a bit of Hero with his wolfish face. She shook her head and mounted Moon Dance, who waited patiently nearby.

"Thanks Moon Dance, you were brilliant," she whispered, patting the black mare on the neck.

Moon Dance held her head high with pride for a minute before walking alongside Isabell, who was already making her way toward the path. Jacquelyn peered back at the battlefield and saw Jeru poke his head out of the forest again, watching them with a smile. She also thought she could detect another shape in the trees, maybe the blind brother? She smiled and turned back to the path. The forest grew thinner, which meant that it couldn't be too much longer.

"We can camp here for the night," Merrick said as they entered a meadow.

Jacquelyn sighed, the thinning trees only led to the large meadow, not the way out. The ground was covered with a thick grass of a lush green color. She dismounted and let Moon Dance graze for a while before tying her reins to a nearby bush. Merrick cleared away a circle of grass and dug a small pit. When he finished, he lit a fire in the pit and took out some dried meat.

"This is the last of our food," he sighed. "We'll have to restock in the next town."

"I hope it isn't anything like Cuth," Jacquelyn complained.

"Believe me, some cities in Feruh are a hundred times worse. But we don't have to go through them luckily," Merrick said.

Jacquelyn took her share of meat and looked up at the sky. It was cloudy, and she could see no stars. She wondered again about the mysterious boy they had met in the forest. The more she thought about him, the more he seemed to look similar to Hero in some way. As if he, too, were a wolf. She shook her head and forced herself not to think about him. Thinking about him made her think of Hero, and it was too painful to think about the man she loved.

Chapter 25

Jeru and Hero made their way to the meadow, where they saw a small fire. They stopped at the outskirts of the trees and watched the two figures as they ate their dinner.

"I don't know why you don't want to go to them," Jeru whispered.

"I can't face them yet. I have to do this alone," Hero replied softly.

"Does that mean you want to leave me behind too?" Jeru asked.

"No. There is just something different between you and them. Maybe because you were a wolf and remind me of home. I don't really know," Hero sighed. "But I know if I join up with them again, then we'll grow way too close, and then it will hurt too much when I have to return to Verinaul."

"What about when you have to leave me behind?" Jeru asked slyly.

"I don't know. I mean, I'll miss you, but I used to admire you when I was younger. You were like a hero to me and the other pups. I don't think I'll be able to become very close friends with you because of that," Hero replied slowly.

"I know what you mean. I still remember you as a pup, and it is hard to see past that," Jeru chuckled. "So, do you want to go around the meadow and keep traveling?"

"Yes," Hero said, somewhat reluctantly.

He gave his friends one last look before following Jeru back into the trees. They silently made their way around the perimeter of the forest, being careful not to leave the cover of the trees as it was still quite light out.

Once they circled around the meadow, Hero stopped and looked back. Jeru waited politely for him as Hero said a final silent farewell. He wanted to meet up with them again, but he knew he couldn't face them yet. He sighed and followed Jeru as they ran through the forest.

"Do you know how much longer it will take us to get out of Feruh?" Hero panted as they ran up a steep hill.

"I'm guessing about three more weeks," Jeru answered.

Hero sighed and sped up a bit. He knew they wouldn't make it in time, but maybe they could help the King somehow. He slowed as the edge of the forest came into view. Jeru stopped as Hero replaced the bandages around his head to hide his eyes. He grabbed hold of Jeru's hand, and they continued running. He knew every second counted so he tried to run even faster.

"We have to get out of this country. What's the next gate?" Hero asked.

"I think it's called the Ruroshiken Gate. It leads to the plains that stretch out before Delring," Jeru replied.

"How long will it take to cross the plains?" Hero asked.

"About four hours. Then we'll hit the Hivina Gate that leads into Hasrath. It's only a mile to Delring from there," Jeru said.

"We'll have to lend our help to King Dervik," Hero said. "Jeru, we should keep moving during the day too," he said.

"Okay," Jeru replied shortly. "What about your injuries?"

"I think they're okay now. They don't hurt anymore," Hero replied. "So we'll run until we can't run anymore."

"That might not be a good idea, Hero. What if we wear ourselves out?" Jeru asked.

"We won't! We have to reach Delring! Something in my heart tells me that we have to be there," Hero replied determinedly.

They ran as fast as they could throughout the night, and didn't even stop as the sun slowly rose into view. In fact, they ran until midday when Jeru finally collapsed. Hero removed the bandages from his eyes and pulled Jeru into a thicket for cover.

"I'm exhausted," Jeru panted.

"I think we should rest for about five hours," Hero replied. "Then we have to move again."

"Only five hours? But Hero, we're going to kill ourselves," Jeru whined.

"We can handle it," Hero smiled.

Jeru looked at him doubtfully and then took out some food. They didn't have much left so he divided it into small portions. Hero wolfed his down and curled up to sleep. Jeru sighed and followed suit. He hoped that Hero wouldn't wake in five hours.

Hero opened his eyes with a start. The sun was setting, and he knew that the time had come to move on. He woke Jeru up, and, after a lot of complaining, the younger boy got up. Hero prepared to tie the bandages around his head, but he let them drop.

"We need all the haste we can muster. I'm too slow with those on," he explained as Jeru looked at him.

"But if those soldiers see you, they'll try to capture you," Jeru pointed out.

"Let them try," Hero growled, putting a hand on his sword's sheathe.

Jeru gulped and followed Hero as he started to run toward the north, to Delring. He didn't want Hero to start taking any risks, but he understood that they were running out of time. Hero ran as fast as he could, ignoring the burning pain in his legs and lungs. He hadn't rested enough, but that wasn't going to stop him.

They didn't encounter many interesting things in Feruh in the next two and a half weeks. The soldiers had moved out of the towns and cities and most of the men had gone to fight in the war. Hero and Jeru stopped in the inns along the way, which were usually filled with old men and children.

"I think we're almost through Feruh," Jeru whispered as they sat at a small table in an inn.

"So we have to go through the Ruroshiken Gate first, and then cross the plains and then go through the Hivina Gate?" Hero asked.

"Yes, but I'm not totally sure how far the Ruroshiken Gate is," Jeru admitted.

"Excuse me," Hero said as a waitress came over. "Do you know how far the nearest gate out of Feruh is?"

"Well, tha' depends on where you're going," the waitress answered. "If ya wan' to help the other men in the war, which ya should, then I suggest headin' to the Ruroshiken Gate. It's about three days from 'ere on horseback."

"Thank you, ma'am," Jeru replied. "That's the one we want."

"Do you know where we can get some horses?" Hero asked.

"Yeah, tha' farm at the end of this town is full of horses. Not real beautiful, but they're stronger than any other horse around here," the woman answered.

"Thank you," Hero replied.

They ate their meal in silence. Three days and the great battle would begin. Hero felt awful that the war had already been raging for a week or so without him on hand to help. He wanted to find out why he was mentioned in all the legends. He had to be able to do something. He stood up and with Jeru following went to buy some horses.

"I don't know how to ride," Jeru pointed out before they reached the farm.

"Just hold on tight and don't let go. Try not to be too nervous or your horse will feel it and get frisky," Hero explained.

They walked into the well-kept farm and saw two men pitching hay into the horse stalls. They stopped their chore when they saw they had customers.

"Ya folks lookin' to buy some horses?" one asked.

"Yes sir," Hero said with a smile. "How much for two horses with a lot of endurance?"

"Well, I'd say aroun' 1000 coins an' no less," the second one replied.

Hero and Jeru looked through their bags and found that they came 20 coins short. The farmers noticed their dismay and laughed.

"If ya have any valuables, then we'll take 'em instead," they said.

"Well, I have this dagger," Jeru said.

"Tha will do jus' fine," the first farmer smiled.

He took the money and the dagger and led them to two giant horses. They weren't as pretty as most, as their coats were scraggly and slightly matted, but they were of great build and looked powerful. One was silver with a black mane, while the other was brown with a white mane.

"Forest and River are the names," the second farmer said. "Have fun wit' 'em."

"Do we need tack?" Jeru whispered.

"No. Just hold onto his mane and you'll be fine. Try not to tug it too much though or you'll annoy him," Hero smiled.

They led the horses from the barn, and Hero mounted the silver one called River. He turned back to see how Jeru was doing. The boy had somehow managed to mount the horse so that he faced backwards. Hero sighed and went over to help. When Jeru finally faced the right way, they set out.

"How are you going to fight without a weapon?" Hero asked.

"Don't worry," Jeru smirked. "That wasn't a weapon. It was a decoration. I figured we might run out of money, so I grabbed it before we left my house."

Hero shook his head as he spurred River into a gallop. The horse wasn't the smoothest runner, and jostled Hero around a lot. But Hero was a lot more comfortable than Jeru, who tried desperately just not to fall off. He was nearly sitting on the side of the animal when Hero turned to check on him.

"Are you sure we need horses?" Jeru complained.

"Positive. Besides we can't let them go after paying for them," Hero pointed out.

"I don't think Forest likes me very much," Jeru said.

Hero looked back and saw that Jeru was hanging onto the horse's neck and trying to use the mane to pull himself upright.

"Don't yank on his mane," Hero called out. "Use your legs to stay balanced. Clutch with your knees…there you go."

Jeru had righted himself and followed Hero's instructions. He now rode upright and beamed with joy at his success. Forest relaxed when he realized that his mane would not be torn from his head. He caught up to River, and the horses trotted side by side.

"This isn't so bad," Jeru smiled.

"See? You just have to get used to it," Hero replied. "Horses are great. I had one named Phoebus a while back."

"Where is he?" Jeru asked.

"He was killed by a demon," Hero replied quickly.

"Why would they ever kill a horse? That's really mean!" Jeru snarled.

"Phoebus protected me from them. He was a fine animal. Shone like gold when the sun shined on him," Hero smiled.

"I'm sure he was happy with you," Jeru said. "And I bet River will be too."

Hero nodded and fell silent as they continued on. He was rather tired of waiting to see what would happen. He wanted to know how he was to help.

"Jeru, do you think that Arlyn will be in this battle?" Hero asked suddenly.

"No. I doubt it," Jeru replied. "She probably won't ever be at a battle. You can bet that Muryn will lead them though."

"I will have to settle on killing him then," Hero growled.

"Then Arlyn will hunt you down and kill you. She and Muryn are very close, and if he is even scratched she will be beyond reason."

"Whether she gets angry or not, Muryn has to die," Hero thought. "And I will be the one to do it."

"I think we should slow our pace a bit so that the horses don't get exhausted. That woman said three days, and we'll be sure to make it in that time," Jeru said.

Hero agreed, and they slowed the horses into a steady trot. Jeru looked a lot happier with the slower pace. Hero realized that the horses were still fine, but the young boy was not.

"Are you sure that it's the horses that need a break?" Hero asked slyly. "Or were you referring to yourself?"

"Shut up, Hero. I'm not used to this," Jeru pouted.

"Well, we have three days of hard riding ahead of us, so you better get used to it," Hero laughed, spurring River into a canter.

"Wait for me!" Jeru yelled, digging his heels into Forest.

The brown horse frisked his head and galloped off, passing River and carrying a terrified Jeru with it.

"*Help me!*" Jeru bellowed as Hero laughed loudly.

When Forest had finally let off all his steam and slowed down, Jeru's hair was windblown and his face, flushed. Hero stopped River beside him and gave him an arrogant grin.

"Looks like the old hero from back in the day can't even handle riding a horse," he joked.

"Oh, shut your mouth," Jeru snapped, dismounting from the large horse.

They tied the horses to a nearby tree and camped nearby. Jeru complained about sore legs and asked if they could walk the rest of the way.

"Well, if you want to then that's fine, but I shall have to go ahead of you. Unless you can keep up with River that is," Hero said.

"Never mind," Jeru grumbled.

"Oh come on, Jeru. Riding isn't that bad. It's really fun," Hero said with a smile.

"The only fun part is dismounting," Jeru pouted.

"Could you ever run that fast by yourself? I don't think so. I love being able to move that fast without having to work too hard," Hero sighed.

"Without having to work? Riding that beast is the hardest thing I've ever done in my life," Jeru shouted.

"Don't be so loud," Hero said seriously. "You never who could be nearby."

"Oh come off it," Jeru groaned.

"I'm serious. There could be soldiers nearby. We don't want to run into trouble now," Hero whispered.

"Whatever, I'm going to sleep," Jeru muttered moodily.

He stretched himself out on the ground and refused to speak another word. Hero sighed. He knew his friend was just tired from the ride and hungry. But they barely had any food left and with the coming battle, they were not in cheerful moods. Hero gazed up at the stars and wondered again how he was expected to stop the fight. How was one inexperienced swordsman supposed to fight off an entire army? He was no match against Muryn, and he bet his life that other captains and lieutenants were more skilled than he. He sighed and turned on his side. He wished he were back home, running through the woods with Nakoomu at his side. He wanted to run over the snowy hills of his land with his pack following closely behind. He wanted to return to Verinaul, but at the same time, something made him want to stay in Nazberath.

"But what?" he wondered aloud. "Why would I ever want to stay in this turbulent world where bloodshed seems to be the only thing important to its people."

He knew that the something that made him want to stay was someone with long black hair and bright blue eyes and a smile that flashed at him whenever they were together. He sighed; he knew that he should never have let things go this way. How could he love more than one?

"Sorry, Jacquelyn, but I won't betray Nakoomu no matter what I feel for you. I wonder…do you even feel this way about me?" Hero said softly.

Chapter 26

For the next two days, Hero and Jeru pushed their horses to the limit. The powerful animals were gasping for breath by the time they stopped on the third day. The Ruroshiken Gate lay just ahead of them. It was wide open, and they spotted some wagons coming through—wagons loaded with people and catapults.

"We have to stop them," Hero snarled, urging River forward.

"There are too many," Jeru called after him.

He groaned and followed his friend into battle. The soldiers turned in surprise, and then they laughed at the few number.

"All right boys," said one. "Looks like those there boys are wantin' an early death!"

They drew their swords and charged, while the wagons continued their slow path to the plains. Hero stood up on River's saddle and jumped off the horse when the first soldier caught up. He couldn't afford to lose his horse now. The soldier gave a startled yelp before Hero slashed his throat.

Jeru had dismounted and charged at the soldiers with his large dagger at the ready. When the soldiers paused with amusement at finding a kid as their opponent, Jeru snarled and lunged at them. He kicked one in the groin and stabbed the other in the forehead. He then turned to finish off the one he had kicked.

"Tha's not right," one of the soldiers cried. "They shoulda' been dead by now."

"Here me, men of Feruh!" Hero bellowed. "I am Hero Red Eye, son of Serval Red Eyes and known as the Lone Wolf in your world! I will stop this fighting and end that foolish Queen's reign!"

"Tha's Lone Wolf?" a soldier gasped.

"Can't be, too young," another argued.

"Whether you believe me or not is up to you, it doesn't matter," Hero growled.

He rushed ahead and killed another soldier, quickly slamming his fist into another who tried to sneak up behind him. The man saw his red and yellow eyes and cried out in panic. He fell to the ground and begged Hero to spare him. Hero smacked him in the head with the flat of his blade and knocked him out.

"Surrender or die," Jeru barked, knifing another soldier.

"We ain't surrenderin' to you," a large man snarled. He was obviously the leader of the group.

"If I beat you, then your men will surrender," Hero said.

"You can't beat me, ya fool," the leader laughed.

He drew a sword and charged at Hero, who dodged it and kicked the man in the back. He went sprawling a few feet before regaining his balance. He snarled and rushed at Hero again, who jumped into the air and slashed at the leader's shoulder as he came down. The leader managed to block the blow.

"How's this?" he shouted, pulling a whip out of nowhere.

He smiled, and, with a crack, the whip wrapped around Hero's wrist with a sharp snap. Hero ground his teeth with pain, but he wasn't about to give up. He smirked and dug his teeth into the whip and started to gnaw it apart. The leader's eyes widened, and he tried to tug the whip away. Hero dug his heels into the ground, which made it impossible for the leader to pull him anywhere. Once he successfully chewed through the whip, he ran to the astounded leader and stabbed him through the heart.

"The rest of you leave the wagons and return to your homes!" Hero ordered while Jeru nodded.

The soldiers dropped their weapons and fled. Jeru looked at Hero with amazement.

"You were really scary," the young boy whispered.

"Was I? I didn't even realize," Hero smiled.

"Your eyes blazed and power seemed to emanate from your body. Very impressive," Jeru commented.

"Maybe that's the way to win this war—through intimidation," Hero wondered. "Come, the plains are here and Delring only about five hours away."

"I can't believe we actually made it in one piece," Jeru said, rounding up River and Forest.

They mounted and rode through the plains, making sure no soldiers waited to ambush them.

When they finally reached the Hivina Gate, they gasped. It had been broken down and smoke billowed into the sky. Hero and Jeru forced their tired horses into a fierce gallop, both praying that they were not too late.

"We need more time," Hero said angrily. "We can't defend the city if there isn't anyone to defend!"

They rode through the gate and saw the bodies of Hasrath soldiers strewn about the place. Hero wished they could give them a proper burial, but there was no time. He and Jeru continued forward and prepared for battle. Although fear filled his body, Hero also felt excited.

"There, look. They've broken through the city's outer wall!" Jeru cried out as they neared the city.

"Now is the time, Jeru. There's a whole army in front of us. We have to ride through them," Hero said softly.

Jeru gulped and looked at the huge mass of people ahead of them. There were about 50,000 soldiers from Carthafell, Zenbin, Feruh, and Gelda. Hero told his young companion to act as Feruh soldiers while they were in the presence of the enemy soldiers. Jeru nodded and sighed deeply. He stiffened up and urged Forest toward the army.

Hero soon followed, and within minutes horses, people, catapults and shouts surrounded them. Soldiers cursed as the two horses pushed by them and more than one shot an arrow at them. Hero and Jeru leaned down and kept yelling that they were Feruh men who had come to help. But no one listened, so they just had to hope that they did not get killed.

When they passed through the destroyed doors of the first wall, Hero saw him. Muryn sat astride a large black stallion with a pure white mane. The General looked over at him, but he had already ducked his head and buried his face in River's mane. When he peaked up again, he saw Muryn order more catapults to be loaded. Jeru and Hero dismounted and ran to the second wall, heavily guarded by Delring's soldiers who were shooting arrows down upon the enemy forces.

"Come on, there must be a place where they'll let us in," Jeru said, dodging an arrow.

Hero nodded and they raced off the find an entrance. They ran all the way to the back of the city, dodging Delring arrows, and trying to tell anyone would listen their true identity. Once they reached the back, they saw that a number of men waited for them on the walls, arrows pointed directly toward them.

"You have two seconds to tell us who you are," one of them threatened.

"I am the one known as Lone Wolf," Hero replied calmly.

"Ha. You think we're going to believe you?" another one scoffed.

"Take a look into his eyes," Jeru challenged.

One soldier disappeared and soon opened a small metal door in front of them. The others tensed and prepared to shoot in case Hero or Jeru moved. The soldier looked into Hero's eyes and was at a loss for words.

"We're saved," he shouted. "It really is him. His eyes are red and yellow, like the stories!"

The soldier invited them in, and the one who came to inspect them, Jon, led them toward the actual city.

"Wait until King Dervik sees you. He'll be thrilled!" Jon smiled. "Our reinforcements were due to come three days ago."

"I don't know exactly what I can do, but whatever may help I will do," Hero stated.

"And me too," Jeru exclaimed.

"Me three," a familiar voice said.

Hero and Jeru whipped around to see Molly leaning against a tree. She didn't look like the little girl they had met before though. Her eyes were pink and purple again, but her hair was dark green. She had light blue skin and wore a pink dress. She also had translucent wings that seemed to sparkle with their own light. She smiled with purple lips and floated over to them.

"The Fairy Queen...oh I give up pronouncing your real name. Molly has been helping us for five days now—healing the men and singing them songs to keep their spirits up. She's been too kind," Jon said.

"But you lived in Shiboo. They sided with Queen Arlyn," Jeru pointed out.

"That doesn't mean the fairies supported that awful woman. We lived there first, and we gave the people permission to settle there so they left us all alone," Molly explained.

"Come on you two, the King is waiting," Hero said, following Jon along a white cobblestone road.

They had entered the city, which was bigger than any city Hero had ever seen. All the houses stood about one inch apart, and the smallest was two stories high. Vendors filled the streets, still selling their goods despite the harsh battle going on around them. White roads all led to the palace in the distance. Even the palace was white, and big enough to fit two cities the size of Cuths. Hero glanced at the top-most tower and saw that it practically touched the heavens.

"This place is amazing," Jeru said in wonder.

"I wish you could have dropped by before the invasion," Jon sighed.

"Can the reinforcements get here any sooner?" Hero asked.

"Not possible," Jon moaned. "The King has tried many times to hustle them, but they can't move as fast as he needs them to."

"Then we'll just have to fight with the men we have," Hero mused, "which may be suicide."

"King Dervik is doing all he can to think of a way to defend the city," Jon replied sadly. "But we've already fallen to the inner wall as you could see."

"Fear not, Jon. We will find a way," Molly whispered reassuringly.

Jon nodded and for the rest of the way he remained silent. Jeru glanced around the city nervously, as though expecting the enemy to come charging at them at any minute. Hero stood looking straight ahead at the large palace where the King he had heard so much about waited for him.

Not long after, they passed through the huge oak doors that led into the palace. The large entrance hall had a beautiful woven rug spread across it, and many chambers branched from the hall, but Jon walked up a broad flight of stairs. Hero and Jeru looked around eagerly at the fine furnishings and paintings that seemed to fill the palace completely.

"We're here," Jon said, stopping in front of a door with the crest of Hasrath on it. A hybrid of man and lion, the crest featured the head of a lion and the body of a man with a lion's tail. This creature held a large sword in one hand and a bouquet of flowers in the other. Jon opened the door and bowed low to a figure looking out a large window.

"Sire, I have brought you someone you will be very pleased to meet," Jon said, still bowing.

"Thank you, Jon. Return to your post now, please," the King replied in a deep voice that was rough but very warm.

"Yes, your Majesty," Jon replied.

He straightened up and left the room, giving Hero a small pat on the shoulder. Hero smiled at him and entered the room with Jeru and Molly in his wake. King Dervik turned to face them, and they all bowed.

"Please," he said, indicating that they should rise.

They did so, and the King smiled. He was a man in his mid-forties with long black hair that fell neatly to his shoulder blades. He had a large mustache that fell past his chin. His eyebrows were bushy and his eyes, brown. He had a wide face and a broad nose. His mouth was slightly too large, but not overly so. He had a look to him that inspired trust. He waved his hands to the chairs in front of his large throne, and the companions sat.

"So, what brings you to this city whilst we are in war?" he asked kindly.

"We offer you our service," Hero replied.

"What is your name?" Kink Dervik asked.

"My name is Hero, Milord, or as you know me, Lone Wolf," Hero answered politely.

"Lone Wolf?" Kink Dervik gasped. He looked into Hero's eyes and nodded. "So it is. We are truly lucky that you have come."

"Excuse me, but I've never been trained for battle, your Majesty," Hero gulped. "I'm not sure how much use I will be."

"Sir Hero, you were once a wolf, yes? How would your pack handle this?" King Dervik asked.

"Our pack wouldn't waste time defending," Hero replied. "I know it sounds crazy, but we should launch an all out offensive. Keep some of the men on the walls to use bows and man the catapults, and send the rest to confront Muryn and his army."

"Hm…It has risk, but we can't rely on the reinforcements any longer. They will not get here in time if we keep this up," Kink Dervik said softly.

"I think it's a good idea, your Majesty," Molly spoke up.

"Yes, I believe it is our only hope," King Dervik replied.

"I also suggest attacking from both sides," Hero said. "Their main force is concentrated right at the center of the inner wall. So many are jammed in the opening of the outer wall that they won't be able to retreat quickly. Send two forces at them at once. Have your best generals leading them, and you'll be sure to win."

"I thought you weren't trained in war," King Dervik smiled. "Well, I think one unit should be led by General Sunyin. And if you wouldn't mind, I would like you to lead the other."

"I will lead the second unit, the one that attacks from the left. We must call General Sunyin into the room," Hero replied.

"You are correct. Molly, would you please find the General?" King Dervik asked.

"Right away, your Highness," Molly replied.

She got up and disappeared on the spot. King Dervik fixed his eyes upon Jeru and had a questioning look upon his face.

"This is my friend, Jeru," Hero smiled. "He helped me get here."

"I see. It is nice to meet you," King Dervik said.

"And to meet you, Sire," Jeru replied nervously.

"Jeru was also a wolf," Hero said.

"Really now? This is a surprise!" King Dervik exclaimed. "So you two are in the same deal, eh?"

"Not really," Jeru explained. "You see, I was a wolf that died and was reborn into Nazberath. Hero was still alive as a wolf when he was sent here."

"I wonder, can humans change into animals and go to Verinaul when they die?" King Dervik mused.

"That's a good question, Sire," Jeru replied.

"I think they can," Hero blurted out. The other two looked at him. "Think about the Wise Ones. They knew all about this world, and it's not as if we have books about it."

"Oh my, you may be right," Jeru yelped.

At that moment, the door opened and Molly returned with a woman in full battle armor. She had dark brown hair tied up in a high ponytail. She had hard, black eyes and a small face that was pretty, but not beautiful. She also had a small scar on the side of her neck. She bowed to the King and looked at Hero and Jeru curiously.

"Please be seated, General," King Dervik said.

She sat next to Hero.

"This is Hero Lone Wolf and his friend, Jeru. Hero just created a battle plan that may win us this fight," King Dervik explained.

"This is Lone Wolf? I'm honored," Sunyin said, bowing her head to him. Hero nodded back in return. "What is this plan?"

Hero explained his plan again. By the time he finished, Sunyin had an excited glint in her eyes and nodded with approval. She agreed to lead the first unit and strike the enemy from the right.

"I pray for your health and victory," King Dervik said as they got up to head off for battle.

"You can't fight unprotected," Sunyin said. "We'll have to stop by the armory and get you ready. I also suggest going to the smithy to sharpen your swords."

She led them to a large room where many suits of armor hung from the walls. She looked Hero up and down and reached for a heavy looking breastplate. She then went to the other side of the room and selected a chain mail shirt and battle boots. She set them down in front of Hero and went to find the same for Jeru.

Hero reached down and slipped the chain mail shirt on over his tunic. It was very uncomfortable. He frowned as he placed the heavy breastplate over his torso and wondered how he was expected to move. He replaced his worn boots with the new ones, and Jeru gave a nod of approval.

"Sunyin, how do I move in this gear?" Hero asked as the General gave Jeru the same armor.

"Believe me, it just takes getting used to. By the time you reach Muryn, you won't even remember it's there," Sunyin smiled.

Jeru placed the armor on and frowned as it weighed him down. He sighed and followed Sunyin as she led them to the smithy. They reached the hot room about five minutes later. Sunyin shoved Hero toward the first available blacksmith, who immediately sharpened his sword. Another sharpened Jeru's dagger. Sunyin then led them from the smithy and instructed them to follow her to the troops. Hero gulped nervously and nodded his head.

The troops had been called to assemble in a rear courtyard of the grand palace. They whispered excitedly to one another. Obviously the news of Hero had spread from Jon. When Sunyin came into view, they all turned their heads in her direction and stood in salute.

"At ease," Sunyin ordered, and they all sat back down. "As you probably know by now, Hero the Lone Wolf has come to help us battle. This is Lone Wolf."

The men cheered as Sunyin placed a hand on Hero's shoulder quickly before starting to pace in front of the large army. Hero would have thought it impossible for the men in the back to hear, but the entire army remained perfectly silent and listened attentively to their General.

"Hero, since it is your plan, you may explain it to the men," Sunyin decided.

Hero gulped nervously again and stood before the army. "My plan is to attack Muryn's army from both sides in a pincer attack. The majority of his force is concentrated on the front gate of the inner wall. General Sunyin will lead the first unit from the right, while I will take command of the second unit, which will attack from the left. We have to act quickly before they get through that second wall," he explained. "I'll leave the units to Sunyin."

"Okay men, everyone from the 50th row back will be in Hero's unit, and the rest will come with me!" Sunyin called.

The soldiers gave a loud cheer, and Sunyin placed her helmet over her head. She turned to Hero and clasped his and Jeru's hands tightly before leading her unit to the right of the city. Jeru gave Hero a comforting smile and followed his friend as he made his way to the left. The soldiers stopped him and bowed before him.

"It is a tremendous honor serving in your unit," they said.

"I am grateful that you feel that way," Hero blushed. "Now, let's go kill those intruders!"

The men gave a shout and followed Hero and Jeru toward the left end of the city. Hero gazed at the sky and wondered vaguely where Jacquelyn and Merrick were. He hoped against hope that they didn't make it to the city to witness the battle, but he knew in his heart that they would come no matter what. He sighed and glanced over his shoulder at the men, who were now un-tethering horses. Jon appeared with a grin, leading Forest and River over to them.

"And so comes the battle," Hero murmured. "It is time for Lone Wolf to strike."

Chapter 27

Once Hero's troops were ready, he signaled them to make haste toward the center of the city where a great loud bang carried on the wind. The enemy soldiers must have positioned a battering ram at the gate while Hero and his troops were preparing. Hero knew that if he and Sunyin didn't make it in time, then the whole plan would fail. He looked at the sun and knew they had half an hour, almost exactly how long it would take to move his whole unit to the battle.

"Men of Nazberath," Hero called. "We ride to the center of the city at all haste. Follow me!"

He nudged River into a canter and heard the loud din of the soldiers following him. Jeru had his eyes closed, and Hero knew he was saying a silent prayer. Hero would have asked the younger boy if he wanted to stay from the fighting, but he knew that the once revered wolf would never allow such a thing. Hero heard the banging more and more clearly as they rode on. The Carthafell army had almost breached the gate. He quickened the pace.

When he reached the center of the city, he saw Sunyin's unit already charging the enemy soldiers. He smiled because the enemy focused all of their attention on the unit at the right.

"CHARGE!" Hero bellowed.

He and his unit galloped toward the startled soldiers in the middle. They tried to form ranks to defend against the rapidly approaching second unit, but Hero and his men collided with them before they could respond.

Instantly a sea of noise surrounded Hero. He tried to focus on his unit as well as himself, but it was extremely difficult. Carthafell soldiers and their allies struck at him from all sides, and he barely had time to lift his sword from one man before another set upon him. He also saw that his opponents were not all human. Occasionally his blade would strike down a man or woman with purple, blue or red hair.

"Hero...*Watch out*!" a voice shrieked.

Hero turned in time to see a soldier with a spear coming at him. He pulled back on his reins and River reared up. The strong horse brought his hooves down upon the warrior, crushing the air from his lungs. Hero turned to see Jeru giving him a wink. He thanked his friend silently as another man engaged him in battle.

He saw Muryn across the sea of armored bodies. The General of Carthafell wore a smooth smile on his face as he cut down many Hasrath soldiers. Hero knew that they were overwhelmed, but the surprise attack had turned the battle in their favor for the moment. They could only hope that the reinforcements from Jurik and Olkina arrived in time. While he watched the General, a highly dressed officer, most likely a Lieutenant, smashed his war horse into River. The move unseated Hero, and he fell to the ground with a snarl.

The Lieutenant laughed and thrust his spear at Hero, who dodged and grabbed it. The Lieutenant tried to yank it from his grasp, but Hero wouldn't relinquish the weapon. Instead, he gave a mighty pull and the Lieutenant fell from his horse. Hero quickly thrust the spear through his heart. He mounted River again and re-sheathed his sword, using the spear instead.

"Come on men of Delring!" Sunyin yelled above the noise. "Send these vile creatures back where they belong!"

The brave General steered her horse into the thick of battle and began to hack down enemy soldiers. Hero saw Muryn charge his horse after her. He spurred River on to intercept the skilled General. Muryn saw him at the last moment and turned his horse to face him. Hero smiled as he held the spear out like a javelin. He prepared to spear the evil General through the heart, but Muryn simply jumped out of his saddle and tackled Hero to the ground. Hero lost his spear and drew his sword to make ready to fight against the General.

"I thought you'd be dead by now," Muryn said mockingly. "Well done."

"Prepare to die, Muryn," Hero snarled.

He lunged forward and slashed at Muryn's neck. The skilled General simply stepped aside and followed up by stabbing at Hero. Hero ducked under the deadly blade and punched Muryn in the chest, which didn't do much since the General wore armor. Muryn laughed and kicked Hero in the face where he was unprotected. Hero fell to the ground and growled, now sporting a bloody lip and nose. He felt his teeth grow back to his wolf teeth and looked up to see Molly sitting upon a rooftop. He sent her thanks silently, since only she could change his teeth to wolf's. Hero ran at Muryn and, at the last moment, jumped to the left to try and strike at his side. Muryn jumped back lightly and blocked the blow. Hero pushed Muryn's blade aside with his sword and threw a punch at the General's face. Muryn raised his own free arm and blocked it. He pulled his sword away and thrust it at Hero's knee.

Hero tried to jump back, but a Carthafell soldier blocked his way. Muryn's blade sank into his upper leg, causing him to let out a grunt of pain. The ruthless General then slammed his elbow into the side of Hero's head, and he crashed to the ground. Hero rose as fast as he could and jumped at Muryn. He buried his teeth into Muryn's arm and was pleased to hear Muryn's gasp of shock as the teeth dug into his flesh. However, Hero had let his guard down, and Muryn slipped out a knife, which he slammed into Hero's side, where the armor was not as tough.

Hero yelped and backed away, holding his side. He wondered whether Muryn would wound him as much as Hynraz had back in the mountains. Seeing Muryn's cocky grin erased that thought. The man would probably just kill him straight out. Ignoring the throbbing pain in his side, Hero swung his sword at the General's face, but he just laughed as he blocked it. Hero brought his sword closer to defend himself, but Muryn threw his knife at him. He couldn't use his sword to block it or else Muryn would render him totally defenseless. He clenched his teeth together and took one hand off his blade. With that hand, he caught the deadly knife and growled as it slit his palm open. He threw the knife aside and blocked Muryn's blow.

"Tell me, Wolf," Muryn said as they paused to catch their breaths. "What happened to my brother?"

"None of your business," Hero replied angrily.

He charged at Muryn once more, and once more Muryn dodged his attack. The General kicked Hero in the back and sent him sprawling. Hero tried to get up, but he felt a sword point at the back of his neck.

"Surrender now, or I kill you," Muryn said.

"You'll have to kill me," Hero shot back.

Muryn gave a quick bark of a laugh, and Hero felt the sword dig a little deeper into his neck. Suddenly, Muryn let out a curse and the pressure lifted from Hero's neck. Hero sat up and placed a hand on his neck, where he felt warm blood trickling under his armor. He saw a familiar face above him and a hand in front of his face. Hero smiled as he took Merrick's hand, which pulled him to his feet.

"Finally caught up to you it seems," Merrick grinned.

"Not at the best time," Hero replied.

"Oh, Hero, you're okay," Jacquelyn cried.

"For the moment," Hero said. "Now let's focus back on this battle before saying our hellos."

Hero looked around for Muryn, but couldn't find the General anywhere. He spat disdainfully, but saw he had more to worry about. Carthafell and its allies had pulled a fancy trick. While the others busied fighting, they had loaded their catapults with Minotaurs, which would easily survive the thrust into the air and would crash into the city.

The enemy launched the Minotaurs into all parts of the city. They stood at least eight feet tall and had hefty arms that carried massive, spiked hammers.

"To the city," Hero yelled. "They're breaking into the city!"

The Minotaurs had opened the gate of the inner wall, which allowed the remainder of the enemy troops into the city. The Carthafell, Feruh and Zenbin soldiers gave a whoop of joy and streamed into the city. Hero groaned and knew that the tide had turned, and it was their turn to defend. He did, however, hear the sound of multiple horns in the distance, which meant that the reinforcements had finally arrived.

The only problem that Hero now faced was the fact that almost none of his troops had heard the order to get back into the city. They were still just trying to kill the soldiers outside the inner wall. Hero yelled again, but in vain. He grew increasingly frustrated. He took a deep breath and was about to let out a yell. When he opened his mouth, however, a howl filled the air. It was a long, clear note that hung in space. The fighting slowed, and Hero could finally be heard over the dead silence that followed his howl.

"To the city!" he yelled.

He rushed toward the gate and saw the Hasrath army following him. He grinned to himself and stabbed a Feruh soldier. He ran to the nearest Minotaur, which was smashing a house to bits with its spiked hammer.

"Get ready," Hero snarled, more to himself than the beast.

He jumped up and sliced the Minotaur across the chest. It roared in anger and nearly impaled him with the hammer. Hero ducked and stabbed at the Minotaur's knee. The Minotaur just stepped on his sword and trapped it under a hoofed foot. Hero dove away from the monster as it swung the hammer at his head. He saw two figures join the fray and realized the Merrick and Jacquelyn had stayed with him. He smiled in gratitude as they pushed the Minotaur away from Hero's sword. Hero grabbed the weapon and he and his two friends attacked the beast.

"Like old times," Jacquelyn called with excitement.

"Exactly what I was thinking," Hero laughed.

"This is how it should be," Merrick added.

They all dodged the Minotaur's next attack and drove their swords into its chest simultaneously. The Minotaur let out a cry and fell to the ground in a pool of blood. Another beast came to avenge its fellow, but it was also slain by the three companions.

"General," a soldier gasped, stumbling over to Hero. It was Jon.

"Jon, you've been wounded," Hero said with concern, glancing at the man's bloody side.

"That's not important. Some of the enemy soldiers are making their way to the palace. The King doesn't have enough guards up there," Jon explained quickly. "We need to get men there quickly!"

Hero nodded and prepared to try to howl again, when the sound of trumpets filled the air. The reinforcements came crashing through the enemy lines, swinging their weapons about them and cutting a path to the city. Hero ran over to meet them and saw the General of the new force stop to face him.

"Sir, please come with me and help destroy the forces in the city," Hero said. "We need to protect the King."

"I will lend you half of my number. More soldiers are coming from Carthafell. Rumor has it that the Queen may come," the General replied.

He split his army in half and told one unit to follow Hero. Jon blew a horn, and soldiers from Hero's original unit came to him as well. Hero saw Sunyin close by and ran over to her to tell her the plan.

"I'm going to lead this unit into the city. I need you to stay here with the Jurik soldiers and help keep the enemy out of the city," he explained.

"As you wish, General Hero," Sunyin saluted.

She started to re-group as Hero led the other soldiers with him to the city. They made it to the center square before running into problems. The Minotaurs had all gathered together, and archers stood behind them.

"CHARGE!" Hero bellowed.

His men ran forward as the Minotaurs came crashing toward them. The archers let the arrows fly, and Hero saw some of his soldiers fall. He saw that Jacquelyn and Merrick hadn't been hit and breathed with relief. The Minotaurs let out a roar and picked up speed.

Within seconds, the two forces collided. The Minotaurs' sheer weight knocked many men down, Hero among them, and he had to hasten to his feet to avoid being trampled. Too close to one to use his sword, he took out his small hunting knife and stabbed it in the side. It roared and punched him in the face. Hero took a step back and wiped the blood from his chin.

He saw one of the Jurik soldiers finish off the wounded monstrosity. Hero gave him a smile, and the soldier returned the smile with pride. They all knew they were taking orders from the Lone Wolf, and it boosted their morale to know that he of legend was with them.

"Hey, Hero," a voice said.

Hero looked to his left and saw Jeru. The former wolf had a large but shallow cut running down his right cheek, but he had a grin on his face and a glint in his eyes. Hero smiled back, and the two faced yet another Minotaur.

"We have to take care of those archers," Merrick snarled as another wave of arrows penetrated their force.

"Leave it to me," Jeru bragged.

He ran in between two of the Minotaurs and rushed at the archers. They scrambled to notch another arrow, but Jeru moved quickly through them, slashing them with his long dagger. One almost managed to shoot him, but Jon had thrown a small knife into his throat before Jeru was hit.

The ground was soaked with blood by the time they had slain all of the Minotaurs. They had lost a large number of their own men and were tired and irritable. Hero stood in front of them and tried to get them to hurry along to the palace.

"This is crazy," one of them complained. "We can't fight anymore."

"Yeah," a few others agreed.

Hero's eyes blazed with anger, and the soldiers shrunk back in fright.

"Listen to you!" Hero snarled. "How can you give up now? Don't you care about this world? If we let them win, then Nazberath will fall to ruin as will Verinaul. Now I don't know how humans feel about the well being of their world, but I for one will not sit back and watch the ones I love be annihilated!"

"But there are so many," someone whined weakly.

"There are plenty of us to take them," Hero shot back. "We are not going to give in. Do you want to be thought of as weak? Or do you want to be the men I know you are?"

The soldiers glanced around uneasily. No one spoke. Hero watched them with his blazing eyes, astounded at the humans gathered before him.

"Well, Hero it seems none of these cowards is going to help," Merrick said, looking at the soldiers with disgust.

"Yeah, we should get moving if we want to get to King Dervik," Jacquelyn agreed.

"I agree," Jeru added.

"You men disappoint me. I thought it was an honor to fight with you, but you have shown me your true nature," Hero spat at the frightened soldiers.

He turned to go with only his three friends behind him. He heard nervous feet coming as well and turned to see Jon, who gave him a weak smile. Hero smiled back, and they pushed farther into the city.

"It is way too quiet," Jacquelyn whispered as they neared the palace.

"I don't like the looks of this," Merrick said softly.

"We couldn't have killed them all back in the square," Hero said.

A sudden yell sounded all around them and about a hundred men came pouring from all sides. They were quickly surrounded. Hero cursed and grabbed his sword. He looked for a possible way out, but there was none.

"Ambushed, I knew this would happen!" Jon cried.

"We won't go down quietly," Jeru snapped.

The enemy forces advanced upon the five companions menacingly. Hero ordered them to put their backs together and stand in a circle.

"This will be fun," one of the adversaries sneered.

They charged, and Hero and his friends started to fight with everything they had. But no matter how good they were, they were outnumbered, and victory did not seem possible. Hero felt his vitality start to ebb away, but shook himself mentally and fought even harder.

"Charge!" he heard a voice yell.

His army had followed him and had launched an assault on the enemy troops. Hero let out a laugh and felt his spirits rise. Their force outnumbered the attackers now. Soon, they had defeated the force. Hero looked at his men with renewed respect.

"I guess I was wrong about you," he said.

"No, General. We shouldn't have let ourselves drown in despair," one of them replied softly.

"We must fight to redeem ourselves," others called.

"Very well then. I shall look forward to your help," Hero grinned. "We should head into the palace now, in case they've made their way inside."

"Yes sir," the men saluted.

"Well Hero, you've become quite the accomplished soldier since we last were together," Merrick chuckled.

"I think you're doing a great job," Jacquelyn complimented.

"Thank you," Hero said, blushing slightly at her praise. "Now let's go!"

By the time they reached the King's palace, the front doors had already been ripped apart. Hero cursed violently and forced his men on faster. King Dervik couldn't be killed at this point. Then the Queen would have a much stronger hold on Nazberath. He practically flew up the stairs and burst into the King's throne room. King Dervik was there, sword slashing at the enemy and face set into a battle snarl.

"Advance, quickly now!" Hero bellowed. He and his men charged at the attackers, and soon killed them all. Blood seeped into the carpets and gave the room an eerie red glow. King Dervik sagged down into his throne and clutched a wounded side.

"Thank you, Lone Wolf. If you hadn't gotten here when you did, well..." His voice trailed off. "What is the situation now?"

"My Lord, I am afraid we are being overrun," a voice said sadly.

Molly drifted lightly through the window with a worn expression. She sat down on the floor and sighed deeply.

"Even with the reinforcements, we cannot drive them back," she said.

"Is there *nothing* we can do?" Hero snarled.

"I can't see any hope for us," Molly replied.

"What do we do then? We can't just sit here and let them kill us," Merrick said coldly.

"We should fight," Jeru agreed.

"We will," Hero said. "But we have to fight smart, not rush blindly in."

"If only we could find a way to outnumber them," Jacquelyn said. "Or make them *think* that they're outnumbered!"

"You have a plan?" King Dervik asked.

"If I may, your Majesty?" Jacquelyn asked with a curtsy. When the King waved a hand in acceptance to hear her plan, she took a deep breath. "I know of some herbs that can shroud an area with mist. If we can trap them in such a fog, then they will end up fighting each other instead of us. Also, we can use the fog as cover and strike at them when they can't see us."

"Do you have the herbs?" Molly asked.

"Please tell us you do," Jon pleaded.

"I still need a few red mountain herbs. I think they can be found on Demon's Peak," Jacquelyn said softly after checking her satchel.

"But we can't go back there," Jeru exclaimed.

"What if there was another way to make the mist," Molly suggested.

"What if we use smoke instead?" Hero asked. "Or better yet, lure them into the smoke and pull our men back. We can set up archers in the buildings and on the roofs so they can fire down onto them without the risk of killing each other."

"I like that idea," Merrick smiled. "What will we burn?"

As if in answer to his question, a loud roar was heard in the distance. They all crowded by the window and saw a large shape hurtling through the air toward the city.

"That's a dragon!" King Dervik gasped. "I thought Arlyn had destroyed them all!"

"Hero, that must be Barudokai," Jeru exclaimed excitedly.

"You're right. He must have come to help us," Hero laughed.

He rushed out of the room and made his way to the roof with Jeru, Merrick, Jacquelyn and Molly behind him. Clouds hid the dragon, which was good since the enemy hadn't seen him yet. He must have seen Hero and the others, however, as he soon landed on the roof with them. He gave them a smile and showed off his large teeth.

"I thought you boys might need some help," he said.

"Thank you, Barudokai," Hero said softly.

The dragon shrugged nonchalantly, but they noticed a contented gleam in his eyes.

"Now here's the plan, Barudokai," Hero began. "We need you to trap the enemy soldiers in smoke. You can add a little fire in there, too, to burn some. Before you do so, I need to tell our men to pull back, that way they won't get caught in it too."

"How are you going to tell them all at once?" Merrick asked.

"I'm going to howl," Hero smiled.

"You mean like a wolf?" Jacquelyn asked with surprise. "Is that what we heard earlier?"

"Yes," Hero said. "Thanks to Molly, I have redeemed some of my wolfish qualities for the time being. Now let's get those men out of there."

He filled his lungs with air and let out a long, clear howl. He saw the fighting pause, and then to his immense relief, King Dervik's army retreated back to the main city. Barudokai lifted himself into the air and flew down upon Arlyn's army, which cried out in despair when they saw the beast. Barudokai let out a burst of fire and smoke that smothered the army in thick smog.

Hero and the others ran to the retreating forces with the rest of Hero's unit remaining to guard the King, excluding Jon who refused to leave Hero. Hero saw Sunyin storming over to him and winced when she caught his ear and dragged him to a private house.

"Why did you order the retreat?" she snarled. "Are you giving up?"

"No, it is part of the plan," Hero yelped, pulling her hand away. "I called a retreat so that you and your men wouldn't be trapped in the smoke and shot with arrows."

"Oh, I see." She smiled.

She walked out of the house ignoring Hero when he called after her to apologize. Hero sighed and exited the house to tell the rest of Sunyin's men the plan. When he had, the best archers made their way to various rooftops and began to shoot arrows down upon the smoke like rain.

"Sir, Hero," Jon cried. "Some are coming!"

Hero turned around and saw a unit of about fifty soldiers charging at them. At the head of the unit was Muryn. Hero stepped up to meet the General, but Merrick got in his way.

"What are you doing?" Hero demanded.

"Muryn is mine, Hero," Merrick growled. "Nobody else gets to kill him but me."

"I know how you feel, Merrick, but let me handle this. I'm more, well," Hero didn't finish.

"If you were about to say 'more experienced,' then you know that's a lie. I'm the one who taught you, if you recall. I think I have a bit more experience anyway, seeing as I am a human and have been fighting for years, while you just arrived in our world a few months ago," Merrick said harshly.

"Very well," Hero admitted. "But if I feel that you're about to die, I'm stepping in, okay?"

"All right," Merrick said with a nod of his head.

"Well, it has been a while hasn't it, brother?" Muryn smiled.

"Shut it. Your miserable life will end now," Merrick snarled.

They both rushed toward each other, swords raised and battle snarls set on their faces. Hero and Jacquelyn watched in fright, hoping that Merrick would be able to take on the Carthafell General. Muryn smiled with sadistic pleasure as he successfully fended off all of Merrick's attacks. Merrick growled in frustration and lunged once more. Muryn sidestepped and kicked Merrick in the ribs.

"Not good enough, brother. Fight me like this, and you'll be dead very soon," Muryn taunted.

"Shut up," Merrick ordered.

He rushed toward his older brother. Muryn prepared to counter, but at the last moment, Merrick jumped to the side and brought his sword down in a quick slash. Blood splashed through the air and Muryn staggered back, clutching a bloody cheek.

"You!" he roared with rage.

He ran forward and punched Merrick in the stomach. Merrick spit out some blood and blocked the wildly swinging sword. Muryn looked absolutely livid. Blood ran down his face and splattered his shoulder and neck. His eyes blazed, and he fought harder than he had ever fought before. This violent turn in his brother threw Merrick off balance; he had always thought that Muryn kept a calm head no matter what the situation. Merrick just couldn't keep up with him.

"Oh no, Merrick's in trouble," Jacquelyn gasped as her Muryn cut her friend across the chest.

"I won't stand by and let him die," Hero said. "Hold on, Merrick, I'm coming!"

He rushed into the fray. Just as Muryn raised his sword to deliver a death-blow, Hero moved in the way and blocked the strike. It was so powerful that it chipped his own sword and shook his arm until it went numb.

"Time for you to die, Lone Wolf," Muryn sneered.

"Forget about me?" Merrick growled.

He struck at Muryn, but the General dodged the blow. Unable to dodge the strike from Hero, however, he felt the sword stab him in the thigh. Muryn stumbled away from the two fighters and glared at them with hatred. A Carthafell soldier ran up to them.

"Sir, I have bad news," he said.

"Can't you see that I am busy?" Muryn yelled.

"But General Muryn, sir, we are being defeated. We need to regroup," the soldier pleaded.

"What? Defeated? Are you telling me that one dragon is destroying our whole army?" Muryn roared.

"It's not just that, sir. They have archers shooting from all directions, and we can't see anything!" the soldier cried.

"You don't think we will just let you escape do you?" Merrick snapped.

"That is not for you to decide," Muryn replied sharply. "Arlyn, we need a little help retreating!"

"Is he mad? Arlyn is not here," Hero said.

"Maybe not. But she can still hear me," Muryn smirked.

He started to fade away. Merrick and Hero gasped as Muryn and the soldier disappeared into thin air. Soon after, they heard other cries of astonishment and anger. The whole enemy army had vanished as well. In a flash, the battle was over and the enemy spirited back to Carthafell.

"We did it," Sunyin said softly.

"I don't believe it," Jon laughed.

The rest of the army and Barudokai came into view. Hero gazed up at the dragon and nodded in gratitude.

"Thanks, Barudokai. We would not have been able to win that battle if you hadn't shown up," Jeru smiled.

"My pleasure," Barudokai grinned, showing rows of sharp teeth.

"Hero, King Dervik wishes to speak to you," Molly said.

"Very well. Merrick, Jacquelyn, I'll see you later," Hero sighed.

"We'll be waiting," Jacquelyn said.

Hero nodded and followed the Fairy Queen back to the palace. They made their way into the throne room and saw King Dervik upon his throne. He beamed fondly at them both.

"On this day, we recognize the warrior Hero, Lone Wolf, who led our men to victory against the evil forces of Nazberath," King Dervik said. "I bow before you."

And so he did. The King of all Hasbeth bowed to the former wolf of Verinaul. Hero smiled with pride and bowed his head to the King as well. He had done it. He had saved Delring from Arlyn's forces. The legend of Lone Wolf rang true.

Chapter 28

Late that night, the city of Delring blazed with lights. The party that followed their victory would be one to talk about for centuries. Everyone had attended. The best part happened when the women and children returned from the mountains where they had been hiding. They returned with looks of absolute joy and gratitude. The whole city echoed with noise and laughter. No one was in a sour mood, even though they might have lost friends in the battle. They all knew that friends and loved ones would not want them to mourn.

Hero sat by a fountain with Jacquelyn and Merrick. They had been silent for a while. Both had given a detailed story of what had happened after they split company. However, Hero still felt as though he should say something about his decision in the first place. He cleared his throat, but his two friends just shook their heads.

"We know why you did it," Merrick smiled.

"You just didn't want to get too close. Otherwise it would be too painful to leave Nazberath, right?" Jacquelyn grinned.

"That's right," Hero replied sheepishly. "I kind of regret that choice, because I care for you both. But I didn't want anything to keep me here, you know? I have to make sure I get back to Nakoomu."

"You'll get back to her," Merrick said. "We'll make sure you do."

Isabell stepped gingerly over to them. Her leg had been badly wounded in the battle. She would never fully recover, but she would be able to carry Merrick after she healed a bit. She gave a snicker and rubbed her head on Hero.

"It has been too long since I last saw you," she said.

"Hey, Isabell. I hope you're feeling well," Hero said, patting her head.

"I'm a lot better now knowing you three are safe," Isabell snorted.

"Hey there, General," a voice said.

They turned to see Molly and Jeru. Merrick and Jacquelyn looked around at Hero, who blushed and gave a little shrug.

"You are a General?" Merrick asked in disbelief.

"Yeah," Hero replied.

"Congratulations!" Jacquelyn beamed.

"Thank you," Hero said.

"So what's our next move, Hero? Are we just going to sit around in Delring for a while?" Jeru asked.

"That's the plan. I think I'll rest here for a few weeks before thinking about moving on. Besides, I don't really know where to go from here," Hero admitted.

"Have you ever heard about the Desert's Rose?" Molly asked.

"I've heard a little bit about it here and there," Hero answered.

"Why don't you try to find it? Supposedly, it has the power to transform anything into what they want. You could have it return you to your true form," Molly explained.

"But I can't stay a wolf in this world forever," Hero argued. "It would be like a beacon for Arlyn and her men."

"That is the miracle of the rose," Molly giggled. "You change whenever you want. All you have to do is think about changing, and it will happen."

"That sounds interesting," Merrick said.

"Can anyone use it?" Jacquelyn asked.

"Yes. Though I heard it works better if you are like Hero. You know, if you were an animal beforehand," Molly replied.

"So then, I could use it too?" Jeru asked hopefully.

"There is only one Desert's Rose, and it only works for one person. The person who finds it gets its powers," Molly said. "And I'm not sure, but I think it boosts your strength and gives you the ability to use magic."

"Well, then I guess it will belong to Hero," Jeru laughed.

"What do you say?" Jacquelyn asked slyly.

"I suppose it may come in handy," Hero smirked. "Once I'm rested up, I'll head off to find it."

"Do you even know where this desert is? Or what it is called?" Merrick asked Hero.

Hero shook his head.

"The desert can be found in Tulek, thankfully a neutral country. The desert is called Maneat Desert," Molly sighed.

"That's the plan then," Hero said, gazing at the stars.

Later on, while Jacquelyn, Molly and Jeru danced, Hero and Merrick sat together. They were silent for a time, watching the festivities.

"Hero," Merrick said, glancing at him. "You know that it isn't over."

Hero looked at him without replying.

"Muryn got away and Arlyn will be furious. Once her forces recuperate, she will strike again," Merrick continued.

"I know," Hero said finally.

"One year," Merrick said.

"Huh?" Hero asked.

"I'm betting she'll strike again in a year," Merrick replied.

"I see. It looks as though I shall remain here for some time," Hero said.

"Seems that way," Merrick agreed softly.

"I won't rest until my job is done," Hero said gravely.

"I will help you until your job is done," Merrick replied.

Hero smiled. The two friends clasped each other's hand, sealing the promise.

When Hero woke up in the middle of the night, he realized that the celebration continued. However the noise had abated to a mere whisper compared to earlier. He got out of bed and stepped out onto the balcony. He saw a shape on the next balcony and straightened up, ready for an attack. He heard a woman laugh and saw that the shape belonged to Jacquelyn.

"What are you doing up?" Hero asked.

"I could ask you the same," Jacquelyn chuckled.

"I just couldn't sleep," Hero whispered. "I have a guilty feeling."

"Why?" Jacquelyn asked, concern in her voice.

"I didn't only leave you both because I was afraid of being hurt," Hero sighed. "I also wanted to draw the enemy away from you. I remember Merrick once telling me that they would have a harder time capturing us if we were together, but I think it only makes it easier. I believed that you were both better off without me and that I could go faster without you. Sorry."

Jacquelyn was silent for a minute. Then Hero heard her sigh and saw her lean out over the balcony.

"You don't have to apologize," she said. "I understand how you feel, and I'm not offended or anything. However, I absolutely refuse to let you leave for that desert without me. I don't care what your reasons are, I'm going with you no matter where you go."

"Jacquelyn," Hero said softly.

"I don't want to be away from you," Jacquelyn admitted.

Hero was about to respond, but another voice cut in. "I hope you two weren't thinking of leaving me behind."

"Merrick? Is that you?" Jacquelyn asked.

"It is indeed," Merrick replied.

"I can't possibly win over you two. I promise that I won't leave you behind when I go to find the Desert's Rose," Hero laughed.

Hero gazed at the full moon hanging in the sky. He was at peace for the moment. He could rest without fearing for his life. Lone Wolf had done his job and protected the city of Delring against the enemy. What had once seemed impossible was finished. He smiled to himself as he remembered all of his self-doubts. He knew he had a long way before his job was complete. Much larger battles loomed in his future, and Arlyn was still out there, waiting to strike. He knew in his heart that only after her death would the Storm of Endless Tears stop and the creatures of Verinaul be saved.